MANHUNTER

"Are you saying you're looking for a *husband*?" Cal Delaney asked.

"That's exactly what I'm saying," Rachel replied.

He stared at her for a long moment, and then threw back his head and started to laugh uproariously. Rachel felt her ire rise. So, he was taking this proposal as some sort of joke, was he? Well, she would throw in the bait and see just how funny he thought it was.

"I'm talking about a business arrangement, after which time I would expect the man in question to disappear in exchange for twenty thousand dollars."

Cal Delaney stopped laughing.

Books by Donna Grove

A Touch of Camelot
Broken Vows

Available from HarperPaperbacks

Broken Vows

Donna Grove

HarperPaperbacks
A Division of HarperCollinsPublishers

In memory of my friends
Teresa Smith and Linda Bowers

HarperPaperbacks   *A Division of* HarperCollins*Publishers*
10 East 53rd Street, New York, N.Y. 10022

Copyright © 1995 by Donna Grove
All rights reserved. No part of this book may be used or
reproduced in any manner whatsoever without written
permission of the publisher, except in the case of brief
quotations embodied in critical articles and reviews. For
information address HarperCollins*Publishers,*
10 East 53rd Street, New York, N.Y. 10022.

Cover illustration by Aleta Jenks

First printing: March 1995

Printed in the United States of America

HarperPaperbacks, HarperMonogram, and colophon are
trademarks of HarperCollins*Publishers*

❖ 10 9 8 7 6 5 4 3 2 1

Prologue

Elena Rose Ranch, Fort Worth, Texas, April 1878

When a man knows his days are numbered, his perspective on life changes. Galen Girard knew this for a fact.

He stood with his back to the others as he gazed through the polished glass window of his study, surveying his second greatest achievement, the working section of a sprawling cattle ranch known as the Elena Rose. Over the years, he had invested his sweat, his fortune, his heart, and his soul into the Elena Rose, and had built it into one of the largest, most profitable spreads in the state.

In his youth, Galen had cut a fine-looking figure, and now that he had reached middle age, he was proud that he still retained a full head of chestnut hair and that his body, worked hard by ranch life, had never gone to flab. That body, however, was now turning traitor on him, falling prey to an invisible disease that was likely to claim him before the year was out. His mind was as sharp as ever, though, and he fully intended to see that certain things were done before he was forced to bid adieu to this world and continue on to the next.

Now, he disregarded the impressive scene outside his study window and faced his single greatest achievement of all, that which far surpassed the phenomenal success of the Elena Rose—his only surviving child, Rachel. She was a grown woman and magnificent to behold. This morning she stood straight and tall, dressed smartly in a navy blue riding habit, with her coppery mane loose and wild. She had her late mother's high cheekbones and flashing green eyes, but that square jaw and the stubborn, determined set of her mouth, they were Galen's own. Oh yes, Rachel was his daughter, in spirit as well as in flesh, and he was proud of her.

And knowing her high spirits almost as well as he did his own, he eyed her warily, aware that her apparent calm in the face of his latest pronouncement was only a prelude to the storm. After all, she had no way of knowing the truth about his condition. He had sworn his old friend, Doc Bowers, to secrecy.

"Married?" Rachel spat out the word like a piece of spoiled meat. "What in the blue blazes do you mean I have to get married? That is the most outrageous piece of poppycock I've ever heard in my entire life!"

Galen's sister-in-law, Charlotte, rose from her chair in one corner of the study and glided to Rachel's side. She rested a calming hand on her niece's forearm. "I'm sure your father didn't mean it like it sounded, did you, Galen?"

Galen flipped open the lid of his cigar box and extracted a Havana cigar. As he moved to light it, he squinted at his sister-in-law, irritated with her pawing, whining manner, as usual. There was only one reason he had planned to have her sit in on this exchange, and that was because he knew her presence would exert a certain subtle pressure on his daughter. "I meant it exactly like it sounded, Charlotte," he said. "Don't go trying to dance around the issue."

So many years ago, Galen had warned his twin brother not to become involved with Charlotte, but she was comely and flirtatious, and George had toppled like a house of cards. When Charlotte became pregnant, George naturally did the right thing by her, and then lived just long enough to rue that day. Now it looked as if George and Charlotte's son, Nicholas, had inherited George's weakness for enticing coquettes. A person had only to look at Nick's new wife, Daisy, to see that history was about to repeat itself.

Rachel shook off Charlotte's hand and pointed a finger at her father. "You have rounded the bend! You're crazy if you think I'm going to get married just because you've suddenly got the addle-pated idea you want an heir! Well, take a look in front of you! I *am* your heir!"

Galen feigned a thoughtful expression as he puffed on his cigar. "Why, I hadn't thought that far ahead, my dear, but an heir *would* be nice. I must consider that as a point in your favor when I make out my will."

Charlotte interjected eagerly. "Well, Galen, you needn't fear for the Girard name. There is Nicholas, you know, and given time, I'm sure he and Daisy—"

Galen shot Charlotte an annoyed glance that caused her to clamp her mouth shut.

Rachel tried to collect herself, closing her eyes and sucking in a deep breath. "Daddy, you aren't being reasonable. I've worked hard to earn the Elena Rose. You've always said—"

"You're right. I've always said it would be yours when I'm gone, but I'm still breathing, Rachel Elena, and until that fact changes, I still call the shots."

"But—"

He pointed his cigar at his daughter. "You *will* get married, and your husband *will* be capable of running the Elena Rose, and he will *not* be some weak-kneed pansy you can walk all over whenever you have a mind to!"

It was only now Galen realized he had begun to shout in an effort to intimidate his defiant offspring. It wasn't working. Rachel now wrinkled her nose at him as if he'd turned into some kind of loathsome, scaly reptile. He cleared his throat and lowered his voice. "Now, I'm giving you a chance to pick him out for yourself. Two months is plenty of time as I see it. If you haven't found yourself an acceptable man by then, well, by God, if you want to inherit the Elena Rose, I'll pick one out for you myself."

"And if I refuse?"

With great dignity, Galen lowered himself into the chair behind his massive mahogany desk. "The ranch will go to Nicholas"—and now he chose his next words very carefully for maximum effect—"and Daisy, of course, since she's his wife."

Rachel dropped all pretenses of control. Her green eyes shot sparks of rage. *"Daisy? Daisy Parker? You would leave the Elena Rose in the hands of Daisy Parker?"*

"She's Daisy Girard now, Rachel," Charlotte cut in

tactfully, "I know you two have never gotten along, but I think—"

Rachel shot her aunt a look that would have wilted a newly bloomed rose. "Daisy Parker is *not* a Girard! She will never *be* a Girard, and she will *never* get her greedy hands on any part of the Elena Rose!"

Charlotte pressed her lips together and held her tongue, but it was obvious by her expression that she was not pleased.

Rachel narrowed her eyes at her father suspiciously. "What's brought all this on so suddenly, Daddy? All this foolish talk about retiring from ranch work and writing up a will and . . ." She paused. "Is there something wrong with you?"

Galen took the cigar from his mouth, fixed his beloved daughter with his unflinching blue gaze, and lied through his teeth. "My dear, I am healthy as a horse. It's just come to that time in my life when I feel the necessity to set matters straight once and for all. In fact, I've been meaning to get to it ever since your mother passed away."

Rachel stared at him hard, trying to discern if he was telling the truth or not. After a moment, she scowled. "You are a totally unreasonable crusty old bastard."

Galen tried not to smile as he plunked the cigar back into his mouth and started shuffling through the papers on his desk. He had always admired people with guts enough to speak their minds. That went for his business associates and staff as well as his own daughter. "I've said all I need to say. I've got work to do."

Rachel stood, her mouth opening and closing as if to make a retort, but ultimately she decided against it. She spun around to leave the room, bumping into a desk lamp with her elbow. Galen almost laughed out loud as her hands, so practiced from years of similar mishaps, shot out in the nick of time to steady it before it could crash to the floor.

She fixed him with one last determined glare for good measure. "I will never do it! *Never!*"

She stormed from the room with such dramatic flourish, Galen thought she might have done even her legendary mother justice. It had been two years since Elena Rose Girard passed away, and there were many times, times like these, when Galen missed her so badly it was like a physical ache in his chest.

He slid back in his chair and puffed on his cigar. He knew that after all the ballyhoo and bellyaching was done, Rachel would do it, all right. She would do it because she was obsessed with the Elena Rose.

Charlotte raised a hand to smooth her carefully arranged chignon. "Quite frankly, Galen, I am also at a loss to understand this sudden turn of mind. You never seemed overly concerned about Rachel's status as a . . . uh, er, unattached woman. I mean, you and Elena raised her to be so . . ."

"To be so what, Charlotte?"

She seemed to cast about for a tactful word. "To be so . . . well, outspoken. Not many gentlemen find that to be an attractive trait in a young lady."

Galen drummed work-worn fingers on his desk top. "Nothing wrong with a woman who can speak her mind. Shows she's got one."

"Well, regardless, I still don't understand your sudden hurry, Galen."

"She'll be twenty-one soon. It's nigh on time—past time if you go by them silly society rules you're always concerned with, am I right?"

Charlotte fluttered, "Well, I hardly thought you cared much for—"

"Rules or no rules, I think it's time she settled down, Charlotte. Maybe I just want to see to it she makes a good choice while I'm still around to have a say in the matter." He gave her a teasing smile. "You wouldn't want her to end up marrying some slick fortune hunter after I'm dead and gone, now would you?"

Charlotte raised a hand to her breast and gasped in horror. "Most certainly not!"

Galen could practically see the dollar signs flashing in Charlotte's greedy eyes at the very thought of some stranger siphoning off the Girard family fortune. Why, that had always been *her* responsibility!

In actuality, he had no fear Rachel would fall for the wiles of a fortune-hunting lothario. She was too sharp for that—too sharp and too suspicious. No, his fear was that his daughter would never marry at all.

It wasn't that Rachel was an unattractive woman. On the contrary. She had, seemingly overnight, transformed into an eye-popping beauty. Galen had always seen the light within his daughter, even when she seemed nothing but an awkward adolescent, but now that her beauty was obvious for all to see, his daughter was bombarded with hopeful suitors. These local men were no match for her sharp intellect and scathing tongue, and they all, sooner or later, ended up creeping away like shamed dogs.

Galen, however, was astute enough to see the writing on the wall. He was concerned that his proud and independent daughter wouldn't recognize the right man when he *did* come along. In all her efforts to become a practical-minded business woman, Rachel had hardened herself to the point where she was fearful of her own heart.

Would he really leave the Elena Rose Ranch to Nicholas and Daisy? Probably not. But he had to make damn sure Rachel thought he would—even if she ended up hating him for it.

Very subtly, for he knew his scheming sister-in-law was still studying him, he raised his eyes to the ceiling. *Elena Rose, I know you wouldn't approve of the clumsy way I'm going about it, but the pot's already on the flame. Now we'll just have to wait and see how the stew turns out.*

1

Red Panther Hotel, Fort Worth, Texas

 Lacey Holloway, saloon waitress and fallen angel, pulled a rumpled bed sheet over her plump breasts, rolled onto one side, and propped up her curly blond head with one hand. Smiling the sleepy, languid smile of a sated woman, she observed Cal Delaney, naked and splendid, as he sat up and reached for a cigar from the scarred night table.

He struck a match and proceeded to light it with what Lacey considered very fine grace. As far as she was concerned, Cal did most everything—and she fought off a salacious giggle at this thought—with thoroughly practiced skill. Now, as he shook out the match and rose to retrieve his boots and discarded clothing from the floor, Lacey noted the clean line of his profile, the strong jaw, the straight line of his nose, and the tousled blond hair that reached just to the nape of his neck. He needed a shave, but that didn't take away from his appeal. In fact, Lacey thought it only added to it. She was tickled pink that for the last two nights—ever since he blew into town—he had chosen her to keep his bed warm.

As he climbed into his denims, Lacey admired his flat belly, his broad chest and shoulders, and the smooth curve of sinewy muscle in his arms. The only thing that marred such utter male perfection was a handful of old scars. When he turned his back to cross the room to the dresser, her curious gaze settled on two jagged slashes. These, she could tell, were still tender and new.

Although he claimed to be a cowpuncher and had arrived in town with Ezra Evans, an independent drover, rumor had it that back in Dodge City, Cal had been a fearsome gunslinger. Even though Lacey had never seen him wear a gun belt, and he had not yet spoken one word about his past, she suspected that the rumors were true. Ever since meeting Cal, she had often caught herself daydreaming about what it might be like to be a famous gunslinger's woman.

Caleb Delaney, however, had all but forgotten the dreamy-eyed girl in the bed behind him as he searched through his travel-worn saddlebags and pulled out a clean shirt. A Colt .44 Peacemaker clattered onto the dresser top. Frowning, he picked it up. The grip still fit his hand as if he had been born to it. The sight had been filed down to facilitate a clean, quick draw. The trigger notch had likewise been filed away so that, once drawn and in the right hands, its rapid-firing ability was unmatched, even by the more modern double-action pieces. In Cal's experienced hands, the weapon was capable of getting off all six shots in less than two seconds.

He ran his thumb over the smooth surface of the ivory grip and felt an unwelcome wave of nostalgia wash over him. This, the civilian model, he had worn on his right hip for so long it had become a part of him. Its partner, a long-barreled Cavalry model, had ridden comfortably well on his left.

When he looked up from the revolver to stare out the grimy window of the hotel, he didn't see the dusty thoroughfare one story below or the few early morning stragglers who now roamed along its length. The image he saw mirrored back at him in the dirt-streaked glass wasn't even his own. It was an insolent face, the face of a sneering young cowboy. It had been over a month now, but the memory still stuck with him like the bad taste that follows a long night of downing rotgut whiskey.

"Hey, Delaney! You think you're somethin' special, do you? Show us what you got! You ain't so fast as they say, are you?"

The overexuberant cowpoke had baited Cal earlier that evening, and seeing that his young antagonist was on the shy side of sixteen, Cal had turned away from him. The boy, drunker than two judges and enraged at being ignored, came stumbling out of the saloon after Cal, still shooting his mouth off like a hotheaded fool.

Dodge City had an ordinance against carrying weapons. It wasn't only because of Cal's reputation among the lawless that he couldn't afford to abide by that ordinance; it was because of the increasing frequency of senseless confrontations like this one. It was common knowledge that up in the Dakota Territory, Wild Bill Hickok had been shot in the back of the head while playing an innocent game of poker. These days, Cal opted to pay a nominal fine for breaking the ordinance rather than take a chance on ending up like Wild Bill.

The kid stood with his thin legs planted before the flapping batwing doors of the saloon. The fandango houses were in full swing. Tinny piano music drifted on the air around them. Only two of the kid's friends and a few others had bothered to step out to witness this impromptu skirmish.

He was lucky Cal was an even-tempered fellow. There were many who would have killed him with much less provocation. Cal, however, was looking for a good night's sleep and just wished the boy would pass out where he stood or listen to his friends and shut up. Very deliberately, Cal turned and started to walk away.

"Don't you walk away from me, you yella skunk! You turn your back, and I'll put a bullet in it! I can take you or any two like you! Whyn't ya fight? Whyn't ya fight?"

Bad shooting, even among some of the West's most notorious gunfighters, was the rule rather than the exception, and this quarrelsome greenhorn was not bucking that convention. His first shot, brazenly fired when Cal's back was still turned, cleanly missed its intended target.

When Cal turned around, he saw the kid had stepped off the boardwalk in front of the saloon, ignorant of the fact that his silhouette now made a perfect target against the ghostly lamp glow cast from within. And Cal Delaney never missed a bull's-eye.

When the kid moved to get off a second shot, Cal drew and fired. He didn't see that he had much choice. He had no desire to sacrifice himself for the sake of greenhorn pride.

At thirty paces, Cal took his opponent in the knee, forcing him down in the street, but even that didn't muffle the youth's bravado. Perhaps liquor had combined with shock to numb his sense of physical pain. As the boy raised his revolver to fire again, Cal winged his right wrist, decisively ending the ill-balanced confrontation then and there.

It had also ended Cal's career. When he shed his gun belt that night, it was for the last time. He realized, quite suddenly and unexpectedly, he just didn't have the stomach for it anymore.

A sigh from the girl in his bed brought him back to the present. "You sure you got to be going so soon, Cal? You don't have to meet Ezra for another hour."

Cal stabbed out his cigar in an ashtray atop the dresser and shoved the Colt back into one of the saddlebags. "Just enough time to grab me a hot bath and a shave downstairs," he replied, putting on his shirt.

She giggled suggestively. "Or, just enough time to grab yourself a little more of something *else* if you have a mind to."

Cal didn't bother to answer as he crossed the room to the door, stopping only to fish some paper bills from his pocket. He tossed them onto the bed. "That good with you?"

Lacey's hand snaked out to pluck up the bills. "It sure is, honey."

He rested one hand on the door latch and fixed her with his blue gaze. "Be gone when I get back, okay?"

Lacey couldn't disguise her hopeful tone of voice. "See you tonight, though. . . . Right, Cal?"

He didn't look back as he stepped out into the squalid hallway. "Sure, Lacey. See you tonight."

At just about the same time Caleb Delaney was treating himself to a hot bath and a shave on the bad side of town, Rachel Girard was storming through the kitchen of the palatial Elena Rose ranch house.

Before her father summoned her to his study and
threw down the gauntlet, Rachel had been planning to
spend her morning out on the southeastern section of
the ranch overseeing the start of spring roundup. Now,
as she blew like an ill wind past their housekeeper,
Dolores Cortez, Rachel felt more like heading west
where she knew she could ride Misty, her finest
palomino, for hours without running into a blessed soul.

Dolores, straight-faced as always, intoned after
Rachel's departing back in an exaggerated Mexican
accent. "This mean you no want lunch today, *Señorita*
Girard?"

In no mood for Dolores's dry sense of humor,
Rachel growled an unintelligible reply before yanking
open the back door and marching down the porch
steps. She set out for the stables.

Paco Rodriguez, one of their ranch hands, jauntily
raised his hat before noticing the livid expression on
Rachel's face and the furious pace at which she moved.
"Good morning there, er, uh, Miss . . . *ahem.*"

Rachel's mind was not on observing friendly for-
malities. She barely noticed the befuddled cowpoke.
What good had all her years of learning and hard work
done for her now? Her father was suddenly ready to
hand it all over to Nick, who had never even expressed
an interest in the Elena Rose, and Daisy, who couldn't
tell a longhorn from a Brahman even if her life
depended on it!

"Rachel! Hey there! Rachel!"

She recognized that voice and she didn't want to
talk to him. She didn't want to deal with that even-
keeled, reasonable male demeanor of his. What she
wanted was to hate him for a while. She was entitled
to that much.

Acting as if she hadn't heard her name, Rachel yanked the stable door open with frantic desperation.

"Rachel Elena!"

Nick was not giving up.

As the door slapped closed behind her, she stopped to catch her breath. The dark stable smelled of horses, fresh hay, manure, and leather. As a child, Rachel had loved it here.

She heard the heavy wooden door creak open. Morning sunlight streamed in like a carpet runner unfurling before her feet, then narrowed and disappeared as the door swung closed again.

"Rachel?"

She took a deep breath, gathering up her anger like a protective cloak. When she turned to face him, her voice was calm. "What do you want? I thought you'd be on your way into town by now."

Nick appeared amused. "I was, but when I saw you flying out of the house like you'd been shot from a cannon, I knew something had to be up."

Rachel felt her eyes growing accustomed to the murk as she looked up at her handsome cousin. He had inherited his mother's ebony hair and the Girard family's blue eyes—a deadly combination as far as the ladies were concerned. She dropped her gaze. When had she stopped looking at Nick as a brotherly childhood playmate? When had they both grown up? "And why should you think it's any of your business?" she asked.

His tone softened. "Come on, Rachel. What's the matter?"

Rachel steeled herself not to fall prey to this familiar ploy. He had always been able to get around her fits of anger by posing as a sympathetic listener. They used to understand each other as instinctively as if they'd been born twins, but that all changed when he'd started courting Daisy Parker.

She glared at him. "*You.* You are what's the matter."

"Me?"

"If you think you're going to take the Elena Rose from me, you've got another thing coming!"

"Wait a minute. Take the Elena Rose? What are you talking about?"

Rachel felt her anger surge, felt it tear around at a furious pace in her veins, and she relished it. "It's not going to happen, Nick! It's mine! It's always been mine, and it always will be!"

"You're not making any sense."

Rachel jabbed a finger at his chest. "You have the stockyards and I have the Elena Rose! That's how it's supposed to be!"

Nick shook his head, clearly bewildered. "Rachel, where have you been getting this?"

Despite her efforts to hold on to it, Rachel felt her anger start to dissipate, start to flow right out of her, like water, into a useless puddle at her feet. It was her father she was really angry with, not Nick.

Her reply was bitter. "Talk to your mother. I'm sure she can't wait to tell you about it. She's probably bending your wife's eager ear as we speak."

He looked wary. "What's Daisy got to do with this?"

Rachel ignored the question. "He can set down all the ridiculous conditions he wants. It doesn't matter because I'll meet them. I'll meet *every damned last one of them!*"

Nick eyed her cautiously, then backed off. "All right, Rachel. I'm going to leave you alone right now because it's obvious you're too upset to talk about this. But tonight, I'll try again."

Rachel pressed her lips together and turned her back.

"You hear me, Rachel?"

She folded her arms and didn't answer.

After a moment, she heard him leave, and she breathed deep in an effort to collect herself. It wasn't Nick she was angry at, it was her father. She had to remember that. She knew in her heart that she nursed past grievances when it came to Nick. Sometimes it served her conveniently, like now, but she had to be careful in the future that it didn't cloud her judgment.

The past was in the past.

She had been devastated when Nick first courted Daisy Parker. That girl had been a thorn in Rachel's side for years. Even as a child, Daisy had always been as pretty as a Botticelli painting—petite with cornflower blue eyes and wavy, sun-yellow blond hair—almost like an angel. Her spiteful disposition, however, left no doubt as to her earthly origins.

When Nick announced that he was actually going to marry that girl, Rachel had fled the room, fighting off tears of rage and frustration. She convinced herself that it was because she loathed Daisy Parker. She had only recently begun to face the troubling possibility that it might have been because she had fallen a little bit in love with Nick herself.

2

Rachel knew she wasn't pretty. As a young girl, she had spent enough time agonizing in front of the mirror to have reconciled herself to that fact. And it wasn't just that her jaw was too square, her cheekbones too sharp, and her lips too wide. It was her hair. Daisy Parker had commented once at school recess that Rachel's hair stuck out worse than the pins on a hysterical porcupine. But that wasn't the worst of it.

As a child, Rachel had always been tall, too tall, and throughout her adolescence, while the other girls were growing bosoms and rounding out nicely, Rachel had continued to sprout up and up and up. It was Daisy Parker, of course, who had finally dubbed her "Rachel the Beanstalk," and the horrid nickname had stuck for years.

Even today, if a man on the street stared at her, Rachel's first thought was that her skirt hem must be dragging or that her hair was sticking wildly out of place. Surely, it wasn't because he considered her attractive. When her suitors told her she was beautiful, she accepted the compliment suspiciously and wondered if it might not be Elena Rose greenbacks they were imagining reflected in her eyes. She didn't like the idea of any man marrying her for money. She liked even less the idea of sharing the Elena Rose with a husband. Unfortunately, her father had other ideas.

Paco, her father's ranch hand, followed her out of the mercantile, a hefty box of purchases tucked under one burly arm. To those who didn't know him, the barrel-chested, half-breed Mexican was an intimidating physical specimen, but now he appeared no more threatening than a giant puppy as he lumbered along behind Rachel on the busy Fort Worth street.

"You get everything you wanted, Miss Rachel?" he asked in a hopeful tone.

Rachel glanced at the shopping list she clutched in one gloved hand. "Not quite."

Actually, after one full afternoon of shopping, she *had* procured all the items on her list, but at Paco's timely inquiry, she couldn't help being reminded of one item in particular, a very large item, and one not specified on said written list. It was, in fact, this item that was her most pressing concern—finding a suitable candidate for the title of husband. She had been keeping a sharp eye out all week with less than encouraging results.

Paco spoke again. "We best be getting back. It'll be dark soon."

"That suits me just fine, Paco. It's been a very long and disappointing day, and I've got one humdinger of a headache."

Oh, it was true. It had indeed been a very long and

very disappointing day. Rachel had been reduced to measuring up carefully each male of marriageable age they passed on the street. By now, she was getting desperate.

Just as she and Paco reached their buckboard, a young cowboy passed and politely lifted his hat. "Evenin' ma'am."

Rachel nodded in response. She assumed he was from out of town, one of the many cowboys employed by the independent drovers who came to Fort Worth at this time of year to gather and brand their consignments of cattle.

Out of habit, Rachel turned to size him up from behind. Tall enough, but just barely. Wouldn't crack a mirror. Much too young, she decided. Eighteen if he was a day.

Rachel started to turn away, stopped, then turned back to stare after the departing figure on the street. She was struck with the glimmer of an idea.

Paco, who had apparently not missed the alert expression on Rachel's face, wrinkled his brow. "Ready to go, Miss Rachel?"

She wasn't paying attention. She was thinking. Her father had stipulated that she must get married, but he hadn't said one word about how long she must remain married. Would it be Rachel's fault if the no-good lout ended up deserting her?

"Uh, ready to head back, Miss Rachel?"

Rachel smiled. All she really needed was a temporary husband, preferably a man decent-looking, intelligent, and most importantly, *tall* enough to spare her embarrassment. What she needed was a man who wanted money badly enough to consider going along with the elaborate farce that was taking shape in her mind.

Paco deposited the box of goods into the back of the buckboard. "Miss Rachel?"

What she needed was a mover, a man whose feet got itchy if he stayed in one place for too long. That eliminated all of the local men she had been screening, men with family and business ties to this area. What Rachel needed was an out-of-towner, perhaps an independent drover, a man who came and went with the seasons. What Rachel needed was . . .

Her gaze drifted down the street in the direction the young cowboy had gone, toward a part of town where respectable ladies had few occasions to wander. What Rachel needed might be, at this very moment, settling his wandering male self down to a drink at the Red Panther Saloon. She squared her shoulders, feeling suddenly rejuvenated. "Just one more stop, Paco."

Then she started moving with great purpose, and Paco called after her, clearly panicked. "Oh no! No, Miss Rachel! You are going the *wrong way!*" He hurried to catch up to her. "Don't you remember the last time we went in one of those saloons?"

In fact, Rachel remembered it vividly. Two years before, out of sheer curiosity, she had intruded upon the male confines of the Red Panther Saloon, and her father hadn't been too happy about it when he had gotten the hefty bill for damages. Still, she didn't think it was fair that she'd been blamed for the disastrous saloon brawl that had taken place. It wasn't as if Rachel had actually broken anything herself.

Her brisk pace didn't falter as she waved a dismissive hand. "That was years ago, Paco. I was much younger then, and I didn't know what I was doing. Now I know *exactly* what I am doing."

"But we got into a big fight! And your daddy ended

up paying for all those tables and chairs!" Paco started to wail, "Oh, if your daddy only knew!"

"But he doesn't know does he?" Rachel was determined that her trip into town should not be completely wasted, and the only way of doing that was to go where the men were. And the men were at the Red Panther.

At the Red Panther Saloon, the evening was young but already into full swing. Cigar smoke floated in hazy clouds around the kerosene lamps that hung from the ceiling. Pretty waitresses in short frilly skirts circulated through the crowd, winking and laughing at bad jokes as they served drinks. Big Bart, the piano player, a hefty man with flabby jowls and a severe perspiration problem, was launching into a tinny rendition of "Sweet Betsy from Pike."

Howard the barkeep chewed on the butt of a corona as he served up three-finger glasses of rye whiskey and foaming mugs of beer. As always, he was dressed immaculately in a white shirt and red vest. Howard had kept bar at the Red Panther Saloon since its inception, and although no one had ever died with his boots on in this establishment, he was a cautious man and never far out of reach from the Smith and Wesson Schofield revolver he kept hidden beneath the bar.

Dolly Jordan, madam and proprietress, leaned against the backbar just beneath the lower right corner of her finest piece of Saturday night art, *Aphrodite Emerging from the Bath*. Typical of her ancient profession, Dolly's fleshy white breasts nearly overflowed the dipped neckline of her scarlet satin dress. Bright red and blue ostrich feathers adorned her highly wrapped platinum tresses, and flashy diamond rings and earrings attested to the profitability of her business enterprises.

At a table in the middle of the room, Cal Delaney examined the cards in his hand. A six of hearts, an eight of clubs, two black nines, and a king of diamonds. He threw down the six and the eight. "Give me two, Ezra."

His luck was running high. Not that it mattered much. It was a friendly game of draw poker, played for pitifully low stakes. Still, since Cal had sworn off his former, much more lucrative occupation of bounty hunting, he was painfully conscious of his dwindling finances.

It was probably ironic that now, when for the first time in his life he was ready to set down roots and stake a claim for himself, he was the least able to do so financially. His wages as a cowpuncher didn't add up to much more than chicken feed.

Lacey Holloway appeared at his side and slapped down a fresh beer mug. "There you are, Cal!"

He didn't look up even though he knew the girl would continue to hover. Cal thought she was all right on her back but was rapidly discovering she could be something of a nuisance when standing on two feet.

Ezra Evans, the independent drover Cal had joined up with during his last stop in Dodge City, grinned as he rearranged the cards in his hand. "She's smiling on me tonight, boys!"

Cal's expression didn't reflect any pleasure at the sight of his last two cards. His poker face came without conscious effort. He had long ago learned to bury his emotions, all except anger, of course. He had always considered anger, when it was carefully and precisely channeled, to be a valuable asset, at least in his former profession.

All at once, a discernible hush fell over the crowd. Heads turned and men gaped at the attractive, obviously respectable young woman who had just stepped in the door. A two-headed purple steer lumbering into the saloon would have elicited a similar reaction. When Big Bart's sausagelike fingers stilled on the yellowed ivory keys, the atmosphere surrendered to a sudden, heavy silence.

She stood like a princess, tall, aloof, and unsmiling. Even from where he sat, Cal could see the ethereal color of her eyes as her pale green gaze swept the room. For a jarring moment, those incredible eyes connected with his. Something like recognition flickered between them. But that, of course, was impossible. Cal had never met her before. He would have remembered her.

She blinked, then abruptly looked away. And that slip was the only sign of self-consciousness that he could detect. He read in those eyes that she was young, not in her teens, but young; much younger than her self-assured manner indicated. What the hell was a girl like that doing in a place like this?

A large Mexican entered behind her. Beneath his ragged cowpuncher's garb, Cal figured he packed about 220 pounds of pure muscle. The Mexican glared at the crowd, and, as a direct result, most of the men wisely returned to their former distractions. The customary murmur of the crowd resumed, and Big Bart started tapping out the first notes of "Yellow Rose of Texas."

Ezra's deep voice intruded on Cal's thoughts. "You wanna put yer eyes back in yer head? Are you gonna call or throw in?"

Cal ignored the question. "Who is she?"

"You don't want to know."

Cal tore his attention from the girl and looked at Ezra. "If I asked, I want to know."

The older man sighed. "Her name's Rachel Girard. She's Galen Girard's daughter."

From across the table, Vernon Humphrey snickered and tossed in a chip to start the betting. "Yeah. Don't look, don't touch, don't even *think* about it!"

Cal didn't bother to acknowledge this advice. Young Vern, he knew, was ruled by his newly blossoming glands. Cal suspected that Vern thought about it a lot; that he was, in fact, thinking about it at this very moment. Cal looked to Ezra. "Galen Girard, the rancher?"

Ezra nodded.

Impressed, Cal whistled low through his teeth. She was a princess, all right. A bona fide cattle princess.

"Either call or get out of it, Cal." This was Ezra.

Cal tossed in three chips. "Call and raise two."

Ezra snorted. "Two? What're you trying to do, put me out of business before we get started?"

"Call or get out of it, Ezra."

"Sheee-it."

Cal returned his attention to the girl as she boldly approached the bar, stepping into line near the end and hooking one heel neatly over the brass rail.

Lacey leaned down close to Cal's ear. "She's just a spoiled rich bitch. Known her all my life."

Ezra matched Cal's two dollars and passed the betting to Juan, the third cowpuncher at the table. Juan muttered something wicked in Spanish, then threw his hand facedown onto the table. Vern followed suit.

Dressed like a persnickety schoolteacher, the girl wore a snowy white shirt-blouse tucked into the small waist of an unadorned tan skirt. A stylish straw hat perched ever so primly atop her head, and her hair, pulled into a knot at the nape of her neck, was an odd color, cinnamon spice with rampant streaks of gold. *Gold as Kansas prairie firelights.* This last thought popped into Cal's mind like a bolt from the blue.

Dolly moved to face the primly garbed young woman from across the bar just as Ezra nudged Cal with his elbow. "Well, whatta ya have? We ain't got all night."

Cal reluctantly returned his attention to the game and showed a full house.

Ezra's voice turned petulant. "How the hell do you call for two cards and end up with a full house? Damn it all, Cal!"

Cal raked in his negligible winnings. "Mind if I take a short break, gentlemen?"

With two fingers, Ezra flicked his cards away in mild disgust. "Take a mighty long break if you want."

Cal offered the man one of his rare smiles. "How about if I buy you all a round on me? That fair?"

Ezra's slumping shoulders rose just a little bit. "Yeah, that might ease the pain some, I reckon."

Cal pushed back from the table and stood. Lacey pressed up against him. "Say, Cal, you don't have to do that. I'll get it for you."

"Relax," he said, moving away. "I need to stretch my legs."

His curiosity had gotten the better of him. When he came up behind the girl at the bar, he caught the faint scent of roses, a most uncommon aroma in the middle of a smoky saloon. Her hat now hung loose down her back, secured by a ribbon cinched around her neck. A few coppery tendrils had come free from the knot at her neck and wisped to curl about her face.

Cal felt a passing urge to reach out and tug at her hairpins, to send that entire mass of curls cascading down her back. He thought about that hair fanning out on a pillow in a bed with her lying beneath him, and it caused a sudden, unbidden stirring down below. Cal, who was unaccustomed to being attracted to one woman when experience had taught him any woman would do, made an effort to control himself as he listened to the conversation that now passed between the flamboyant Dolly Jordan and her unlikely customer.

"You must realize, Miss Girard, that it's in my best interests not to offend your father in any way, but the last time I served you, if you'll excuse the expression, all hell broke loose."

"Well, Miss Jordan, my father isn't here right now, so if I were you, I'd stop worrying about offending him and start worrying about offending me."

Dolly batted her eyelashes and thought about this deeply for a moment. "Just what is it you're really after, Miss Girard?"

"I told you before, Miss Jordan. A drink. You do serve drinks, do you not?"

"We do."

"Fine. I'll take a brandy sour if you please."

Dolly rolled her eyes. "You have *got* to be joking."

"Well, a cordial then. You do serve cordials, don't you?"

The corners of Dolly's bright red lips twitched. "Do any of these big, strapping boys look like they order up cordials?"

Rachel gave Dolly a hard look. "Make it bourbon. Neat."

Dolly held the girl's prickly gaze for a long moment

before she inclined her head in the barkeep's direction. "Get it for her, Howard."

Rachel Girard reached into her silk reticule and extracted a silver coin as Howard poured out a small portion of the liquor and pushed it across the bar.

She slapped the coin down triumphantly. "Keep the change."

The barkeep managed to keep his amusement confined to the glint in his eyes. "Much obliged, Miss Girard."

Cal stepped up to the bar beside her and motioned for Howard's attention. "A round of beers for my friends."

As Howard set to work, Cal turned to see Rachel Girard's white-gloved fingers curl around the glass of bourbon before her. Before she could lift it to her lips, however, her head tilted and her gaze traveled up to take in the immodest feminine figure in the huge painting behind the bar.

Cal watched in amusement as full, wine-red lips pressed together prudishly. As if sensing Cal's interest, she jerked her head around to stare at him. Up close, Cal thought those eyes were even more dazzling, emeralds flecked with bits of amber. He was gratified to see a tinge of color rise to her cheeks when he didn't look away. So, she *was* human. Her tone of voice, however, was cool as winter winds on the prairie.

"What are you staring at? Haven't you ever seen a lady take a drink before?"

"Yes, I've seen many ladies take drinks before."

"Well then, this shouldn't be anything for you to be especially concerned about, should it?"

Cal couldn't help the slow smile that curved his lips. "No, ma'am, I reckon not."

She picked up the glass, poised to drink. To her right, a shabbily dressed cowboy, drunk as a boiled owl, staggered up to the bar. He steadied himself, then turned bleary eyes on the beautiful girl standing aloof and unaffected to his left. He blinked at her, then opened his mouth. "Hey—*hic!* . . . little girlie."

Cal saw Rachel's delicate jaw tense as she tried to ignore him. The huge Mexican that had followed her in started to move up close behind the cowboy.

"Hey little—*hic!* . . . little girlie."

Rachel looked at him. "Are you addressing me?"

"I sure—*hic!* . . . I sure am."

Howard set down a tray of foaming mugs by Cal's elbow. Cal removed a bill from his pocket and slid it across the bar.

A voice rose from the crowd somewhere behind the wavering cowpoke and the looming Mexican. "Hey, Benny-boy, you know who you're talking to?"

Benny-boy's forehead crinkled as he pondered the inquiry, then he turned around, apparently oblivious to the menacing Mexican behind him. "I yam speakin' to the—*hic!* I yam speakin' to the—*hic!*"

Losing all track of his most recent thought, he turned back to squint at Rachel. "How come ya don't lift yer skirts, little girlie?"

Cal could only imagine her icy stare. "I beg your *pardon?*"

"I said, lift yer skirts! We cain't see yer—*hic!* . . . legs!"

"Well, I can't see your hick legs either, and I can only thank my lucky stars for that."

Benny-boy squinted at her fuzzily, no doubt trying to discern whether he had just been insulted. Unbeknownst to him, the Mexican now loomed like a black thundercloud directly over his right shoulder.

"Hey!" the cowboy demanded. "Whaddaya mean by that? Come here a minute!" No decision to reach for Rachel Girard would have been a wise one, but where he touched her, swiping drunkenly for her arm and instead landing an open palm across the rise of her breast, was akin to setting off a keg of dynamite.

The Mexican's warning, which started at a low, threatening rumble, rose to a thundering roar. "Get your hands off her *NOW!*"

The cowpoke turned around to peer up into the Mexican's furious countenance. "Whaaat? A greaser? I don't follow no damn orders from no—*hic!* . . . no damned greaser!"

The Mexican's full face suffused with blood. His black eyes bulged with fury. He wrapped hamlike fists around the open collar of Benny-boy's shirt and lifted him straight up. After holding him suspended for a moment, the Mexican grunted and gave a mighty heave.

Benny-boy flew across the room as surely as if he had grown angel wings. He landed with an earsplitting crunch, smack-dab in the middle of a table full of serious poker players. The table splintered and collapsed like a circus tent. Playing cards and poker chips flew as five shocked cowpokes staggered back out of their chairs. One of them sprang back up, snagged Benny-boy by the collar. Yanking him to a standing position, he pulled back a fist. "I was holding four aces, you son of a bitch!"

Cal lost track of the exact sequence of events soon after Benny-boy was sent careening back into yet another group of surly onlookers. Mayhem erupted. The waitresses, well-accustomed to the occasional free-for-all, scattered and beelined for the far corners of the room, holding their drink trays up like shields when the debris started flying. Big Bart jammed his bowler hat down onto his head and made a break for the door.

As unbridled confusion descended, Rachel took an inadvertent step backward. Cal was not at all displeased to feel her pressed up against him. Immediately upon contact, she jumped and whirled around to stare up at him in shock.

Out of the corner of his eye, he caught a flash of brass behind her. A cowboy had just rammed one arm into a foot-high brass cuspidor and was preparing to swing it like a battering ram. Cal wrapped an arm around the astonished girl's waist and yanked her down onto the floor with him.

She gasped as the cuspidor whizzed over their heads and she offered no resistance as Cal proceeded to inch them backward, with her on his lap, through a tangled mass of denim-clad legs. It was miraculous that they made it behind the bar without any mishaps.

Once settled, Cal was in no hurry to release her. Even in the midst of all this ruckus, the feel of her hind quarters snuggled so neatly in his lap was quite pleasant.

Apparently unaware of the delightful effect her movements had on his personals, she wiggled and twisted around to face him. He expected to see fright or shock or panic. What he saw instead was righteous indignance. "I'm not paying for all of this!"

Howard and Dolly cowered close by. Dolly looked up as a whiskey bottle shot through the air and smashed into the portrait above the backbar, spattering the canvas and leaving a gaping hole where Aphrodite's head had been. She glowered at Rachel

Girard. "This is all your fault! Your daddy's getting the bill!"

The knot in Rachel's hair was coming loose. Cal got a neat slap in the face from a swinging tress as she whipped her head around to face the livid madam. "This isn't my fault, Dolly Jordan! I'll see this place closed down before I pay one cent!"

Dolly sneered. "We'll see what your daddy says about that!"

Apparently deciding it was high time to take matters into his own hands, Howard rose to his feet, his Smith and Wesson Schofield revolver aimed high over his balding head. He fired at the ceiling.

The blast had no discernible effect on the confusion within the saloon, but it did manage to free a set of kerosene lamps hanging overhead. With its suspending chain severed, the chandelier crashed down onto Howard's carefully polished bar and shattered into many expensive pieces. The barkeep sank back down to his haunches and gave Dolly a sheepish look.

Cal spoke next to Rachel's ear. "Let's get out of here."

Horrified, she pointed at the melee. "Through *that?*"

Cal released his grip on her waist so she could scramble free. "Through the back."

On hands and knees, Cal navigated a route to the rear exit. Once outside they both got to their feet. The cool night air was a refreshing contrast to the smoky interior of the barroom.

Rachel had gathered her skirt up into a bunch at her knees to facilitate movement, and Cal caught a brief glimpse of shapely calves wrapped in black stockings before the skirt once again dropped like a curtain to her ankles. He thought Benny-boy would surely have appreciated the view if only he had been awake and present to see it.

Rachel peered around them in the gathering dusk. To their right was the dilapidated rear of the Red Panther Hotel. In front of them, at the end of a long wooden walk, rose the two-story house occupied by Dolly Jordan and her girls. Rachel's eyes narrowed as her gaze stuck on the telling red lantern burning in the second-floor window above the front entrance.

She turned away from the sight with a little *harumph* and reached up to adjust her hat. Upon finding nothing there, her hand started hopping around the top of her head like a jumping spider. "Oh no!"

Both hands then flew to her neck to discover that the bow ribbon cinched there earlier was nowhere to be found. Her next words would have brought sympathy from any cowpoke worth his salt. "My hat! Blame it all! I lost my hat!"

Cal folded his arms. "I wouldn't advise going in there after it just now."

She muttered under her breath. "Rowdy bunch of animals."

"The boys just needed to let off a little steam."

Rachel fixed him with a look that might have pierced the shell of an armadillo. "Well, you didn't seem to feel the need, I see."

"I've found other ways to vent my steam, Miss Girard."

Her lips parted just slightly, revealing the tips of white, very straight teeth, and her eyes widened. Even in the fading light, Cal couldn't miss the scarlet flush that rose to stain her cheeks. He hadn't meant his comment to be taken in a suggestive sense. What was on this prim young lady's mind, anyway?

She bit her lip and stammered. "I—I'm sorry, it's just that it's been a long and very, uh . . ." She trailed off, cocking her head to one side, adopting an odd, contemplative expression. It was as if she were seeing him for the first time. "That is, it's been a long and very interesting day," she finished.

"You have a way home?"

"Yes. Our wagon is down the street, and I'm sure Paco will be along soon." She raised a hand to smooth back a curl that had fallen across her face. "Thank you for your help, Mr. . . . ?"

"Delaney."

"Mr. Delaney." Having regained some of her original dignity, she started across the barren yard.

Cal watched, amused, as she stumbled over a gopher hole and barely managed to catch her balance before limping around the corner of the saloon to finally disappear from view.

3

Rachel hovered just inside the closed door of her father's study, well aware that she was probably giving the impression of a skittish filly preparing to bolt. Unfortunately, she couldn't help it. She felt jumpier than a toad on a hot griddle.

Ezra Evans and his new foreman sat across from her father's desk discussing the drover's needs for the season. There was nothing about their conversation that differed from those in years past, but it wasn't the conversation that made Rachel nervous. It was Ezra's foreman, Cal Delaney. The memory of scrambling across the floor of the Red Panther Saloon with him was still all too embarrassingly fresh.

Having already clarified just what livestock Ezra was looking for and just what Galen was prepared to sell, the two men launched into price negotiations. Normally, Rachel was fascinated just observing her father, who was a master at this art, but she couldn't bring herself to pay much attention to the haggling today. Instead, she studied the man who had, up until now, sat virtually silent by Ezra's side. So far, he'd said nothing of their episode at the Red Panther, and Rachel was glad for that. She hadn't quite found the words to explain the incident to her father yet.

Ezra finished scratching out purchase prices on a list of stock and pushed it across the desk for Galen to inspect. "That look about right to you?"

Galen scanned the sheet. "You know I've always had a soft spot for you, Ezra. Otherwise, I wouldn't let you take advantage of me like this."

Ezra hooted good-naturedly. "You hear that, Cal? He says it every damn year! And look at which one of us is sitting behind the big fat desk wearing a flashy vest and which one of us is poking cow butts up the trail with holes in his boots!" Ezra caught himself and touched his hat brim apologetically. "Excuse the language, Miss Girard. Sometimes I plumb forget there's a lady present."

Rachel was all too aware of Delaney's measuring gaze as it settled on her from across the room, but she did her best to ignore it. "No need to apologize, Ezra. I've heard a foul word or two in my time, and my ears haven't burned off yet."

Galen chuckled. "Lord knows she's *used* a foul word or two in her time, and her gums haven't stopped flapping yet either."

Rachel smiled grudgingly. Her father could be difficult, but he was also just about the only man Rachel had ever known who seemed willing to treat women with the same respect he accorded men. Rachel could thank her dear departed mother for that.

Galen proffered the sheet in her direction, and

Rachel crossed the room to take it, quickly checking the figures as Galen and Ezra continued to chat. When she was finished, she handed the paper back to her father, addressing Ezra. "When do you figure you'll be ready for trail branding?"

The older man scratched his chin. "Well, most of my boys'll be here by the end of next week."

Galen pushed the sheet back across the desk. "Mr. Delaney, why don't you take this to my ranch hand Paco Rodriguez? You'll find him out by the corral helping with the green mounts. He'll be able to give you an idea about when we can have these beeves rounded up."

Rachel watched as Cal Delaney rose to full height, her gaze taking in his lean hips, muscled thighs, and long legs encased in a pair of snug-fitting denims. She felt a spot of warmth come up on each cheek and hastily jerked her attention back to where it belonged. Well, he easily topped six feet, anyway. Tall enough, even for Rachel the Beanstalk.

Cal took the paper. "I'll do that." He touched the brim of his hat. "It's been a pleasure, Mr. Girard."

Galen nodded. "Maybe we'll do business again."

"I hope so." Then those enigmatic blue eyes moved to touch Rachel. "It's also been a pleasure to meet you, ma'am."

Did she detect a hint of sarcasm? "Likewise, Mr. Delaney."

When he was gone, Galen reached for his cigar box and offered one to Ezra. The drover took one, clearly thrilled by the opportunity to smoke something that cost more than a penny.

Rachel scrutinized her father's innocently complacent features. He was buttering Ezra up, and when Galen stooped to buttering anything other than his morning toast, there was good reason for it. She wondered what he was up to.

As Ezra slid back in his upholstered chair, Galen settled into his own seat like a lazy bear. His eyelids drooped as he interlaced his fingers across his middle. "Tell me, Ezra, this Delaney fella. Where did you find him?"

Ezra blew out a frothy smoke ring. "Met him in Dodge City last month. I'd heard of him before, but we never exchanged words until then. He wanted a job. Said he wanted to learn about the cattle trade, maybe start a ranch of his own someday."

"Is that right? A man with ambition? That's good to hear."

Ezra grinned. "He's got a good head on his shoulders too. Works hard and learns fast."

"Was he in another line of work before this?"

"I'm surprised you never heard of him. Then again, I guess his reputation doesn't extend to Texas. You ask about Cal Delaney around Kansas, though, and most people will recognize the name."

"Come again?"

"He was a bounty hunter for some years, a damned good one too. Earned quite a reputation with his gun."

Galen was quiet for a moment, and Rachel took the opportunity to sift through this new information. She had seen many a wanted poster hanging outside the marshal's office in town. REWARD: $1000, REWARD: $1250, REWARD: $5000. She wondered how Cal Delaney was going to adjust to a cowboy's salary of thirty dollars a month. She assumed that if he had managed to save any of his previous earnings, he would have gone ahead and bought a spread of his own by now.

Galen narrowed his eyes at the drover. "I didn't see he was wearing a gun belt."

Ezra shifted in his seat uneasily. "Well, that's a subject that don't sit well with him, Galen. All he'll say about it is that he's hung up his guns for good, and that's that. I can tell you one thing for sure, though."

"What's that?"

"When he says something, he means it."

Rachel mused to herself. Why *had* Cal Delaney given up his guns? Surely, he could earn his stake money quicker doing what he did best. "Daddy, you don't need me here anymore, do you?" she said suddenly.

Galen glanced up. "No, I don't suppose so."

Rachel flashed the visiting drover a polite smile. "Ezra, it was nice to see you again."

"Yes, Miss Girard, it was nice to see you too." Ezra started to scramble to his feet, but Rachel waved him down as she crossed the room and opened the door to leave.

When she reached the front porch seconds later, she spotted Paco and Delaney standing by the small corral where Sam Callahan, a contract bronco buster, was hard at work breaking in this spring's selection of wild horses. Their backs were turned to her, and this gave her some time to think over just exactly how she should go about proposing marriage to him.

She would handle it in a businesslike manner. She would offer him a sum that would be impossible for a man of his means to refuse. Still, something in her stomach curled sickly at the possibility he might turn her down flat.

When Paco finally moved off, she steeled herself for the plunge. By the time she reached Delaney's side, he had parked one booted foot on the lower rung of the fence and was leaning both forearms over the top of it, observing the activity in the ring.

She stepped up beside him and mirrored his pose. "His name is Sam Callahan," she said, indicating with a nod the man who was engaged in roping an uncooperative bronc. "He's the best around."

"That doesn't surprise me."

Rachel looked up. His gaze was still fixed on the figures in the corral, his broad-brimmed hat pulled low over his eyes. She thought his profile was exceptionally handsome. His nose was straight, the curve of his lips undeniably sensual, his jaw, strong and angular. She returned her attention to the action in the ring. "What doesn't surprise you?"

"That you would have only the best."

His voice, she noticed, was low but smooth as imported India silk. It caressed the ears. A woman could lose herself in the seductive sound of that voice, lose track of what he was actually saying, but Rachel was determined not to fall victim to that. "Where are you from, Mr. Delaney?" she asked.

"I'm from a lot of different places, Miss Girard."

"Originally, I mean."

"I grew up mostly around Abilene, Kansas."

"A cow town. Is that where you learned the trade?"

He looked at her, casually nudging the brim of his hat back with one finger. "The cattle trade?"

The expression in those cerulean blue eyes was startlingly clear. It was probably because of this that her reply came out huffier than she intended. "Certainly the cattle trade. What did you think I meant, the cotton trade, the button trade, the snake oil trade?"

He smiled. "Well, to answer your first question, no, that's not where I learned the cattle trade. I'm still learning the cattle trade, Miss Girard. My parents had a very small farm, and about the only cattle I came in contact with growing up was a mean-tempered, crotchety old cow named Daisy."

Rachel blinked, surprised. "Your cow's name was Daisy?"

"That's right."

She had to look away and bite her lip to keep from laughing out loud. What would snooty Daisy Parker Girard think of that? Another silence. A long one this time. Sam had cross-hobbled the pony's forefeet with ropes. Now, he struggled to hold the rearing animal while lifting a heavy saddle onto its back. No easy task.

Cal Delaney turned back to the action, leaning forward to rest his forearms comfortably on the corral fence. As he did so, Rachel couldn't help noticing that he had unusually fine-looking hands for a man. His fingers were long and slim and unmarred, the nails trimmed short and surprisingly clean. His skin was tan from years in the sun, and the fine hair curling on his wrists gleamed like strands of spun gold in the sunlight. She remembered how intimately those hands had held her as they inched together across the dusty floor of the Red Panther Saloon. They had felt warm and strong and quite capable of . . .

Mortified at the direction of her thoughts, Rachel caught herself. What in blue blazing hell was the matter with her?

She straightened. "Thank you for not saying anything to my father about that little incident at the saloon yesterday."

"Mmmmmm. They were still sweeping up this morning."

Rachel pressed her lips together indignantly. Not "You're welcome," not "My pleasure," just "They were still sweeping up this morning." She wasn't sure if she could stand having this man around—even if it would be only temporary. He had a way of getting under her skin that was most annoying. She forced herself to press on. "Ezra tells us you're planning on buying some land. That takes money these days."

"That it does."

She gave him a sideways look. "More money than a cowpuncher earns, I'll wager."

"You oughta know."

Sam twisted the bronc's ear as he tried to mount, obviously hoping the pain would distract the animal enough so he could get a foothold in the stirrup. There were some lively hoots and claps from the ranch hands as Sam finally managed to swing a leg over the wild horse's back.

Rachel rested her forearms on the fence again, steepling her fingers and gathering her thoughts. It was now or never. "I have a rather unusual business proposal for you, Mr. Delaney."

Now, he did look at her, and Rachel could feel those eyes burning into her skin like two firebrands. After what seemed like an ungodly long span of time, he urged her on. "And what is that?"

"You see, my father can be rather eccentric at times. He's made an unusual request of me." Rachel grimaced and corrected herself. "Not a request, a demand. It's a stipulation to my inheritance."

"A stipulation that I can help you with?"

"If you decide to."

"Well?"

"My father is setting his affairs in order and has insisted that I marry. Otherwise, he's threatened to leave the Elena Rose to my cousin."

There. It was out. Rachel fought the urge to squeeze

her eyes shut and hunch her shoulders as if awaiting the sound of a large explosion.

There was no explosion, just a hesitation. Two slow beats. "Are you saying . . . you're looking for a . . . *husband?*"

"That's exactly what I'm saying."

He just stared at her for a long moment, and then without warning, he threw back his head and laughed—quite uproariously, as a matter of fact. Rachel felt her ire rise. So, he was taking this proposal as some sort of joke, was he? Well, she would throw in the bait and see just how funny he thought it was!

She had to raise her voice to be sure he could hear her over all that guffawing. "I'm talking about a business arrangement, Mr. Delaney. A six-month business arrangement, after which time I would expect the man in question to disappear in exchange for the sum of twenty thousand dollars."

It worked. He stopped laughing. He lowered his foot from the corral fence and faced her. His words came out as six very distinct, disbelieving syllables. "Twen-tee-thou-sand-doll-ars?"

"You heard right, Mr. Delaney."

"Let me get this straight. You want me to marry you, then leave you after six months. In return for this, you'll pay me twenty thousand dollars?"

"That's correct."

"I don't understand. If your father wants you married, why won't he just disinherit you when your husband disappears?"

Rachel couldn't resist a smug smile. "I said my father can be rather eccentric, Mr. Delaney. I doubt he would be so cruel as to kick me when I'm down."

"What does he expect to get out of this?"

Rachel avoided his eyes. "I don't know."

"Grandchildren?"

She looked up at him sharply. "Well, he won't get them!"

The corners of his lips turned up. "How can you be so sure?"

"Because, Mr. Delaney, this marriage is to be in name only. It's to be a business arrangement, nothing more."

He nodded, but that grating smile didn't fade. "Oh, I see. Well, what am I to do if, after I pack up and steal off in the night, your father takes it into his mind to send his bulldogs after me with vengeance to serve?"

Rachel tossed her head and pretended to be observing the action in the corral. "I'd do my best to dissuade him, of course, but in either case, you strike me as a man who can take care of himself."

"Mmmmmmmm."

She glanced over to see his eyes following Sam Callahan's adventures in the ring, but she could tell that he was thinking about other things—about twenty thousand dollars earned in six months as opposed to the approximately $180 he might earn working the cattle trails north.

After a few moments, he asked, "Why me?"

"You seem suitable for the job."

"You don't know anything about me."

"I know all I need to know. It's not like we'll be spending our lives together."

They passed a few more moments in thoughtful silence. Inside the ring, man and animal engaged in a lively battle of wills, the kicked-up dust forming low-hanging, swirling brown clouds. It was evident that both the bronc and its buster were beginning to tire.

Cal turned to her. "All right, Miss Girard, you're

telling me you have twenty thousand dollars in your own name to hand over to me, in cash, after six months, is that about the size of it?"

"I have a dowry. Well, actually, it's a trust account."

He snorted doubtfully. "You have a twenty-thousand-dollar dowry? I wonder why some man hasn't kidnapped you and dragged you by your hair to the altar by now."

Rachel gave him a wilting look. "No, but I have part ownership in my cousin's stockyards, and that's good enough collateral against any loan I might want to take out. As it is, there's ten thousand dollars sitting in an account at the bank right now, ready to be put into my name when I turn twenty-one. Go check it out with Mr. Van Zandt."

"I might just do that."

"You think about it, Mr. Delaney. The offer's on the table for three days. Paco goes into town every Thursday morning. I'll tell him to stop by the Red Panther Hotel. I assume that's where you're staying?"

He nodded.

Ignoring the maddening little grin that curved his lips, she pressed on, "I'll tell him to stop by the hotel. You tell him yes or no. If it's yes, I'll expect you for supper here at the ranch at six o'clock sharp." She pointed a finger at him. "And there'll be no maybe's about it, either. After Thursday morning, the offer is rescinded, is that clear?

"Rescinded. Clear. Yes, ma'am."

She turned to leave. "Good day, Mr. Delaney."

That night, Cal lay awake and restless until well past two in the morning. Lacey had sidled up to him, snoring like an old beagle in his ear, and he wished again that he hadn't gotten into the habit of letting her stay over in his room.

He turned on his side, gingerly disengaging himself from the girl's slumbering clutches. Rachel Girard's bizarre marriage proposal had been turning over in his mind all evening. He hadn't been able to stop thinking about it even during sex, and that amounted to a waste of five good dollars as far as he was concerned.

There was a time when five dollars hadn't meant anything to him, whether he was flush or not, but now he had a goal. Each dollar earned and saved represented one more step toward accomplishing that goal. A place of his own. No more guns. No more death or revenge. No more past.

Rachel Girard's face, in every exquisite detail, now formed a compelling picture in his mind's eye. It was not an easy face to forget. Neither was her temperament. She was one sharp-witted woman. Sharp-witted and sharp-tongued. He wasn't sure he could stand being around her for six months, but . . .

Twenty thousand dollars. Even aside from the money, if he were to take the long view, there was another opportunity to be taken advantage of. After all, he wanted to start a small ranch of his own someday. From whom better to learn the ropes than Galen Girard himself?

Later that night, for the first time in years, Cal dreamed not of bad things like murder and flames or men with empty, black eyes. He dreamed instead of good things, hopeful things, things thrusting toward a future that held bright promise. In fact, the following morning, he vaguely recollected making love in a bed full of greenbacks to a beautiful, faceless girl with firelights in her hair.

4

Dusk had not yet fallen when Cal reined in at the Elena Rose ranch house for the second time in one week. He stepped down from the saddle and tethered his black stallion Friday to a hitching post near the corral.

The opulent Girard home was a grand monument to the prosperity of its wily owner. It was an imposing two-and-one-half-story redbrick structure, its uppermost floor formed by a sharply sloped mansard roof. Arched windows as tall as a man faced the sprawling front lawn. A balcony ringed by a stone balustrade graced the front of the second story and formed the roof of a spacious front porch.

Cal's first impression of the house where Galen Girard and his extended family lived was one of awe tempered with amusement. *Showy,* he had thought, *like a peacock strutting its stuff.* Galen Girard, although professing to be a man of humble beginnings, was obviously not ashamed of flaunting his present success.

Cal patted his stallion's nose. "Well, Friday, here goes nothing."

As Cal strolled up the flagstone walk, he saw that Rachel awaited him on the porch swing. She wore a very proper navy blue skirt with a white, high-necked blouse. Not a bow or a ruffle in sight. She looked even more frigid than usual, prompting him to wonder if he was just special or if she greeted all her suitors so starchily dressed.

His spurs jingled as he took the porch steps. Rachel rose to her feet. "I see you've decided to accept my offer."

Cal looked down on the lovely young cattle princess. "To be quite frank, Miss Girard, for twenty thousand dollars, I'd probably consent to marry one of those cows your father raises."

"How flattering."

Cal folded his arms. "So, tell me, have we set a date?"

"Well, I suppose there's no sense in wasting time. The sooner we get started, the sooner we can go our separate ways. I thought that after supper you could request a private conference with my father and ask him then."

"Ask him what?"

Rachel looked a trifle put out at his stupidity. "Ask him for my hand, what do you think?

Cal laughed. "What's the point? Isn't he the one instigating all of this?"

"Well, you do have to pass inspection. Are you worried?"

"I suppose it depends on what the requirements are."

"I know my father pretty well, Mr. Delaney. I can assure you that he'll find you eminently qualified."

"Hmmm, I see. Then what happens after tonight? Courtship? Poetry? Flowers?" Cal smirked. "You'll have to excuse my ignorance, but I've never accepted a lady's proposal of marriage before."

"In that case, you'll be greatly relieved to know that none of that will be necessary, Mr. Delaney. My father may be tyrannical and demanding, but he's no fool. Love at first sight isn't one of his requirements. A valid marriage certificate is. Shall we go in?"

"Hold it. I have something for you." Cal pulled a folded sheet of paper from his vest pocket.

She gave him a wary look before taking the sheet and unfolding it. She started to read aloud, "I, Rachel Girard, promise to pay to Caleb Delaney twenty thousand cash dollars upon completion of the following terms." She looked up, narrowing her eyes. "What is this, Mr. Delaney? Don't tell me that between bounty hunting and cowpunching, you've somehow found the time to attend law school?"

"What this amounts to is just plain old horse sense. Business is business."

"We agree on that much at least. Perhaps there is a chance we'll get along."

"I wouldn't go getting my hopes up."

She smiled coyly. "I don't have a pen."

"Miss Girard, I'm confident you'll manage to locate one before the evening is over."

Rachel folded the sheet and tucked it into the pocket of her skirt. "Is there anything else we need to clear between us before we go in to face the lions?"

"I can't think of a thing," Cal said, offering her his arm.

Rachel ignored this gallant gesture and turned her back to open the door for herself. Cal rolled his eyes before following her inside. He suspected he would be earning every penny of those twenty thousand cash dollars before six months was up.

Rachel's reference to facing the lions had seemed a good example of her dry sense of humor. But when Cal met the rest of her family he was forced to reconsider this interpretation. Supper with the Girards was like a lesson in genteel warfare.

Rachel's aunt Charlotte was polite enough, but her incessant questioning soon turned pointier than a goose quill pen.

"Where are you from, Mr. Delaney?"

"What is it exactly that you do, Mr. Delaney?"

"Is this your first visit to Fort Worth, Mr. Delaney?"

Cal was just waiting for her to inquire after what fashion of underdrawers he happened to be wearing this evening.

Charlotte's son, Nick, said little throughout the meal, but Cal would have had to be blind to miss the hostile glances that kept coming at him from across the table. Although Nick and Rachel were technically cousins, Cal thought Nick was acting more like a big brother out to defend his sister's virtue.

Daisy Girard was a blatant flirt. She and Rachel sat on either side of Nick, looking and acting like the two sides to every story—diametric opposites. Daisy, small and delicate and blond, was the epitome of the coquette. This evening, with a male guest at the dinner table, she sparkled like fine champagne.

Cal couldn't help noticing that whenever Daisy opened her mouth to speak, Rachel clammed up and

her posture grew stiff. It was clear that those two were
engaged in a family feud.

Cal did his best to ignore the undercurrents that
ebbed and flowed around him, concentrating instead
on enjoying supper, a sumptuous meal of thick steaks,
baked potatoes smothered in creamy butter, and warm,
fresh-baked bread. As a man who had lived much of his
life either on the back of a horse or drifting from one
shabby hotel to another, he had learned to appreciate a
home-cooked meal when he could get one.

He was dragged into the crossfire only once. With
clear purpose, Daisy had settled those bright blue eyes
on him and smiled sweetly from across the table.
"Why, it's so nice to have one of Rachel's beaux to
supper. It's so seldom that one actually gets this far."
She looked to her husband for confirmation. "You
remember poor Vincent Jenkins? He never made it
past the front porch."

She turned back to Cal, her blond ringlets bouncing.
"Why, when he hightailed it out of here, I swear the
dust kicked up by his horse was still hanging in the air
the next morning!"

Nick gave his wife a warning look. "Daisy . . ."

She blithely ignored him. Her eyes danced at Cal
invitingly. "Just how was it that you two met again?"

Cal glanced at Rachel, who was busy stabbing at her
steak as if she was trying to kill it all over again. "Well,
we met right here at the house just the other day."

Daisy gave Rachel a smirk that went pointedly
unacknowledged. "So, she's not had time to scare you
off yet?"

Nick interrupted. "Daisy, we all know you're just
teasing, but Mr. Delaney may not be able to appreciate
it just yet."

Daisy laughed and looked back at Cal. "Oh, Mr. Delaney, you knew I was just teasing, didn't you?"

"Of course, Mrs. Girard. Anyone can see that you and Rachel get along just like two peas in a pod."

Oh, yes. Supper had been a brief but very revealing introduction to the working dynamics of the wealthy Girard family. Cal thought it was no wonder Rachel had armed herself with a tongue as sharp as a cat's claw.

Rachel excused herself from the table just before dessert was finished and reappeared moments later as everyone was rising from their seats. Cal realized what she had been up to when she sidled over to him casually. With her back to the others, she produced their contract from her skirt pocket and pressed it into his waiting hand. "I believe that seals our deal."

Cal slid it into his vest pocket. "I believe it does."

She cocked her head and smiled, her green eyes shining. Cal doubted she had any idea how seductive she looked at that moment. "Aren't you going to check it over?"

"I trust you, Miss Girard."

"You're going to have to stop calling me Miss Girard. It sounds a little formal, considering."

Cal nodded seriously. "Right. Considering."

Galen interrupted their conversation by approaching them from behind and draping a fatherly arm around Rachel's shoulders. He grinned at Cal. "Do you have a taste for brandy and cigars following a fine meal, Mr. Delaney, or would I be tearing you away too soon from my lovely daughter's charming company?"

Cal and Rachel exchanged a significant look. Galen's offer couldn't have been better timed if they had planned it themselves.

A few minutes later, Cal followed the man into a study furnished in dark masculine colors. The walls were adorned with gilt-framed ranch scenes. There were no crocheted doilies, crystal figurines, or fresh flowers in ceramic vases to lighten the atmosphere. In fact, all of the feminine touches present throughout the rest of the house were noticeably absent. It was clear that the study had been designed as a haven where men could retreat to conduct business or simply relax and enjoy each other's company.

It wasn't long, however, before the atmosphere became anything but relaxed. The Big Question had been posed. The older man was pacing. And Cal was on the grill.

"You got a past, son?"

Cal eyed him warily. "Everyone's got a past, Mr. Girard."

"Ezra tells me you hunted bounty for a few years."

"That's true."

"Ready to hang up your guns, are you?"

Cal swallowed a mouthful of expensive brandy. It jolted his taste buds and burned a trail down his throat. It helped to shut out the fleeting image of a boy, not more than sixteen, down in the street, his kneecap shattered, his arm soaked from wrist to elbow with dark blood. Cal took a deep breath. "I already have, in case you haven't noticed."

Girard chuckled. "What else you been into, son?"

Cal fought an urge to tell the old man to mind his own damned business. "I worked a while as a shotgun messenger for Wells Fargo out of Virginia City."

"Virginia City, you say? Visited there a few times on business. Spent some time at the Washoe Club. Took Rachel and the wife along once. We stayed at the

International Hotel, and neither one of 'em could get enough of that fancy elevator! We must have spent the better part of that week just ridin' up and down, up and down."

Cal tried to picture the aloof Rachel Girard gushing and excited, but the image just wouldn't come. "I take it that was a few years back?"

Girard flipped open the handsome cigar box that rested on the corner of his desk and offered Cal a stogie. Cal accepted. "A couple. I guess Rachel's grown up some since then." Girard smiled slyly. "As I recall, the Wells Fargo agency was located on the west side of C Street."

Cal rolled the cigar back and forth between two fingers. "That's the east side. A man by the name of Farley is heading it up these days. You can check it out if you want."

"Oh, you can bet on it." The rancher struck a match and held it for Cal. "You've been around. I'll say that for you. How old are you?"

"Twenty-seven."

Girard lit his own cigar and shook the match out. "Done a lot in twenty-seven years."

Cal puffed experimentally. He recognized the quality immediately. He shrugged in answer to the cattle baron's observation. "Been on my own since I was fifteen."

Girard's dark blue eyes glittered as he tipped his head back and finished off his liquor. He coughed once and brushed the sleeve of his shirt across his mouth. "I reckon you've had occasion to kill some men."

Cal looked away. "When I had to."

"You ever heavy-hand a woman?"

Cal looked up to clash with Girard's wily gaze.

"Hell, no. I wouldn't have the stomach for it. Besides, I never met a woman who deserved it."

Girard let out a hoot. "You never met up with my Rachel before either!"

Cal allowed that comment to pass without a reply. Galen Girard certainly had no illusions about his daughter's notorious reputation.

"Why do you want to marry her?"

"She's a wonderful girl. Why wouldn't I want to marry her?"

Galen chuckled at this. "Tell me what it is that's so wonderful about her."

Cal thought for a moment. The old man supposedly wanted his headstrong daughter married, but he was setting traps just the same. What was his game? "Well, she's pretty. She's smart. I . . ." Cal almost choked over his next words. "We, uh, got a lot in common . . . I think."

Girard looked skeptical. "We'll find out about that soon enough." His voice turned cagey. "She's rich too. I suppose you were aware of that."

"It's not hard to figure out."

Girard changed the subject without warning. "Why'd you give up hunting bounty?"

Cal sighed and decided to tell him at least part of the truth. "After a while, Mr. Girard, I developed a certain reputation. When that happens, you're a walking target for any fool who wants to make a name for himself. Unless you have eyes in the back of your head, your luck is bound to run out sooner or later."

"So you decided to try your hand at cow punching."

"For the time being."

"It don't pay much, does it?"

Cal realized where the old man was leading. He met his penetrating gaze but didn't answer.

Finally, Girard spoke again. "Rachel's fixing to earn her inheritance, son. She tell you about that?"

"She told me about it."

"Most men hereabouts don't know what to do with a girl like Rachel. She's beautiful, she's smart, and she's strong-willed. She scares the hell out of 'em. If she was to get hitched with any of the bellyaching pansies I've seen sniffing around her in the last few months, she'd have them broken and under her thumb in no time. That's not good enough for my girl. You understand?"

Cal finished his liquor in one shot. "I think so."

"I raised her to be just exactly what she is, Mr. Delaney. I taught her to shoot a gun, ride a horse, and muck out a stall as well as strike deals with cattle brokers. I taught her to love the Elena Rose with every fiber of her being, and I'll never apologize for that. Her mother wasn't just a raving beauty, she was the salt of the earth, and I loved her more than life itself. Rachel's a lot like her. All I want for our daughter is a chance to be happy. She thinks the Elena Rose will do that for her. I know different. You think you can handle my Rachel, Cal Delaney?"

"I've handled bloodthirsty, murdering outlaws, Mr. Girard. You think I can't handle one strong-minded woman?"

Girard lifted a bushy eyebrow. "That remains to be seen. You think you can earn a piece of the Elena Rose in the bargain?"

"I want something of my own, Mr. Girard. I'm not asking you or anyone else to hand it to me for free."

Girard laughed heartily. "And I'm not in the habit of giving gifts with no strings attached, son. I want to ensure a solid bloodline to follow me, but what I

decide to pass on has to be earned. And that goes for
Rachel and Nicholas as well as you, Cal. That is, if you
marry my daughter in good faith."

"I understand, Mr. Girard."

The older man's smile was cunning as he reached to
refill Cal's glass. "I hope you do, son. If any man ever
has the gall to hurt my daughter while I've still got a
breath left in my body, he'd better make damn sure he
can get very far away from here very fast because I'll
see to it that he pays. And I don't care how good he is
with a gun. You understand *that*, Mr. Delaney?"

Cal watched as the cattle baron calmly poured from
the decanter. It would seem that his uncompromising
reputation was well deserved. Cal smiled as he
accepted another glass of brandy. "I do, Mr. Girard."

Rachel stood in the hallway, her arms crossed, her
toe tapping. She looked up irritably at the sound of
male laughter. One question. One answer. What could
be taking so long? The two of them had been in there
for over thirty minutes, tossing down drinks, smoking
like chimneys, laughing it up, and shooting the bull
like two long-lost war buddies.

She had known from the first word exchanged with
Cal Delaney that her father would heartily approve of
him. Delaney was a drifting ex-bounty hunter without
a dime to his name, and her father was a filthy rich
cattle man, but Rachel sensed that underneath, those
two were a lot alike. At the moment, however, their
camaraderie was annoying, as it left her standing out
here like some empty-headed piece of chattel ready for
exchange.

The door finally opened and the two men emerged.

Rachel scrutinized Cal's face to determine what had transpired, but his expression was maddeningly blank.

Her father broke the suspense. "Well, Rachel, Cal's asked me for permission to marry you. I suppose that doesn't come as a surprise?" His eyes were so sharply discerning, Rachel had to look away lest he see the deception in her own. "No, Daddy, it doesn't come as a surprise."

"Have you two decided on a date for the wedding?"

Cal and Rachel looked at each other blankly before Rachel replied. "Well, no, we haven't had the time to discuss it, but I don't see any reason to wait. With Dolores to help, I could put something together in maybe . . . two weeks?"

Rachel looked at Cal for confirmation. He shrugged and nodded. Not surprising since he had nothing to lose and everything to gain by tying the knot as soon as possible.

Galen eyed them both for a long moment before a sly smile curved his lips. If Rachel didn't know better, she would have thought her wily father knew exactly what sort of double-dealing she and Cal were up to.

"Two weeks," he said, "sounds fine. I'll leave the details to you." Then he went back into his study, leaving them quite alone in the foyer.

Cal looked at Rachel. Rachel looked at Cal. For once, the expression on Caleb Delaney's face betrayed his thoughts in no uncertain terms. And Rachel was thinking the same thing.

What have we gotten ourselves into?

5

Albuquerque, New Mexico Territory

The cantina was a small, thick-walled adobe square. Two kerosene lamps hung over the bar, and candles made of sheep's tallow dripped onto each of the tables scattered about the room. The place was nearly empty of customers at this time of day.

Carlos picked a coin from his cash box below the bar and gave it to the dark-haired boy by his side. He spoke swiftly, in Spanish, partly so the boy would understand and partly so that the dark man seated at the center table would not.

The boy nodded, then sprinted through the open doorway and out into the late afternoon. Carlos rubbed the surface of the bar with a soiled chamois and pretended not to notice the gringo who was devouring a plateful of *huevos rancheros*.

To a casual observer, the dark man looked like any

saddle-worn traveler passing through Albuqueque—dirty, tired, and maybe a little loco from spending too much time in the sun. But to Carlos's discerning eyes, the dark man reminded him of a vulture, patiently circling, circling, circling, waiting for his time to feed, to feed on exactly what Carlos had a feeling he would rather not know.

The man had come with questions.

Carlos had been running the cantina for fifteen years. He learned a long time ago to keep his mouth shut and his ears open. He knew Leo Walsh, the dark man's brother who had come to town a little over a year ago, and he had tolerated the man only because of Juanita. Carlos had a soft spot for Juanita, who had fancied herself in love with Leo for a time. Luckily, Leo had been gone now for over three months, and Carlos thought she was finally getting over the fast-talking bandido, but still, it was her place to answer any questions this man had about Leo's whereabouts, not his.

A few minutes later, Juanita appeared in the arch of the doorway and crossed to the bar. "*¿Dónde está?*"

Carlos inclined his head in the stranger's direction.

Juanita's soft brown eyes settled on the man. "*¿Qué le has dicho?*"

Carlos shook his head. "*Nada.*"

Juanita nodded. "*Bién.*" She eyed the dark man for another minute before making her decision. "*Le hablaré.*"

Eli Walsh scooped up the remainder of the eggs on his plate, then took a gulp of the Old Towse the tight-lipped bartender had brought to his table. The hard-edged alcohol burned a trail down to Eli's stomach and boiled there for a long minute before fading away. Unfortunately, it did little to dull the thudding pain in his head, the one just behind his left eye. The headache had crept up on him early this morning and had been growing worse all day. He ignored it.

Sensing the girl's presence, he looked up. She was young and large-breasted, with shining thick black hair tied back into a single braid. She wore a dowdy, off-the-shoulder peasant blouse and a faded brown skirt. Small, well-formed café-au-lait toes peeked out of leather sandals on her feet.

She oozed a visceral type of sensuality that would attract most men like a magnet. Eli was not most men. He simply observed and cataloged these facts in the same detached manner he analyzed any of his immediate surroundings.

She spoke first. "You are Leo's brother?"

He realized now who she was. "You're Juanita?"

She nodded.

The thought that his brother had been lying with this obviously half-breed Indian made Eli sick to his stomach, but it didn't really surprise him. His little brother had never been long on good taste, or brains for that matter, and women had always been his greatest weakness. Eli motioned for her to sit.

She pulled out a chair across the table from him. Her long-lashed brown eyes seemed to glow in the flickering candlelight. "He is not here."

Eli pushed his empty plate away. "The bartender said as much. When did he leave?"

"Over three months. He got the letter . . ." She frowned, then started again. "No. He got the fast letter."

"A telegram."

"The telegram, *sí*. He got the telegram, then he leave for a place I never hear of, Garden City."

"Garden City? Where the hell is that?"

"Kansas. A new town in Kansas."

Eli reached into his vest pocket and pulled out a cigar. He lit it as he sifted through this new information. Going back to Kansas was just plain stupid. The Walsh brothers were known quantities in Kansas. Their faces and descriptions were on every town marshal's desk in the state. Leo, in particular, was wanted for killing a federal deputy marshal in Dodge City. After that, the price on his head had grown so lucrative that every lawman and bounty hunter within five hundred miles was dogging him. It was the reason he had been forced to flee to this hellhole in the first place.

"Who was the telegram from?"

The girl pointed to Eli's bottle and raised a curved black eyebrow. He nodded. She motioned for the bartender to bring her a glass. "The telegram came from a man named Billy Wharton. I remember this name. I send him a letter when Leo not come back, you understand?"

Eli nodded thoughtfully. Billy Wharton. He remembered Billy Wharton, all right. Billy was a horse thief and, if Eli remembered correctly, even stupider than Leo.

The bartender brought Juanita a glass, fixed Eli with a dark, measuring gaze, then lumbered back toward the bar as Juanita poured herself a drink.

"What did Billy say that made Leo head north again?"

Juanita shrugged and took a sip of the liquor. "He say that he onto a good thing. Big, easy money. Leo says he go for the money and come back after. Me and him, we live good then."

Eli muttered to himself. "Stupid son of a bitch."

Juanita gave him a sardonic smile, revealing a row of unusually white teeth. "You know Leo, he always go for the big easy money."

"The big easy money. Oh yeah, that's Leo."

She finished her liquor and cleared her throat. "I not hear from him in so long that I send a fast letter to Billy Wharton in this Garden City. I ask, where is Leo?"

"And?"

She leaned across the table. "He say Leo never get to Garden City. He think Leo picked up by the law."

Eli straightened in his chair. "You're telling me they got him? Billy Wharton said some lawman got Leo?"

"*Sí.* This is bad. They will hang him, no?"

Eli didn't answer. He picked up a fork and started tapping it on the table, keeping a beat with the throbbing ache in his head. The pain was a constant reminder of why he had felt compelled to leave California and seek out his younger brother. He knew in his gut that the headaches were not going to go away.

Juanita sat back in her chair. "That is what Billy say."

Eli continued to tap the fork, slow and steady. "The men that got Leo. Did Billy give you any names?"

"No. No names."

"Who else besides Billy knew where Leo was headed?"

Juanita shrugged. "Just me. And Billy."

Billy. *Tap, tap, tap.* Billy Wharton. *Tap, tap, tap.* Eli smelled a set-up.

"You know this Billy, *señor*?"

Eli fixed her with a deadened stare. "I know him."

"He is a friend, *sí*?"

Again, Eli didn't reply.

So, Billy Wharton had sent Leo a telegram with promises of big money—big, easy money just waiting to be had, but only if Leo could meet Billy in Garden City. But Leo had never made it that far. Who knew that Leo was on his way to Garden City? Who besides Juanita and Billy? *Who?*

"Is too late for Leo, *señor?* You think they hang him?"

"I don't know."

"You go after him?"

Eli dropped the fork and moved to rise. "Yeah, I'm going after him, the stupid son of a bitch." He reached deep into his vest pocket and threw down two five-dollar gold pieces. "One's for the grub. The other's yours." He started to turn away.

"I don't want your money, *señor.*"

He turned to look down at her, a chilling smile turning up the corners of his mouth. "Take it. You're a whore, aren't you?"

Her eyes hardened but her voice was quiet. "Only when I have to be . . . and not with your brother."

"Well, Leo's not coming back. You might as well go back to doing what you do best."

Juanita observed the man's peculiar limping gait as he made his way to the door of the cantina. When he was gone, she scooped up a gold coin to squeeze it tight in one fist. Soon, she felt Carlos's hulking form approach from behind.

"You tell him about Leo?"

She nodded, still not taking her eyes from the doorway where the blackened silhouette of Leo's strange brother still burned in her mind's eye. "*Sí.*"

"And he is leaving?"

She sighed. "He is leaving."

Carlos grunted, satisfied, and turned away. "*Está bien.*"

6

Rachel stood before the full-length cheval mirror in her bedroom and tugged at the neckline of her wedding gown. Dolores stood behind her, patiently hooking the back of the dress.

"Stop jumping around, Rachel!"

Rachel stilled her nervous movements and stared at herself in the looking glass. The cream-colored gown was made of delicate lawn and silk with Chantilly lace trimmings. The *cuirasse* bodice was low cut with an off-the-shoulders décolletage, which left little to the imagination. The line of the bodice ended in an inverted V and molded close to her hips before flaring into a long, trained skirt behind her.

The longer Rachel stared at her own reflection, the more horrified she became. She tugged again at the neckline, trying to cover the exposed swell of her breasts.

"Stop it!" Dolores swatted at Rachel's hands.

"What's the big secret? That you are a woman? *Madre de Dios!* I wish your mother was here today!"

Rachel closed her eyes and wished that this was all a bad dream. It was the dressmaker's fault. The woman had gushed over how a girl's wedding day should be the most important day of her life, and Rachel had started to listen. She had suddenly realized that with her temperament and lofty ambitions, this wedding, sham that it was, might very well be the only one she would ever have. Something inside of her had stirred. Once aroused, that something had leaped and clung to the idea of making everyone sit up and take notice.

She wanted to show her Aunt Charlotte that she was not a hopelessly unattractive shrew destined for spinsterhood. She wanted to see Daisy gawk and sputter with jealousy. She wanted to see Nick's expression when she stepped out to light up the room. She wanted . . . she especially wanted to wipe the cynical smirk off Cal Delaney's face and make him think that maybe, just maybe, she was a woman well worth marrying without the promise of a king's ransom in return.

Rachel had seen precious little of her fiancé during the past two weeks, as he had stayed on with Ezra's outfit. Cal had come to call only three times since they announced their engagement, prompting Daisy to start making coy allusions to grooms with cold feet.

It wasn't that Rachel expected the man to fawn all over her. If only for appearance's sake, though, it might have been nice if he had acted his part a bit more convincingly. Even those few times he had come to call, he had spent most of his time with Galen out by the corral. Why, he had practically ignored her. And Rachel was not used to being ignored.

Now, she opened her eyes to see that her dress had not magically transformed itself into something even the least bit more modest, and she groaned aloud. What business did she have trying to impress a man like Cal? She felt ridiculous.

As Dolores pulled up the sides of Rachel's hair to catch in a jeweled comb at the crown of her head, Rachel moaned again.

Dolores's voice was stern. "Stop making sounds like a cow giving birth."

"I think I'm getting sick."

"You are not getting sick. You just wish you were sick. All brides get jitters when they think about the wedding night."

Rachel whirled to face the housekeeper. "That has nothing to do with it!"

Dolores started to offer a wry retort, then stopped as Rachel scurried over to her vanity, her hands dancing nervously over powder boxes, scent bottles, hair brushes, and combs. Dolores's dark brown eyes took on a knowing glint. She had worked for the Girard family for almost twenty years. She had come to this ranch as a young widow, and Elena Rose had hired her on the spot. The two women had grown to be more than mistress and servant over the years, and Dolores remembered Elena as a very dear friend. Rachel was probably the closest thing to a daughter Dolores would ever know.

At times like these, Dolores wished desperately that Elena was still alive. With her reassuring, motherly manner, Elena would have known exactly what to say to quiet Rachel's nerves. Carefully, Dolores approached the girl. "Your mother, did she ever talk to you about—"

"Dolores! Really! I'm twenty years old. Don't you think I've gotten a pretty good idea by now what's involved?"

"I hope not too good of an idea, or your father is likely to shoot the groom before the minister gets here."

Rachel's cheeks reddened. "I didn't mean it like that. I mean, I've heard things, and I've certainly seen enough horses and cattle doing it."

"Horses and . . . cattle?"

Rachel let out an exasperated breath. "Well, the mechanics are the same, aren't they?"

Dolores couldn't control the smile that tugged at her lips.

Rachel's ire was piqued. "Well, *aren't they?*"

"Perhaps, but if you're lucky, it will last longer."

Rachel just blinked at her.

Dolores picked up a ruby necklace from the vanity and motioned for Rachel to turn around so she could fasten it at her neck. "Don't worry. With the right man, it can be very nice."

Rachel thought about this. All this well-intentioned advice was misplaced. Caleb Delaney, of all the men walking this earth, was certainly not the right man for her, and this marriage was to be a fully orchestrated farce from day one. But she couldn't tell Dolores that. She couldn't tell anyone, and that was part of the problem. Not only was her wedding dress turning out to be a scandal in the making, she was also beginning to feel like some kind of conniving sneak.

Just last evening she had run into Nick in the parlor, and they had gotten into an argument. She didn't like arguing with Nick. It was unnatural. When they were children they never disagreed. That was a long time ago.

"I need to talk to you, Rachel."

Nick had said those words with somber conviction as he closed the parlor door and turned to face her. Dressed in an expensive frock coat and trousers, with his white shirt unbuttoned at the collar, Nick certainly looked the part of the young businessman who had just gotten through a particularly long day. "This marriage of yours," he began. "It's insane."

"Ah," Rachel said, folding her arms and preparing to stand her ground. "So, this is to be a dose of brotherly advice."

Nick caught her stance, and a knowing spark lit his eyes. "Don't go all stubborn on me. Hear me out."

"I am hearing you out, Nick."

"You just met this man two weeks ago. How can there be any feelings between the two of you?"

"I don't see how that's any of your business."

"We go back a long way, Rachel."

She started for the door. "This is pointless."

Nick caught her by the arm before she could get past him. "Don't run away. You pull that every time I get you alone."

"Let go of me!"

"You don't even know this man. Why are you marrying him?"

"You know very well why I'm marrying him."

"Rachel, don't do it. Don't marry a stranger just because of some fool idea your father's put into your head. If he actually follows through on his threat to leave the Elena Rose to me, I'll give it to you. Hell, I don't even want it."

Rachel's voice turned cold. "That'll come as a sore disappointment to your mother, not to mention your wife."

"To hell with them. I'm talking about you and me.

There was a time when we were important to each other."

Rachel tried to swallow the lump in her throat. "We were children then, Nick. We're grown up now, and I don't want your charity. I want to earn the Elena Rose on my own."

Nick's voice rose to a bellow. "You call this earning it? I swear, you and your father are both out of your minds! He sets the tune, and you dance right along with him!"

"Well, that's none of your concern, is it?"

Nick's grip on her arm tightened. "It *is* my concern when I see you rushing headlong into marriage with a stranger whose past is shady at best."

"His past doesn't matter."

"Rumor has it this man was a gunfighter, Rachel."

"He was a bounty hunter. He also worked for Wells Fargo. The way I see it, that puts him on the right side of the law."

"Just because the man was once employed by Wells Fargo doesn't make him a hero. I've been talking to some of the drovers down at the stockyards. Most of the ones from Kansas know of him, and he's got a dangerous reputation, Rachel. The word is he doesn't let anything stand in his way when he sets out after a man, including fine points of the law concerning homicide. Most of those bounties are offered for men dead or alive, and quite a few of Cal Delaney's catches have been brought in slung over the saddle. Did you know he once shot a man in the back? And just over a month ago, he nearly killed some cowboy in Dodge City."

Rachel looked into Nick's eyes, trying to gauge if he was speaking the truth. She didn't know Cal very well, but she just couldn't fathom the possibility that he was a cold-blooded killer. She knew that gossip could grow from the size of a pea to the size of a watermelon in less time than it took for a tea kettle to come to a boil.

"That's nonsense," she said. "People love to gossip. Give them a good tall tale, and they'll spread it from here to China."

"Why don't you at least wait? Let me have him checked out."

If Rachel were marrying for life, maybe she would have heeded Nick's words, but that wasn't the case. Nick didn't know the truth, and Rachel was not about to confide in him. Things between them had changed when he turned his back on her to marry Daisy Parker, and it was high time he realized that fact.

Her reply was firm. "No."

"Don't do it, Rachel. Don't marry this man. There's something about him that's not right." Nick's eyes pleaded with her, and Rachel's resolve wavered—but only for a second.

She tore her arm from his grasp. "Why don't I file that advice right along with my advice to you not to marry Daisy Parker? Remember *that?*"

She caught his wounded look just before she turned her back. She had meant to hurt him, to make him feel just a small part of what she felt when he married Daisy, and maybe it had worked.

Now, Rachel thought again about the look on Nick's face and tried to shut out the memory.

Dolores finished hooking the ruby necklace. "One more thing, *paloma*, and you will be ready."

In the mirror, Rachel's gaze dropped first to her naked shoulders, then to her dipped neckline. Her forehead wrinkled. What had she done? This was not her. High-necked blouses, starched skirts, and no-nonsense riding habits, that was Rachel Girard. She was a young woman who demanded and got the respect of every cowhand that worked the Elena Rose. With sudden purpose, she crossed the room and flung open the door to her wardrobe.

Dolores, who was seated on the bed unfolding a lacey mantilla, looked up suspiciously. "What are you doing?"

"I'm looking for something to . . ." Rachel's words muffled as her head disappeared into the array of dresses and skirts that hung inside the wardrobe.

"Stop that! Rachel Elena! You will ruin your hair!"

Rachel's head reappeared as she straightened up, clutching a white, triangular silk scarf in her hand. "How can I ruin hair that starts out and ends up a tangled mess no matter what I try to do with it in between?"

Dolores clucked. "You have pretty hair, Rachel."

"I have *lots* of hair, you mean."

Dolores frowned as Rachel threw the fichu about her shoulders and knotted it in front of her chest. "What are you doing?"

"I'm trying to make do."

"It looks stupid, *paloma*."

"At least I won't catch my death of cold."

There was a gentle knock on the door, and Dolores called out. "Who is it?"

"It's Charlotte. May I come in?"

Dolores emitted a long-suffering sigh. "The door is open."

Charlotte peeked into the room, then slid inside, closing the door behind her. She wore a peach-colored, puffy-sleeved evening gown. Rachel thought she looked like an orange peacock.

"Rachel! Well, I declare to goodness! You look . . . you look . . ." Charlotte's expression grew puzzled. "My dear, what is that *thing* you are wearing about your shoulders?"

"It's a fichu."

"A fichu . . . I see that, yes." Charlotte managed to drag her gaze away from the scarf to meet Rachel's challenging stance. She forced a smile. "Well, lamb child, it's an accessory I never would have thought of myself."

Dolores rose from the bed, cutting off any retort Rachel might have thought to deliver. "Here, Rachel, your mother's mantilla. Bend down so I can put it on."

Rachel did as she was told. Dolores draped the mantilla over the jeweled comb at the crown of her head and arranged it to fall about Rachel's shoulders. The older woman's voice caught in her throat when she spoke. "Oh, you look so beautiful, *paloma.*"

Rachel felt a sudden tightness in her own throat. In choosing to wear something of her mother's, at least she had done one thing right.

Another knock at the door shattered the moment. Tactful as always, Charlotte tiptoed over to the door and opened it a crack. Rachel heard Daisy's voice. "The minister's here, and the groom has decided to show up after all. Do you hear that, Rachel? It looks like he's actually going to go through with it!"

Rachel snatched up a hairbrush to wing at Daisy's pert little nose, which was just barely visible through the open crack of the bedroom door. Dolores's hand shot out just in time to stop Rachel's arm before she could complete the motion.

Daisy continued, unmindful of the danger she was in. "Is she finished dressing? How does she look? Can I come in?"

"If that two-faced, sniping little witch thinks I'm going to let her step one sneaky foot in this room, she's got another thing coming!"

Charlotte looked pained at her niece's purple language. "Well, dear, why don't I just go tell everyone you're ready?"

Before Charlotte closed the door behind her, Rachel heard Daisy's inquiring voice. "What did she say? Why can't I go in?"

Charlotte was calm and reassuring. "She's feeling a bit light-headed and . . ."

Rachel tore her arm from the housekeeper's grasp and threw down the hairbrush. "You should've let me do it."

"Vengeance is mine, saith the Lord."

Rachel muttered as she clipped ruby earrings to her lobes. "Well, the Lord sure is taking His own good time about it."

Dolores handed her a pair of white gloves. "Be calm."

Rachel pulled on the gloves. "I look stupid."

"No," Dolores said firmly, reaching around to unknot the fichu and yank it from Rachel's shoulders. "*This* looks stupid."

Another knock at the door, only this time Rachel knew from the sound that it was not her aunt Charlotte or Daisy. It was her father. She gave Dolores an uncertain look, then called for him to enter.

Today, he wore a black, single-breasted waistcoat and trousers, his white shirt collar set off by a stylish cambric bow tie. Rachel had never seen him look more handsome.

However, his expression made her hesitate. Had he found out about her deception? "What's the matter, Daddy?"

He shook his head. "Nothing, Rachel. It's just that you remind me so much of your mother today."

Rachel, who never cried, suddenly felt tears sting the corners of her eyes. Guilt rose like a black, sinful phantom in the back of her mind. She was deceiving him.

"You are a vision of beauty, my Rachel Elena." He smiled wistfully and offered her his arm. "Shall we go downstairs?"

The infernally long day was done. Ezra and the few other guests that had attended the discreet parlor room ceremony were gone. Dusk had fallen, and instead of following his bride up to her bedroom, Cal had loitered in the parlor. He thought perhaps a considerate groom might extend that courtesy in order to give his nervous bride some time to collect herself before he went upstairs to ravish her virginal body.

Although Cal had no experience with virginal bodies, he thought that, judging by the way Rachel had stood straight as a pine needle when he had simply placed an arm around her waist to pose for their wedding photograph, it was probably a pretty safe bet that tonight was not going to spoil his record.

Now, he stood outside her bedroom door, his saddlebags slung over one shoulder, debating whether he should knock before entering. Despite her nervous agitation during and after the ceremony, Rachel had surprised him.

He wasn't sure what he had been expecting to see when she first appeared on her father's arm in the parlor, but for the first time in many years, he'd had to put some serious effort into maintaining his poker face. When Galen had placed her smaller hand in Cal's, the scent of roses had assailed his senses, distracting him almost as much as the sight of all that ripe, nubile flesh straining at the neckline of that dress.

Cal smiled at the memory and decided against knocking. When he stepped inside, the lamp burned low, casting a sleepy glow over expensive furnishings: a woman's vanity, an armoire, a prayer desk, a nice-sized brass bed—big enough for two. His eyes lingered there before a gasp from one corner of the room snatched his full attention.

Suddenly, he was helpless to control the huge, stupid grin that spread over his face. Cal had seen quite a few women in various states of undress, but none had looked quite like this. The prim and proper Rachel Girard was full of surprises today.

Her curls fell freely over her bare shoulders. A black satin corset, cinched tightly at the waist, rose to cup breasts that looked as if they might spill out at the first sign of a strong breeze. Her petticoats were gone, revealing impossibly long legs clad in snug-fitting, lacey drawers that fired his erotic imagination. Below her knees, black stockings clung to shapely calves and narrow, feminine ankles.

At the sight of her, Cal felt his body preparing for action that it was clear from the mortified expression on her face was *not* going to take place. Not on *this* night, anyway.

But what about tomorrow? he found himself musing. Or the night after that? Six months was a long time to keep saying no.

"Oh my God!" Rachel exclaimed. "It's you!"

"You were expecting someone else?"

She scurried across the room to the bed and snatched

up a yellow cotton wrapper. "No, I was *not* expecting someone else!" She jammed her arms into the sleeves and pulled the garment closed to cover herself.

"What's the matter?"

"What's the matter?" she repeated furiously, tying the belt into a frigid little knot. "Haven't you ever heard of knocking?"

"Yeah, I've heard of knocking."

"Well, you ought to try it sometime."

"Maybe sometime I will. Where should I put my things?"

"What things?"

Cal patted his saddlebags. "My things. You know, personal belongings?"

"I—I don't know. I never thought of that."

"Maybe you could spare a drawer?"

Rachel crossed the room to the huge armoire, yanking open a drawer and extracting various items of clothing—mostly lace-trimmed underthings, from what Cal could tell. "You could have at least given me some time to get decent before you came barging in here like a wild animal," she muttered.

Like a wild animal? Cal squinted at her shapely behind for a moment before deciding to move on to a less volatile subject. "I couldn't stand it much longer down there. If I had to take one more black look from Nick, I probably would've been obliged to ask him to step outside to clear the air."

"He's just being overprotective," Rachel said, yanking open another drawer and stuffing her displaced garments into it. "All of a sudden he's taken an interest in my personal life."

"Well, your aunt Charlotte has taken quite an interest too. I had a hard time putting off all her questions.

She has a very polite way of going about it, but she manages to circle back to her target like a ravenous vulture. Are you sure she doesn't have any idea of what's really going on here?"

"She's just sniffing around. She'd like nothing better than if Nick inherited the Elena Rose."

"And what about Daisy?"

"What about her?"

Cal eyed the vanity. It was littered with doodads, *female* doodads—powder boxes, perfume bottles, a carved wooden jewelry box, ribbons, hairpins, brushes, combs, *junk*. With the back of his hand, he nudged some of them out of his way.

"What about Daisy?" Rachel repeated.

"I imagine she would like for Nick to inherit the ranch, wouldn't she?"

"Are you joking? She'd sell her body for it."

Cal flipped open one of his saddlebags. "She was still pouting when I left. I think you stole all her thunder."

"Isn't a bride supposed to be the center of attention on her wedding day?"

Cal laughed as he pulled out three sets of clean clothes. "Well, you were, anyway."

"You can't complain about Daddy. He's pleased as punch."

Cal crossed to the armoire, dropped his clothing into her emptied drawer, and shoved it closed with one knee. "No, I suppose not. Your little plan seems to be working out just fine as far as he's concerned." He turned to Rachel, looking down at her with a slow smile. "Now, all we have to do is figure out how it's going to work for us."

Rachel's hands went to the lapels of her wrapper, clasping them closer together. "What do you mean?"

"I'm talking about that robe. You're clutching it around that delectable body of yours like your hard-earned virginity depends on it. Are you planning to finish what you started?"

Rachel paled. "What I started?"

"Undressing. You do undress for bed, don't you?"

She turned huffy. "Yes, I do, when I don't have strange men salivating over me."

Cal swiped at his chin with the back of one hand. "Sorry. Was I drooling?"

"You know, if you'd wipe that stupid smirk off your face, maybe we could conduct a normal conversation."

"Sure. But maybe you need to be reminded that my status as a salivating stranger changed drastically as of this afternoon. Salivating or not, I'm now your husband, and if I'm not mistaken, most husbands get to see their wives without clothes."

"I made it perfectly clear to you from the beginning that this is to be a marriage in name only."

Cal raised his hands innocently. "Who said anything about consummation? I'm merely thinking of convenience. Six months is a long time. Aren't you going to get tired of sneaking around and hiding in closets whenever you need to change your clothes?"

"I'll manage."

"I bet you will. Do I have to hide from you too?"

Rachel blew out an exasperated breath. "You're being crude."

"I'm sorry you think so. I'm just trying to establish the rules." He reached out to finger a lock of her hair. "I've never played this game before."

Rachel stiffened. "Well, neither have I, but it seems that a little common courtesy extended both ways might . . . might help to make this situation more . . . more . . ."

Slowly, very slowly, his index finger slid down the side of her neck to the V-neck of her robe. Her voice cracked. "More . . . *tolerable!*" She backed away. "Will you stop that?"

"Stop what?"

"Touching me!"

Cal smiled. "Jumpy, aren't you?"

"I can see you're in no mood to be reasoned with."

"No," he said, reaching up to unknot his tie, "I'm in the mood to get some sleep."

"What are you doing?"

He tore off his tie and took off his suit coat, throwing them both over the open door of the armoire. He started to unbutton his shirt. "I'm getting ready for bed."

Rachel blinked at him. *One button, two, three . . .* "What do you normally sleep in?"

"It depends where I'm at. If I'm outside, I sleep in my clothes. If I'm inside . . . I don't."

Four buttons, five . . . Rachel's brows knitted together as he removed his shirt. She had seen bare-chested men before. This was certainly nothing new. So, why did she suddenly feel like the walls were closing in?

He tossed the shirt over the armoire next to his coat. Rachel was only vaguely aware of the smirk on his face as her gaze traveled helplessly over the lines and contours of firm pectoral muscles. A mat of hair, three shades darker than that on his head, narrowed down a flat belly to a point where sun-bronzed skin met the waistband of his trousers. *All man,* she thought, her throat suddenly going drier than a desert gulch, *every God-blessed inch of him!*

Before her gaze could drop any lower, she caught herself and looked up guiltily to see his amused expression. It wasn't just his physique, she decided, it was everything, everything about Cal Delaney that seemed to scream out raw masculine virility. His eyes, his mouth, his stance, his attitude. Especially this last, his attitude, which she could read clearly in those unsettlingly blue eyes of his. As if he knew every scandalous thought that tripped through her rattled brain, as if he could—contract or no contract—claim his husbandly rights at this very moment if he so pleased, and . . . she would like it.

One callused hand dropped to the buttons on his trousers, and Rachel emitted a little gasp, turning away before she could stop herself. Damn! He was probably getting a good laugh out of this!

She crossed the room to a linen chest and yanked out two folded blankets and a pillow. Whirling around, she threw the whole pile at him. He caught the blankets but missed the pillow. "You'll be sleeping on the floor, Mr. Delaney!"

He snatched up the pillow. "Why am I not surprised?"

"Since you insist on peeling off all of your clothes like some shedding snake, I'm turning down the lamp."

"Suit yourself."

Rachel turned and extinguished the bedside lamp. They were plunged into darkness. She listened to him rustling around and wondered if he would really have the audacity to take everything off. The idea of having a naked man in her bedroom was bad enough. The idea of having *this* particular naked man in her bedroom just about made her stomach heave.

She sat on the edge of her bed. "I trust you'll be all right?"

"Well, I *am* in the lap of luxury, aren't I? Or did I take a wrong turn somewhere?"

Rachel made a face in the dark as she loosened the belt of her wrapper and let the garment slide from her shoulders.

She heard a movement, then a loud thump, then, *"Jesus H. Christ!"*

"Are you all right?"

"What the hell was that?"

"Well, judging by the direction all that swearing is coming from, I would guess you tripped over the stool to my vanity."

"What? Damned thing! What the hell's it doing in the middle of the . . . ?"

He muttered this last bit under his breath, and so Rachel decided it would be best to treat it as rhetorical. She unclipped her garters and reached behind her back to struggle with the ties of her corset. When it finally fell away, she pulled her night dress from under her pillow and struggled into it before removing her stockings. After a short while, the room was quiet.

Rachel slipped between the sheets and buried her face into the pillow. What a God-awful day. She had broken two champagne glasses and tripped over the exposed edge of the carpet in the parlor twice.

She cringed at the remembrance. It never failed. Whenever she became the least bit agitated, she transformed into a walking calamity. It served as a painful reminder of her rocky adolescence, a time when she seemed to be nothing but a bundle of gawky arms and legs.

She rolled onto her back and tried to relax. It was not an easy task—not with *him* in the room. She thought about today, when the minister had tactfully suggested that Cal might want to kiss his new bride. She had frozen like an icicle.

When it came to kissing, her experience was severely limited. Only one of her suitors, Harold Prescott, had ever gotten up the necessary nerve and proximity even to chance it, and Rachel had come away holding the opinion that Harold's lips had felt as wet and squashy as underdone scrambled eggs.

Today, however, when Cal had brushed his lips over hers, Rachel had experienced an unexpected, fleeting thrill, like a butterfly tickling the bottom of her stomach. She had marveled that a man's lips could feel so warm and soft and yet firm all at the same time, and she had wondered if she might have been a little hasty to jump to the conclusion that all kissing was unpleasant when maybe, with certain men . . .

His voice suddenly stabbed the darkness, startling the bejesus out of her. "I've been thinking."

Rachel swallowed hard, willing her pounding heart to slow. "Well, congratulations," she managed to croak.

He ignored the barb. "If you should change your mind, feel free to let me know."

"Change my mind?"

"About consummation of the marriage. I might be willing to renegotiate."

Rachel wrinkled her nose in the dark. "Go whistle for it, Mr. Delaney."

He laughed. "Sleep well, Mrs. Delaney."

7

They had been married for exactly six days, and Cal thought Rachel was already pressing her luck.

He had spent the early part of the week out on the south end of the ranch, separating the last of the beeves for Ezra's consignment. It was time spent by Galen Girard's side—time well spent.

Cal liked Galen. He respected the older man's common sense and his down-to-earth style. Galen made a fine father-in-law. It was just too bad that being married to his headstrong daughter was necessary to the bargain.

As far as Cal could tell, having Galen for a father-in-law was just about the only redeeming virtue of being married to Rachel. Not only was there no sex—a particularly glaring omission—it was now becoming clear that Rachel's notorious reputation as a man-hating shrew had been understated at best. Without a little bed-warming at night to smooth over the day's rough spots, Cal was finding the road of holy matrimony very bumpy indeed.

Then, after Galen went to Dallas on business for a few days, leaving Cal alone with Rachel to oversee the ranch, Cal soon came to the conclusion that his new wife was just about the bossiest, know-it-all female he had ever met in his life.

Her pet project was raising quarterhorses. By the looks of them, Cal thought she was probably good at it. She rode astride with her back straight and her head high, and even Cal had to admire the cut of her figure as she exercised the splendid animals. Everything would have been fine if she had just kept to her own business and left him to his.

She had been baiting him for two days now. It seemed he couldn't even turn around once without her being there, her sharp eyes following his every move, just waiting for him to make a mistake. She wasn't shy about pointing them out, either—right in front of every ranch hand within earshot. She criticized everything from his technique with the half-broken cow ponies to what knots he chose to use with a lariat.

Yesterday, as they were extending the corral fence, she'd even had something to say about Cal's placement of the post. They had argued long and hard, and Rachel hadn't backed down until Cal tossed the heavy digging iron at her feet and told her that if she wanted the post moved, she could damn well dig the hole herself.

She left him alone then, but she'd been in one holy hell of a snit. The two of them had not made so much as eye contact over dinner, and the atmosphere in their bedroom that night had been chilly enough to bring on a spring blizzard.

This morning, Rachel had mounted a golden palomino and disappeared into the vast distance for almost three hours, leaving Cal in a welcome state of peace. She had returned in time for lunch, though, and afterward had taken to busying herself in the vegetable garden.

Now, from the corral where he stood, he caught sight of her on her knees in the garden as she raised her face to the beating sun. She turned her head in his direction, and Cal felt her gaze settle on him as surely as if a big black vulture had alighted on his shoulder. She rose to her feet, removed her gardening gloves, and brushed loose dirt from the folds of her skirt.

When she started across the greening yard toward the big corral, Cal felt the muscles in the back of his neck start to tense. He thought he was going to end up killing her this time.

Soon, she hovered just on the other side of the fence, and he could practically feel her eyes boring into the space between his shoulder blades. "You're not planning on selling that bull in the holding pen to Charlie Canfield this afternoon, *are you?*"

Cal stopped coiling some rope and turned. She wore a white linen blouse tucked into a light tan skirt. The collar was open-necked, and he could see a fine sheen of perspiration coating the exposed skin of her slender throat. If it weren't for the fact that he was on the verge of wringing that lovely neck, the effect would have been quite erotic.

"Do you see a problem with that?"

Paco and the other ranch hands stopped what they were doing and looked up. They had been observing the sparring newlyweds for two days now.

Rachel sucked in a deep breath before her eyes

locked once again with her husband's. "Yes, as a matter of fact, I do."

Silence, like a death shroud, descended over the rapt group as Cal set his jaw. He didn't say anything for a long time. Finally, he tossed his lariat to Paco. "I'll be back in a minute."

He crossed the distance to the fence and quickly scaled it. If she wanted a showdown, she'd get a showdown. Cal was being paid to act the part of her husband, not that of her trained lackey, and he'd be damned if he was going to let her get away with it.

Upon seeing the silent fury on his face, Rachel's eyes widened. She recovered quickly, though, and donned that go-ahead-and-try-it expression Cal was becoming all too familiar with. He snagged her arm in passing, swinging her around in a semicircle and forcing her to stumble along after him toward the stable. "We have to talk, Rachel my sweet."

"What? What do you think you're doing?"

As they put some distance between themselves and their avid audience, Rachel became more vehement. "Stop it, Cal! Let me go! You're acting like a brute!"

"Well, that makes perfect sense because right now I feel like a brute, Rachel." He pulled the stable door open and shoved her inside.

The door slapped closed behind them. After the bright sunlight outside, they were bathed in murky shadows. Rachel tried to pull away. "Get your hands off me!"

Cal only tightened his grip on her arm. "What are you trying to do? See how far you can go?"

She stopped struggling. "What are you talking about?"

"You're deliberately trying to make a fool out of me, and I want to know why."

"I can't help it if you don't have enough confidence in yourself to take a little advice."

"A little advice? You've been undermining my authority for two days now!"

"I have not! You just can't take advice from a woman. If my father, or even Paco, mentioned to you that we might get a better price for that bull elsewhere, you'd think about it, wouldn't you? When I say it—"

"When you say it, it sounds like a dressing down from some dried-up old prune of a schoolmarm."

Rachel's eyes narrowed. "Dried-up old prune of a . . . ?"

If Cal's eyes had had time to adjust fully to the dark, he probably would have caught her palm before it made contact with the side of his face. As it was, he missed, and she landed a solid open-handed slap.

This did nothing to improve his temper. Without thinking, he grasped her by the shoulders, spun her around, and pushed her, none too gently, back up against the wall below the hayloft.

"You bitch," he whispered.

Her reply was breathless but stubborn. "Well, I've been called that before."

He pressed up against her, leaving no room for her to squirm away. "Don't you ever try that again."

She raised her chin, and even in the dim light, Cal could see those green eyes glimmering with impudence. "What are you going to do, Cal? *Hit me?*"

She was breathing in quick, shallow gasps from the exertion of struggling against him. Oh yes, just a short moment ago he had been almost mad enough to hit her. Almost. Right now, with their sweating bodies pressed so close together, he was beginning to feel more like rucking up her prim skirts and taking her right there on the filthy, earthen stable floor.

He swallowed hard and concentrated on cooling his temper. "I don't hit women. Just rest assured there are other ways of evening the score between us."

Rachel eyed him coldly, then looked away without saying a thing. Cal knew she had sensed his thoughts and had read into his words a threat he hadn't intended. There was a hint of fear in her. He knew she would never admit it or give into it, but he could feel it, like an electrical charge passing from her body to his.

He let go of her and stepped back, disgusted. Maybe she was right. Maybe he couldn't take advice from a woman, even if the woman knew her business. There was one thing he was sure of, though: Rachel could stand to take a few lessons in diplomacy. Maybe he could learn to swallow the tonic a little better if it didn't taste so much like axle grease going down.

When she didn't say anything, Cal spoke. "If you have something to say about how I do things, do me the courtesy of talking to me alone. I don't think every cowhand on the place needs to hear it, do you?"

She pressed her lips together and glared at him.

Cal adjusted his hat. "Fine. We'll consider this particular point of contention settled." He turned, punched the door open with the palm of his hand, and stepped back outside.

Left alone, Rachel nearly glared a hole through the stable door. She was burning. She was *up-to-here* with Cal Delaney! She must have been out of her mind the day she'd picked him to play the part of her husband. He was so damned cocksure of himself, he couldn't even take a constructive suggestion without getting all hot about it.

And the way her father was doting on him. First thing Monday morning, when Rachel appeared at breakfast dressed and ready to ride out to roundup with her father, just as she had done for over four years now, Galen had informed her that it wasn't necessary for her to accompany him. He was taking Cal along to show him the ropes. Rachel could stay home and relax. *Not necessary?* Stay at home and relax? What was Rachel supposed to do? Go find herself a quiet corner in the parlor and take up knitting?

Rachel still simmered at the memory. She massaged her arm where Cal had gripped it so tightly. He was a brute, a bully, an animal. The look on his face when he pushed her up against the wall had turned her blood cold. She had thought for one awful moment that he was going to force himself on her. It was perhaps ludicrous to think so, here in the stable in the middle of the afternoon with four of her father's ranch hands just outside, but there it was. She had seen the look on his face.

Rachel scowled as she smoothed her skirt. She reached up to check her hair, wondering if their little tussle had loosened her hairpins. She spent the next few minutes tucking away stray hairs before straightening her shoulders and pushing the stable door open.

She spotted him right away, swinging up into the saddle with the effortless grace that defined all his movements. She knew he was planning to meet Ezra at the edge of town, so she waited as he imparted instructions to Paco before urging his stallion out onto the dusty drive.

When he was safely out of sight, Rachel rounded the corral fence and approached Paco. The burly ranch hand looked up. "What can I do for you, Miss Rachel?"

"Which bull did Cal decide to sell to Canfield?"

Paco replied cautiously. "He didn't change his mind, Miss Rachel, if that's what you're asking."

Rachel squinted into the sprawling distance, thinking. "Well, he's wrong. Get the other one ready to show."

"Oh, I don't know, Miss Rachel. Mr. Cal, he seemed real set on offering this one."

Rachel grew annoyed. "That's because he's too stubborn to admit when he's made a mistake. This one's younger and healthier than the others. This one's worth top dollar, and Canfield won't be paying top dollar."

Paco winced. "Charlie Canfield's got a small spread, Miss Rachel. He can't afford to pay top dollar. I think Mr. Cal was taking that into mind when he decided—"

"Mr. Cal isn't the one losing money by making a bad deal. I'd like to be soft-hearted too, but we don't stay in business by practically giving away our prime Brahman bulls. Charlie Canfield will be getting exactly what he's paying for."

"I know, Miss Rachel. It's just that Mr. Cal—"

She cut him off, and this time her tone of voice brooked no further argument. "You just do what I told you, Paco. I'll handle Mr. Cal."

8

Dolores hummed as she folded the last of the laundry in her basket. Her biscuit dough was rolled out and cut. The spicy aroma of chili, one of her many culinary specialties, filled the kitchen. Mr. Cal had praised it so highly that she decided to make it for supper twice in one week, a gesture she rarely made for anyone.

Dolores liked Cal Delaney. She was well aware that the laconic young man was said to have been a gunfighter and that he had a reputation for being cold-hearted, but Dolores trusted her own instincts better. Her instincts told her that he was a man who had long ago learned to bury his feelings, a man who carried a past hurt locked in his heart. What that hurt was, Dolores didn't know or care. He was strong and smart and ambitious. He was good for Rachel Elena. Dolores also suspected that Rachel was good for Cal Delaney. The only trouble was, neither of them seemed to know it yet, and judging from the briny silences boiling over between them at mealtimes, Dolores thought it might be quite awhile before the fact dawned on either of them.

Realistically, Dolores saw little she could do to smooth things over, but she thought it couldn't hurt to prepare the young man's favorite meal. Perhaps if his stomach was kept full and happy, he would be less likely to strangle Rachel Elena before realizing that she might be the best thing that had ever happened to him.

Dolores's idle musings were cut short by the sound of spurs slamming and ringing against wooden porch steps. The kitchen door flew open, and she was startled to see Cal Delaney framed in the doorway. Having just returned from town, he looked tired, dusty, hot, and . . . *not happy*. His tone of voice was calm, *too* calm. It didn't match the expression on his face. "Where is she?"

Dolores hesitated. She considered trying to get him to sample some chili before confronting the subject of his discontent, but judging by the look on his face, Dolores doubted even two bowlfuls would help matters at this point. She tried to stall. "Where is *who*, Mr. Cal?"

"You know who."

"Well, I am not sure. Let me think." Dolores finished folding a towel and dropped it in the wicker basket at her feet. When she looked back up, she stopped and sighed. That intense blue gaze was compelling. "She's in the back room taking a—" But she didn't get to finish her sentence. Cal was already halfway down the gallery hallway.

*   *   *

Rachel rested her head against the back of the porcelain tub. The rose-scented bath water, piping hot only ten minutes before, was now barely tepid, but it didn't matter. Her body had grown accustomed to it as it had cooled. For the first time in a week, she felt truly relaxed. The muscles in her shoulders had slackened. Her forehead was no longer creased with tension. She thought she might even doze off.

The door opened and closed behind her. She heard footsteps on the hardwood floor, but the fact that these sounded more like heavy boots than Dolores's practical shoes did not occur to her.

"Dolores," she said, not bothering to open her eyes. "Could you bring me that pitcher of water? I'd like to wash my hair."

Life was good. Rachel was not about to let Cal Delaney or anyone else spoil her mood tonight. Tonight she would be calm and collected. Tonight her supper conversation would sparkle. Tonight . . .

"AIEEEEEEE!" She screeched and sat bolt upright as a flood of cold water was dumped over her head.

"Allow me, darling."

Rachel sputtered and batted soaking curls from her face only to focus bleary eyes on the imposing figure of her new husband. He loomed over her, his feet planted apart, a hand resting on each hip, and his expression was . . . *not happy*.

All at once, Rachel became aware of her naked state. She sank down to her neck in the dwindling bubbles. "What are you doing here? Never mind! Get out!"

Cal dropped to his knees by the tub and rested his forearms over the curved edge. His gaze dropped to the distressingly thin veil of froth that rode the surface of the bath water.

Rachel pulled her knees up and folded her arms over her breasts self-consciously. The muscles in her shoulders had tensed up again. "Get out."

"Not until we've had a little talk."

"We've already had a little talk."

"I thought we had an understanding."

"*You* had an understanding. I didn't agree to anything."

The anger in his voice was barely controlled. "And so you decided to sneak around behind my back and undercut my decision. Very honorable."

"You were wrong and too stubborn to admit it."

His laugh was not mirthful. "Oh. *I* was being stubborn. Maybe it's something in the water." Then, with sudden purpose, he unbuttoned his shirt sleeves and started rolling them up.

Rachel stiffened. "What are you doing?"

He stuck one arm into the bath water and began groping. "I want to help, darling."

Rachel felt his fingers brush her shin, and she kicked out with one foot, thoroughly soaking his shirt. "Get away from me!"

"Now, now, don't get testy, princess. I'm just trying to act the part of your faithful manservant. Apparently that's the way you rich girls like it. Now, I know you've got a sponge around here somewhere."

He grazed her thigh with his fingertips, and Rachel kicked out again. The water in the tub lapped over the sides and splashed onto the floor.

"Careful now," he warned. "You knock any more water out of that tub, and I might catch a glimpse of something important. Ah! Here it is!" Grinning, he produced a wet sponge. "Where shall we start?"

"Don't you even dare to think—"

He snatched the bar of soap from the silver dish at his feet and made a grand show of lathering up. "How about your lovely neck?"

He dropped the soap and reached around to cup the back of Rachel's head. Entangling his fingers in her dripping curls, he yanked her forward and pressed the soapy sponge to her throat. Rachel reached up and wrapped both of her hands around his wrist. "Stop it!"

But Cal was too strong for her. He squeezed the sponge, sending rivulets of warm soapy water down her neck. Despite her resistance, he started to move the sponge in small, lazy circles over the glistening wet skin of her chest, lower, lower . . . "But, honey, we've barely gotten started."

Rachel gritted her teeth and closed her eyes, squeezing his wrist as hard as she could. "Cal . . . don't."

After a moment, his ministrations stopped, and Rachel let out a pent-up breath. The sponge nestled cozily between her breasts. He bent his face down to hers, and when Rachel opened her eyes, she was looking directly into his hard blue gaze.

"Stop crossing me, Rachel."

She gave him what she hoped was a withering glare. "You're despicable to come in here and take advantage of me like this."

"Take advantage of you? Is that what you think? Honey, I only wish it was nearly as enjoyable for me as I know it was for you."

Enjoyable? Rachel was speechless. He was an ogre! A despicable worm! When she found her voice, it screeched. *"Get out!"*

He released her, dropping the sponge back into the bath water with a splat. He stood and reached for a towel to dry his hands. "Good evening, Mrs. Delaney."

She watched him cross the tiny room in three broad strides. "Good evening?" she called after him indignantly. "What do you mean, 'good evening'? Where do you think you're going?"

"Don't bother waiting up for me, princess." He didn't even glance back before slamming the door behind him.

"This is it, Cal, honey!"

Fearing that he might wander off somewhere in a drunken stupor, Lacey made sure she kept a grip on his shirt sleeve as she pushed the creaking door open with her other hand.

"Come on. That's right, honey." Lacey eased him inside and kicked the door closed behind them. "Stand right there, Cal. I'll light the lamp."

"You know . . . your floor is moving, Lacey."

She giggled. "Only in your head, Cal. Don't move or you'll trip right over the bed."

Lacey knew the layout of her tiny crib like the back of her hand. Her steps were sure as she made her way over to the nightstand. She pulled open the drawer and felt around for a box of matches. "You still awake, Cal?"

There was an unusually long moment of silence. She had been joking. She didn't really think he'd fall asleep, but—

"Awake? I'm awake. Sure thing. Right here."

She struck the match and saw that he stood next to the door with his back up against the wall. His arms were folded and his eyes were closed. Despite his assurances, he was about as close to asleep on his feet as a man could get.

Lacey returned her attention to the kerosene lamp, lifting the globe and touching the match to the wick. The flame caught and flared. She waved away the smoke as she replaced the globe and dimmed the flame to set the proper mood.

"There," she said, pleased with the effect. She skipped over and took Cal's arm to lead him to the bed. "Come on over here, sugar, and take a load off your feet."

Cal dropped his saddlebags onto the floor, then pulled her along with him down onto the bed. Lacey reveled in a deep kiss before he abruptly broke it off and collapsed flat on his back. "Oh, hell," he groaned, closing his eyes. "Your bed's moving, too, darlin'. I shoulda got us a room at the hotel."

"Well, I know just the thing to fix you up, sugar."

Lacey tried to sound confident as she unbuttoned his shirt and brushed her fingertips along the familiar expanse of his chest, but all her high hopes were plunging faster than a thermometer in December. She had never seen Cal consume liquor like he did tonight. She wondered if this binge was a reflection of how married life was treating him.

Disturbed at being reminded of Cal's unexpected marriage to Rachel Girard, Lacey concentrated instead on regaining his attention. She leaned down close to his ear and whispered. "Cal? Honey?"

He didn't move.

Frowning, she took his jaw in one hand and turned his face toward her. "Cal? Sugar? Sweetie?"

No response.

Hell's bells! He was out.

She let go of him and sat up, disappointed. She knew from experience that trying to rouse a cowboy from a drunk was like trying to breathe life into a stone.

She gazed wistfully at Cal's slumbering form. Oh, he was magnificent. She loved the look of him, the feel of him. Even if there would be no physical connection with him tonight, she knew she would bask in the joy of just sleeping next to him.

Lacey continued to caress his handsome face with loving eyes until an awful realization struck her. It came like an apple falling from a tree, thunking her square on the forehead. This was *not* how it was supposed to be! Dolly always warned her girls not to turn sweet on a customer, and here Lacey was, mooning like a pup and pouting like a deprived child because one of them had fallen asleep on her before they could—*And he was married!*

Lacey covered her face and turned away from him. He was married to the richest girl in town, no less! Talk about being in a pickle. This was a pickle of the sourest persuasion. This was the pickle of all pickles!

Lacey knew she needed to talk to Dolly. She jumped to her feet and started toward the door, almost tripping over the saddlebags Cal had dropped to the floor earlier. She bent to retrieve them, then saw that one flap was open. Inside, among other, very normal things, she caught sight of a book.

A book? She had pictured Cal as many things: a gunfighter; a lawman; a gambler; a desperado, even; but a highfalutin' intellectual? Her curiosity was up.

She pulled it out, flipped open the cover, and peered at the first page. Lacey had never been much for reading and writing, but she had learned enough to sound out the words emblazoned there. She bit her lip, then mouthed the title to herself. *Uncle Tom's Cabin.* She flipped through some pages.

A folded sheet of paper fluttered to the floor. A letter? A letter from his mother, maybe? She frowned. Or a sweetheart? Somehow the thought of Cal having a sweetheart disturbed her even more than the thought of him having a wife, even if that wife *was* Rachel Girard. Lacey picked it up.

After unfolding the sheet, she saw right away it wasn't a letter at all. It had something to do with Rachel. This fired up Lacey's curiosity like nothing else, and she set about concentrating on the words on the sheet: *I, Rachel Girard, promise to pay to Caleb Delaney, the sum of twenty thousand cash dollars upon completion of the following terms.*

It took her awhile, but in the end she got the gist of it. She folded the paper, tucked it between two pages, and slid the book back into the saddlebag before rising to face Cal's slumbering figure on the bed.

Rachel Girard might have grown into what some men considered a looker, but she was still as cold as the wicked north wind. To Rachel, everything boiled down to cattle, dollar signs, and business deals. It always had. Why, Rachel was so scared of ending up a spinster, she had offered to pay an unheard of fortune to Cal Delaney to marry her—even for just six short months. Cal wasn't sweet on that girl at all. He had married her for money.

Lacey sidled over to the bed and bent to the task of removing her best man's boots. "You go right on ahead and rest up, sugar."

In six months Cal would be a free man. He would be leaving this two-bit cowtown twenty thousand dollars richer, and Lacey thought maybe, just maybe, if she could show him what real loving was all about, he just might take her with him.

9

Two days later, after the men left the breakfast table and before Rachel could follow them outside, her aunt Charlotte pulled her aside and insisted they have a talk.

When Rachel walked into the parlor and caught sight of Daisy, fiddling with the ivory keys on the Chickering piano, she immediately became suspicious. Charlotte secured the double doors, sealing the three of them in the room, and Rachel felt as if she had just been waylaid and hog-tied. Trapped.

She faced her aunt. "What is *she* doing here?"

Charlotte raised a hand. "Don't get upset, Rachel. There's something we need to talk about, something you need to know. Sit down."

Rachel stood for a moment with her hands on her hips before she reluctantly complied. What she really wanted was to get this over with as soon as possible. She chose one of the upholstered chairs opposite the tea table. Charlotte took the one facing her.

Rachel narrowed her eyes. "Spit it out."

Charlotte fingered her ruffled linen skirt delicately. "I am sure, my dear, you are not going to like what it is I have to tell you."

Rachel glowered at Daisy, who was plucking out single notes on the piano. Rachel herself rarely played the instrument, but her mother had adored it. Some of Rachel's fondest memories were of the family gathered in front of the hearth while her mother played "The Blue Danube" on the Chickering.

Rachel sat back and folded her arms. "Would you please stop that, Daisy? It's annoying."

Daisy stopped and looked up wearing a haughty expression. "Of course, Rachel. I can certainly understand why you're so easily annoyed these days."

Rachel sat up, rising to the bait. "So easily annoyed? What's *that* supposed to mean?"

Charlotte interrupted before a full-fledged argument could ensue. "Girls! This is no time to start bickering! Daisy, it was you who came to me out of concern for the family. Try to remember that. And Rachel, you would do well to hold your tongue until we're through. As I said, you have Daisy to thank for bringing these facts to our attention. I doubt anyone would've said anything to your face for quite some time."

Rachel turned to her aunt impatiently. "All right! Enough of this shilly-shallying! Out with it!"

"Daisy came to me yesterday with some information she'd overheard. It seems there are rumors that your husband . . . that Cal has been seen at the Red Panther Saloon."

Rachel frowned. So that was where Cal had gone night before last. Well, it didn't surprise her. He had shown up late the next morning looking as if he'd been kicked in the head by a buffalo—obviously hurting from a night of hard drinking. That had suited Rachel just fine. He deserved a good buffalo kick in the head as far as she was concerned.

She met her aunt's gaze evenly. "Is that it?"

"Well, um, not quite, dear." Charlotte paused tactfully, then continued, "He was seen drinking—drinking quite a bit, I might add—at that awful saloon, but afterwards, he . . ."

Daisy's grating voice reached Rachel's ears and what she said left them ringing in shock. "Afterwards, he left with one of the girls. You know, one of the girls who—"

"Daisy!" Charlotte exclaimed.

Rachel barely noticed her aunt's agitation. Cal had spent the night with one of those girls. He had gone and gotten drunk and spent the night in a whorehouse. *That no-good, low-life bastard! That vile, disgusting, fornicating . . .*

"Rachel? Are you all right?"

"Of course."

"Did you hear what Daisy said?"

"Yes."

"Well, dear, while I might have worded it a little differently, Daisy speaks the truth. I myself went into town yesterday and spoke with a certain few people who shall remain nameless. I'm sorry to say, it appears that what Daisy says is quite true."

Rachel squared her shoulders. "Well, naturally I can't accept such a story without investigating it first." And then she would kill him in his sleep.

Charlotte gave her a sympathetic smile. "I wouldn't expect you to, dear. He is, after all, your . . . er, husband."

"Who was he supposedly consorting with?" Rachel demanded.

Charlotte's eyelids fluttered. "Well, dear, it hardly matters who. They're all—"

Rachel leaned forward in her chair. "Who?"

Out of the corner of her eye, Rachel saw Daisy rise from the piano bench. "One of the girls at Dolly Jordan's place."

Rachel turned to lock eyes with her smirking nemesis. She knew that, if only out of malicious delight, Daisy would at least be honest with her. "Which girl at Dolly Jordan's place?"

Charlotte tried to intervene. "Rachel, I don't think knowing the identity of the—"

Daisy smiled. "Lacey Holloway."

"Lacey Holloway." Rachel repeated this familiar name from the past as if to affirm that she had heard correctly. *Lacey Holloway?* A picture flashed in her mind's eye; that of a ragtag eight-year-old child, her thin shoulders habitually hunched beneath tattered clothes, her dirty blond hair hanging in her eyes as she painstakingly scratched out sums on her slate. Rachel had sat in the row next to her in Mrs. Kuppenheimer's class. Even in those days, Rachel had had little in common with Lacey Holloway except for the fact that they had both suffered the sting of young Daisy Parker's cruel wit.

Daisy seemed happy to elaborate. "Word has it that Cal spent quite a bit of time with Lacey before you two were married. Right up to the night before your wedding, as a matter of fact."

Rachel felt as if she had just been kicked in the stomach. "Who told you this?"

Daisy moved back to the piano bench. She sat down

again and started poking at the keys. "Cal wasn't being very discreet. He was seen by more than one person." She stopped and looked at Rachel. "It's not exactly a secret that the two of you haven't been getting along."

Rachel sprang out of her chair, fists clenched at her sides. "That is none of your business!"

Charlotte half rose from her own chair in an attempt to forestall an all-out catfight. "Calm down both of you! Rachel, we understand this isn't easy to take, and if you weren't a strong woman, I would have insisted you not be told."

Rachel glared at Daisy before turning back to her aunt. "How sweet of you to be concerned."

Charlotte shook her head disapprovingly. "I understand that this news has disturbed you. It would disturb any self-respecting woman, but it could happen to anyone, Rachel. A dashing stranger comes to town and sweeps you off your feet. Suddenly you're saying 'I do,' and the man has effectively smooth-talked himself into inheriting a family fortune."

"It wasn't like that at all!"

Charlotte's tone turned conciliatory. "Rachel, we all know the pressure your father was placing on you to wed. It's no wonder things have turned out this way. Why, I wouldn't even hesitate to place the blame for this fiasco right at Galen's feet. You, my dear, were a victim, and that's absolutely nothing to be ashamed of."

"You're darn tootin' I have nothing to be ashamed of!"

Daisy added her own log to the fire. "He's just a fortune seeker, plain and simple."

Rachel turned on her. "It takes one to know one."

"Nicholas and I are in love."

"Oh, pah! More like he had an itch and you were there to scratch it!"

"Rachel!" Charlotte exclaimed. "That was uncalled for! You're taking your anger out on poor Daisy! Why not try directing it at the man responsible?"

"I will direct my anger wherever I please, Aunt Charlotte."

Charlotte rose from her chair with great dignity. "Fine. But when you're through with that, give some serious thought to taking the proper action."

"What do you mean, 'the proper action'?"

"While it may be considered acceptable by some of the baser elements of our society for a married man to be consorting with, well, fallen women, I'm sure that you'll agree it certainly cannot be overlooked by a woman of your—"

"So, what exactly do you deem to be the proper action?"

"Well, considering the short duration of the marriage, an annulment might not be out of the question. Certainly a divorce, while unsavory, would not be unreasonable under the circumstances. I doubt anyone would look askance at you, my dear. On the contrary, I think you might be admired as being a woman who can recognize a mistake when she's made one and act decisively to rectify it. Most people would see you as a woman able to take charge of her own destiny."

With that little inspirational speech, Aunt Charlotte finally laid all her cards on the table. An annulment. A divorce. How convenient for both Charlotte and Daisy. A divorce so soon between Cal and Rachel would land Nick right back in the running to inherit the Elena Rose, wouldn't it?

"I'll take it under consideration," Rachel said.

"Does that mean—?"

Rachel went to the door, ending the discussion. "That means, Aunt Charlotte, that I will handle this problem myself."

Rachel was handling the problem herself. Well, at least *part* of the problem.

She clutched a small box of groceries to her chest as she inched her way alongside the Red Panther Saloon. It was early afternoon, and the saloon and the area surrounding it looked deserted. She peeked around the corner of the building and saw that Dolly Jordan's parlor house was quiet.

Rachel had asked around and learned that Dolly usually ran her errands about this time every afternoon. She was hoping today would be no different. If Dolly were to catch sight of Rachel, she would run her right off the property lickety-split. That would never do. Rachel needed to get inside that parlor house undetected.

Fate was on her side. She didn't have to wait long before the front door opened and the buxom madam emerged into the light of day. Dolly wore a low-cut royal blue day dress with gaudy white ruffles. Rachel watched her rearrange a shawl about her broad shoulders and step down off the rickety porch, not even glancing in Rachel's direction as she set off across the yard toward the respectable part of town.

Pleased with her luck thus far, Rachel flattened herself against the side of the saloon. Somewhere in the back of her mind, where rational thought still reigned, she realized that Cal's flagrant infidelity would only lend more credence to the day when, according to their agreement, he finally deserted her. But she wasn't thinking with that part of her mind today. Her fur was up. Way up.

She knew he was getting back at her for thwarting him the other day. He was dangling a mistress in front of her nose—in front of the whole town, in fact—in order to embarrass her. She could just imagine the talk. *Did you hear about Rachel Girard's new husband? Married less than a week, and he's already playing around with Lacey Holloway down at Dolly Jordan's place! Why, that Rachel Girard must be a sorrier specimen of womanhood than we'd ever thought!*

Rachel caught herself grinding her teeth and stopped it. She despised Cal Delaney! The thought of him pawing Lacey Holloway and the two of them laughing together and . . . Well, it made her blood boil. He was acting just like a *man*, just like the vile, untrustworthy, despicable creature that he was! His actions only reinforced her conviction that she would never let a man get close enough to hurt her. Thank heavens she wasn't in love with him. Rachel wondered how other women ever endured the heartache of such callous betrayal.

She peeked around the corner again to make sure the coast was clear before she crossed the yard. Today, she had chosen to wear a nondescript calico dress with a large floppy sunbonnet to hide the telltale color of her hair. It was safe to assume no one would recognize her from a distance.

As she climbed the porch steps, the uneven plank boards heaved and groaned, making her wonder if the rotting wood might actually collapse beneath her. The old frame building appeared even more dilapidated close up. Not only was it afflicted with peeling paint and cracked windowpanes, Rachel now saw that the exterior was liberally pocked with bullet holes, no doubt the work of high-spirited cowboys on a drunken spree.

Rachel balanced the box of groceries on her left hip as she pushed open the front door. Cal had crossed this disgraceful threshold only two nights ago. That galling thought alone was enough to propel her through the archway and on inside.

She stood alone in a large living area, or, at least, that's what she thought it would have been if this were a respectable dwelling. The place smelled of cheap perfume, cigar smoke, and stale beer. Tacky red velvet draperies with gold braid tiebacks hung in the windows. Shabby divans and chairs were set back against all four walls of the room, and an old upright piano sat silent in one corner. With disdain, Rachel noted a number of oil paintings, female nudes similar to the one she had seen in the saloon.

"Who are you?"

Rachel jumped, startled at the shrill voice that accosted her. A tiny woman with a flocculent mane of flaming red hair had entered the room. Barefoot, she wore a tattered plaid wrapper. "I said, who are you?" she repeated.

This girl wasn't local, and there was no hint she recognized Rachel. Her suspicious tone was probably due to discovering a strange woman in the house. No doubt a male would have elicited a much warmer welcome.

Rachel offered the girl a bright smile. "Why, howdy! I'm Rachel Holloway, Lacey's cousin. You know if she's here?"

The redhead eyed Rachel up and down. "Well, I suppose she's here. Her cousin, are you? You don't look like her."

Rachel laughed. "Well, you know how it is. She takes after one side of the family, and I take after the other."

"She never said anything about no cousin."

"Oh, there are lots of us. We all grew up together, but I left Fort Worth a few years ago. Lacey always said if I got back into town, I was to stop by. Only trouble is, she never told me which room she's in."

The woman seemed to relax and gestured vaguely behind her. "You go up those stairs and down the hall. Her room is the third on the right. She's probably still in bed, though. She had a late night, if you know what I mean."

Rachel's smile froze. A late night? Not with Cal. Cal had spent the night on Rachel's floor. But the night preceding last, he had been here—up those stairs, down that hall, and behind the third door on the right.

Rachel recovered her voice. "Yes, well, much obliged." She started across the room.

"Where do you all come from?"

Rachel stopped. "Uh . . . Corpus Christi."

"Corpus Christi? That's south, right?"

"Right."

"How's business down there?"

Rachel looked at her blankly. Business? What could this girl know about business? "Well, business is just fine."

"Oh." The redhead smiled. "Me and my sister are heading north next week. Business should be booming up there."

Rachel smiled back hesitantly. "Well, best of luck to you."

The redhead chuckled and crossed the room to flounce down onto one of the empty divans. "Why, sugar plum, luck has nothing to do with it!"

Rachel forced a nervous laugh before turning to leave. "Oh, right! So right!"

Rachel hurried from the room before the little tart could ask any more questions. She rolled her eyes in disgust as she passed still more oil paintings on her way up a shadowy staircase. Either Dolly Jordan had a passion for Greek mythology or she had once had a love affair with a very bad artist.

After Rachel reached the top of the stairs, she had no trouble locating Lacey's room. She steeled herself before shifting the grocery box to her hip and trying the door. It was open.

The room was sparsely furnished and pitifully small. A huge bed took up most of the floor space. In one corner stood a washstand with a ceramic wash-bowl and pitcher. The flowered wallpaper was faded, peeling, and riddled with water stains. For an instant, Rachel felt a twinge of compassion for the girl who lived in such dismal surroundings.

The female figure wrapped in a cocoon of sheets and coverlets on the bed didn't stir. Her face was turned away, but Rachel easily recognized Lacey Holloway's tangled mass of blond curls spread out on the pillow behind her.

Rachel stared at that bed for a moment, picturing Cal and Lacey together, and all traces of compassion fled. The bone she had to pick with Lacey had nothing to do with poverty or privilege. It had to do with the fact that Lacey had spent the night with Rachel's husband. This was personal.

Resolute once again, Rachel closed the door. She set

her box down on the floor and rummaged inside until she found what she was looking for: a Colt revolver.

"Lacey?" Rachel kept her voice soft and soothing as she moved to the bed. She didn't want a whole lot of screaming and hollering just yet. Even in a whorehouse full of snoozing tarts, Rachel thought someone might come running if a girl made enough racket.

Rachel perched on the edge of the bed and shook the other girl's shoulder gently. "Lacey Holloooowaaaay."

The girl stirred and moaned. "What?" She turned over, yawning wide. "Oh, honey, not again." It took a moment for her sleepy eyes to focus on Rachel and register recognition.

Her jaw unhinged, she popped up like a shooting spring.

"Rachel! Oh my Lord! Rachel Girard! Oh my Lord!"

"Well, good afternoon, Lacey. My name isn't Girard anymore, though. But maybe you didn't hear. I got married last week."

Lacey's hands grappled with the coverlet as she yanked it up to her neck. "What are you doing here?"

"Just visiting, Lacey. We haven't seen each other in so long. What's it been? Eleven years since we last spent time together in school? Do you remember Miss Kuppenheimer's class? Weren't those the days? Me, you, Nick, and Daisy."

By now, Lacey had come fully awake and was gathering her scattered senses. "You don't have any business here! You get out of my room right this minute!"

Rachel smiled. "Well, that depends on your definition of business." She moved closer on the bed and raised the revolver so the other girl could get a good look at it.

Lacey's complexion paled. "What's that?"

Rachel opened the cylinder and removed first one cartridge, then another from the loading gate. "This here is a Colt .45 revolver."

"What are you doing?"

"I'm unloading it."

"Why?"

Rachel removed a third cartridge. "Well, my daddy taught me to shoot passably well, you see, but it just occurred to me on my way here that walking around town with a loaded gun could be dangerous. Know what I mean?"

"You get out of here, Rachel, or I'm gonna yell for help."

Rachel rolled the cylinder back with a click and raised the barrel, holding it so the muzzle hovered about five inches from Lacey's tiny, upturned nose. "I wouldn't do that if I were you. I haven't finished unloading this yet. I could be startled very easily, and my finger might slip."

Lacey snorted bravely, but Rachel detected a note of false bravado in her words. "You don't scare me."

"Why in the world do you think I would want to scare you, Lacey? We're old friends. Unless, of course, I had some reason to be upset with you. Now, that would be a different story."

"You wouldn't dare shoot that thing in here."

"Wouldn't I?"

"They'd hang you for murder."

"I doubt it."

Lacey swallowed hard. "You still wouldn't."

"Oh, I might," Rachel assured her. "And the next time my husband visits you, you can bet I will for sure. Understand?"

"You're crazy. I'll go to the sheriff."

"Oh? Who's he going to believe? Me or you?"

Lacey's tongue flicked out to wet her dry lips. "Maybe not now, but if I was found dead—"

"If you were found dead, I'd make sure they buried you in the finest pine box money can buy. Don't you worry about a thing."

"They'd hang you!"

"Like I said, I don't think so. Remember, I'm a wife whose husband is cheating on her with the town tramp."

Lacey seemed to weigh this previously unconsidered factor before glancing around the room for an avenue of escape. Things didn't look good. Her back was up against the wooden headboard, not to mention she was still too tangled up in the bed sheets to move very far. Still, when she looked back at Rachel, she made a feeble attempt to set her chin defiantly. "You'll never get back in this house."

"I got in today, didn't I?"

"I'll lock my door!"

"That flimsy little thing?"

"Just stop it, Rachel!"

Rachel lowered her voice. "No, Lacey, you stop it. Stop playing around with my husband."

"Cal doesn't even want you! If he did, he wouldn't come to me!"

Rachel shoved the gun closer and was gratified to see Lacey jerk back, her eyes big and riveted on the muzzle.

"What Cal wants isn't your concern."

Lacey's face mottled bright pink. She began to tremble, whether with fear or rage or a combination of both, Rachel couldn't tell. Then, she squeezed her eyes shut, sucked in a huge breath, and let out a holler to wake up heaven. *"Get out!"*

Judging that her mission was now satisfactorily accomplished, Rachel lowered the revolver and stood. "Oh, I'm leaving, all right. For today. But remember, next time . . ."

"Get out! Get out!"

Rachel dropped the revolver and cartridges into the grocery box and picked it up. "It's been nice seeing you again, Lacey."

She opened the door and stepped out into the dingy hallway. With the door safely closed behind her, she collapsed back against the wall to catch her breath. Her heart was chugging like a runaway locomotive. Now all she had to do was get out of the house without running into anyone who knew her.

With her free hand, she reached into her dress pocket and pulled out three .45 cartridges. She clutched them tight in the palm of her hand and smiled. She'd removed them before leaving the house this morning. The revolver she'd held on Lacey had been empty, perfectly harmless, but Lacey had no way of knowing that, did she?

Rachel started for the stairs. She felt better. She felt rejuvenated. She felt satisfied that she had, as her aunt would have chosen to put it, taken the proper action.

The next move was up to Cal.

10

Cal took the stairs at Dolly Jordan's parlor house by twos. He had missed dinner at the ranch for the second time in one week to come into town, only this time it was not by choice. This time it had been at Lacey Holloway's request.

It was bad enough that Lacey had sent her message through a leering Elena Rose ranch hand. The truth was, Cal didn't much appreciate being summoned at all. He was responding to Lacey's message mainly in order to tell her not to send him any more messages.

His rapid footfalls echoed in the narrow, dark hallway leading to Lacey's room. He rapped on her door impatiently. "Lacey! It's Cal! Open up!"

He heard her scrambling around. Then, she was framed in the archway, dressed in her skimpy waitress outfit. Her eyes were big. "Cal!" She grabbed his elbow and dragged him through the threshold before shoving the door closed behind him. "I thought you weren't going to make it before I had to go to work!"

Cal eyed her dubiously. The girl was getting clingy. It had been a mistake for him to come back to her room the other night. He probably should have picked one of the other girls, maybe one of the redheads. Not that it would have mattered, anyway. He had rusted his boiler but good that night, an uncommon occurrence for him.

In his former profession, he had learned early on to nurse his liquor, leave his right hand free, and always sit with his back to the wall. It was a true testament to his new style of life that he had relaxed his guard to the point of getting drunk and passing out colder than a dead fish on Lacey's bed.

"What's so important that you've seen fit to drag me all the way into town, Lacey?"

"It's Rachel. She came here yesterday."

"Rachel came . . . *here?*"

Lacey started pacing, her short ruffled skirt flouncing up and down with each step. "She told me to stop seeing you."

"She what? How did she even know I did see you?"

"She tried to kill me."

"*What?*"

Lacey started waving her arms frantically. "She held a gun on me, Cal!"

"A gun?"

She stopped pacing. "Are you listening to me?"

"Oh, I'm listening, all right. I'm just having a little trouble believing what I'm hearing."

"Well, believe it! She was gonna pull the trigger!"

"Say again?"

"She tried to kill me! She said the next time she

finds out that you and me been together, she's going to come back!"

Cal smiled. "Oh, I doubt Rachel would actually kill you. At least, I don't think so."

"What are you smiling about?" Lacey shrieked. Even as she uttered the words, the realization came to her that she had never seen Cal Delaney really smile before. She had seen his smirk, and she had heard his laugh, dry and sardonic, but she had never seen that light in his eye or the truly amused grin that curved his lips at this moment. It galled her to think that Rachel Girard could make him smile like that, especially when she'd gone and pointed a loaded six-shooter at Lacey's nose!

"What in hell is that woman up to?" Cal wondered aloud.

"She's crazy as a loon! You'd better get away from her as fast as you can!"

"She's my wife. How do you propose I get away from her?"

Lacey stamped her foot. "Just leave!"

Cal shook his head. "I don't think so." He reached into his vest pocket, pulled out a five-dollar gold piece, and flipped it onto the bed.

Lacey stared at it, feeling as if Cal had just ice-picked her in the heart. "What's that?"

"It's for your time," he said, turning to leave.

Lacey shot forward and snagged him by the arm. "Cal, where are you going, honey? Since you're here, we might as well have some fun. I mean, we—"

"It's for your trouble, then."

Lacey rubbed up against him. "But you've already made the trip, honey. Don't worry about me, Cal. Hell's bells, I'm not scared of Rachel Girard."

"Oh? Maybe you should be."

At his tone, Lacey stiffened and her voice turned cold. "If you think you're going to get any good loving from that she-devil, you're sorely mistaken. She'll chew you up and spit you out like garbage!"

Anger flashed in Cal's deep blue eyes, and Lacey stepped back, suddenly apprehensive despite her indignation. She had never seen Cal angry before, and she had the idea that it might not be in her best interests to rile him any further.

"You don't know me very well, do you, Lacey?"

Lacey blinked back tears as he slipped his arm from her limp grasp. "Cal . . ."

"Don't send me any more messages."

Lacey stood rooted to the floor as the door slammed in her face. Trembling, she sank down onto the bed, tears of humiliation and anger running a path down freshly powdered cheeks. Dolly had warned her about taking on customers that could play with a girl's heart.

She glared through burning tears at the gold piece lying on the bed where he had tossed it. On impulse, she snatched it up and flung it across the room. "Every dog has its day, Cal Delaney, and when I get mine, you'll be sorry!"

It was late by the time Cal arrived at the ranch. When he passed the open door of Galen's study, the older man lifted his head and gave little more than a grunt in acknowledgment. Cal knew that he had scored no points with Galen when he took off the other night. The man naturally saw it as shabby behavior toward his beloved daughter, and Cal couldn't very well blame him. After all, Galen didn't know the real story between Cal and Rachel, did he?

As he climbed the stairs to the room he shared with Rachel, Cal fought to control the grin that kept tugging at his lips. He still didn't know whether to be angry or amused at Rachel's latest stunt. Damn! She was a hell-cat, wasn't she?

Well, he knew one thing for sure. He would have to bring her to heel. He wanted that twenty thousand dollars, and he was going to have to find some way of sticking it out here for at least six months in order to get it. He meant for those six months to be peaceful, and the only way they were going to be peaceful was if he found some way to force his feisty little bride to knuckle under and start acting like a normal wife—at least in public.

As expected, he found the lioness in her den, tucked into bed but wide awake. He noticed that she didn't bother looking up from her book at his entrance. It was a fine tactical move on her part.

Her voice was cool. "I see you made it in tonight. Not too much of an inconvenience, I hope."

Cal dropped down onto Rachel's vanity stool, stretching his legs out in front of him and crossing his ankles. "No inconvenience at all, darling. Anything to be by your side, you know that."

"Mmmmm. How sweet."

"What are you reading?"

"*Tale of Two Cities* if it's any of your business."

"Ah, yes. One of my personal favorites."

Rachel raised her gaze to meet his. "That's surprising."

"What? That I read?"

Rachel simply rolled her eyes and returned to her book.

"You'll never guess who I ran into while I was in town."

"I'm sure I couldn't care less."

"Lacey Holloway." Cal watched his lovely bride for any sign of surprise, but she was just too darned good for that.

"Lacey Holloway, Lacey Holloway, Lacey Holloway," Rachel muttered vaguely as if trying to place the name. "Oh, yes. Her. Pitiful girl. Such a shame."

"A shame?"

"How she turned out."

"You two are old friends, I hear."

She turned a page. "Well, I wouldn't exactly say that. Acquaintances maybe."

"You've got no reason to be upset with her, then?"

Rachel still didn't look up from her book. "Upset with her? Why would I be upset with her? Just because she sees fit to fornicate with my husband from time to time? Fiddlesticks. Why should that upset me?"

"Then what she says can't possibly be true, because according to Lacey, you tried to kill her yesterday."

"Kill her? Why?"

Cal shrugged. "Oh, I don't know. Because you're jealous of her, perhaps?"

Rachel slammed the book shut, betraying herself for the first time. "Jealous?"

Cal grinned.

She recovered quickly, her voice cooling once again. "What have I got to be jealous of her for?"

"You tell me."

Rachel snorted. "Well, it wouldn't be because of what your conceited self might be thinking."

"You can't possibly know what my conceited self is thinking."

"Oh?"

"One thing I'm thinking is that you sure went to a

lot of trouble to get Lacey out of the way. I think you'd be just thrilled if she left town."

"If I wanted her out of town, I'd have offered her money. She'll do anything for money, which I suppose you've already noticed."

Cal smiled. His lovely wife had a sharp tongue.

Rachel adjusted her pillows and leaned her head back. Lustrous copper curls billowed out behind her, much as Cal had once imagined they would. "Lacey's father was a drunk. A mean son of a gun too. I remember she used to come to school more often than not with a black eye or a fat lip. Fell off the porch, she'd say, or ran into a barn door."

"Sounds like she had a rough life."

"Yes, I'm sure she did. Much rougher than mine, as you're probably thinking right now. She was always spiteful, and I guess I can't blame her. She never liked me, and I never liked her. Oh, I'm sure she appreciated the fact that Daisy Parker used to pick on me, that Daisy had someone else to make miserable besides poor little Lacey, but life's funny. Now Daisy and I are related by marriage and forced to live under the same roof. Lacey . . . well, you can see how Lacey turned out."

"Can you blame her?"

"Blame her? I suppose not. I'm sure she does what she feels she needs to do to survive." Rachel's eyes narrowed to slits. "But she's not going to do it with my so-called husband. Not while I have anything to say about it."

Cal took off his vest and tossed it over the vanity, then bent to remove his boots. "And just what makes you think you have anything to say about it?"

Rachel propped herself up on one elbow, being careful to hold the sheet over the bosom of her cotton nightdress. "I have something to say about it because we are supposedly married, and that is a fact known by each and every soul in this county! And as long as that's so, I will not be publicly humiliated by you visiting the local cathouse!"

Cal didn't reply as he removed his shirt.

"Well?" Rachel demanded.

Cal unbuttoned his pants. "Well, what?"

"Do we have an understanding?"

He laughed. "An understanding? I doubt it, sweetheart. You and I haven't managed to reach any understandings before this. Why start now?"

Rachel's eyebrows rose nearly to her hairline as he stripped down to his drawers. "What are you doing?"

"Why, I'm getting ready for bed, wife."

"Your blankets are in the linen chest. You'd best go get them before I turn down the lamp."

Cal started toward the bed. "Oh, I think not."

Rachel stiffened. "You—you can't be thinking that you're getting into this bed!"

As far as Cal could tell, Rachel didn't scare easy, but he suspected she had a maidenly fear of at least one thing—sex. "That's exactly what I'm thinking," he said. "If I'm going to be a good husband, I might as well start now."

Rachel looked horrified. "You can't. You wouldn't!"

Cal sat on the edge of the bed. "What's the matter, princess? You're looking a little peaked."

He turned down the lamp, then slid smoothly beneath the top sheet. Despite the darkness, Cal knew Rachel was still sitting ramrod straight next to him. For once in her life, she had been struck speechless, and he heartily congratulated himself on this monumental accomplishment. It was a start.

He moved over and rested a hand on her hip. It felt warm and inviting and very female through the thin material of her nightdress. "What's the matter, Rachel? You mean, you don't want me going to see Lacey anymore, but you haven't come up with any alternative activities for me? That's not planning very far ahead, is it?"

"Cal Delaney, if you're even thinking of . . ."

He rested an elbow on the pillow and propped his head up with one hand. "Of what? Claiming husbandly rights to my wife? Who are you going to tell? Daddy? He might be surprised that it's taken so long."

She drew in a deep breath, and he knew she was trying to collect herself. "Just don't forget we have an agreement. And I pay off when you've held up your end of the bargain."

Cal sighed, rolling onto his back and clasping his hands behind his head. "Bargains, deals, contracts, and wedding vows. You know, after a while, it all gets so confusing for us simpletons."

Rachel was furious. She reminded herself that he was just trying to rattle her. He was angry at her over the episode with Lacey, and this latest move was his way of getting back at her. Well, it wouldn't work. She would simply ignore him!

She scooted as far away from him as she could without falling out of bed, then flounced onto her side, presenting him her back.

"Oh, no you don't." Cal reached out, wrapped one arm around her waist and yanked her back across the bed, smack up against the hard length of his body. He laughed, infuriating her all the more as she struggled valiantly to free herself. It wasn't long before she was forced to surrender.

She squeezed her eyes shut, hardly daring to breathe as she waited for him to finish what he had started. But he didn't move. Apparently, holding her captive was going to be the extent of his revenge for now.

She willed herself to relax. She couldn't help noticing that his body felt warm and solid and very, very strong next to her own. It was difficult not to feel oddly comforted by this new discovery, but after a few minutes, her eyes flew open again, suspicious and alert.

What was that . . . that . . . thing? Then her breath caught as she suddenly realized the source of that growing pressure against the curve of her buttocks. With a yelp, she tried to wrest away, but he jerked her back and held her still.

His voice was low next to her ear. "Face it, princess, there's a fox in your henhouse. I think you'd better get used to it."

11

Wearing a spanking new blue-and-white party dress, Daisy collapsed onto the porch swing and sighed fretfully. "I declare! What is taking her so long? We're liable to miss the bonfire lighting."

Nick replied in a flat tone, "What are you worried about, Daisy, that it'll be too late for you to make a grand entrance?"

Daisy wrinkled her nose but didn't respond.

Galen frowned and pulled a watch from his vest pocket. "She's probably just lost track of the time."

"Someone should look in on her," Charlotte said.

A heavy silence ensued. Cal looked up from contemplating his boots to find that all heads had turned in his direction. He stared back at them blankly, then straightened. "Oh. I guess that should be me."

Galen's tone was dry. "I guess it should."

As Cal turned to go into the house, he felt all four pairs of Girard eyes boring into his back. It had been weeks now, and still he sometimes forgot that the rest of the world saw him as Rachel Girard's husband.

As far as he could tell, his relationship with Rachel bore little resemblance to that of a marriage. It was more like a boxing match, a daily pugilistic exercise, each of them dancing and feigning, ducking and swinging. So far, their match was a draw.

He climbed the stairs reluctantly, not at all in the mood to confront his bride. He didn't really give a damn if they showed up late for Old Man Sutter's barn dance. This was to be their first public appearance as husband and wife, and it couldn't be over soon enough as far as he was concerned.

When Cal pushed the bedroom door open, what he beheld made him stop and gape in disbelief. It looked like a ransacked dressmaker's shop. Dresses, skirts, and blouses had been flung everywhere—across the bed, over the brass headboard, and over the armoire door.

In the midst of this mayhem, Rachel stood before the mirror, holding a blue satin frock up to her figure and scowling. She looked up at his entrance. "What are you doing here?"

"Everyone's wondering what's taking you so long."

"I haven't decided what to wear."

Cal's exasperated advice was offered in the tradition of all men everywhere. "Wear what you got right there!"

"I can't. It makes me look too . . . tall."

Cal strode across the room and snatched up a blue gingham. "What about this?"

Rachel shook her head. "No, I've let the hem out of that one so many times, it looks like—"

"It looks like what?"

Rachel started to get angry. "You wouldn't under-stand!"

Cal snorted. "You're sure as hell right about that!"

"Swearing at me will not help matters."

"Fine. I'll stop swearing if you stop pussy footing around like some flighty female and get dressed."

Her green eyes flashed. "Well, being the flighty female that I am, I guess I have a right to change my mind! Why don't you go downstairs and tell them I'm not going?"

"What do you mean, you're not going?"

"Am I not speaking English? I mean, I'm not going!"

"Everybody's going!"

In a fit of petulance, Rachel forgot her modesty and flung down the blue dress. "Well, not me!"

With her slim figure clad only in a thin camisole and white pantalettes, Cal was hard pressed not to notice the tantalizing upward tilt of his wife's breasts, the promising curve of her hips, and tapering length of her coltish legs.

When he looked up to meet her gaze, he saw that her cheekbones were tinged with color, but she was apparently more stubborn than embarrassed. She didn't scurry to find her wrapper or stoop to recover the discarded frock.

Cal let a moment of silence creep by as they stared each other down. They were getting nowhere. He knew that if he was forced to go back and inform her family that Rachel was refusing to go to the barn dance, Galen would assume that his daughter's sudden fit of temper was somehow Cal's fault.

Galen was a good man, but he had a blind spot when it came to his spoiled daughter. Cal had no desire to receive the cold shoulder from his mentor just because Rachel couldn't decide what damn dress to wear. "All right," he said. "Truce."

Rachel blinked at him, surprised. "What?"

"Truce."

"Truce?"

"It's temporary, I assure you. Just for tonight."

Rachel studied him suspiciously.

"You haven't been able to decide what to wear, right?"

"I . . . well, no, not yet."

"It's certainly not for lack of selection, is it?" Cal moved about the room, fingering each of the discarded garments briefly, looking them over. "Why don't you let me pick something out for you?"

Rachel stared at him as if he had just suggested they take a walk on the Trinity River. "You? Why should I do that?"

"Because I happen to know what looks good on a woman."

Rachel snorted. "What you think looks good on a woman they don't permit in public."

He forced a smile, refusing to be baited. "Indulge me."

He felt Rachel watching suspiciously as he sauntered about the room, picking up first this dress, then that. Finally, he spied an emerald green dress lying in a heap in one corner. The color, he knew, would match her eyes and set off that magnificent hair. He crossed the room and held it out to her. "This."

She took it hesitantly—as if she expected the sleeves to be packed with sticks of sputtering dynamite—then turned again to face the mirror. She held it up and frowned. Cal stood behind her, looking over her shoulder. He had been right. It did match her eyes. The effect was breathtaking.

"Well, I don't know," she said, wrinkling her nose.

She didn't know? Cal almost lost his carefully cultivated self-control before he realized Rachel was not deliberately trying to be difficult. For the first time, it occurred to him that the image he saw of Rachel and the image she saw of herself were two very different things.

She cocked her head to one side. "It'll have to do."

Cal shook his head in silent exasperation as he crossed the room to sit on the bed. Rachel draped the dress over the open door of her armoire and started searching through one of the drawers. She was preoccupied and, for the first time since they had married, seemingly unconcerned about dressing in his presence.

He had come to regret his rash decision to share her bed. He had done it to bother her, and it certainly accomplished that purpose, but if the truth were told, it was probably bothering Cal a heck of a lot more than it was bothering Rachel.

It was not an easy thing—sleeping next to her and not giving in to the ever-growing temptation to touch her. But he couldn't remedy the situation by returning to his place on the floor. That would be admitting defeat, and he had too much pride for that. Thanks to his precious pride, though, he was paying an excruciating price. Now, as he slowly took in the feminine curves of his wife's appealing figure, he was beginning to feel randier than a jackrabbit in springtime.

As Rachel pulled a corset from her drawer, she tried to ignore Cal Delaney's silent, yet all-pervasive, unmistakably male presence in the room. He had declared a truce, but warfare could be a subtle thing, and at the moment, she could feel his appraising eyes on her almost as surely as if he were running his hands over every inch of her body. As she struggled with her corset, she fumbled with the ties, suddenly feeling clumsy.

Cal materialized behind her, stilling her hands with his. "Don't wear it."

Rachel slowly lifted her gaze to meet his in the mirror. "Of course I'm going to wear it."

"You don't need it."

"Yes, I do."

"No. You don't."

Rachel was stunned as, with inarguable finality, Cal loosened each tie until the undergarment fell to the floor at their feet. He accomplished his purpose with such ease and efficiency, she couldn't help wondering irritably at the multitudes of corsets he must have removed in his lifetime.

She gave up and reached for the dress. As she pushed her arms through the sleeves, she noticed he hadn't moved away. He was still watching her. She cursed her trembling hands as she struggled with the tiny buttons on the back of the dress.

Seeing her frustration, Cal pushed her hands away, and took up the chore himself. Their eyes locked in the mirror as his fingers slowly worked their way up her spine.

He had foregone his customary denims and work shirt and had donned tan trousers with an open-collared white shirt. His hair, three shades of blond, was combed back from his forehead, and he was freshly shaved. He smelled of soap and bay rum.

When he was done buttoning her dress, he reached up unexpectedly and pulled the hairpins from the knot at the nape of her neck. "Now, as for this . . ."

Rachel's hands shot up too late to save her curls from falling in an avalanche past her shoulders. "Hey!"

"Rachel, this is supposed to be a festive occasion. There's no need to look like you're going to a prayer meeting."

As Cal moved to snatch a hairbrush from her vanity, she folded her arms. "So, you have a problem with the way I wear my hair, do you?"

"Well, now that you mention it . . ."

She was puzzled by his strange behavior. One minute he was swearing a blue streak at her and the next he was gently running a brush through her hair. "You know, Cal, it sounds like you're almost looking forward to this ordeal."

"Aren't you?"

Rachel let out an exasperated sigh. "It started out small, with only Joshua Sutter's family, ours, a few friends, and the ranch hands. Soon, half the town had invited themselves."

"I heard Sutter and Galen go back a long way."

"They were stationed here when Fort Worth was a military post. When the army moved to Fort Belknap, Sutter was discharged. He decided to stay and stake a claim. Daddy came back a few years later, staked his own claim, branded his first cow, and the rest, as they say, is history."

Cal continued to run the brush through her hair in soothing, gentle strokes. "So, they got rich together, is that it?"

"They both worked at it, Cal. You make it sound like coins were dropping from heaven. Even before the war, Joshua Sutter was one of the few cotton growers smart enough to make a tidy profit without the use of slave labor."

"Commendable."

Rachel eyed Cal curiously in the mirror. "You told me once that you were from Kansas. Were your parents abolitionists?"

"My father was killed in Lawrence when Quantrill's Raiders attacked. I doubt they stopped to question his sentiments."

Rachel looked away. "I'm sorry."

"It's all right."

Patiently, he worked out the tangles in her hair. Cal had never volunteered much information about his family, only that they were dead. Even now, his facial expression gave away none of his feelings.

He finished brushing out her hair and sauntered over to the vanity. Rachel turned to see him flip open one of her carved jewelry boxes, searching for something. He pulled out two jeweled tortoise-shell combs, closed the box, and returned to her side, offering the ornaments to her.

"What's this?" she asked. "You're letting me do something?"

"I have a feeling you'll do a better job of placing these than I will."

She took the combs and turned back to the mirror. "Oh, so I get credit for something."

Cal stood behind her as she pulled her hair back at the sides and secured it with the combs. His tone was musing. "To tell you the truth, I'm not sure what to expect tonight. I've never been to a dance before."

Rachel was incredulous. "Never?"

"Never."

"You mean, even when you were growing up, you—"

Cal interrupted, "Wait." He reached over her shoulder and gently tugged a few strands loose from the combs so that soft curls fell to frame her face. "There. Perfect."

He rested a hand on each of her shoulders. For some reason, this simple contact seemed to Rachel a most intimate gesture, but she couldn't bring herself to move away. Once again, their eyes brushed and locked in the mirror.

"My parents were strict Methodists," he said. "Dancing was forbidden."

"Methodists?" Rachel repeated, surprised. "Well, you've certainly strayed from the fold, haven't you?"

His grin was crooked. "Do you think so?"

Rachel smiled then, despite herself. "Cal Delaney, let's see how you stack up, shall we?" She held up one hand and began ticking off sins with each finger. "One, you swear; two, you drink; three, you smoke—"

"You've noticed that, have you?"

"Four, you've led a life of violence."

"But that's all in the past."

Rachel narrowed her eyes. "And, last but not least, you consort with women outside the bounds of marriage."

"But never *within* the bounds of marriage. Don't I get any credit for that?"

"No. We're not really married."

He started running his fingers through her hair, making her scalp tingle. "At least I don't dance. You can't pin that on me."

Rachel fought the little shivers that ran through her as he played with her hair. She felt her face starting to wash over warm, and she turned around abruptly, making him stop it before her cheeks could burn scarlet. She looked up at him, keenly aware that they were standing much too close and his eyes were much too knowing.

"I suppose we'll have to dance together," she said. "For appearance's sake."

"Do you think you can manage it?"

"I think so." Rachel felt like a schoolgirl experiencing her first crush. Lord, but he was a handsome man, distractingly so, even for a girl with enough good sense to be on her guard against it. She averted her eyes. "My shoes. I've got to find my shoes."

Rachel proceeded to flutter about the room like an addlepated fool, finally retrieving her shoes from under the bed. As she pulled them on, working diligently with the button hook, she was careful to avoid meeting his gaze. Truce indeed! She thought she preferred war. At least then they were on surer ground.

When she was finished, she stood and faced him resolutely. "I'm ready."

"Sound the trumpets."

She threw him a haughty look as she moved to the door. "If it's not too much to ask, you might try to curb your wit tonight so as not to embarrass me in front of the entire community."

"It'll be difficult."

"Try to remember, you *are* a Girard."

Cal followed her out into the hallway, closing the door firmly behind them. "Not so, princess. *You* are a Delaney."

It was some time later that Cal leaned against the trunk of a gnarled oak, observing the festive crowd. It seemed as if the entire population of Fort Worth had shown up. There were old and young alike, from screaming infants to doddering old men. Everyone, from the well-to-do Girards to the most impoverished of the town's inhabitants, had dressed in their colorful best to kick up their heels and join in the revelry.

Fort Worth was a hospitable place. The country was wide open and green, the climate mild, the people down-to-earth and accepting. Cal could feel at home here—if he were a man so inclined. But what was home really?

Virginia City—had that been his last real home? He had spent two years there, working out of the Wells Fargo office, forging friendships with honorable men like Jason Farley and Tex Granger. Tex had been the best tracker Cal ever worked with. Jason had been country smart and wily as a fox. During their time together, the three of them had made a formidable team. When the time came for Cal to move on, however, he had packed up and left without so much as a backward glance.

And what of Abilene? That was where he had spent a good portion of his youth. It was there he had met the old gunhand named Grady, the man who first taught him how to handle a six-shooter. It was on the back streets of Abilene that, at sunup each morning, Cal had foraged behind the deadfall saloons for empty tin cans and whiskey bottles, enough to fill two large burlap sacks. Every day for almost a year, Cal tramped out beyond the city limits to set those bottles in a neat line and practice shooting until his wrists grew numb and his eyes bleary. In Abilene and Wichita he grew into a man. How was it that he never called either of those places home?

Perhaps home had been the old sod house. Cal remembered that first planting season as if it was yesterday. With a straw hat perched on his head and an old Sharps rifle slung over one shoulder, Cal's father had bent to drive his axe into the newly broken sod. Cal, no more than seven years old at the time, had followed in his father's footsteps, carefully dropping a single grain of corn into each new cut.

Certainly home had been the fine frame house, the one his father built much later, the light-filled home that had brought a gleam of pride to his mother's eye. It was in this house that Cal could remember his mother and his older sister, Jessica Anne, singing "Oh! Susanna" as they ground up corn to make johnny cakes for supper. That was the house where his mother had given birth to Rebecca, the light of their lives, the beautiful child who later succumbed to diphtheria.

Cal remembered the day they wrapped her tiny body in a sheet and laid her to rest forever on the small rise behind the hay shed. Even now, the recollection ached like an old wound that had never really healed.

Cal recalled then what home was. It was the endless flat prairie. In the summer, the sweltering heat would rise from the sun-baked earth in shimmering ripples. In the winter, ice-dusted winds could freeze a man's eyes shut. Home was hail and lightning storms, firelights sparking off the horns of the oxen, fireballs bouncing and crackling across the prairie. Home was the never-ending, dispassionate wind that whipped across the land and the gritty dust that never seemed to wash from his hair. Home was lost dreams, withered crops, and death—always that. Some people called it the heartland.

Cal's attention was wrested back to the present as the fiddler atop the grandstand drew his bow, emitting a screeching note. This was a signal that another round of dancing was about to begin.

Sutter's hoedown was being celebrated this evening

under a nighttime sky that glistened with winking stars
from one cloudless horizon to the next. The air was
warm and breezy, perfumed with the aroma of crackling wood from a roaring bonfire. Cal didn't like that
smell—it stirred up bad memories—memories best left
buried.

The man on the grandstand called out. "Salute your
partners! Join hands and circle to the left!"

Daisy Girard approached Cal's side and let out a
sigh. "Poor, poor Rachel!"

Cal had no trouble finding Rachel in the dance
crowd. She had just tripped over Nick's foot.

"Poor, poor girl."

"Poor, poor girl, what?" Cal asked, as if he didn't
know very well what Daisy was hinting at.

Daisy waved a splayed pink fan in front of her face.
"Well, look at her out there, stumbling all over the
place. Some things never change."

"Always a little awkward, was she?"

Daisy laughed. "I'd say so! Smart as a whip, but she
never could manage to put one foot in front of the
other without tripping over something. I suppose no
one's perfect."

Cal didn't allow his irritation to show. "That's a
fact."

Daisy peeked up at him coyly. "You know what
Rachel's real problem is?"

"No, what is Rachel's real problem?"

"She can't take a joke. Never could. So serious all
the time. Now me, I say if you can't take some pleasure
out of life, what's the point?"

"Interesting philosophy."

A silence rose between them as they observed
Rachel stumble once again, then jump back, wearing a

disgruntled expression. Nick bent to whisper something in her ear, and Rachel's frown smoothed out. She laughed as Nick took her about the waist and led her back into formation.

Daisy verbalized the obvious. "They get along well. He has a way with her. Always has. They're like brother and sister in some ways. Then again, in some ways they're not. Have you ever really watched them together?"

"How do you mean?"

"He's the only person who can make her laugh."

Cal's gaze followed the two cousins as they weaved in and out of the circle. "And Rachel," he said thoughtfully, "does she make Nick laugh too?"

"Sometimes."

"Does that bother you, Miss Daisy?"

"Bother me?" Daisy's fan flapped back and forth more rapidly. "Heavens, why should it bother me? They're cousins, aren't they? What could possibly be going on?" She paused, then continued in a plaintive tone, "Still, this thing they have between them, like they understand each other without having to speak out loud, it does get tiresome."

"Does it?"

"You watch sometime when Rachel is in one of her fits and Nick just happens to be there to smooth things over. Why, easy as you please, he'll pull her aside and coo into her ear, just like Rachel does with one of those prized horses of hers. You watch, she'll come away purring like a contented kitten."

Cal was doubtful. "Really? From what I've seen, Rachel usually treats him as if she's got a bone to pick."

Daisy tittered. "Oh, well, you're right about that.

She's never forgiven him for marrying me. The very idea of it still sticks in her craw. He knows it, too. He's been spending the last year trying to make it up to her like a repentant lover. Why, if Nick ever did inherit the Elena Rose, I wouldn't put it past him to offer it up to her on a silver platter."

Daisy's choice of words lingered in Cal's mind. *Like a repentant lover.* He adjusted his hat. "But it probably won't come to that, will it?"

"Probably not. Not since you rode over the horizon."

"How's that?"

"Oh, come now, Cal. I think we both know the answer to that. It doesn't take much to figure out that you and Rachel didn't exactly come together out of mutual attraction."

"Now, how do you figure that?"

"Knowing Rachel as well as I do, I daresay she's a cold woman, a woman with room for only one great love in her life, and that great love is the Elena Rose. It consumes her. She'd do anything to keep it all to herself."

Daisy's cornflower blue gaze became unmistakably bold. "I don't imagine there's much passion left for a man like yourself, Cal, a man well used to the kind of attentions a real woman can offer. I can almost understand why you may feel the need to, shall we say, step out to seek greener pastures."

Cal would have been a fool to miss the proposition that had just been flung in his face. He let his eyes slide down over her dainty figure before once again meeting her unflinching gaze. "You wouldn't be applying for the job, would you, Miss Daisy?"

She feigned innocence. "Why, what job are you speaking of?"

"Taking up the slack."

She flashed a white smile. "Cal, you say that in such a way that it almost makes me blush! Why, the very thought! And me being a married woman!"

Cal didn't reply. Instead, he returned his attention to the whirling dancers. Nick was leading Rachel into a relatively difficult maneuver. To his credit, he got her through it without missing a beat.

Daisy had a point. Rachel and Nick got along well together. Unusually well. Cal had never thought much about it before. Now that it had been brought to his attention, however, he wondered how he had ever missed it.

At the conclusion of the dance, the crowd started clapping and hooting as the group of hoofers broke and scattered. Nick and Rachel soon made their way back through the milling crowd to where Cal and Daisy waited.

With her curls loose about her shoulders, her green eyes lambent in the light of the bonfire, and her cheeks flushed from exertion, Cal thought Rachel looked like a woman basking in the afterglow of lovemaking.

Daisy piped up. "Why, Rachel, honey, I do so admire your spirit, keeping at it like you do when most people would have given up long ago!"

Rachel scowled. "Some of us have better things to do with our time than practice our dance steps, Daisy."

Accustomed to their habitual squabbling, Nick interrupted calmly, addressing his wife. "I trust you and Cal found enough to talk about while we were gone?"

Daisy placed a proprietary hand on Cal's arm. "Why, we found plenty to talk about, didn't we, Cal?"

Before Cal could even open his mouth, Daisy turned

to Rachel and gushed, "You are such a lucky, lucky girl to have found such a handsome and charming husband!"

Cal wasn't sure whom Daisy was trying to annoy more—her husband or Rachel. It didn't matter. Judging by their faces, she was doing an admirable job of irking them both.

Nick's mouth thinned into a grim line. "I should have known you'd manage to entertain yourself."

Rachel reached out to swat Daisy's hand away from Cal's arm. "Let's just remember whose husband is whose, shall we?"

Daisy laughed. "Isn't that cute? Why, Rachel's jealous!" She folded her fan and linked arms with a recalcitrant Nick. "Even when she knows I'm a perfectly happily married woman!"

Rachel glowered at her. "The air's getting a little thick. I'm going to wait in the wagon." She marched off toward the barn where most of the wagons and horses were tethered.

Daisy smirked at Rachel's back and turned gleeful eyes up at Cal. "See? I told you. Rachel never could take a joke."

"Maybe it's just your jokes she has a problem with," Nick said.

Daisy pouted. "Why don't you just forget about your grumpy old cousin and ask your own wife to dance?"

"I'll go check on her," said Cal.

Nick gave him a pointed look. "I'm sure that couldn't hurt. Getting some attention from her husband for a change."

Cal absorbed Nick's criticism without comment. He watched grimly as Rachel's cousin led his gloating wife back into the crowd. Cal had known from the beginning that Nick didn't much like him. At first he had chalked it up to family protectiveness. Later, after he had married Rachel, he figured Nick's continued hostility had something to do with Cal's less than exemplary past. Now, after seeing Nick and Rachel together in an entirely new light, he wasn't so sure snobbishness was all there was to it.

He headed up the incline toward the darkened silhouette of the barn. The moon was near full, illuminating enough to make up for the bonfire's waning light behind him. When he rounded the corner of the hulking structure, he had little difficulty spotting their buckboard, one in a long line of deserted vehicles.

Rachel stood with her back to the wagon, her arms folded stiffly across her chest. She didn't acknowledge him as he approached and broke her sulky silence. "Let me just see if I understand the situation. When Daisy insults you, your answer is to go barging off to sit out the evening in the dark while she stays behind to dance with her husband."

"Shut up."

"Well, I've got to hand it to you, Rachel, you sure know how to teach her a lesson."

"No one asked for your opinion."

"That comes free with the marriage contract."

She fixed him with a cold stare. "Thank you so much. And now, if you're through, why don't you head back to the party? I certainly never expected you to tear yourself away from Daisy's sparkling company on my account."

"Don't start turning martyr on me, Rachel. Remember, you're the one who left me alone in the first place. It's a little stupid to be acting all jealous over—"

"Jealous? Oh, please! You flatter yourself!"

Cal smiled. "That's okay. I won't tell. Besides, Daisy's not my type."

"And here I thought Daisy was every man's type. What is your type, then? No, never mind. I already know the answer."

"Do you?"

"Lacey Holloway."

Cal laughed. "Are we back to that sore point again? There was nothing more between me and Lacey than there is between us. A business transaction, pure and simple. Monetary compensation in return for services rendered. Only in our case, I'm the one rendering the services, much different services, unfortunately, but services nevertheless."

"You can be so crude sometimes."

"I'm just speaking the truth. But now that we have me all figured out, that brings us back to you. What's your type, Rachel?"

"I don't have a type, but if I did, it certainly wouldn't be you."

Cal moved in close and touched her hair. "Too crude."

"For starters."

Cal looked down at her face. She was so lovely. He hadn't, as of yet, grown indifferent to it. He found her just as entrancing now as he had the first day he set eyes on her at the Red Panther Saloon.

Rachel's hand shot up to bat his fingers away. "Stop it!"

"Stop what?"

"Stop touching me and towering over me like that. I know what you're trying to do."

"You do?"

"You're trying to intimidate me, but it won't work."

Cal couldn't help but smile at this. "I believe you," he said, although he didn't move away. "Tell me, just how long has this little feud between you and Daisy been going on?"

Rachel looked away nervously. "Since we were children."

Cal traced an idle finger along the delicate line of her jaw and down the side of her neck. Her skin was warm and smooth, flawless. "You mean, you two have been jealous of each other since you were children?"

Uncomfortable with his nearness, Rachel twisted away, but there was nowhere for her to go. Cal had her effectively hemmed in and she was otherwise backed up against the wagon. Exasperated, she turned back, glowering at Cal's amused expression. "There you go with jealous again. That's preposterous."

"No, it's not. You're jealous of her because you think she's every man's idea of the ideal woman. She's jealous of you because you have everything she's always wanted."

They were close, almost-touching close. He smelled like shaving soap and leather and tobacco, a heady mixture of masculine scents that wreaked havoc with her ability to concentrate. She saw now that the soft glimmer of amusement had faded from his eyes, and something fluttered in her stomach.

"Ridiculous," she insisted, cursing her voice for betraying her growing trepidation. What was wrong with her? She cleared her throat and pushed on. "There's nothing for her to be jealous of."

"It's written all over her face when she looks at you."

"Why should she be jealous of me? She's the one who got—" *Nick.* She almost said Nick. In the end, Daisy was the one who had gotten Nick.

Cal's eyes narrowed, and Rachel got the awful feeling she had just rushed headlong into a trap, that he knew exactly what she had been going to say. She plunged on in a weak effort to conceal her confusion. "You're wrong."

Cal studied her for a moment, then took a thankful step back. "All right. I'm wrong," he said evenly. "You two have been at each other's throats for so many years because of temperamental differences."

There was enough space between them so that Rachel felt safe to breathe again. She tried to convince herself it had been her imagination, that knowing look in his eye before. "That's right," she replied. "Except for the two years when she went back East to school. I thought she was finally out of my life forever, but then she came back and sank her claws into Nick."

"Well, I can tell you one thing for sure. Your cousin's marriage is not a happy one."

"How can you possibly know that?"

"It's just an idea I have."

Rachel frowned, then hugged herself and turned away. "He never should have married her. I told him but he wouldn't listen. All she had to do was wiggle her hips and give him just a feel of what was under her blouse, and he was hopelessly snagged. Even Daisy knows that men can't think past their—" She stopped, biting her lip, wanting instead to bite off her wagging tongue. Why she was even talking to him about this subject was beyond her.

"He didn't have to marry Daisy," Cal said. "He could have found that kind of entertainment down at Dolly Jordan's place."

"He's no different from the rest of you," Rachel

said, keeping her eyes glued to the driver's seat of the buckboard. "You all want what you can't have."

"And for Nick, that was Daisy Parker."

"Right. Besides, Nick would never . . ."

"Nick would never what?"

Rachel shook her head. "Never mind."

"Nick would never patronize an establishment like Dolly Jordan's. Is that what you were going to say?"

"I didn't say that. I don't know what Nick did on his own time. I just don't think he would treat it so lightly."

"What do you mean, 'treat *it* so lightly'?"

At his words, Rachel turned on him, feeling inexplicably angry. "I mean that any act between two people that can cause a child to be brought into the world has to be considered meaningful!"

"Not every act has that outcome."

"But it has that potential."

"Not if you know how to prevent it."

"Oh, and I suppose you know all about that," Rachel tossed back sarcastically.

"I know enough."

"Spare me the details of your vast experience."

"Well, it just so happens my very first job was sweeping up and running errands for a cathouse in Abilene. I couldn't help but learn a few things just from hearing the girls talk."

"I thought you said you grew up on a small farm."

"That was before. Circumstances changed."

"I'll bet you learned a lot while you worked there, avid pupil that you are."

Cal gave her a slow smile. "If you mean, is that where I had my first woman, the answer is yes."

"I don't want to hear about it!"

"Good. I wasn't going to tell you."

"Well, I wasn't about to ask!"

"Of course not. Why would a respectable young lady like you want to know how not to get babies, anyway?"

Rachel was out of patience. She'd had just about enough of him for one evening—enough of him and Daisy and Nick and all of Tarrant County, for that matter. "I already know how not to get babies!" she shouted as she pushed by him to leave. "By keeping my distance from men like you!"

12

Western Kansas

The sun was setting in the west, casting a ghostly orange glow over the lonely town. The settlement was nothing more than a whistle stop, a handful of dilapidated buildings stuck out here in the middle of nowhere. Eli Walsh stepped up on the boardwalk outside the saloon and looked over its weathered false front. Billy Wharton was known to show his face here on a regular basis.

Eli crushed the butt of a cigar beneath his boot heel and pushed through the batwing doors. It was a short-bit house—no music, just bad whiskey, half-a-dozen nicked tables, and a pair of slatternly whores hanging around the bar.

Eli let his gaze slide over the dimly lit room. There was Billy, sure enough. A wiry young man, still in his late twenties, with pockmarked cheeks and mousy brown hair, he was engrossed in a poker game with a couple of cohorts who looked like they didn't have two dimes to rub together.

Eli crossed the room to the bar. Billy looked up and caught a passing glimpse of the newcomer before looking down again. A split second later, his head jerked up, and he almost fell off his chair. It might have been funny except Eli had never possessed a sense of humor.

He motioned for the bartender, a hawk-faced man, and ordered a rye whiskey. One of the whores leaned up against the bar and smiled boldly at him. Behind her, above the backbar, Eli saw a faded wooden plaque:

$1—LOOKEE $2—FEELEE $3—DOOEE

Eli ignored her. It wasn't long before he felt Billy hovering by his left shoulder. "Hello, Billy."

"Hey, there, Eli. Didn't know you was in town."

The bartender slapped down a glass and poured the whiskey. Eli pushed a bill across the bar. "Leave the bottle."

The bartender moved away.

"So, uh, Eli, what brings you to town, huh? I thought you was out in California."

Eli lifted the glass to his lips and gave Billy a side glance. "I'm looking for Leo."

Billy swallowed hard. "You . . . you come after Leo?"

Eli finished the liquor and poured out another shot. "That's right."

There was a short silence during which Billy's stomach gurgled. "Well, Eli, Leo . . . he, uh, he ain't here."

"That's what Juanita tells me."

Billy drummed his fingers on the bar. "You talked to Juanita, then. Leo's girl in Albuquerque, right?"

Eli turned to him and nodded.

"Well see, Eli, I don't know if she told you or not, but Leo . . . well, it looks like he got picked up."

Eli just looked at him.

Billy continued, his weasel brown eyes downcast. "See, I did a dumb thing, Eli. Lookin' back, of course, I guess it was stupid."

"What was the big job, Billy?"

Sweat started popping out on Billy's forehead. "Well, it was a livestock thing. It kind of fell through."

"Fell through."

Billy wiped his mouth with the back of one sleeve. "Yeah."

"So, how do you figure the law knew Leo was back in Kansas?"

"Oh, I don't think they knew, Eli. I hear it was just one of those things, you know, they just got lucky . . . you know."

Eli reached into the pocket of his duster to pull out a pouch of Bull Durham tobacco and a wad of cigarette papers. He laid out a sheet and opened the pouch. "One of those things," he mused aloud. "Lucky for them. Unlucky for Leo."

Billy tittered nervously. "Yeah. Unlucky for Leo."

Eli sprinkled some tobacco on the paper and lined it up with one finger. "You hear who picked him up?"

"No, I didn't. Probably some deputy marshal."

Eli finished rolling the cigarette. He licked the seal. "You hear where they took him?"

"Well, I heard Dodge City."

Eli struck a match with his thumbnail. "They're liable to hang him in Dodge City."

"Well, I don't know. I don't know about that, Eli. All I know is what I heard."

Eli nodded as he drew deeply on the cigarette, then exhaled twin streams of smoke though his nose.

Billy's voice became wheedling. "Look, Eli, I feel real bad. It's partly my fault, I guess, asking him if he wanted in on the job and all, but I just never thought it would come to this. You understand that, don't you?"

"Sure I do, Billy. You couldn't have known, right?"

Billy let out a relieved breath. "Yeah, that's right, Eli. I couldn't of known. It was just one of those things."

"Just one of those *unlucky* things."

"Y-you going to Dodge?"

"Yeah." Eli paused. "You want to ride with me?"

Blood drained from Billy's face. "Me? Well, I, uh, I would, Eli, I would, except that I got things going here. I mean, nothing big, mind you, but things . . . just things."

Eli watched gray smoke rise and curl from the end of his cigarette. "Sure. I understand. That's all right, Billy."

"Say, uh, you think you want to sit in on our game, Eli? I mean, since you're here and all. For old times' sake and all."

"No. I'm going to finish my drink and take a room. I want to head out at sunup. Got a long ride ahead."

"Oh, yeah. Sure you do. Maybe next time." Billy started backing away. "Maybe next time then, huh?"

"Next time."

Billy returned to his table. Eli poured himself another drink. He finished his cigarette. When he looked up, the whore was still leaning up against the bar, staring at him. She winked. Eli thought she looked like hell.

He turned and walked out of the saloon, affording Billy Wharton nothing more than a parting nod on his way out.

Billy let out a huge sigh of relief when he saw Eli Walsh disappear through the swinging batwing doors. He felt very lucky indeed. The shadow of a hawk had just cruised over the field, and Billy the mouse had lived to tell the tale.

Boots Cassidy, an aging saddle tramp, was dealing cards around the table. "Who was that?"

Billy threw in his ante and watched his cards pile up. "Just a guy I used to know a long time ago." He picked up his cards. These days, it seemed like one hell of a long time ago, a lifetime ago. Billy was as green as a new grass blade when he had hooked up with the three Walsh brothers to pull off a couple of bank jobs. The idea was to go in when the buildings were empty of customers, leaving only a couple of nervous cashiers to deal with. It was Eli who had done the killing. Eli was always picky about leaving witnesses.

Billy's job was to wait outside and hold the horses, and that had been just fine and diggety-dog dandy with him. Billy was a thief, a liar, and a cheat, but he'd never had the stomach for cold-blooded killing.

Boots cleared his throat. "You in or not, Billy?"

Billy tried to concentrate on his hand. It wasn't anything to hop and holler about. He did, however, have a pair of fours to open. He threw in his bit.

Boots matched Billy's bet and passed to Stan Daniels, the half-deaf drunk who completed their bedraggled trio of players. Stan threw in. Boots looked at Billy with red-rimmed eyes.

Billy sighed. "Three. Gimme three."

Boots gave him three. Billy arranged his new hand absently. A pair of fours, a pair of twos, and a nine.

Billy had always gotten along with Leo Walsh well enough. Leo, at least, knew how to have a good time. And as for Max, the oldest of the brothers, he had been a born leader, the type of man Billy would have been happy to follow, if only it hadn't been for Eli. Eli was like a rogue animal, vicious and unpredictable, his natural inclinations barely held in check by respect for his older brother's authority.

Billy had once seen Eli drill some fella straight through the heart with his Colt .45 just because he claimed the guy had been looking at him funny. Just asking for it, he'd said. Well, that had been about enough for Billy. Eli wasn't only mean, he was crazy too, and it hadn't taken Billy long after that to find an excuse to drop out of the gang.

He had kept in touch with Leo from time to time, that was until Leo killed that federal deputy in Dodge City. Leo hightailed it south then. And rightly so. He was hotter than a burnt griddle cake. The price on his head went up to a thousand dollars.

Billy had thought he was through with the Walsh brothers for good. At least, until that night a few months ago—the night in Dodge City. Billy's luck was running pretty high that night. He had come out ahead sixteen dollars.

Billy had followed a sporting gal nicknamed Jelly up the stairs and down a squalid hall, his eyes glued to her swishing hips. The room was dark. It was only after Jelly closed the door behind them that Billy froze up. It was that sound—a purely unmistakable sound—four distinct clicks, the sound of a Colt's hammer being cocked. He and Jelly were not alone.

"Glad you could make it, Billy."

Billy didn't recognize the voice, and as for the man sprawled in a chair in one corner of the room, he couldn't make out much more than a silhouette. He was tall, long-legged, wearing Mexican boots and fancy silver spurs. His broad-brimmed hat was set down low, casting his features in black shadow. The Colt was trained casually on Billy's chest.

By now, Billy had lost his amorous mood. "Who . . . who—"

"Thank you, Jelly." The man spoke to the saloon girl, who still stood by the door. "Billy and I have a few things to discuss in private."

The girl gave Billy a shrug before she slipped back out into the hallway. "Sorry, honey."

Billy gritted his teeth and tried to keep from moaning out loud. Set up! Set up and caught like a possum in a trap! His voice shook worse than a turkey's gobbler. "You—you gonna shoot me, Mister?"

"I haven't decided yet."

"Who—who are you?" Billy asked, carefully eyeing the revolver that was cocked and ready and still aimed at his chest. He briefly considered making a run for it.

The man obviously read Billy's thoughts. "You wouldn't even clear the doorway."

Billy started sweating. "You got a name, Mister?"

The stranger laughed, but somehow the sound didn't lift Billy's spirits any. "Cal Delaney. Pleased to meet you, Billy."

Billy winced. He recognized the name, and it didn't bode well for him.

Delaney went on. "There's still a warrant out on you from your horse-thieving days around Winfield. It's been awhile, but a lot of those folks have long memories, and I reckon a few of them are still pretty put out over the whole sorry deal."

Billy's shoulders slouched.

"They still hang fellas for horse-thieving, Billy. That has to be a powerful bad thought for you at the moment."

"Awww jeez, that was years ago."

"It's a shame people hold grudges like that, especially when I'm sure you've stayed out of trouble ever since."

"All right, you got me clean. You ain't gotta rub it in. You gonna take me back there?"

"That's the plan."

Billy tried to think of a way out of this situation, but nothing came to mind. He had heard enough about Cal Delaney to know that Delaney usually went after the big fish. Billy wondered what he had done to merit this particular bounty hunter's attention.

He gathered up his nerve and threw up the question in what he hoped was a bold manner. "I ain't got more than a hundred dollars on my head. What's a guy like you doing messing around with the likes of me?"

"Well now, that's a right smart question, Billy."

"Yeah, so?"

"You just might be able to buy yourself out of this."

Billy groaned. "I ain't got no money, Mr. Delaney. I got sixteen dollars in my pocket and a broken-down roan tied out front. I swear, I ain't got nothin'."

"Not so. I think you have something I can use. Information."

Billy's heart leaped hopefully. He sensed a way out, a light at the end of a very long, very dark tunnel. But his tone was still cautious. "I don't follow."

"Well, follow this, Billy . . . Leo Walsh."

Billy gulped. *Leo Walsh.* The light at the end of the tunnel flashed and winked out. "Walsh, you say? Who's that?"

"You're not a very convincing liar."

Billy scratched his head. "Well, come to think of it, I remember a Leo Walsh, but I haven't seen him around these parts for quite some time."

"That doesn't surprise me. Where *would* Mr. Walsh be parking his boots these days?"

"Well, uh, I heard he left the state, headed south. Mexico, I think."

"Where in Mexico?"

"I ain't heard where."

"You're not trying, Billy."

"All right, all right! New Mexico. Last I heard, Leo was in Albuquerque. You gonna let me go now?"

"I don't think so."

"Awww, dang it! I told you all I know!"

"You're going to send a telegram."

"I'm gonna what?"

"You're going to invite Leo up for a visit."

Billy was incredulous. For a moment, he almost forgot the gun that was still trained on his chest. "Are you crazy? Leo won't step foot in Kansas! I heard he killed a deputy! You boys is the ones who chased him south in the first place!"

"You have unusually acute hearing, Billy."

Billy was confused. "I have cute ears, you say?"

Delaney sighed. "You hear a lot."

"Oh."

Delaney continued. "He'll come back. You're going to issue him an invitation he won't be able to resist."

Billy shook his head, worried. "I don't know."

"If not, you're going to stretch hemp, Billy."

"How do I know you'll let me go like you say?"

"You ever see a man hang? It's not a pretty sight."

Billy was starting to sweat so bad his shirt was soaking through. "Stop talkin' like that!"

"This is a one-time offer, Billy. It's simply a matter of my own convenience. I can take you in, then go after Leo myself. It might take me a little longer, but I reckon the outcome will be just about the same."

Billy sighed long and hard. His head was starting to hurt. Too much barrelhouse whiskey. Too much thinking. "You don't understand. Leo's got a brother that's crazier than a—"

"I heard they aren't riding together anymore."

Billy snorted. "You got cute ears too, Mr. Delaney."

"And I keep them to the ground. Word has it Eli is somewhere in California."

Billy shook his head. "Aw, jeez. I just don't know."

"That's the deal, Billy. Take it . . . or leave it."

And so Billy had taken it. He had set Leo up to save his own miserable hide. He wasn't proud of it, but hell, Leo was doomed to catch it sooner or later. With a thousand dollars on his head, dead or alive, Leo's watch had just about run itself out of ticks.

Boots Cassidy's voice brought Billy crashing back to the present. "Don't just set there with yer teeth in yer mouth! You gonna throw in yer bit or what?"

Billy threw in two bits just to shut the old man up.

He had almost managed to forget about the whole ugly Leo Walsh affair. Until tonight, that was, tonight when his worst nightmare had sauntered, big as a buffalo at noon, into the bar. Billy had feared that Eli knew about the whole sorry, rotten, dirty deal. But it wasn't so. Eli didn't suspect a thing. He had come to town for information—information about where they had taken his brother. Billy had given him that information, and Eli was going to be gone by sunup. That was good. That was better than good. That was *good riddance.*

"Show us what ya got!" Boots shouted in his ear.

Billy threw down his hand.

Boots Cassidy's raspy face split into a toothless grin. "Yahoo! Deuces and fours! Is that all?"

Billy downed the last of his warm beer as the older man reached for the kitty. "I gotta go," he muttered, pushing back his chair.

"Oh, sure you gotta go! Sure!"

"Hey, I gotta take a leak, that okay with you? Why else would I be leaving?"

"Cause yer losin' yer shirt, that's why!"

Billy forfeited a retort by settling the hat on his head and turning to leave. He could still hear Boots chortling as he pushed through the doors and out into the early evening air. It was already getting dark.

It was the supper hour, and the street was empty. Billy rounded the corner of the saloon and headed down the narrow alley that separated the saloon from the livery next door.

He whistled to himself as he unbuttoned his pants, his stomach rumbling hungrily. As he proceeded to relieve himself on the ground, he looked up at the narrow strip of darkening sky above. There might be enough change in his pocket for a hot meal at the boardinghouse before he headed back into the saloon.

Billy had already buttoned up his pants and was turning to leave when his sixth-sense alarm went off. Someone was behind him, but he was a split second too late. A forearm, hard as steel, closed around his throat, yanking him back with such force, it almost knocked him off his feet. The man behind him squeezed, hard, and Billy felt his windpipe collapsing.

Billy tried to wrest the arm away, but it did no good. His attacker had him in a disadvantageous position, not to mention the guy was strong as hell. Then Billy heard the man's voice, low and growling next to his ear, and he thought that if he hadn't just made water a minute ago, he would surely be wetting his pants now.

"You set up my brother."

Billy tried to talk, to deny the accusation, but he could do little more than emit a strangled bleat.

He had never been so scared in his life, not since he had stared down the barrel of Cal Delaney's six-shooter. He didn't know which was worse. No, scratch that. He knew which was worse. *Now* was worse. Eli was worse.

"Let's get down to cases, Billy boy." Eli's viselike grip didn't falter. "You set up my brother, and since you're too stupid to think up something like that by yourself, someone must have put you up to it."

Eli slid his forearm up to lift Billy's chin, releasing the pressure on his windpipe. Billy sucked a rush of sweet, fresh air into his burning lungs. At the same time, he tried to turn his head and slip out from beneath Eli's forearm, but his chin got in the way. He let out a yelp as his neck cracked, sending a warning jolt down his spine.

Out of the corner of his eye, he caught a flash of moonlight as it reflected off the cold steel blade of a stiletto. Eli yanked Billy's chin up and back, exposing his throat and gently resting the blade against Billy's jugular.

"Who put you up to it?"

Billy was breathing hard and fast as he tried to think

of a way out. He was alone with Eli, and Eli was bigger than he was, stronger than he was, and had one helluva mean-looking little knife. Things didn't look good.

Billy had no choice but to squeal. "It was Delaney! The bounty hunter! It was Delaney!"

There was a pause as Eli absorbed the name. "Delaney put you up to it. He got Leo, then he took him to Dodge City. That right?"

Billy tried to nod, remembered it was impossible, then put his answer into words. "That's right! He made me do it! He was going to take me back to Winfield cause of that horse-stealing warrant! They'd a hung me! Don't you see? I didn't have no choice!"

"Did they hang him? Hmmm? Did they hang Leo?"

Billy was shivering like a mutt in a thunderstorm. His only hope of getting out of this alive was to give Eli what he wanted—information—and then try to reason with him, make him understand that Billy had been a victim, same as Leo had been a victim.

One thing was for sure. He wasn't about to tell Eli that his little brother was already dead, that he had never made it to Dodge City.

"I don't know! I swear on a stacka Bibles! I don't know nothin' about it! Maybe—maybe it ain't too late! Maybe you could still get there in time to bust him out!"

Billy felt the knife sink ever-so-slightly into the flesh at his throat, and his insides turned to water.

"You wouldn't be lying to me again, would you, Billy? Because if you're lying . . ."

Billy's voice spiraled to a high-pitched shriek. "No! No! I ain't lying, Eli! I swear I ain't! I didn't have no choice! It was either hang or do like he said! I always liked Leo! I liked all you fellas!"

Eli's voice turned soft as a lover's. "And we liked you. Especially Leo. He liked you a lot."

Tears ran straight back from Billy's eyes to tickle his ears. "You got to understand, Eli! This Delaney, he's a real bad fella to have on your tail! I didn't know what to do! I mean, either he'd shoot me or they'd hang me and—"

"You wouldn't want to die with a lie on your lips."

"No! No! I don't want to die at all! I'll help you! I'll ride with you!"

Eli seemed to think this over for a minute, and hope, just a tiny spark of it, sprang to life in Billy's heaving chest. *Maybe, maybe, maybe . . .*

Eli spoke then, his voice quiet but his words, and their meaning, horrifyingly clear. "Much obliged, Billy, but I think I'll go this one alone."

13

Cal couldn't think why the dream came back this particular night to haunt him. Perhaps it was because he had been remembering, remembering too much, and remembering always seemed to come to no damn good.

He was in the cornfield, as always, and the burning was in the air. He was fifteen and tall and strong for his age. He knew this, and yet for some reason, he couldn't see over the towering cornstalks, couldn't see over them or through them or around them. This was especially bad because he was lost and he had to get home. He had to get home *now*.

Rebecca was dead and Pa was gone too, but Mama and Jessica Anne, they were still alive. Keeping them alive—that was why he had to get home because, this time, *this time* he knew what was going to happen. If he could just get home before those men came, he could yank his father's rifle down from the gun rack before they had a chance to set foot inside the door.

But he was lost. And they were coming. He heard their voices inside his head, or maybe they carried on the breezes all around him. He couldn't tell.

"Hey, sweet face, what's your name?"

"You ever had a man before, sweet face?"

Cal started to run, blinded by panic. He swung at the shriveled cornstalks, using his arms like flying machetes, his heart slamming in his chest. But the stalks kept coming at him. Was he running in circles?

His father's disembodied voice sprang to life in his head. *"You're the man of the house while I'm gone, Cal. You take care of your mother and sister now, you hear?"*

He could smell the burning. It was searing and acrid in his nostrils, almost choking him as he sucked in great lungfuls of spoiled, black air. He screamed out, "I'm sorry, Pa! I didn't have a gun!"

"What's your name, sweet face? You ever had a man before, sweet face?"

Cal fell to his knees, gasping, pounding the earth with his fists. *"I didn't have a gun!"*

Then came the screams, screams all the more soul-shattering because he had never actually heard them, not in reality. He had only had time—twelve years of time—to imagine them, over and over, as they might have been.

Cal bolted awake in a cold sweat. Rachel was shaking him, her worried face barely visible in the darkness.

"Cal! You're dreaming! Stop it!"

He pushed her away as he sat all of the way up, burying his face in his hands. "Jesus."

Moonlight spilled in the open window. Filmy curtains

billowed softly in the night breeze. She spoke in a subdued voice. "You were having an awful dream."

"Very astute, Rachel."

He could tell by the abrupt silence that he had hurt her feelings. He raked an unsteady hand through his hair. "I'm sorry."

"I couldn't get you to wake up. You kept talking . . . saying things."

"What things?"

"I don't know. Names mostly."

Cal lay back down and waited for his heart to stop pounding. He was aware that Rachel was watching him in the darkness.

"Who's Jessica?"

"My sister." Cal closed his eyes and felt Rachel lie down again beside him.

"I didn't know you had a sister."

"She's dead."

There was a pause. "I'm sorry."

She sounded wretched, and he was stabbed with guilt. He rolled over onto his side and propped up his head with one hand. "It's all right."

"It's just that . . ."

"What?"

"Every time I ask you about your family, it ends up . . ."

Cal sighed. "It was a long time ago, and I just don't like to talk about it."

"Whatever it was, it must have been terrible."

Cal was silent for a moment. "Maybe I'll tell you about it sometime, but just not now, all right?"

Her eyes met his in the dimness. "All right."

He looked down at her for a long time. Her hair was loose, spreading out on the pillow beneath her head, her full lips parted, revealing just the tips of her teeth. He felt a tightening in his loins, and, on impulse, he reached over to pull the blanket away from her. He could just make out the peaks of her breasts beneath the thin material of her nightdress. She stared up at him, lying very still, her luminous eyes expectant.

"Come here, Rachel."

She didn't move—either toward him or away from him. He wanted to touch her. He wanted to touch her so bad it hurt. Very slowly, he inched next to her and lowered his head to brush his lips over hers. They were soft and warm, like petals.

But she stiffened. "I—I don't think we should be doing this, uh, here."

"Why not? It's the most natural thing in the world." He kissed her.

Rachel's thoughts were jumbled and confused. Was she imagining that she could feel his heat? It seemed to be emanating from him in waves, warming her.

He had been hurting just a few moments ago, suffering and vulnerable, exposing, however briefly, a side of him that she never suspected. She had reacted to it instinctively, wanting to reach out to him, to touch him, to hold him and comfort him, but she knew, just as instinctively perhaps, that he would only push her away. Now, all of a sudden, he had changed. He wanted to reach out to her, to touch her, but his intentions were quite different, weren't they?

She was all too aware of his masculinity, the overpowering essence of it, and it was like a magnet, drawing her to him. His hand came to rest very lightly on her waist, and her whole body tensed, primed and waiting.

"*This* is natural, Rachel." His words were soft, whispered, soothing. She wanted to close her eyes, drift into his voice, let him do whatever he wanted with her. "What is unnatural is you and me sleeping in this bed night after night and not making love." He kissed her again, a little longer this time, his tongue flicking out to trace her lips. His fingers made lazy little circles that tickled through her nightdress.

Hesitantly, Rachel turned to him. She closed her eyes and let him gently urge her lips apart. When his tongue touched hers, she was at first shocked, then intrigued, then . . . she didn't know what.

He buried his face in her hair, and Rachel felt him kiss her neck as his hand skimmed up over her nightdress to cup one breast. She caught her breath and gripped his arms, feeling the heat of his skin, the incredible smooth hardness of muscle.

He tugged at the ribbons of her nightdress. "Just let me touch you."

His voice, his words, so persuasive and seductive and low next to her ear, murmured against her neck, were mesmerizing. A work-callused hand touched her bare breast beneath the gown, then he was kissing her neck again, moving down, raining gentle kisses down over the rise of her breast, and Rachel couldn't think anymore. When he pushed aside the open flap of her gown and took her nipple in his mouth, a compelling glow began to warm in the depths of her stomach.

Beneath the blanket, he inched her nightdress up, sliding his hand up the length of her leg. Then she felt him *there*, urging her thighs apart, and her eyes flew open. She wasn't really married to this man. He didn't love her.

His fingers delved into her, and she let out a gasp as reality caught up in a hurry. "We can't . . . Cal, I'm not ready," she whispered hoarsely.

Withdrawing his fingers, he raised his head enough

to kiss her on the mouth. "You feel ready to me." Then his thigh was between her legs, urging them apart still farther as he moved over her, fitting himself against her, his erection pressing and demanding, and Rachel suddenly realized with shock that it wasn't just his fingers she wanted inside of her *there*, it was his—

"No! Get off of me!" Her words came as a desperate plea, an act of sheer, unadulterated panic. This was happening too fast.

He lifted his head and looked down at her, one hand coming to rest on her outer thigh. "Why? You want it as much as I do."

She was confused, stammering, unable to get the words out. "You're not—You're not . . ."

His demeanor abruptly changed. She felt the muscles in his back tense beneath her fingers, the resentment building within him almost as palpable. "I'm not *what*? I'm not Nick?"

Stunned, she gaped at him. The shadowed contours of his face were clear enough to make out the unmistakable set of his jaw, the anger that blazed in those cold blue eyes. What had he said? What did he mean? That she wanted Nick in her bed? How could he even think such a thing, much less say it? Nick was her cousin! It was unthinkable!

Her retort was an act of self-defense. "I was going to say you're not really my husband, and if you remember our agreement, the question of marital relations is clearly spelled out!"

"Don't play games with me, Rachel."

"I'm not playing games. We had an agreement."

"The hell with our agreement."

"Get off me!"

He leaned down close to her face, almost close

enough to kiss her, only that was clearly not his intention this time. His words were low and distinct. "I never took a woman against her will, and I'm not about to start now, but you'd better make up your mind, then think hard about the signals you're putting out."

Rachel's thoughts were spinning. He had used her body against her. He had made her want him. Hadn't he? He knew so much more than she about these things. She wasn't sure what to think.

Then, he did get off of her, and Rachel was left cold and quivering inside. She hated him. She wanted him. She couldn't think straight. She was beginning to believe that Cal Delaney had permanently and irrevocably robbed her of all rationality.

They lay side by side, not touching, neither of them speaking for what might have been one minute or fifteen. She knew he wasn't sleeping. Finally, she spoke, her voice coming out hoarse. "Are you . . . are you going to be all right?"

An eternity seemed to drag by. Then, he said, "Yeah."

Rachel swallowed a lump in her throat and fought back an urge to cry, something that she had not had to do in a very, very long time. "I'm sorry."

The subdued bitterness in his voice was unmistakable. "It's okay, Rachel."

"I . . . I just . . ."

"You were right. Spreading your legs for me wasn't in the contract."

His bluntness stung like a slap in the face.

After a while, she felt him rise from the bed. She listened as he dressed in the dark, then left, the bedroom door clicking shut quietly behind him.

But he hadn't put on his boots. Wherever he was

going, he wasn't leaving the house. He wasn't going to Lacey. She felt some consolation, small as it was, in that.

Rachel turned on her side, fastening the silk ties of her nightdress. He had called it making love. She reached beneath the blanket to push her gown back down over dampened thighs. She clamped her knees together tight, still feeling a slight tenderness between her legs where he had invaded her.

Love had nothing to do with it. He had just been too long without a woman. Rachel happened to be the closest, most convenient receptacle for his lust. Lacey Holloway would have done just as well if she had been lying next to him this night.

Rachel blinked back more tears. Lacey would have done better! Lacey didn't have the common sense God gave a gopher, but she sure knew what to do with a man in her bed. Rachel hadn't a clue. She had just proven that tonight.

Cal lit the lamp on Galen's desk and crossed the room to the liquor cabinet, pulling out a decanter and a glass. He hadn't had the dream since Dodge City, since the night he shed his gun belt for good. By vowing never to wear it again, he had chosen a new life. He had hoped that maybe his past would finally be behind him. But that had been naive.

He had been feeling much too settled here. He was getting soft, living like some heir apparent in this damned palace Galen Girard had built for his filthy rich family. He didn't belong in this world any more than Rachel belonged in his.

He poured out a splash of scotch whiskey and capped the decanter. Maybe he had started to forget who he was. It had taken the dream to remind him, to remind him where he had come from, of what he had become, and what he would always be—a drifter, a hunter . . . a killer. For it was true. He had finally joined the ranks of the murdering outlaws he spent his adult life stalking. It had come to that. Perhaps it had been inevitable from the beginning.

"Does Galen know you're drinking up all his good liquor?"

Cal turned to see Nick framed in the open doorway. He had been so lost in his own musings he didn't hear the other man approach. Now he knew for sure he was getting soft. In the past, a mistake like that might have gotten him killed.

Cal took a healthy swig from his glass. "I couldn't sleep."

Nick's eyes flicked over him. "Neither could I."

"Problems at the stockyards?"

"Nothing I can't handle."

"I'll bet." Cal held up his glass. "You want to join me?"

Nick stepped over the threshold. "Why not?"

Cal pulled a second glass from the cabinet and poured out a drink. He handed it to Nick, who had collapsed into Galen's chair behind the desk. "You look real comfortable sitting there, Nick."

Nick ran one hand over the smooth leather arm of the chair. "It's nice, but not quite my style. What about you, Cal? You want to try it sometime? What's your style?"

Cal laughed drily. "The only kind of leather I've ever been comfortable in is a well-worn saddle. I think you know that."

Nick raised his glass to his lips. "Yeah, I thought as much. So whatever made you think you could stay in one place long enough to make a girl like Rachel happy?"

Cal held Nick's skeptical gaze. "Is it important to you that Rachel be happy?"

"Of course it is."

"You two get along real well considering you're her main rival for the Elena Rose."

Nick swirled the liquid in his glass thoughtfully. "It's not much of a rivalry, Cal. I've got my own row to hoe. The stockyards are mine. Galen backed me, sure, but I'm close to paying him off, and then that'll leave just me and my partners, free and clear. I don't want or need the Elena Rose."

"I get the feeling your mother and sister are of a different opinion."

Nick threw his head back and laughed. "Ah yes! Mother, she's always dreamed of owning this place, and Daisy, well, she would bask in the sheer social status of it."

"But not you."

"That's right. Not me. If Galen ever left the ranch to me, I'd just as soon hand it over to Rachel. She deserves it."

"It's my guess she wouldn't want it that way."

Nick raised an eyebrow in mock surprise. "I'm amazed."

"Why is that?"

Nick's smile was not friendly. "That you've bothered to get to know even that much about the woman you married."

Cal rested his elbow on a bookshelf. "You don't like me much, do you, Nick?"

"You haven't shown me much to like, have you?"

"Oh, I don't know. Seems to me you had your mind made up before I even walked through the door."

"That's not true at all. It's the way you treat Rachel."

"Maybe little Miss Rachel has been getting her own way for far too long."

Nick looked annoyed. "You have no idea what she's about."

"But I'll bet you're going to tell me, aren't you?"

Nick set his glass down. "You probably think she wants the Elena Rose because she's spoiled and rich and greedy."

"But, of course, that has nothing to do with it."

"It has precious little to do with it. Why do you think she wouldn't want to take it from me?"

"Because she wants it to come from him."

"Very close. Rachel *needs* it to come from him. She's always striven for his approval."

Cal laughed. "Has anyone ever thought to inform her that she's always had it?"

"Rachel is an unusual young woman, Cal."

"I've noticed."

"No, I don't think you have." Nick snatched his glass and tossed off the rest of his whiskey. "You know, I once saw my wife reduced to tears over the fact that her waistline had expanded half an inch. Her skirt was too tight."

Nick held the empty tumbler up to the light of the lamp and studied it for a moment before continuing. "When Rachel was nine, she got some fool idea about trying one of the cow ponies in the corral. The animal was only half-broken, and it took off like a shot as soon as her foot touched the stirrup. She was thrown in two seconds flat. When she screamed, everyone came running. Her arm was broken. It must've hurt like hell. When Galen carried her out of that corral, he walked right by me. I could see the tears coming to her eyes, but she wouldn't give in and cry. Nine years old,

Cal. She wouldn't cry—not in front of her daddy. Not in front of anyone."

Cal finished his drink. "Don't worry about Rachel. She can take care of herself maybe better than you think."

"I'm not so sure of that anymore. She's always been a pretty good judge of character, but I think she's way off the mark this time. She fights you, but for some crazy reason, she seems to trust you. A hell of a lot more than I do."

Cal offered up his empty glass as if in toast. "Well, they say love is blind."

Nick ignored the sarcasm. "I've had you checked out."

Cal strolled over to the liquor cabinet and poured himself another stiff one. He had a feeling he was going to need it. "Did you find out anything interesting?"

"Oh, plenty. People remember you, Cal. They remember you in Virginia City. They remember you in Abilene and Wichita. The saloonkeepers, the confidence men, the drunks, even some of the older prostitutes remember you. They remember that you turned up on the streets when you were just a kid, but none of them seem to recall where you came from. Why is that, Cal?"

"You know so much. You tell me."

"Because you aren't from Abilene at all. Where *are* you from? Where does a guy like you get his start?"

Cal evaded the question by posing one of his own. "Tell me, have you had a chance to pass all this on to Rachel yet?"

"Why? Is there something you don't want her to know?"

"Hell no, Nick. I just want to make sure I reserve a front row seat, that's all."

Nick nodded to himself. "You're cocky. I'll give you that. But you never answered my question."

"I must have missed it."

"Where are you from?"

"Since you enjoy playing detective, why don't you find out for yourself?"

"So, there *is* something you'd like to keep hidden."

Cal shook his head in grim amusement. "You Girards. You all take the cake. You really do."

"We look out for our own, Cal. Same as anyone else."

"Well then, try putting your feelers out around Lawrence, Kansas, and see what juicy tidbits you come up with. And if there's anything else I can help you with, just let me know, Nick. Maybe you'd like a list of all the women I've ever screwed while we're at it?"

Nick rose to his feet. "Oh, I don't know. Would it even begin to rival the list of kids you've crippled?"

Their eyes locked and held for a tense moment before Cal replied. "You figure it out."

Nick smiled coldly. "Maybe I will, maybe I will." He crossed the room to the door. "In the meantime, you just take care to treat my cousin right, or—"

Cal interjected. "Or else you'll come after me—you and Galen and every gun for hire in the great state of Texas. Right?"

The satisfied smile on Nick's face didn't fade as he turned to leave the room. "Thanks for the drink, Cal. It's been a real eye-opening pleasure."

14

Kansas, 1866

Cal tried to lie still as his mother covered his forehead with one palm, searching for any hint of fever. He was fifteen—too long for his bed, too tall even to stand up in the attic loft without cracking his head on one of the ceiling beams, certainly too old to be fussed over by his mother.

He had come down with the fever and ague almost a week ago and had been fighting its devastating effects ever since. He would no sooner be back on his feet than it would sweep over him again. His latest bout hit yesterday morning, and he was only now getting over the worst of it.

Elizabeth Delaney frowned, deepening the worry lines on her forehead and around the edges of her sky-blue eyes, the lines that were now a permanent part of her once porcelain complexion.

Cal brushed her hand away impatiently. "I told you I'm feeling fit as a fiddle! If you'd just let me—"

"You're still flushed."

"I'm not flushed! I'm hot!" Cal kicked at the old army blanket that half covered him.

"You're flushed."

"Ma, I'm a grown man, and you're treating me like a—"

She ran her fingers through his hair. "You're able to do a man's share of the work around here, but a man you're not. Not just yet, Cal. Don't be in such a hurry to—"

He interrupted. "And there's more than one man's share of work that needs to get done! If we don't get that corn in—"

"If we don't get that corn in, nobody's gonna die of it," she finished. "You've got to save up your strength. You know what happened to Mrs. Paxton's son."

"I ain't Mrs. Paxton's son."

His mother set her jaw, indicating her mind was not about to be swayed. "That's right. You're my son, so stop sassing me and lie still."

"Ma!" Jessica Anne's anxious voice carried from the kitchen area below. "The bread's burning! Should I take it out?"

Elizabeth rolled her eyes and muttered under her breath. "Well, I don't know, Jessy. If it's burning, what do *you* think?"

Cal had to bite his tongue to keep from making a wise comment. His older sister had not inherited their mother's talents in the kitchen.

Elizabeth rose, smoothing the wrinkles from her calico skirt. "Take a nap. I'll bring your supper up when it's ready."

Cal folded his arms mutinously, but his mother ignored the gesture as she brushed aside the curtain that separated Cal's sleeping quarters from his sister's, then disappeared from view. He heard her stepping back down the loft ladder to the kitchen.

With a grunt, he pushed up to a sitting position and swung his legs over the side of the bed. Darn if he was going to waste the whole day lying around like some bump on a log. He stood up too fast, smacking his head into a ceiling beam with a loud thwack. He tottered on his feet, riding out the dull, thudding pain that reverberated throughout his skull. Black splotches swam before his eyes, obscuring his vision so he had to just stand there like a blamed fool, leaning with one hand up against the wall until the spell passed.

Disgusted, he snagged up blue jeans that had been lying across the bottom of his bed and climbed into them with the same kind of painful slowness observed in old people with rheumatism. As he shrugged on a shirt, he thought ruefully that maybe it hadn't been such a good idea to get out of bed, after all.

He shuffled over to the tiny loft window and bent to peer outside. The sun hung over the roof of the old sod barn, ready to begin its downward slope toward the western horizon. From somewhere below his window, their dog, Laddie, started barking. Cal saw nothing out of the ordinary. Laddie was a good dog, friendly and eager to please, but he barked like a fish swam. Perhaps a butterfly had crossed his path.

Cal craned his neck to see around the side of the barn to the edge of the spreading cornfield. Tall green stalks leaned in the late afternoon breeze. He could barely make out the top of Luke MacGregor's hat as it bobbed in and out among the shoots.

Luke's father was their closest neighbor. He had been quick to send his oldest son over to the Delaney farm to help cover for Cal while he was down. It was no secret that Luke was sweet on Jessica Anne, and as for Jessica, her reaction to Luke's attention was obvious. Ever since last week, when Luke had started coming over to help out, Jessy had been acting as flighty as a hummingbird. Cal had heard her at dawn this morning as she had agonized in front of her mirror for over half an hour, fussing with her hair and mumbling to herself.

Feeling undeniably weak, Cal turned away from the window and made his way back to his bed. He wondered if Luke's sister, Hannah MacGregor, ever bothered to fuss with *her* hair when she expected that Cal might be around. Somehow, he doubted it.

He collapsed onto his bed with a thump. Supper smells were starting to fill the house, making his stomach rumble despite the fact that he hadn't done a lick of work to deserve an appetite.

He reached beneath the straw mattress and pulled out a worn copy of *The Life and Strange Surprising Adventures of Robinson Crusoe*. He had read it dozens of times, but books were scarcer than hen's teeth. He folded his feather pillow over double, propped his head up on it, and flipped the book open.

It wasn't long, though, before his concentration began to stray from the magical words of Daniel Defoe. Instead, in his mind's eye, there appeared an arresting image of Hannah MacGregor.

She and Cal had grown up together, but Cal had never noticed until the last few months how pretty she was. Now, whenever Cal was alone with Hannah, which was not nearly often enough, his heart started to pound and his palms grew sweaty. Time either seemed to speed up or slow down. His spirit leaped, his ambition soared. His head filled with lofty Shakespearean sonnets: *"Shall I compare thee to a summer's day? Thou art more lovely and more temperate."* But, in direct contrast, every word he tried to utter in her presence seemed to grow to the size of a boulder and jam in his throat.

Cal figured he must be in love with Hannah MacGregor. He closed his eyes, shutting out the sound of casual conversation passing between his mother and sister in the kitchen below. He imagined Hannah's lingering smile, her long-lashed eyes, her tiny waist, and the gentle swell of blossoming young breasts beneath the bodice of her calico dress. Beautiful.

His lips curved into a whimsical smile as supper smells continued to rise from the kitchen. His mother and Jessy were down there fussing over something insignificant. "Now, where in tarnation did that ladle get to?" Then his mother was humming again. *"'Greensleeves,'"* he thought, just before drifting off to sweet dreams of Hannah MacGregor.

It seemed only seconds later that Cal's eyelids fluttered open, but he knew time had passed. For one thing, the sun's rays were slanting through the loft window, casting a golden, mote-filled rectangle onto the loft floor by his bed. He pushed up onto his elbows, blinking, confused, feeling that something was different, out of kilter . . . *wrong*.

Then his sleep-befuddled brain finally registered what it was: Laddie *wasn't* barking. The abrupt cessation of that sound was what had awakened him. It had been cut off all at once, ending with a yelp and a pitiful mewl, leaving only a sudden, preternatural silence in its wake.

He couldn't have moved fast enough, even if he had been able instantaneously to interpret the strange precognitive feelings that had been washing over him ever since he opened his eyes.

Just as Cal bolted from the bed, sending both his aching body and his open volume of *Robinson Crusoe* thudding to the floor, he heard the front door bang open. The whole house shuddered with the impact. Crockery shattered.

Cal heard his sister shriek. Then, his mother's voice, straining to remain calm. "What do you want? Who are you?"

Indians! Cal thought. The word ricocheted around the inside of his head like panic gone wild. Renegade Indians! There had been some raids by the Cheyenne and Sioux, mostly in Nebraska, but they had been known to strike almost anywhere without warning. His head filled with imaginary horrors—homesteads burning, men scalped, women violated.

"Evenin' ladies! What's for supper, Mama?"

The booming male voice brought all thoughts of Indian massacres to a skidding halt. No Indian he had ever heard spoke with an accent that sounded like it came straight out of southern Missouri.

Another voice, this one chuckling. "Hey, pretty girl, what's your name, hmmmmmm?"

Cal rolled onto his stomach and crept to the edge of the curtain to peer down at the scene below. There were two of them, white men, and they were well armed, revolvers hanging at each hip. One of them aimed the barrel of a rifle straight at his mother's head, and Cal's stomach cramped into a knot of disbelieving terror.

The one with the rifle spoke again. "Who else is in the house, Mama? Your man ain't wandering around somewhere, is he?"

"N-no. He's not here. Just me and my daughter."

The man let a few moments of uneasy silence tick by. He was tall and had black hair. His eyes, beneath the brim of his hat, were dark and glittering and intelligent. His mustache was thick, his scruffy beard maybe a week old. "You telling me the truth?"

Cal saw his mother stiffen and nod. "Of course. What is it you want from us?"

"I'm looking at three plates on the table, Mama. You better think again."

Even over the aroma of fried potatoes, gravy, and cornbread, Cal caught the rancid odor of men who had been on horseback for days—old sweat, horse, dirt. Elizabeth Delaney was not answering his question fast enough. The one with the rifle moved toward her threateningly, and Cal almost cried out, *I'm up here!*

The one who had badgered Jessica stepped forward so his face came into Cal's narrow line of vision. Beneath his wide-brimmed hat, Cal caught a glimpse of coffee-brown hair. The whiskers on his cheeks were downy, barely noticeable. That was because he was young, not much older than Cal.

"If you're trying to protect your boy out in the field, you're wasting your time, Mama!" he bawled gleefully. "He told us to let you know he ain't gonna make it in for supper!"

"What have you done with Luke?"

The young one laughed again but didn't answer.

The one with the rifle wasn't nearly as amused as his companion. "One, two, three," he said, as if counting plates and heads to his satisfaction. "Fine and dandy. You serve us up some grub, Mama, and you won't have anything to worry about."

"If food was what you were after, all you had to do was ask," Cal's mother said, turning away and moving to the stove, bluntly ignoring the rifle that was trained on her.

The young one spoke up. "Say, this is a right nice place! Hey, Max, we could hole up here for a while, what do you think?"

"I think," the one with the rifle answered tightly, "that's as stupid an idea as you've come up with all week, Leo." He nudged the rifle at Elizabeth, who had turned around to look at him, questioning. "You just keep on with what you were doing, Mama. We're gonna eat our fill and be on our way."

A sprig of hope rose in Cal's chest. Maybe it would be like the man said. Maybe they would eat their fill and be gone.

"Hey, sweet face, what's your name?" The one named Leo approached Jessy, who was hunched silently in the corner behind the table, trying to make herself invisible. "Whatta you say there, pretty girl? Cat got your tongue?"

Elizabeth Delaney looked up, her face pale and tense. "Leave her alone, please."

Leo ignored the request. His face split into a lecherous grin. "You ever had a man before, sweet face?"

"Shut the hell up, Leo."

Leo swung around, glaring. "Don't tell me to shut up, Max! I can talk to her if I want!" He looked back at Jessica, his voice taunting. "Ain't hurtin' anything, am I, sweet face?"

Elizabeth Delaney raised her voice. "I asked you to leave her alone!"

"Awww, don't fret, Mama. She's gonna be all right. I wouldn't hurt her. Not a sweet face like that."

Jessy's head was bent, her hair, the hair she had fussed with that morning, pulled into a loose coil at the base of her blushing neck. Pale blond tendrils hung down over her eyes. Cal couldn't see her face, couldn't see the tears he knew were starting to trickle down her cheeks.

He swallowed hard, trembling with the effort it took to keep still. His hands were clenched into fists. Cold anger roiled in his stomach. Rage urged him to act, to spring from his hiding place and attack his sister's tormentor. Only the barest thread of rationality kept this basic instinct in check. He knew that if he moved now, it would only ignite an already potentially explosive situation. He knew this in his head, but his heart was a different matter.

Cal ducked farther down, making himself flatter to crawl forward another few inches. There were two firearms in the house, the Henry and the shotgun. Both would be hanging on the gun rack beside the front door.

He craned his neck to assure himself that they were still there. That's when he saw, to his utter dismay, that there was yet another member to this party. As if two didn't make for bad enough odds, he thought grimly.

This one had been perfectly silent and remained so now as he leaned against the wall next to the gun rack, cutting off even the remotest possibility of access to the weapons there.

There was nothing about this man's face that was wrong. On the contrary, his features were almost too normal, too agreeably placed. There were no scars or abnormalities or anything unpleasant that might put one off in passing. It was only his eyes, now fixed unconcernedly on the others in the room, that made Cal shudder with dread. Those eyes were black and completely innocent of emotion. *Empty.* It was this man's eyes that made Cal realize, with inexorable, damning finality, that his family's predicament was very serious indeed.

Cal eased back behind the curtain that separated Jessy's side of the loft from his own. His mind raced, searching for anything he could use or possibly improvise to fight them, but there was nothing more lethal at hand than Jessy's hairbrush. He had to get out of here and find out what happened to Luke.

When Cal rose to his feet, his head swam, threatening to toss him off balance, and he cursed the sickness that made him fuzzy and weak now when he needed all of his wits and strength.

Moving to the attic window, he stole one last glance over his shoulder. He heard that familiar hooting laughter, and a hand squeezed his pounding heart. It was the young one, the one called Leo. *If you so much as touch my sister, I'll kill you, you son of a bitch,* Cal thought.

Going out feet first, he squeezed through the open window. He had done this many times and had never failed to land gracefully on both feet. This time, though, his knees buckled, throwing him back onto his behind with a rude jolt.

Out of the corner of his eye, he caught a flash of something blond in the scrubby grass, and he turned his head to see Laddie, splayed out on his belly, limp. He stared, dry-eyed and numb, as dirty blond fur fluttered in the breeze.

The thought that, at any moment, one of the men inside the house could glance out the window snapped Cal from his momentary stupor. He scrambled to his feet, and, stepping over the dead dog, started across the yard.

When he reached the hay shed, he rounded a corner, safely out of sight from the house. Breathing hard, he scanned the barnyard and the edges of the cornfield, searching for any sign of Luke. Nothing. It was quiet. Only the clucking of the chickens and the dull thunking of Daisy's cowbell as she and her calf moved lazily about their pen. Too quiet. Wrong.

Maybe Luke had already gone for help. But a voice whispered inside Cal's head, a voice he didn't want to acknowledge. *And maybe he didn't.*

Cal saw no sign of the horses the three men must have ridden in on. It occurred to him that they might have spotted the isolated homestead and planned their approach. After hobbling their horses out in the middle of the field, one of them could have walked up to Luke wearing a friendly smile while the other two crept up from behind to knock him out cold. . . . Or kill him.

Cal squeezed his eyes shut, willing himself to stop it. No one had been killed except Laddie, and he was just a dog. Killing a dog was a far sight different than killing a human being. He opened his eyes, blinking away sweat.

"You're the man of the house while I'm gone, Cal. You take care of your mother and sister, now, you hear?" His father had spoken those last words to him thinking he would be gone for a few days, a week at the most, but Richard Delaney had never come back

at all. And Cal, only twelve at the time, had become the man of the house sooner than expected.

A helpless panic began to rise in his chest. *How can I take care of them if I'm out here with nothing better than a pitchfork to fight with? How do I take care of them now, Pa? How?* But his father's voice had fallen silent, offering him no answers.

Cal tried to think rationally. What he needed was a gun. But that wasn't going to happen. Even if he could find Luke, sprawled unconscious out in the cornfield somewhere, it would do him little good. Two unarmed men still had no chance against three who wore loaded revolvers at each hip.

He had no choice but to go for help. Still, something inside of him cringed at the thought of leaving his mother and sister here, even for a minute, and he knew going for help would take a lot longer than that. Cal raised anxious eyes to the western sky where the sun was already dipping behind the corn shoots.

Quickly, he rounded the blind side of the barn to eye his only source of transportation. Old Lucy was a swaybacked draft horse who had long ago outlived her usefulness. Unsaddled and tethered by the water trough, Lucy looked worse off than any crooked horse trader's snide.

Cal untethered her and swung up onto her back. He gripped her mane, urging her away from the Delaney homestead. Once he had her out past the edge of the field, he bent forward and kicked the old horse into a raging gallop. "Move!"

And she did. She didn't have much choice. The boy on her back was riding to beat the devil.

*   *   *

The ride to the MacGregor farm was the longest of his life. Lucy was sweating and blowing out beneath him, but she kept going just the same. It was as if she somehow sensed this might be her last, most important mission, and she was determined to make it a good one.

As the sun dropped lower and disappeared beneath the flat horizon, however, Cal was forced to slow her down lest she misstep and lame herself. That would have put him on foot, and he couldn't afford that.

Luke's father, Jasper, was at home, along with Nelson Riley, another neighbor who was bartering for some livestock. It was the only lucky thing that had happened so far, finding an extra man to head back out with them, and Cal allowed himself to hope it might be a good omen.

Cal barely had time to blurt out his story before Jasper called for his other two sons to grab their rifles and mount up. Nelson wasn't far behind. It was a dark night. The moon played hide and seek with a band of clouds, making their navigation difficult and time consuming.

Cal prayed, prayed to a God he only half believed existed, but it wasn't long before an orange glow on the horizon put a sudden, heart-wrenching stop to those desperate prayers. Cal kicked his horse into a heedless gallop.

The others had seen it too. Nelson Riley bellowed something about a prairie fire, but by then, Cal was racing too far ahead to understand the words.

Time spun out, unraveling like a crazed spool of thread. One minute he was pushing ahead into the night, pushing ahead toward flames licking at the black sky far, far into the distance—and the next, he was skimming past their cornfield.

If you have a passion for great historical romance, here's an offer you'll love...

4 FREE NOVELS

SEE INSIDE.

Reader Service.

Yes! I want to join the Timeless Romance Reader Service. Please send me my 4 FREE HarperMonogram historical romances. Then each month send me 4 new historical romances to preview without obligation for 10 days. I'll pay the low subscription price of $4.00 for every book I choose to keep--a total savings of at least $2.00 each month--and home delivery is free! I understand that I may return any title within 10 days and receive a full credit. I may cancel this subscription at any time without obligation by simply writing "Canceled" on any invoice and mailing it to Timeless Romance. There is no minimum number of books to purchase.

NAME

ADDRESS

CITY   STATE   ZIP

TELEPHONE

SIGNATURE

(If under 18, parent or guardian must sign. Program, price, terms, and conditions subject to cancellation and change. Orders subject to acceptance by HarperMonogram.)

Cal's mount, the one he had exchanged for Lucy at the MacGregor's, stopped and pranced sideways, balking at going any farther. Cal dropped the reins and slid off the skittish animal. He stood, wavering on two legs, staring stupidly at the horrific conflagration before his eyes.

What had happened? What in God's name had happened?

Jasper, behind him a moment later, was awestruck. "Jay-sus Christ!"

Cal's mind reeled. It had been that blamed hay-burning stove! Hadn't they always feared it would catch fire one day? But, where was Mama? Where was Jessica? Surely they would have had time to get out. Surely they would be here to greet Cal and his group, wouldn't they? *Wouldn't they?*

Cal scanned the empty yard.

Jasper motioned to his boys. "Jed! Tobias! Check the field for Luke!"

Maybe they're on the other side of the house, and they just don't know we're here yet. Maybe . . . He wanted to call out their names, but he couldn't—or wouldn't—because if he did, and they didn't answer . . .

A voice spoke to him, the same voice which had hinted earlier that maybe Luke MacGregor's reward for helping the Delaneys get their corn in had not been just a nasty bump on the head, maybe it had been something more like a slit throat or a broken neck. *Mama and Jessica are in there . . .*

Cal moved forward on legs that felt as alien as two sticks beneath him. A wall of heat slapped his face, forcing him to stop.

. . . dead.

An almost peaceful sense of unreality, light as a

gossamer veil, settled over Cal. Something inside of him shut down.

Nelson Riley's voice, faraway, unreal. "Looks like the work of redskins to me, Jasper!"

"No, he said it was white men! Are you sure, Cal?"

Heat blasted in malefic waves, baking Cal's upturned face, cooking the front of his shirt so that white bone buttons singed the skin on his chest. He barely felt it. He was too busy watching his home, along with what was left of his family, burn to the ground.

He thought about the three men, the ones who were now riding off to parts unknown. Scot-free. He saw their faces. He remembered their names.

Nelson Riley's voice started to fade, to pull back into the distance until it was a hundred miles away. "Haven't seen the likes of this since Quantrill's Raiders."

Tobias—or maybe it was Jed—called out, running in from the field, his voice rising to a panicked scream. "Pa! Pa! We found him! We found Luke! He's—"

"You take care of your mother and sister, now, you hear?"

Cal sank to his knees, grief clotting in his chest. They would still be alive if only he'd had a gun.

15

A *week had passed* since he and Rachel argued in bed. Famished, Cal attacked his eggs and bacon with abandon. He hadn't been this hungry, it seemed, in days. He was feeling better. The dream hadn't come back.

Nick, Charlotte, and Daisy had already left the table, leaving only Galen, who still nursed a cup of coffee, but that was fine with Cal. He preferred Galen's company to that of the others anyway.

He glanced up as Rachel appeared in the archway, her hair tied back in a single braid crazy with stray hairs. She looked unusually pale.

"Good morning, pumpkin," Galen said pleasantly. "Looks like it's gonna be another scorcher out there today!"

Rachel mumbled something unintelligible as she pulled out a chair at the table.

"What's the matter, pumpkin?"

"Daddy, pumpkins grow in the garden. I am your daughter."

Galen chuckled as Dolores came into the room, balancing a serving tray on one hip. "You want your eggs scrambled or fried, Rachel Elena?"

At this inquiry, Rachel whitened even more. "No eggs. Just a biscuit with some jam and coffee, please."

Galen finished his coffee and threw Cal a wink. "And maybe a piece of pumpkin pie if you've got it, Dolores."

Rachel shot her father a warning look.

Dolores cleared some dishes from the table. "A biscuit is not breakfast, Rachel Elena. You should have something hot. Do you want your eggs scrambled or fried?"

"No eggs."

"What day is it, Rachel Elena?" the housekeeper asked, raising a dark brow.

Puzzled, Cal looked from one woman to the other as they eyed each other tensely. Finally, Rachel spoke. "All I said was, no eggs. Just a biscuit and some jam."

"Hmmmph!" Dolores picked up another plate and banged it down onto her tray. "And I said, a biscuit is not breakfast!"

"Well, it isn't your breakfast we're discussing, is it?"

"Scrambled," Dolores replied breezily, pushing through the door to the kitchen before Rachel had a chance to argue.

Rachel glared at the closed door. "No eggs, damn it!"

Galen, knowing a cue to cut out when he saw one, rose from his chair and tipped his head in Cal's direction. "See you outside."

After Galen left, Cal poured another cup of coffee and eyed his sullen wife from over his cup. What was stuck in her craw this morning?

Dolores blew back in from the kitchen and slapped down a brown medicine bottle next to Rachel's elbow. Cal frowned to himself. Laudanum?

Rachel gave Dolores a chilling stare. "That will not be necessary."

Dolores snorted. "Just take it like I say and be done with it. No need to go making life miserable for everyone, is there?"

Rachel reached out and, with one finger, pushed the bottle away. "I said, that will not be—"

Dolores interrupted by addressing Cal. "You be learning soon, Mr. Cal, to stay away from the little woman this time of the month. She is mean enough to kill a bulldog."

Rachel's cheeks were suddenly ablaze with color. The look she gave the plain-talking housekeeper was indeed enough to kill a bulldog—perhaps even a half-dozen Brahman bulls to boot. "Thank you, Dolores. I think you've done about enough."

Cal hid a smile behind one hand as the two women stared each other down. Finally, Dolores tossed her dark head and stamped back into the kitchen.

Rachel glared at Cal, her voice tight. "And what are you staring at?"

"You, my darling."

Rachel pressed her lips together, then abruptly closed her eyes and rested her forehead on one hand, muttering, "Sometimes, I hate that woman."

Cal fought to keep a straight face as he downed the rest of his coffee and rose to his feet. At least now he knew what the problem was. "Really? And I was just beginning to like her."

Rachel didn't look up.

"So, are you going to take it easy today?"

Now, she did look up. "Why? I have a little headache, that's all. What's the big hoorah?"

Cal shrugged. "You look like hell."

"Thank you so much. I wasn't aware that beauty was a prerequisite for ranch work."

"I wasn't referring to your desirability, princess, just your state of health. You look like you aren't feeling well."

"You men! You're all alike! A bunch of simpering, arrogant, patronizing—"

"Don't go getting your feathers up, Rachel."

"The state of my feathers is none of your concern!"

"Enjoy your eggs." Cal turned to leave, not glancing back to catch the murderous glare he knew his disheveled bride shot him as he left the room. He set his hat firmly on his head as he stepped out onto the front porch and grinned. What a prospect! Confronting Rachel on a day when she actually had a reason to be temperamental. Incredible.

He was halfway out to the stables when he heard Dolores. "Mr. Cal! Mr. Cal!"

He stopped and turned.

She reached his side in seconds and placed an open palm across her chest as she struggled to get her breath. "Whoa! Mr. Cal, you move pretty damn quick when you put your mind to it!"

"You want to stop with the Mister stuff, Dolores? You're old enough to be my mother."

She looked insulted. "Not quite, Mr. Cal. You will want to be careful with that. I can still swing a pretty mean rolling pin."

Cal threw his head back and laughed, actually feeling good for the first time in days. He did like Dolores. She didn't pull her punches. "What do you want, Dolores?"

"There will be a special supper tonight."

"Why?"

The housekeeper nodded, as if to herself. "As I thought. She didn't tell you?"

Now Cal's curiosity was up. "Tell me what?"

"It's her birthday today."

"Rachel's?"

Dolores nodded. "She doesn't like a big fuss, but leave it to her not to tell her own husband."

Cal mused to himself. Rachel hadn't given him so much as a clue. He didn't have a whole lot of experience with women outside of the bedroom, but it sure didn't fit in with the usual mold, did it? Women liked presents, didn't they? Why wouldn't Rachel tell him it was her birthday?

Then, the idea struck him that maybe he hadn't exactly been approachable this week, not since he had the dream, not since they argued in bed. Okay, so maybe he had acted like a lout.

Dolores interrupted his thoughts. "Mr. Cal?"

"What?"

"You will be sure to be there, *sí*?"

"Yeah, *sí, sí*," he answered absently. Then, just as Dolores was turning away, he changed his mind. "No, wait a minute. Maybe you'd better not count on me."

The woman stopped to stare at him. "But . . ."

He smiled reassuringly. "There's some work I've got to get done around here and then something I've got to do in town. I'm not sure I'll be back in time. Understand?"

Dolores blinked at him, then slowly the corners of her mouth started to turn up. "Yes, Mr. Cal. I think I understand. *Está bien*." She turned to move away once again.

"And Dolores?"

She stopped. "Yes, Mr. Cal?"

"Thanks."

She winked. *"De nada."*

Dolores had made Rachel's favorite pecan pie for dessert, and by now, Rachel had already opened most of her gifts. Her aunt Charlotte had given her a beautiful Chinese fan, Nick had given her a handsome Mexican saddle, and Daisy had presented her with a pink parasol, of all ridiculous things. Now, Galen handed her a small gift box. "Happy birthday, Rachel Elena."

Rachel lifted the lid to see a single sheet of paper inside. It was a banker's draft. The draft itself was a symbolic gesture, Galen's way of telling her he had released the funds of her trust account for her personal use. They both knew she would leave it in the bank—for now. That was, until the day she would have to hand it all over to his son-in-law.

Rachel forced a smile. "Thank you, Daddy."

"Well, you're twenty-one now, Rachel. Old enough to know your own mind."

Nick laughed. "She's known her own mind since she was seven. You remember when she packed her bags and ran away only to be discovered an hour later up in the haymow?"

Rachel threw her cousin a menacing look. "I could come up with a few childhood anecdotes about you too, Nick, so I'd stop right there."

Nick raised his eyebrows at her from across the table and closed his mouth, still grinning.

Rachel looked down at the draft in her hands.

Twenty-one. Legally an adult. From this day on, the property in her name would no longer be held in trust for others to handle. She had been waiting for this day for a long time. She should have been happy.

Dolores appeared in the doorway. "Anyone want more pie?"

They all declined. Daisy made some remark about watching her figure, but Rachel wasn't listening. She was staring at the one empty chair at the table—*his* chair. He had not even shown up for supper. On her birthday!

"So," Daisy asked coyly, "anyone know where Cal got to?"

Her question was met with a stunned, awkward silence.

Rachel squared her shoulders. "Dolores said he had business in town to take care of. I'm sure it's . . . important."

Daisy was apparently not daunted by the disapproving looks she was receiving from Galen and Nick. "Bizzz-niss?" she inquired, drawling out the word suggestively.

Rachel knew very well she was referring to Cal's past affair with Lacey Holloway, and she felt her ire rising. How dare Daisy refer to that indiscretion, even indirectly, with Galen and Nick in the room!

"Yes," Rachel answered flatly. "Business."

"Mmmmmmmm. Well, it must have been very important *business* for him to miss his wife's birthday supper, wouldn't you think?"

Nick threw down his napkin and rose from the table in disgust. "Daisy! Can't you just leave it alone?"

"What?" Daisy looked up at her husband, the picture of innocence. "Just because you all are afraid to say something about it? Rachel's not a fool." Daisy turned her head to meet Rachel's livid gaze from across the table. "You don't need everyone to tippy-toe around the subject, do you, dear?"

Charlotte cleared her throat. "I'm sure whatever business he had to take care of . . . I'm sure it was very important, or else . . ." She reached out and patted Rachel's forearm. "Lamb child, I wouldn't worry about it if I were you."

Galen sighed. "You know, I like Cal, Rachel, but sometimes I just don't understand—"

Rachel shot to her feet. "That is enough!"

Everyone stared at her in shock.

"I don't need anyone's pity!"

They were still gaping at her. *Pitying* her.

Rachel felt a lump forming in her throat and was suddenly terrified she might burst into tears. "Excuse me," she mumbled, dropping her gaze. "I think I need some air."

She rushed from the room with one hand clamped over her mouth. She hated them! She hated *him* for embarrassing her like this! Picking up her skirts, she flew down the front porch steps.

It was already past dusk. The night was clear and balmy. She ran across the darkened lawn until she reached the pavilion, far enough away to feel safe from prying eyes.

She grasped the wooden railing, trying to catch her breath and calm herself. A cow mooed, low and mournful, and a calf bawled back. She could see the bunkhouse from here. Light poured from the open windows. Distant male voices drifted on the air.

She imagined Cal in bed with Lacey Holloway and waited for the anger to come. She willed it to come, like a conjured spirit, swift and sure and furious. She needed it to come, but it wouldn't. All she felt was a sick sort of churning in her stomach, a maelstrom of emotions she couldn't identify. Cal Delaney, whoever he was, whatever he was, he wasn't good for her. The sooner he was out of her life, the better.

Then she heard it. Hoofbeats, soft and regular, thumping on the dirt drive. She turned to see his tall figure astride Friday, the stallion that had brought him all the way from Dodge City and beyond, the horse that probably knew him better than any person ever would.

With the back of one hand, she hastily wiped at eyes that had brimmed with tears only moments before. Thank heavens the sun had already set. Any redness would be undetectable in this light. She smoothed her skirt and folded her arms, collecting herself. She knew she was visible from the corral where he was now drawing rein. If he had any decency at all, he would approach her and try to explain.

She wouldn't accept his explanations, of course. She would snub him. Actually, he deserved much worse than that. He deserved to be *gelded*, the unfaithful snake.

Cal dismounted and tethered his horse to the hitching post. She recognized the tilt of his hat, the long, easy strides as he turned and started back toward the house—his walk.

Rachel had every intention of waiting for him, but as he approached, she began to feel the anger she had tried to stir within herself only a few minutes earlier.

He was fifteen yards away, close enough for her to see his complacent expression, close enough for her to hear the ballad he was whistling.

Whistling!

It was as if her feet grew springs. She took off down the incline, catching him by surprise. He staggered back a few steps when she flew into him, her fists pummeling his chest.

"Rachel! What the . . . ?"

She did precious little damage as he caught both of her flailing arms, clamping down so she could barely move. She tried to free herself so she could swing out at him again. "You bastard! You missed supper!"

"Yeah, I kinda figured as much. I didn't know you rich folks had such strict supper rules. What the hell's gotten into you?"

She fairly screamed at him. "Where have you been?"

"I told Dolores. Didn't you get the message?"

Rachel tried again to yank free from his grasp. "I got the message!" she said furiously. "Business! Business in town! You don't have any business in town except with Lacey Holloway!"

"Lacey Holloway? Who the hell told you that?"

"No one! No one told me! I can smell her cheap perfume all over you, you worm!"

His grip tightened painfully. "You don't smell anything, Rachel! Now, stop it. I wasn't with Lacey or any other woman."

It took a while for his words to sink in. She stopped struggling long enough to look up into his face. She tried to read deceit there, but there was none. The only thing she saw was indignance.

Her shoulders slumped and she dropped her head. "Oh, damn, I just don't know what's the matter with me today."

Sensing that all the fight had gone out of her, he released her. "It's probably just your—"

She raised her head, her gaze turning unmistakably hostile.

"Your birthday. It's probably just your birthday," Cal finished lamely.

She stared at some vague point off into the distance for a moment as if contemplating, then, "Oh, to hell with everything." She turned and started back toward the darkened pavilion.

Cal then remembered why he had come up here in the first place. He bent to retrieve the small parcel he had dropped when Rachel came flying at him like some locoweed-crazed hellcat.

He caught up with her as she reached the pavilion. "Rachel?"

She turned.

He held out the box. "Happy birthday."

She stared at it. "What is this?"

"What's it look like?"

"It looks like . . . a present."

"Why don't you open it and see?"

Very slowly, she lifted one hand and took the box from him. With the other, she pulled at the elaborate bow. "You didn't actually tie this, did you?"

"No, Harl Davis at the mercantile took care of that for me. Otherwise, you'd probably have to settle for a half-hitch or a figure-eight."

She almost smiled as she tugged the bow loose and lifted the lid of the box. Cal waited.

She let out a small gasp and pulled out the locket. When she held it up, it flashed in the moonlight. "It's a gold heart," she said. "It's real." Her tone was full of awe.

Cal frowned. "Of course it's real. What do you think, I'm going to buy the richest girl in Tarrant County fake jewelry?"

"How did you afford this?"

Cal looked at her flatly. Leave it to Rachel. He had never been exactly destitute, not since he was a kid, anyway. And he'd always managed to earn a good living. But, of course, what he considered a good living would seem like peanuts to a woman like Rachel.

He tried to keep his voice even. "I draw a decent salary."

She didn't seem to hear him. She clicked open the locket. "There's nothing inside."

"I thought I'd leave that up to you." He paused. "It's your heart."

She looked up at him again, and he was shocked to see her eyes were shining . . . with tears! He had a panicky, sinking feeling in his stomach. He had never bought jewelry for a woman before. Hell, he had never bought *anything* for a woman before. Was it all wrong?

"You don't like it?" he asked.

She turned away and sank down onto one of the benches. "I love it. It's . . . it's . . . beautiful."

Cal was completely baffled. She loved it? Then why was she crying? Nick had said she never cried. She had broken her arm and she hadn't cried. What was she pulling this now for?

He stepped up onto the platform. "Look, uh, Rachel . . ." He fumbled for words, feeling like a complete dolt. "The other night . . ."

Her head was bent as she fingered the locket on her lap.

He took a deep breath before continuing. Apologizing had never been his forte. "The other night, I was maybe not so . . . I mean, maybe I said some things that weren't exactly—"

She looked up, waiting.

"Well, maybe I said some things that weren't so, uh, romantic."

"Romantic?"

He shrugged. "Maybe I came across a little harsh."

She frowned. "A little harsh?"

Cal drew himself up to full height, sensing she might be getting her second wind. "Yeah. Harsh."

"You were furious with me."

He eyed her cautiously before answering. "I was *not* furious."

"Yes, you were. You've been angry with me for the last week."

"I wasn't angry with you," Cal said again. "I wasn't angry with anybody." He paused and let out a sigh before looking down at the ground. "Just myself, maybe. I don't know."

He waited for a response. At least she had stopped snuffling, and he was grateful for that.

"I accept your apology," she said finally.

He bristled some at this. Apology. All right, maybe it was an apology, but she didn't have to *say* it. Cal shifted his weight from one foot to the other before looking up. "Yeah, well, I've got to go stable my horse."

Without warning, Rachel jumped to her feet and threw her arms around his neck. Cal almost lost his balance as his hands instinctively closed around her waist. He was assailed by the tantalizing scent of roses as she hugged him tight, letting out a tremulous little sigh that made him feel like gutter slime for what was going through his mind.

He knew this was not intended to be an erotic embrace, but he could feel her breasts molding against his chest, the length of her legs beneath her skirts, the sensual softness of her belly pressed up against his . . . In another minute, he was going to do something that would entail having to buy her another locket complete with a second sniveling apology attached.

Hannah MacGregor. The name flashed unbidden through Cal's mind, bringing with it the fleeting, long-forgotten taste of first love, the naive exuberance of blossoming youth, a time when just about anything seemed possible. He wondered absently what had ever happened to Hannah. He wondered even more what had brought her to mind now when he hadn't thought of her in years.

It was only through supreme willpower that Cal kept his hands planted firmly around Rachel's waist. After a moment, he eased from the embrace. "I'm starving. I hope Dolores kept some supper warm for me."

Rachel's eyes were red and slightly swollen. Her skin was pale, and her hair was still a mess. He wanted to kiss her. He turned away instead. "I'll see you inside."

Before she could answer, he was halfway across the yard, heading for the corral. He had thought he would feel better after giving her the locket. He had thought he would feel better after apologizing to her. Instead, if it were possible, he was feeling worse.

He had acted believably indignant when she accused him of going to see Lacey Holloway. He hadn't gone to see Lacey, but it wasn't as if the thought of visiting Dolly's place hadn't occurred to him this evening.

He was feeling very frustrated. It would have been easy to stop off and indulge himself with a willing female, but his conscience had intervened. Even though his marriage to Rachel was a mutually-agreed-upon farce, he actually felt guilty over the thought of bedding another woman!

He removed his horse's reins from the corral fence and clicked his tongue. The steed followed him into the darkened stable. Cal pulled a match from his vest pocket and lit the kerosene lamp hanging by the door. "Come on, Friday."

He led the horse into an unoccupied stall and knelt down to uncinch the saddle. He doubted that visiting Dolly's place would have done much to relieve him, anyway. It wasn't abstinence that was causing his problems. He had abstained from women for longer periods than this without difficulty. After all, chasing felons across the countryside didn't exactly leave a whole lot of spare time or energy for dallying with the ladies. He had spent most of his nights alone—just him, his horse, and a good book—camping out under the stars in the mountains, on the plains, and in the deserts.

Cal pulled the saddle from his horse's back and set it aside. No, abstinence wasn't the problem. Rachel was the problem. Her proximity and her unavailable availability, if that were an acceptable oxymoron.

As he slid the saddle blanket from Friday's back, the horse raised its head and blew out a snort. Rachel had been right. He couldn't afford the locket. He still owed Harl Davis another two dollars.

Good old Harl had been more than happy to extend the credit, though, stating that since Cal was a Girard and all, he certainly knew Cal was good for it. That offhand remark had stabbed at his pride. He wasn't a Girard. He was a Delaney.

Cal lifted the bridle over the horse's head and removed the bit from his mouth. "That woman is driving me loco, Friday."

With a currycomb in one hand and a body brush in

the other, Cal started grooming his steed's glistening black coat. He deliberately pushed Rachel from his mind and worked in silence.

When he was finished, he patted Friday's nose. "Don't ever get hitched, boy. Just do your thing, then head for the hills. That's my advice."

The horse seemed to nod its big head in agreement.

Cal watered and fed Friday, then left the stable, dousing the lamp behind him. He stood outside the door for a moment, eyeing the great house up on the hill.

He filled his lungs with sweet, clean night air. The cattle in their pens rustled lazily. Crickets chirped. From somewhere behind the stable, he heard two cats hissing and squealing and screeching. Either fighting or making love.

He could hear the ranch hands in the bunkhouse, laughing it up and hollering good-natured insults at one another. That was where Cal belonged—not in the mansion on the hill.

He raised his gaze to the moon. It hung low in the sky, nearly full, huge and yellow and wrapped in a ghostly haze. But it wasn't a cloudy evening. What was that filmy haze swirling like misty fingers over its face?

A familiar chill raced up his spine. It reminded him of the hunt—when he was getting close to one of his prey. But he wasn't a hunter anymore. A bizarre turn of phrase came to mind. Maybe not the hunter but the hunted?

Don't ever let your guard down, Cal. Who had taught him that? The old gunhand Grady? Jason Farley, perhaps?

He stared at the moon. That haze, that swirling mist

put him in mind of the steam that might rise from a witch's caldron as she stirred up some diabolical delight, and he recalled a line from *Macbeth*: *"By the pricking of my thumbs, Something wicked this way comes."*

Unconsciously, his hands dropped to his sides, to his thighs where his Colts used to ride. They were, of course, not there. He clenched his fists and tore his gaze from the giant glowing orb in the sky, resisting an illogical urge to steal a glance over his shoulder. There was nothing back there. Just a stable full of horses and two randy cats going at it like there was no tomorrow.

You're spooking yourself, Cal. He shook off the feeling and headed back up to the big house.

16

Dodge City, Kansas

The yellow moon hung low on the horizon, giving the visual impression of a faded, dying sun against the blackening sky. Eli chewed on the butt of his cigar and regarded the phenomenon with a vapid eye. His head was still pounding, vestiges of the last spell that hit him over two hours ago.

He stood by the stock pens at the edge of town. The pens were full to splitting of restless cattle to be shipped out on Santa Fe Railroad cars the next morning. From across the yard, the occasional flare of a match meant that a lone cowpuncher assigned to guard duty was lighting up his smoke.

Eli had just found out his brother was dead.

"Brought him in slung over his horse, yep." Decker, a bald geezer with a spreading middle, nodded and sucked on a wrinkled cigarette. "Coupla months ago now, yep."

Strains of lively music from the dance halls and saloons carried on the gentle breezes that swept through town. The place was aglow, an oasis of light on the flat Kansas plain. False fronts bustled with nocturnal activity. Cowboys swaggered on the streets, their jinglebobs ringing and clanging on the boardwalks as they strutted from one saloon to the next.

Eli took the cigar from his mouth. "It was Delaney that brought him in, right?"

"Yep. Delaney. That's the one. A farmer hauled him into town in the back of his wagon. Leo was already dead, shot in the back. Delaney wasn't in too good of shape hisself."

Delaney. The name rose in Eli's mind like the curling, wispy tendrils of an old, very bad dream. Their gang in those days had consisted of six men: Eli, Leo, Max, and three cousins named Abbott. Together, they had robbed a Virginia-Truckee bullion car on its way from Virginia City to the mint at Carson City. They had lost one of the Abbott cousins during the robbery, but they had killed two Wells Fargo agents. This, and not the silver they got away with, was the root of the troubles they were to face later.

It had been Max, of course, who spotted their pursuers—ever vigilant, ever cautious Max. They had topped out on high ground and were ready to make camp when Max pointed into the hazy distance, many miles back. A small group of men on horseback.

They stopped only long enough to heat up some grub and to water their horses before pushing on through the night. Bypassing the heavily traveled mountain routes, they elected to go south instead, deeper into the wilderness of the Sierra Nevada.

By dusk on the following day, low on sleep and with

tempers running short, they entered the Yosemite Valley, well southeast of their original destination, Sacramento. It was soon after breaking camp the following morning that they caught sight of the intrepid pursuers yet again.

For days, the Walshes and the two remaining Abbott cousins, Jay and Bobby Joe, continued south through rugged terrain. As an added precaution, they brushed out their tracks and traveled in stream beds and over rock flats whenever possible. But the three riders still came.

It was then that Max decided they should make a break for it to Mexico.

They pushed on, without sleep, beyond the crests of the Sierra Nevada and two miles down into the desert. Death Valley. As the sun rose over the slopes of the Amargosa Range, so did the mercury. Their pace slowed as they traveled over sand dunes and salt formations. Heat rose from the desert floor like blasts from a colossal furnace.

Finally, out of water, exhausted, and irritable, they crossed into the Panamint Mountains. The posse that dogged them followed, closing in. They had no choice but to hole up in an old mining shack, securing their horses around back to shelter them from gunfire. Their only hope was to confront the men that were so determined to catch up with them.

They didn't have to wait long.

An hour before dusk, a man's voice rang out of the wooded stillness. "Surrender," the man demanded, "surrender within the hour and you'll be taken alive."

The outlaws were not holed up under the best of circumstances. There was plenty of rock and forest cover for the three men who were waiting for them outside. Still, surrendering meant only one thing: hanging.

Max wanted them to wait. He needed time to think.

Jay Abbott rebelled. No more thinking. Thinking and planning had gotten them nowhere. He rose up to the open window and fired at the men who waited outside. A split second later, another bullet screamed through the air. Jay staggered back, a look of stunned surprise on his face. He had been hit bull's-eye center in the forehead. One shot. No wasted ammunition. Whoever had pulled that trigger was possessed of a cool head, a steady hand, and eyes like an eagle. Eli had never seen anything like it before in his life.

The shootout that followed was an unmitigated disaster. Max and Bobby Joe were taken out before they even cleared the doorway. Eli didn't stop to look back. He took off on his stallion like a bat out of hell, but whoever was shooting caught him in the leg just before his horse went out from under him. He was barely able to swing up behind Leo and escape, bleeding like a stuck pig.

When they finally made it to Los Angeles, Eli was half-dead from losing so much blood, and his leg was inflamed with putrid infection. Later, after he recovered, Eli made it a very special point to find out the names of the men who had killed Max. The dogged trio had been Wells Fargo agents.

Eli knew that Jason Farley now headed the Wells Fargo office in Virginia City. It was just lucky for Mr. Farley that, because of the bounty on his head, it behooved Eli to steer clear of that particular area.

As for Tex Granger, the second member of the posse, he had left the employ of Wells Fargo soon after the shootout. Eli hadn't been able to keep tabs on him.

Cal Delaney had also left Wells Fargo. He had branched out on his own and was working independently as a bounty hunter. He tended to operate in and around Kansas, but he had been known to track his quarry as far as Canada or Mexico if he were in the mood for it.

Delaney had taken up Leo's trail soon after Leo killed the Dodge City deputy. Leo fled to Mexico first, then drifted up to Albuquerque, convinced that Delaney had given up on him. Leo was wrong—for the last time in his stupid, pathetic life.

Now, as disjointed memories flooded his mind, Eli's chest constricted, clenching tight as a fist. "Where is he now?"

Decker rocked on his heels. "Who? Leo?"

Eli felt like grabbing the old man's shirt collar and twisting it until his eyes bulged. He already knew where Leo was. Leo was planted somewhere up on Boot Hill, probably under a tombstone that read Wells Fargo Never Forgets.

"Delaney. Is he still here?"

The geezer removed his dusty bowler hat and punched out a dent. "No, not here. He left a while ago, shortly after he was patched up, if I remember right. Yep."

"Going where to?"

Decker replaced his hat. "I seem to remember he took off his guns."

"A man like that doesn't just take off his guns."

Decker raised one hand. "No, he really did! I remember it 'cause it was after I seen him shoot that boy in the street." Decker chuckled to himself. "Damned stupid kid come running out after Delaney, hollering up a storm, making a fool jackass out of hisself! Hell! He drew on Delaney while his back was turned! Hell! Stupidest thing I ever seen in my life!"

Eli puffed on his cigar. "Cold-decking a man in the back isn't always stupid, Decker."

"Well, it is when you miss!"

Decker chuckled heartily at his own joke, stirring up a lot of stringy phlegm in the process. Eli waited while he hacked it out before continuing. "Delaney didn't kill him, though. Mite big-hearted of him if you ask me. The kid was a flaming—"

"You said he left town," Eli interrupted.

"Yep, yep. He joined up with some drover . . . uh, whoseamacallit."

Eli was losing patience. He wanted to smash his fist into Decker's bloated face. "Whoseamacallit," he muttered.

"Yep! What's-his-name, that was, uh . . . friendly fella . . . Evans! That's it! Left town with Evans. Headed south to Texas, I'd guess. Evans usually drives herds up from Fort Worth to Dodge. I reckon he'd be headed back up the trail by now."

"Evans." Eli memorized the name. He would be taking the Chisholm Trail.

Decker raised red-rimmed, bleary eyes to peer up at him. "You ain't thinking of going after Delaney, are you, Eli?"

Eli didn't say anything for a moment. *Wells Fargo Never Forgets.* Well, Eli Walsh didn't forget either. When he finally replied, his voice was low, almost inaudible. "That's exactly what I'm thinking."

Decker shook his head and stamped out his cigarette. "You're a crazy sumabitch, you know that, Eli? What do you think you're gonna do with a guy like that?"

Eli drew on his cigar, causing its orange tip to glow bright against the black night. He looked up at the rising yellow moon. "Why, Decker, I'm gonna play the last card. I'm gonna kill him."

17

Day had broken. The bright vermilion skyline had cooled to pink and yellow and blue. The sun was growing warm, but the air was bracing as it moved across the river and out onto the open range beyond. It had rained the day before. The ground was soggy, the grass wet and clean. White billowing clouds drifted lazily overhead. It was going to be a beautiful day.

Cal wasn't thinking about the weather. He was actually trying to think of nothing at all, though that was much easier said than done.

He raised the Cavalry Colt to eye level and lined up the sights. Quite a distance off, atop a low rock formation by the river's edge, a motley collection of twenty-six empty bottles and tin cans sparkled in the early morning light.

Cal worked at clearing his mind of everything but one pure, thin line of concentration. This simple act, possibly the most important skill he had ever taught himself, seemed more difficult to accomplish than ever before. He had indeed gone soft.

Cal pulled the trigger. Its report shattered the virgin stillness of the new morning. His hand and wrist, strengthened by years of practice, absorbed the gun's kick easily as the bottle on the far right popped and shattered. A few birds arose, fluttering and screeching, from a tree nearby.

He lined up the sights and cocked the hammer. Pulled the trigger. *Twang!* The can next to the first bottle flipped into the air and dropped to the ground somewhere near the river's edge. He cocked the hammer and pulled the trigger again. *Pop!* Again. *Twang!* Again. *Pop!*

The trick was to clear his head, to empty his heart and mind, to forget past and present, to concentrate on what was before him and nothing else. That was the trick. That and erasing all doubt. Doubting his own skill was the second stumbling block. There could be no doubt.

He could still pull it off. It just took a little more effort, that was all; just a little more effort to get back into it. *Back into it.* Was that what he was doing? He wasn't sure what had compelled him to saddle up Friday and ride all the way out here just before dawn.

First had come the dream, then, a few nights ago, the undeniable sense that someone, or something, lurked just behind him. Now, here he was out on the southwestern edge of the Elena Rose Ranch picking off a row of targets.

Was it time for him to move on? Had he stayed too long? Was he truly incapable of putting down roots? Maybe it was impossible for a man to escape what he was. Maybe it was foolish even to try.

At the sound of a rider approaching from behind, Cal lowered his revolver but didn't turn around. He knew who it was.

Paco's voice boomed in the early morning quiet. "You aren't thinking of going anywhere, are you, Mr. Cal?"

Cal's smile was mirthless. Paco was a lot smarter than he pretended to be. "You know much about guns, Paco?"

The big man laughed. "Not much, Mr. Cal. I can usually count on my fists, and if they ain't enough, I reckon there's always a shotgun around to do my talking for me."

Cal heard him dismount. "How'd you find me?"

"Well, I saw you leave early on. I just followed the sound of gunfire, and here you are."

"You're an early riser."

"Old habits die hard."

"Ain't that the truth." Cal tucked the empty Cavalry Colt into the waist of his denims. Although he had brought both of his old sidearms, he had not strapped on his gun belt today. That was something he had vowed never to do again. Now, Cal bent to retrieve the Peacemaker from where it lay by his feet. "This one's the best for speed, Paco. A good old single-action Colt, the Equalizer. You wouldn't think it, would you?"

"You're not one for the newfangled double-action pieces, then?"

Cal reached into his vest pocket for some cartridges. "The double-action pieces, they call them thumb-busters for good reason. The trigger pull is too hard, too slow to get off. Now, this one here, if you file down your sight and trigger guard, you get no resistance if you have to draw fast, and as for cocking the hammer, if you use your free hand . . ."

Cal thumbed six cartridges into the loading gate of the Peacemaker. Holding the revolver at just above hip level, he trained his eyes on his targets. "Cover your ears, and hold on to that horse."

Paco tightened his grip on his mustang's reins and watched as Cal used his left hand, palm down, to fan the revolver's hammer, resulting in a staccato firing of all six chambers. Struggling to control his nervous mount, Paco saw that five of the six targets were gone.

Cal lowered the gun, squinting through smoke to see the one bottle left standing. "Speed's not usually worth a damn, though."

"Looked pretty damn good to me."

"Not if the one you miss is firing back at you."

"About the only things we fire on around here are rattlers and lame horses, Mr. Cal. They don't usually shoot back."

"You're lucky." Cal crossed to the tree where his stallion grazed, blissfully undisturbed by the discharge of firearms. He stuffed both revolvers into a saddlebag and pulled a Winchester from the rifle scabbard. "Another good thing about the .44, Paco. Now, you can use the same cartridges in your rifle."

Tethering his horse, Paco followed Cal as he strolled a distance farther from the stream bed. Cal loaded the firearm in silence as he walked.

They covered about thirty yards before Cal abruptly stopped and turned. With both hands, he raised the weapon, lined up his sights, and fired. Paco didn't have to look to know Cal hit what he was aiming at.

"Maybe I won't be betting on you at the next lassoing or bull-wrangling contest, Mr. Cal, but I'll be laying out about a month's pay if you ever enter the target-shooting competition. Looks like what they say about you is true."

Cal lowered the rifle. "Yeah, it probably is."

After a moment, Paco sighed. "It's too bad you never got to meet Mrs. Girard."

Cal pulled the trigger-guard lever and raised the rifle again. He fired. A bottle exploded in the distance.

"Rachel's mother, you mean?"

"A right fine lady she was."

"I've seen her portrait in the parlor. Nice looking woman."

"Inside and out. She had a good heart." Paco paused. "That's not to say, of course, she didn't speak her mind when she had a hankering to."

Cal gave Paco a side glance. "Is that right?"

"She and Mr. Girard had their times."

"Their *times*?"

Paco chuckled. "Things could get lively."

"Are you saying they had some loud discussions?"

"Oh, I remember a door or two being slammed on occasion."

"It must be hereditary," Cal muttered as he yanked on the trigger-guard lever of the Winchester.

"There was the one time she gathered up all of Mr. Girard's duds and tossed them out the door."

Cal tried to picture the look on Galen Girard's face upon discovering his longjohns scattered all over the front yard. He eyed the burly ranch hand. "Is there a point to all this?"

"Point?" Paco tried to look innocent. "No point."

Cal gave him a knowing smirk. "Then, it wouldn't have anything to do with me and Rachel, right?"

"Can't see as how it would."

After a moment, Cal returned his attention to the targets and raised the rifle to line up the sights. He thought about Rachel—her exquisite cheek bones, wine-red lips, flashing green eyes, and wild cinnamon curls. He remembered how she looked the day she was getting dressed for Old Man Sutter's barn dance, the tantalizing outline of her breasts just visible beneath the flimsy material of her camisole, the gentle curve of buttocks when she turned around, and her long, slender legs, which seemed meant to wrap around a man's waist.

He fired.

Nothing. Missed.

Cal lowered the rifle and scowled. Even a passing thought of Rachel Girard played hell with his concentration—damn it, with his sanity, for that matter. That woman was trouble with a capital *T*.

Cal looked at the ranch hand. Paco was looking back at him, his bushy brows raised expectantly. "You about done playing for today, Mr. Cal? We got them colts ready for gelding."

Playing. Cal knew full well he had just been lectured to. He smiled grudgingly. "Yeah, I'm through playing. Shall we head on back?"

Paco straightened, showing just a flash of his big, white teeth. "Why, Mr. Cal, I thought you'd never ask."

Daisy stood behind the mercantile, tapping her foot impatiently and casting furtive glances about her. It was the middle of the morning. Anyone might stumble across her back here. No one had ever caught her yet, though. She told herself to relax. Then, she heard rapid footsteps in the narrow alley that separated the mercantile from Furman's Dress Shop, and she stiffened expectantly.

When Lacey Holloway appeared around the corner, she let out a bated breath. "Do you have it?" Daisy asked anxiously.

Lacey was dressed in a plain blue gingham. Her fine hair was straight today and pulled back into a simple bun. She might have been any young woman of modest means in a town the size of Fort Worth—the daughter of a farmer, perhaps, or a storekeeper. Today, she didn't look anything like the prostitute she was, but everyone knew just the same, and Daisy had no desire to be observed meeting with her.

"Of course I do," Lacey answered peevishly. The two of them were not exactly friends despite the secret they shared.

"Let's have it then. I don't have all day. Rachel came into town with me, and all I need is for her to see us together. She'd never stop digging until she found out what was going on."

At the mention of Rachel's name, Lacey wrinkled her nose. She withdrew two small white paper pouches from her handbag. "She won't find out. I certainly won't tell her."

"Oh, she's got ways, Lacey. She's worse than a bull-dog with a bone when she gets fixed on something."

Lacey passed the pouches to Daisy. "Remember, fifteen to twenty grains to a pint of water."

Daisy shoved the small packages into her reticule, glancing around to make sure they were still quite alone. "I know, I know."

Lacey smiled slyly. "Tannin water before and plain cold water after, as cold as you can get it."

Daisy gave her a withering look. "I'm aware of how to do it by now. Does it look like I'm expecting any babies to you?"

Lacey gave the other woman's waist a disdainful glance. She assumed it was Daisy's obsession with her figure that kept her in terror of getting pregnant.

Lacey had to control an urge to smirk. She knew Daisy kept her ministrations a secret from her husband, who, by now, was probably wondering why his wife was failing to conceive. It was a secret that Lacey was content enough to keep. It would do her no good to reveal it. Perhaps it would prove useful to her someday, but for now, it paid her more to keep her mouth shut. She held out one hand. "Ten dollars."

Daisy scowled as she reached inside her reticule for the bills to slap into Lacey's outstretched palm. "There! What is in this concoction, anyway? Gold dust?"

Lacey shrugged as she tucked the money into her own bag. "I ain't rightly sure, Daisy. Miss Dolly mixes it up herself. She swears by it, and I wouldn't mess with success if I was you."

Daisy gave Lacey a doubtful look. Lacey thought Daisy was finally catching on to the fact that she was being outrageously overcharged, but it didn't really matter. Daisy didn't have much choice. Who else was going to keep her dirty little secret?

Lacey decided to change the subject to one she had an interest in herself. "So, what is Rachel up to these days?"

Daisy shrugged. "She and that husband of hers spend most of their time fighting like two wet hens. Land's sake, I don't know what ever possessed her to marry him in the first place. He hasn't got any money and that reputation of his . . . unsavory, to say the least."

Lacey thought about Cal Delaney, about his eyes,

the color of blue ice, about his body, lean and hard, and his hands, hands that could elicit thrills with such calculated expertise. She started feeling a little warm.

"Still," Daisy continued thoughtfully, "I suppose he *is* rather attractive in a rough sort of way." Her eyes grew dreamy. "He's got that way about him, you know . . . mysterious, rugged, raw, untamed . . ."

Lacey rolled her eyes. Daisy Girard's underdrawers were obviously doing a little overheating of their own at the moment.

Daisy's voice trailed off absently before she suddenly shook her head, snapping back to reality. "What were we talking about?"

"You were saying you can't understand what Rachel sees in Cal."

Daisy tittered and reached up to pat her feathered hat. A splash of pink popped out high on each cheekbone, supporting Lacey's theory. "Oh my, yes! Well, I suppose there is something there to catch a girl's eye, after all. I might be better off wondering what it is *he* ever saw in *her*."

Lacey snorted. "Money. He married her for money."

"Well, of course the Girard fortune had something to do with it, Lacey. How else would Rachel ever manage to snag a husband? She's meaner than a rattlesnake."

Lacey placed a hand on one hip. "I didn't say anything about the Girard fortune. I said, he married her for money. Twenty thousand dollars to be exact. I happen to know—"

The words had come tumbling out faster than apples from an overturned barrel. Lacey clapped a hand over her mouth, mortified by her own gaff.

Daisy's eyes were already narrowing suspiciously. "What do you *happen* to know, Lacey Holloway?"

Lacey shook her head. "I didn't say I knew anything."

"You know something!" Daisy pointed an accusing finger. "I know you've been with Cal. Did he tell you something? Did Cal tell you something about him and Rachel?"

Lacey drew the drawstrings of her purse. "I've got to go."

Daisy's hand shot out and clamped on Lacey's arm. "Oh no, you don't! You're not going anywhere, you little sneak."

Lacey jerked her arm free. "I will do as I please, Daisy Parker." She turned and started to walk away.

"Ten dollars!"

Lacey slowed her steps.

"Fifteen!"

Lacey stopped, her mind starting to calculate, her resolve starting to weaken.

"Twenty!"

Lacey turned and gave Daisy a measuring look.

"All right! Twenty-five. That's my final offer. It's all I've got."

Lacey approached. "Thirty. Not a penny less."

"*Thirty!*" Daisy's voice rose to a squeal before she realized she might attract attention. She glanced around and dropped her voice to a whisper. "Thirty dollars? You little hussy!"

Lacey folded her arms, oblivious to the insult. "Thirty dollars. Take it or leave it. It's no skin off my nose."

Daisy muttered something very unladylike under her breath before plunging one white-gloved hand back into her reticule. She pulled out a roll of bills and counted out thirty dollars.

"If it'll make you feel any better, it's worth that and

more," Lacey assured her, taking the money and stuffing it into her handbag.

"It better be. Now, spill your beans."

"It so happens that Rachel was so scared of becoming an old maid that she offered Cal twenty thousand dollars to marry her."

Daisy's look was dubious. "Did he tell you this?"

Lacey nibbled at her lip hesitantly before answering. "No, he didn't, and that's why you've got to promise not to ever let him know where you found this out."

Lacey suddenly had another fleeting image of Cal's talented hands, only this time they were wrapped around her neck. She swallowed hard. "I mean *never*."

Daisy waved Lacey's concerns away. "If he didn't tell you, then how do you know it's even true?"

Lacey tried to force down another picture that popped to mind. Rachel Girard holding a six-shooter to Lacey's head and pulling the trigger . . . *POW!*

"Lacey Holloway!"

Lacey jumped. "What?"

"If you're not going to tell me any more than that, you can just give me back that thirty dollars right now."

Lacey blinked. "I saw the paper."

"What paper?"

"Their paper," Lacey clarified. "They had it all on a paper, and they signed their names to it."

"You mean to tell me Rachel paid Cal twenty thousand dollars to marry her, and they signed a paper saying this was true?"

Lacey tried to think. "Well, he doesn't get the money until they're divorced."

"They're going to get *divorced*?" Daisy's voice rose high again, only this time she was too excited to check herself. "When?"

Lacey shook her head, suddenly feeling very uncomfortable with her decision to spill the beans. "I . . . I don't know."

Daisy tapped her chin with one index finger. "Well, if that don't take the rag off the bush."

"You said it," Lacey agreed.

Daisy continued mulling aloud, "Of course. That's the only way a man like Cal would get married. If he knew he was going to get out of it eventually, but why would Rachel . . . ?" Her eyes suddenly lit up with understanding.

"What?" Lacey's curiosity was piqued.

Daisy turned back to Lacey urgently. "Are you sure you can't remember if it said when they're to get divorced? Are you sure you can't remember anything else?"

"Only that it was to a be a marriage in name only."

"*A marriage in name only*?" Daisy's eyes widened eagerly.

"That's what it said. Word for word. A marriage in name only. You know what *that* means, don't you?"

Daisy smiled.

Lacey answered for her. "It means no frisky-frisky between the sheets. That's what it means."

Daisy wasn't looking at Lacey anymore. In fact, it seemed she'd forgotten her companion was still present. "It means no heirs for Galen Girard," she said softly. "It means Rachel thinks she's pulled a fast one."

"Imagine that, Rachel being so scared of becoming an old maid she would actually pay a man to marry her," Lacey said.

Daisy gave her a sly look. "Oh, she wasn't afraid of becoming an old maid. That's not why she did it."

"What are you talking about? What else could it be?"

Daisy's eyes shined with secret knowledge. "You were right, though, Lacey. It was worth thirty dollars. It might actually end up being worth a whole lot more than thirty dollars before I get through."

Perplexed, Lacey cocked her head and watched as Daisy Girard strolled away, around the corner of the mercantile and out of sight.

Cal removed his mud-spattered boots on the porch. By now, he knew that Dolores wouldn't hesitate to wield her rolling pin if anyone dared to soil her clean floors. It was already late in the afternoon, but they had gotten some good work done. Rachel had kept her distance. To his great surprise, castrating male colts was not one of her specialties. She was exercising her own horses and staying out of his hair for a change.

Cal entered the house and was halfway up the staircase when he heard his name. He stopped, listening for the voices that were coming from Galen's study. It was Daisy and Charlotte. Now, what were they doing huddling in Galen's study? And what were they saying about him?

Slowly, quietly, Cal backed down the stairs and stood outside the study door. It was cracked open. Charlotte was sputtering. "I simply cannot believe my eyes! This is preposterous, even for Rachel! How in the world did you learn of this?"

Daisy's voice was coy. "I can't tell you that."

"Where did you get this agreement?"

"I —Well, I came across it in some of Cal's things."

In the corridor, Cal's attention was riveted. Daisy had found the contract. But how?

Charlotte sounded doubtful. "You 'came across it'?"

"All right! I searched their room. Would you have believed me if it wasn't staring you in the face?"

"Have you spoken to Nick about this?"

"No, I haven't had a chance, but it wouldn't matter anyway." Daisy sounded petulant. "He absolutely refuses to listen to reason when it has anything to do with Rachel. You know how he is about her. Maybe he'd listen to you."

"No, you're probably right. When it comes to Rachel, Nick has never been able to set his emotions aside."

"Charlotte, we need to go to Galen about this."

There was a moment of silence before Charlotte replied. "Yes. He has a right to know. The problem is, how to go about it. He's almost as blind as Nick when it comes to facing Rachel's shortcomings."

"Well, you know he won't take it well coming from me, Charlotte. It would be better if you told him."

"Oh, I don't know about that."

Daisy pulled the right string. "Nick's inheritance may depend on it."

"But . . . this contract. It's so hard to believe."

"Yes, but it explains a lot, doesn't it? They've never gotten along. Have you ever seen him kiss her or even put his arm around her?"

Charlotte snorted. "Well, they *do* share a bed. What are we to suppose goes on up there?"

"Absolutely nothing! That's what 'marriage in name only' means. It's all for appearance's sake. One thing is for certain. Rachel and Cal will never produce the heir Galen is so intent on having."

"It might help our case if you and Nick were expecting."

Daisy's tone grew annoyed. "I'm sure that, in time . . ."

"Yes! Yes! I've heard it all before. You've been married over a year and still no grandchildren. There's no reason why a healthy girl like you—"

Daisy interrupted heatedly. "Have you ever stopped to think that it might be Nick? It's not always the woman who's at fault! There *are* some men who—"

"There is absolutely nothing wrong with my son!"

"Fine, Charlotte. If that's the case, then, as I said before, in time —"

"Enough! We're getting off the subject."

"That's right. A marriage in name only is no marriage at all. Rachel is welshing on her part of the bargain with her father. Add to that the fact that they're actually planning on divorcing in six months."

"We have to approach Galen with this as soon as possible."

"Tonight. After dinner."

"God help us. He'll be angry."

"Angry with Rachel, though, Charlotte. She's making a fool out of him."

"I hope *he* sees it that way."

"Tonight, after dinner, you get him to meet you here in the study. I'll come along if you think it'll help."

There was a short silence. "All right. But we'll need the contract. Are you sure Cal won't miss it?"

"It was in one of his old saddlebags in Rachel's closet."

"Well, where are we going to put it until tonight?"

"Do you know the combination to Galen's safe?"

Charlotte waffled. "Well, I have had occasion to notice while he was opening it, but I doubt that he knows I know."

"That's no good then. Let's see. . . . I've got it! We'll fold it up and put it in one of these books."

There was a pause.

"What about this one?" Daisy piped up.

"It doesn't matter. Just make sure you remember which one. All we need is to get Galen in here and then lose the infernal thing. He'll chop our heads off."

In the hallway, Cal folded his arms. *Which book, ladies? Don't stop talking now.*

Daisy mused. "What about this cow book?"

Cow book. Cal shook his head in amazement and looked at the ceiling.

Charlotte was impatient. "Oh, for heaven's sake, Daisy. Half the books on that shelf are cow books. Let me see it." She read aloud, *"Historic Sketches of the Cattle Trade of the West and the Southwest.* Ugh. How dull."

Satisfied that he had heard enough, Cal retreated. He took the stairs. Between now and suppertime tonight, he had to think of a way to let the wind out of their sails. Otherwise, he might as well kiss twenty thousand hard-earned dollars good-bye.

18

"Where the hell were you all afternoon?"

Cal had Rachel by the arm, leading her up the steps of the front porch. They had just left the house by the back door on the pretense of taking a moonlight stroll—as if they had ever taken a moonlight stroll yet! Now, he was taking her back in the house, and Rachel was losing patience. "I was exercising my horses. What business is it of yours? And what are you doing, dragging me around in circles like this? I barely got to finish my—"

Cal pulled the front door open. "Rachel, the question was rhetorical. Shut up."

Before she could retort, he pulled her through the threshold into the deserted entrance foyer. The rest of the family was still in the dining room finishing dessert. Cal led her down the hall to her father's study.

He closed the door behind them. Dusk was falling, and Rachel had to squint until her eyes began to adjust to the fading light. "What is going on?"

Cal was already across the room, hunkering down to examine the volumes that lined the bookshelves. Annoyed when he didn't bother to reply, Rachel started for her father's desk. "I'm going to light a lamp."

He swiveled, pointing a finger at her. "No. Sit."

"I am not a dog. I do *not* sit on command."

Cal didn't look up as he thumbed through a book. "If you want the Elena Rose, you'll damn well sit like I tell you to."

Well, he had gotten her attention with *that* statement.

Cal found what he was looking for. He pulled a folded sheet of paper from between the pages of the book. Quickly, he shelved the volume and rose to his feet. "Recognize this?" he asked, holding the sheet up.

As he approached, Rachel's eyes widened and her jaw dropped. "What's *that* doing in *here*?"

"Daisy found it."

Rachel felt faint. "Oh, no. How?"

"Good question." Cal folded the paper into quarters and shoved it into his vest pocket. "But we don't have time to chat about it at the moment." He paused. "Now, will you sit?"

Rachel's knees wobbled. Her head was spinning, threatening to toss her off balance. Oh, she would sit, all right. Sit or faint. Cal caught her elbow and deftly steered her over to a divan in one corner of the room where he sank down beside her.

Rachel mumbled miserably, "It's all over."

"No, it isn't."

She turned to him. "How can you say that? You think she's not going to tell my father everything?"

Cal was unbelievably calm. "No, I'm positive she's going to tell him everything. Tonight, in fact."

"How do you—"

"Long story. You're just going to have to trust me. You still want the Elena Rose, don't you?"

"Of course I want the Elena Rose. What kind of stupid question is that?"

Cal reached up and slipped open the top button of his shirt. "Well, I want that money you promised me, princess, so the way I see it, there's only one thing left to do."

Rachel blinked at him, aghast, as he finished unbuttoning his shirt. He inched over so that he was smack dab up against her on the divan. Rachel stammered, "W-what are you doing?"

"Kiss me."

Her voice rose. *"What? Now?* How can you think about that at a time like this?"

Cal clamped his hand over her mouth and leaned in close to her face. "Kiss me like you mean it."

His hand slid away from her mouth and curved around the back of her neck. Before she could question him, he proceeded to give her a kiss that just about crossed her eyes.

When he lifted his head, Rachel was breathless and more confused than ever. "What is this, Cal? Your way of saying good-bye? Because he's going to kill us both, you know."

He pulled her hairpins free and tossed them to the floor. "We've probably got about two minutes. Not enough time to argue." He started unbuttoning her blouse.

Rachel regained her senses in a hurry and swatted his hand away. *"Cal!"*

He grabbed her wrist. "Trust me, will you?"

"Trust you? Are you crazy? Someone's liable to walk in at any minute!"

He grinned. "Now you've got the idea. We're going to get caught in the clutches."

Rachel barely had time to absorb what he had just said. He was kissing her again, taking her breath away. She felt a slight tugging, then her blouse fell open. Heedlessly surrendering to the spirit of the moment, she let her arms slip around his neck. *Wait a minute. Did he say . . . he wanted to get . . . caught?*

She pushed him away. "We can't!"

"Rachel, we've lived together for almost a month now, and it's been pure hell."

She stared at that incredibly sensual mouth before raising her eyes to lose herself in his gaze. And how was she supposed to think straight with his thigh all pressed up against hers? "Hell," she repeated after him vaguely, trying to recall what they had been talking about.

"Are we going to let all that pain and misery go to waste?" The corners of his mouth tilted up. "Isn't it worth at least one quick grope in the dark to try to save it?"

"A quick what?"

His smile widened as one hand dropped to her waist and slipped around back, unhooking her skirt. Then he was kissing her again, demanding a response. She responded. His other hand was already beneath her blouse, his palm gliding lightly over the tip of one breast.

Rachel couldn't help it. Her body thrilled to his touch. She closed her eyes as he urged her down to a half-reclining position beneath him. The chain to her locket snapped, and it promptly slid down inside her chemise. "My locket!" she gasped. "It fell down my—"

"I'll get it."

Before she could protest, he reached up to slip the top buttons of her chemise. It was not her practice to wear a restricting corset beneath her riding habit, and she had not bothered to don one for supper, either. Now, there was nothing to discourage Cal's explorations as he bent his head to nibble a delightful path down her neck to the opening of her chemise.

Rachel swallowed a tiny squeal when she felt his mouth, his tongue, searching playfully between her breasts. He hadn't shaved since this morning, and the brushing tickle of his beard against her sensitive skin was, surprisingly, not at all unpleasant.

When he raised his head again, the locket chain gleamed in his teeth. Grinning, he let it drop to her chest. "If he's going to kill us, I, for one, can't think of a better way to—" He stopped and tilted his head, listening. Then, Rachel heard it too. Voices in the hallway.

Cal whispered, "Show time." Then, his lips slanted down to brush back and forth over hers. "Let's make this good."

It's already good, Rachel thought as he claimed her again. She closed her eyes and let her hands slide up over his chest.

She was barely aware of the voices in the hallway as they neared. It might have been Daisy and her father or Charlotte or just Daisy. She didn't care. If this was to be the last of it . . . well, then, so be it.

The door opened, spilling a stream of light onto the carpet of the study. Rachel's eyes flew open, and Cal lifted his head.

"What the . . . ? Who's there?" Galen paused. "Cal? Rachel?"

Charlotte's voice. "What's going on?"

A lamp flared to life, illuminating the room. Galen's expression was . . . well, Rachel wasn't quite sure. She had never seen that particular look on her father's face before.

"*What the dickens!* I thought you two were going for a walk! You didn't get too far, did you?"

Cal sat up, feigning surprise. "Galen! We weren't expecting—"

"*I can see that!*" he bellowed. "Don't you two have a room for that sort of thing?"

Rachel didn't have to falsify her own mortification. She knew her cheeks were flaming scarlet—as much from what had been going on before the door opened as from what was taking place at this moment. "Oh! Oh, Daddy! I can explain!"

She struggled to sit up and pull the front of her blouse together at the same time. Her hands flew up too late to catch the locket before it slipped down between her breasts again. Galen's brows drew down into a deep V as he watched his daughter grope about for the lost trinket.

Charlotte clutched at her throat and looked as if she were about to suffer an apoplexy. "Well! I never!"

Galen threw her an annoyed look. "It's probably been a while, at any rate, Charlotte."

"This is outrageous!" Daisy stood in the doorway, staring at Rachel and Cal as if they had suddenly grown an extra set of heads.

Cal buttoned up his shirt. "We just got a little carried away is all. No harm done."

Rachel gave up on fishing for her lost locket and started buttoning her gaping blouse with trembling hands.

Daisy was livid. "This is a grand farce!"

Galen started for the door. "Well, it's something, all right, but farce isn't quite the word I had in mind."

"No!" Daisy started hopping up and down. "Don't you see? They're lying! They're trying to fool us!"

Galen looked at Daisy as if she had lost her senses.

Rachel rose to her feet too fast. She felt her skirt start to slither down over her hips and caught it just in time. "Get her out of here!"

Daisy grabbed Charlotte's arm. "Tell him! Tell him!"

Charlotte appeared to be suffering from the effects of an intestinal gas bubble. "Well, I—I hardly know where to begin."

"What's this all about?" Galen demanded.

Seeing that Charlotte was going to be useless, Daisy flew across the room to the bookshelves. "This! This is what it's all about!" She pulled a thick volume from the shelf and threw Rachel a triumphant glance as she flipped it open.

"What is it, Daisy?" Galen demanded gruffly. "You want to borrow a book?"

"*No!*" Daisy started to thumb through the pages faster and faster. "It was here!"

Galen looked to Charlotte. "What's the matter with her?"

Charlotte's eyes were still glazed. She didn't answer.

Daisy turned the book upside down, gripping the front cover with one hand and the back cover with the other. She shook the book frantically. "It was here!"

Nick stuck his head in the door. "What's going on?"

"Good question!" Galen blustered. "I've got a houseful of crazy women and a son-in-law who can't keep his pants on long enough to make it up the stairs!"

By now, Daisy was shaking the book so hard it was a miracle the spine stayed intact. "It was here!"

Galen pushed by Charlotte in disgust. "I'm going to my room. Obviously my study isn't sacred anymore."

Nick wrested the book from Daisy. "Have you gone mad?"

Daisy's face glowed bright pink. "I had it! The contract!" She whirled and pointed a finger at Cal and Rachel. "They planned this! I don't know how they did it, but they did it!"

Nick took her by the arm. "Calm down."

"I will *not* calm down!"

Rachel couldn't help feeling some sense of satisfaction as she dropped to her hands and knees to gather the scattered hairpins. She had been humiliated, true, but out of it, she had gained the heretofore unmatched satisfaction of seeing Daisy Parker reduced to a blathering, raving lunatic. All in all a pretty fair deal.

Nick wrapped a firm arm around his wife's shoulders and forcibly escorted her from the room. "You're going upstairs to lie down until you get over this."

As Daisy's shrill ranting began to fade, Charlotte stood like a block of ice in the center of the study. Upstairs, Nick closed their bedroom door, and it grew quiet.

The wall clock ticked.

Rachel rose to her feet, blowing an errant curl from in front of her eyes. She smiled sweetly at her aunt. "Well?"

Charlotte was clearly not amused. "Well, Rachel, with the help of your 'husband' here, it looks like you've managed to pull off another humdinger."

Rachel didn't bother to reply.

Charlotte turned to leave, but she paused by the

door before stepping out into the empty corridor. "Rest assured, though, dear, this isn't over yet."

Rachel waited a few moments before scurrying over to the door to see that everyone was gone. She turned back to Cal, clapping one hand over her mouth. "I think we did it."

"Well, I think we gave Daisy just enough rope to hang herself with. For now, at least."

"Cal, I can't believe it!"

"I told you to trust me."

"But how did you know?"

He raked splayed fingers through his hair, tousling it, wearing a devilish grin that caused Rachel's elated heart to flutter. "I just happened to be in the right place at the right time, but if I were you, I'd stick closer to the house to keep an eye on those two."

Rachel thought about this for a minute.

Cal crossed the room to the door. "I swear, Rachel, your family is worse than a nest of vipers."

She smiled coyly. "If you can't take the heat . . ."

"Stay out of the kitchen," Cal finished. "Right. But nobody warned me ahead of time, did they?" He winked. "By the way, princess, you look a mess. Tuck that blouse in before you end up embarrassing yourself, will you?"

Rachel reined in beside Cal, her gelding stamping restlessly beneath her. Behind them, to the south, the sun was still shining. Ahead of them, dark clouds billowed and swelled on the horizon. The soft breezes were already turning cold and picking up speed as they swept across the grassy range.

"This is a fine kettle of fish," Cal muttered, nudging his hat back to peer at the darkening sky.

"If it wasn't so late in the year, I'd swear it was a norther blowing in," Rachel replied.

Cal turned to her wearing a look that clearly communicated the opinion that this foul weather was somehow her fault. "Some day off. This whole thing was your father's idea, you know."

Rachel didn't dare utter the words that were on the tip of her tongue. *Her father's intentions had been good.*

"Due to the, er, uh, incident in my study the other night—" Galen had begun, casting his eyes from the floor to the desktop to the ceiling and back again, anywhere but at his beet-red daughter and smirking son-in-law—"It has occurred to me that, as newlyweds, perhaps the two of you could use some, er, uh . . . privacy, uh, that is, time alone together."

Rachel hastened to intervene. "Oh, I don't think—"

Galen cut her off, raising his eyes for the first time to clash with hers. "You two didn't see fit to take a wedding trip at the time, but maybe now—"

Cal intervened this time. "Galen, I don't think—"

Rachel jumped in. "Now just wouldn't be a good time."

"There's so much work to do," Cal added.

"We couldn't possibly—"

"Maybe another time."

"Yes," Rachel said brightly. "Maybe after fall roundup."

Galen studied the pair of them grimly. "Well, it's delightful to see you two agreeing on something for a change, but that's beside the point. I'm afraid I must insist you take a day off. Two days would be even better."

"Two?" Rachel echoed. "Two *days?*"

Galen smiled. "Two days. I don't want to see either

of you lifting a finger around here, is that understood?"

Cal folded his arms and looked up at the ceiling.

Rachel was horrified. "But what are we supposed to do?"

Galen raised both hands. "How the hell do I know? I never took a day off in my life!"

"Daddy!"

Galen continued, grinning like a crocodile as he addressed Cal, "You haven't been out to the north end, have you?"

"No, Galen, I haven't."

"Well, there you go, pumpkin. If I remember correctly, those are your old stamping grounds," he said to his daughter. "Why don't you take Cal out there? Pack a dinner! Hell, pack your supper, too! It'll take you half a day just to ride out and back, won't it?"

And it had. It was midafternoon. They were already much too far from the ranch house to make it back before the weather caught up with them. Cal looked at her expectantly as the wind whipped Rachel's hair about her shoulders. She pushed a strand from her face and glared at him. "What?"

"You didn't happen to bring a couple of rain slickers along, did you?"

"No, I didn't. It was perfectly beautiful this morning when we left. Did you?"

He shook his head and looked back at the darkening skies.

Rachel reached down to pat her restless mount. "There's a line cabin about a mile from here. We could wait it out there."

Cal urged Friday forward. "Let's go."

They pushed their mounts into a gallop. Still, they

were riding due north, directly into the storm, and it wasn't long before Rachel felt the first smattering of raindrops sting her face. By the time they reached the tiny cabin, the late afternoon had turned to midnight, and the rain poured down in sheets. A flash of lightning slashed the heavens and a roll of thunder followed.

They secured the horses along the south side of the cabin to shield them from the gusting north wind. When they threw open the cabin door, Rachel's teeth were chattering. Between the wind and her soaked clothes, she was chilled to the bone.

Cal peered bleakly at the dingy interior. There were two windows, one on either side of the cabin, both covered with thin sheets of cured rawhide rather than pane glass. On a sunny day, these sheets admitted a rosy glow of sunlight to cheer the one-room shack. On a day like today, it was dark as a tomb.

Cal took off his hat and observed wryly as rainwater poured from its brim to the warped puncheon floor. "Great idea your father had. Take the day off. Have yourselves a picnic."

Rachel bent to wring out the hem of her riding skirt. "Will you please stop dragging my father into this?"

Water trickled from a dozen leaks in the roof. Cal replaced his hat and sighed. "All the comforts of home."

Rachel straightened. "Oh, *this* coming from the man who lives in the saddle, the man who camps out in the desert."

Cal ignored her sarcasm. "Is there anything around to shed some light on the subject?"

"There should be a lantern on the table. If not, there're some candles in a trunk next to the fireplace."

"You know the layout pretty well."

"I come up here from time to time."

Cal slapped their saddlebags down on a small table near the door. "Do you, now?"

"Sometimes," Rachel said, her eyes narrowing pointedly, "I need to get away from certain people."

Cal felt inside his vest pocket. "My matches are soaked."

Rachel moved to the fireplace, then knelt and flipped open the trunk, the same trunk she had brought up here four years ago. It held everything she needed for a stay of several days: candles, matches, playing cards, books, blankets, soap, toothwash, even a bottle of sherry.

Within seconds, the kerosene lamp was lit. Not that it helped much. The line cabin wasn't exactly a palace. The furniture was old—a sawbuck table for dining, four three-legged stools, a waist-high cupboard box, and a straw-filled mattress atop a bed of boards built into one corner.

Still, Rachel liked the place. She'd thought of it as her own personal retreat ever since she was a child and came here to play house on her own. Her father had never been as furious with her since. Lord, those days seemed so long ago now.

Cal cut into her thoughts. "Are there any pots or pans?"

"In the cupboard by the fireplace. Why?"

Cal was already kneeling by the open box, rummaging around. "You'll see." After a moment, he rose to his feet with an armful of pots and pans. He placed them around the room at strategic points. Soon, the cabin was filled by the *rat-a-tat-tatting* of raindrops splashing into metal containers.

Cal brushed his hands together triumphantly. "That should do. Now for a fire. That is, if I can find any dry wood."

"Most of it's outside, but there should be some stacked in the corner behind the door."

"Why don't you unpack the food while I get this started?"

That sounded like a good idea. Rachel was starved. She pulled up a stool and unbuckled the saddlebags.

Cal's voice was nonchalant as he struck a match. "I see you've organized this little sanctuary to suit yourself."

Rachel's mouth watered as she unwrapped the food. Cold fried chicken, apple pie, and biscuits. "And why not?" she asked, pulling out a bottle of white wine and examining it closely. "I spend more time here than the ranch hands. We haven't had problems with rustlers in years, and most of the cattle are grazing on the south end this time of year."

By the time Rachel had set their food and utensils out, she turned to see Cal poking fledgling embers to life. She crossed the room to stand next to him, starting to feel a welcome warmth seep into her bones.

After he got the fire going strong, he stood. "That should improve our circumstances." He reached up to unbutton his shirt.

Rachel's eyes widened. "What are you doing?"

"I don't know about you, but I'm not going to stand around all soaking wet when we've got a nice fire going."

Rachel observed indecisively as Cal shrugged off first his vest then his shirt. He had a point. She would have liked nothing better at this moment than to shed her wringing-wet blouse and riding skirt, but . . .

Cal was on the floor, tugging off his boots. "Are there any blankets?"

Blankets! Of course! Why hadn't she thought of that? She pointed to the trunk as Cal stood to climb out of his denims.

While Cal's back was turned, Rachel stripped down to her chemise and pantalettes. It wasn't long before she felt a blanket roll smack her in the behind. She turned to see Cal wearing a cocky grin. "Let's eat."

They huddled in their blankets as they ate chicken and drank wine from tin cups. They listened to the rolling thunder and howling wind as it battered the cabin, and Rachel started to relax. Maybe it was the food. Or maybe it was the feeling of peaceful solitude that always crept over her when she was here. Or maybe it was just the wine. Whatever it was, it was good.

When they were finished, the rain still showed no sign of abating. Cal rose from his stool, his cup in one hand. "It looks like we're going to be stuck here for a while. We might as well make the best of it."

He sauntered over to the fireplace and knelt down by her trunk. "What else do you keep in this little treasure chest of yours, princess?"

She poured herself the last of the wine. "Lots of things."

Cal perused the contents. After a moment, he let out a low whistle. He pulled out the sherry bottle and held it up tauntingly. "What have we here, Rachel Elena? Could it be the very proper Miss Girard is a closet tippler?"

"That's strictly for medicinal purposes."

"Oh, sure it is. Sure it is." He set the bottle down on the floor and pulled out a book. "Now, what's this?"

"It helps to pass the time."

"I know all about passing time, Rachel. So, tell me, what's the best book you ever read?"

Rachel took a tentative sip of her wine. She let it slide down her throat to tickle her stomach. "*Alice's Adventures in Wonderland.*"

"A children's story?" Cal looked up doubtfully.

"You've heard of it?"

He chuckled and returned to searching through the contents of the trunk. "Mock turtles, mad hatters, and white rabbits with watches . . . tsk, tsk, tsk."

Rachel smiled, feeling her oats by now, refusing to be baited. "Quid pro quo, Delaney. Do you have a favorite?"

"No question about it," he replied. "*The Life and Strange Surprising Adventures of Robinson Crusoe.*"

Somehow Rachel wasn't surprised that his favorite story would be about a man marooned alone on a desert island. She had a feeling Cal had been marooned on his own personal desert island for quite some time now.

"Finally, something useful," he said, waving the deck of playing cards over his head.

"I use them to play solitaire."

Cal slammed the trunk lid closed. "Well, you're not going to play solitaire tonight, princess."

"What do you propose?"

"I propose," he said, dropping his blanket to the floor and spreading it out before the fireplace, "a game of draw poker. Just you and me. May the best man win."

He wore only his drawers and his socks. Rachel tried not to think about the broad expanse of his chest. She wrinkled her nose, disturbed. "Poker? That's gambling."

"You better believe it."

"What are we going to play for?"

Cal chuckled wickedly. "How about your virginity?"

Rachel rose from her stool. "You can be so crude sometimes."

"You know what? Daisy's right about one thing. You have no sense of humor."

"I do so have a sense of humor."

"You, Rachel, are no fun."

"Well, look at the pot calling the kettle black. You don't exactly belong in a circus yourself."

"Maybe it's the company I've been keeping."

"Oh, really? Maybe it's the other way around. Did you ever think of that?"

"What, me? I have a sense of humor, Rachel. It's just a little more subtle than most."

Rachel clutched her blanket around her shoulders, sniffing indignantly. "Subtle. So that's what you call it."

"You see, the difference between you and me is that I know how to relax. I know how to let off steam."

"Well, I'm afraid your method of letting off steam is not an option for respectable women."

Cal shuffled the deck absently. "That's not what I was talking about."

"Oh. Well, that's a switch."

He stopped. "See? There it is right there. That prissy attitude of yours. Maybe you should relax and let the starch out of your corset every once in a while."

"Let the starch out of my corset? Well, for your information, I could let off steam as well as the next fella if I had a mind to. I just don't have a mind to, that's all."

"My point exactly."

"All right! All right!" Rachel stamped across the room and settled down opposite him on the blanket. "Get out that bottle of sherry and pass out the cards!"

He looked at her like she was an idiot. "*Pass out* the cards?"

"Well, what do *you* call it?"

Cal tossed a card facedown on the blanket in front of her. "I call it dealing. You deal the cards, Rachel."

He dealt them each five, set the deck down, and picked up his hand. He mulled silently as he rearranged his cards. Rachel watched him and did the same.

After a moment, he looked at her. "Well?"

"Well what?" Rachel asked back cautiously.

"How many do you want?"

"How many what?"

Cal squinted dubiously. "You don't know how to play, do you?"

"You might have to refresh my memory."

A slow smile curved his lips. "Are you sure we can't play for your virginity?"

"Just shut up and teach me the game. We'll play for matchsticks."

Cal uncorked the sherry bottle and poured them each a healthy portion. "Divide up the matchsticks, princess. We'll ante up one a piece. I can see this is going to be a loooong night."

19

It was black outside. The wind had died down, and the fierce, pelting rain had changed to a light, steady patter on the roof. The corners of the cabin crouched in dark shadow, but the fire in the hearth burned low and warm, cozying the center of the room and transforming the interior from a shabby, broken down shack into a comfortable, homey nest.

Rachel peered at the cards in her hand. Her matchstick pile was dwindling. Cal's looked like Mount Olympus. She picked up her cup, sipped at her sherry, and set it down again. She felt a bit light in the head.

Cal's patience was stretching thin. "How many, Rachel?"

He had explained the basics of the game to her a number of times already. *Easy as falling off a log*, he had said. *Straight flush beats fours beats a full house beats a doohickey beats a thingamabob beats a hickeymadoodle*. She had listened carefully as he had then explained strategy, trying her darnedest to hold it all in her head. Having always been bright, it was a point of pride that most new concepts need not be explained more than once, but tonight . . . well, tonight was different.

She bit her lip. "Did you say that three of a kind beats a full house or that a full house beats three of a kind?"

He spoke through his teeth. "Full house beats three of a kind. How many?"

"Two," Rachel said, then, "No, wait. Three."

Cal moved to draw three cards.

"No, wait. Two."

"Are you sure?"

Rachel nodded, not sure at all. "Absolutely."

He muttered something under his breath.

Rachel changed her mind. "Wait a minute. Make that three." She threw down another card.

"Rachel, you can't—"

Just then, a fat water drop splattered onto the card deck from the ceiling. This was soon followed by another. Then another. Cal peered slowly upward.

"Maybe it's a sign we should quit," Rachel offered hopefully.

Cal picked up the deck and slid his tin cup over to catch the new leak. It lined up perfectly. *Dop! Dop! Dop!*

He threw his cards down. "Maybe it is at that."

Rachel threw in too. "I guess you've had better days off."

Cal gathered up the deck. "Oh, I don't know. If we played a while longer, I might have earned enough matchsticks to build me a fair-sized homestead."

Rachel let this harmless gloating slide as she gathered her blanket around her shoulders. "It's dark, it's wet, it's cold, and the roof leaks."

Cal set the deck aside and stretched his legs. "This is nothing. Try living in a sod house on a rainy day. Everything gets soaked. It leaks for days after a good rain."

Rachel looked at Cal quizzically. This comment, offered up voluntarily and out of the blue, was out of character for him.

He continued, his fathomless eyes taking on a far-away look, a *remembering* look. "We'd have to hang out all of our clothes and bed linens to dry. If the rain was coming from the north, like it is now, we'd have to move everything to the south side of the house to keep it from getting wet." He stopped abruptly, his gaze refocusing, pulling back into the present.

"Where did you live?"

Cal seemed to weigh this question carefully before answering. "On the plains outside of Lawrence."

Rachel pushed one step farther. "Were you born there?"

"No. My parents came from Ohio when I was six."

"Did you travel by covered wagon?"

Cal wondered what it was about women that made them want to pick and probe beneath the surface. "We took a steamer up the Missouri River," he said. "I don't remember much except that the boat was crowded. I seem to recall sleeping on the floor most of the time. I liked that part of it. My sister hated it."

"Jessica?"

"Yes."

Rachel spoke softly. "I've often wondered what it would've been like to have a sister."

"I had two sisters. Jessica and Rebecca. Rebecca was the baby. She took sick and died young."

"It must've been terrible."

In his mind's eye, Cal pictured the tiny grave behind the hay shed. "It almost killed my mother. My father had quite a time with it too. We all did, I suppose."

Rachel's exotic green eyes were soft and lambent in the glow of the fire. Soft with pity, he thought. Cal looked away as silence descended between them like a sheer curtain. He despised pity. He didn't want it, not from Rachel, not from anyone.

After a long pause, she spoke again. "Tell me about what you're planning to do with your money."

Cal looked up, surprised she had chosen to change the subject. "The twenty thousand?"

Rachel nodded, sipping at the sherry in her cup.

"Get a place of my own."

"And raise cattle?"

"I'm not sure yet."

Rachel studied him curiously. "Are you ever going to get married again?"

Cal gave her a wry smile. "After this? How could anything else compare?"

"I'm serious. Don't you want a family?"

"Don't you?"

Rachel swirled the liquid in her cup. "I guess I have enough family to deal with as it is."

"I have to agree with you there."

"You didn't answer my question."

Her question. *Don't you want a family?* What for? Just so some hand of fate could descend and, with the flick of one impassive finger, take it all away? Cal's voice hardened. "The answer is no." He turned to the fire, picked up the poker, and nudged a wood scrap.

Rachel couldn't help but feel the cold slap of his words. She fell silent, letting her gaze wander down over the smooth, bronze skin of his back and shoulders, the shifting play of muscle in his arm as he toyed with the burning embers. Her attention fell to where two pale scars contrasted sharply against the natural tan of his skin.

Apparently sensing her scrutiny, he turned his head and caught her eye. Rachel saw that he knew exactly what was going through her mind. Rather than skirt the issue, she decided now was the time to broach it. "How did you get them?"

He looked back into the fire. "It's a long story, Rachel."

"Well, time's one thing we've got plenty of."

He gave her a quick side glance. "I let my guard down. It was stupid, and I almost got killed because of it."

"Was it an outlaw?"

"A guy named Leo Walsh. I spent over a year tracking him down. I was taking him to Dodge to face murder charges."

"He sounds dangerous."

Cal's voice was low, contemplative. "He was garbage. A thief, a rapist, a killer."

"Is that why you kept after him for so long?"

"It was a little more personal than that."

"What happened?"

"We'd stopped at a roadhouse. The owner's daughter served us up some supper, and I saw her looking at Leo. He was flirting with her, egging her on. I'd already searched him for weapons, but I should've done it again after we left that place."

Cal paused. Raindrops thuttered on the roof. Flames crackled in the hearth. "Either she slipped him the knife or he managed to sneak it himself. I don't know. It doesn't matter. The next night we camped out about half a day from Dodge. His hands were tied in front of him, but I loosened the ropes so he could eat. That was my second mistake. Before I knew it, he was on me, fighting like a wildcat. He had nothing to lose, you see. He was facing the rope."

Rachel listened, transfixed, as he continued, "We struggled. With his hands tied, he wouldn't have had a chance, but the knife seemed to come out of nowhere, from up his sleeve most likely."

Cal was staring hard into the fire now, his face a studied blank. "He stabbed me twice. It didn't hurt too bad at first, but I knew it was serious. Blood was everywhere. He knocked me senseless, but only for a few seconds. When I came to, he was taking one of the horses, making a break for it. I assume he was leaving me for dead."

Rachel prodded. "So, he got away?"

"I thought he was going to. I'd been after him for years, and I just couldn't let that happen. I didn't think I was going to live long enough to find him again, you see?" The question hung like an unwelcome visitor in the stillness between them.

"What happened?" Rachel asked.

"He'd taken one of my sidearms, but I still had the other. It was dark. I could barely make him out with my eyes, but I could *hear* him. I really thought I was dying. I thought . . ." Cal hesitated, then shook his head before continuing. "I pulled the trigger and he dropped. Just like that. It was over. He was the first man I ever shot in the back. And the last too."

Cal closed his eyes. "I don't remember anything after that. If some farmer hadn't found us the next morning, I'd probably be dead too."

Rachel remembered Nick's words. *"Quite a few of*

Cal Delaney's catches have been brought in slung over the saddle. Did you know that he once shot a man in the back? And just over a month ago, he nearly killed some cowboy in Dodge City."

She pushed these words away. There was more to this story than Cal was telling her. She was sure of it. "He would've hanged anyway," she said.

Cal opened his eyes, his jaw set. "My job was to bring him in, not execute him."

"But he was getting away. He might have hurt more people before he was caught again."

Cal turned, pinning her with eyes that had turned to shards of blue ice. "Why are you making excuses for me, Rachel?"

"I—I'm not."

"Well, then stop it. You weren't there."

Even as Rachel felt the harshness of his reproach, she knew it was his way of pushing her away again, just as he had when she had awakened him from that awful nightmare. Well, she'd be damned if she was going to just shy away this time. "Is that why you took off your guns and gave up bounty hunting? Because of Leo Walsh?"

"Part of it."

"What was the other part of it?"

Cal tossed the poker aside angrily and stood. "You're just chock full of questions tonight, aren't you?"

"Well, we *are* married. We shouldn't keep so many secrets from one another."

Cal smiled dryly. "Most married people do more than just sleep together in bed. Shall we change the rules on that subject, too?"

Rachel opened her mouth to reply, then closed it

again, gazing up at him with wide eyes. She had given some thought to that subject—quite a lot of thought, actually. Ever since he gave her the locket for her birthday. The plain fact was, Rachel had no intentions of ever marrying again. The very idea of it interfered with her ambitions. Was it to be, then, that she would never experience physical intimacy with a man? Was it to be that she would always have to wonder what all the brouhaha was about?

When she finally sorted through her conflicting emotions, she had come to the logical conclusion that it might be all right to try it—just once—with a man like Cal, a man who was obviously experienced, a man whom she suspected some forthright women might refer to as a skilled lover. Perhaps that would settle the matter for good. Once it was done, she could wash it right out of her hair and get on with more important things, things like running the Elena Rose.

Rachel saw immediately that her hesitation had given her away. A cunning smile played about the corners of his mouth. She felt the color in her cheeks rise all the way to her ears and knew it wasn't just because of the alcohol she had consumed.

She gulped a hearty swallow of sherry to fortify herself. "Well, I've actually given that some thought."

"Have you?"

"Yes and . . well . . ." Rachel set down her cup. Her palms were sweating. "I thought if we were to . . ."

"Yes?"

Was he deliberately trying to make this difficult? Rachel began again. "That is, if we were to consider . . ." She ran out of words and her throat went dry. This was not coming out very well at all.

"Have sex?"

Rachel winced. "Must you use that word?"

"All right, let's see . . . nice words . . ." He seemed to be thinking. "How about, a roll in the hay? Tumble between the sheets?"

Rachel covered her face. "Why did I even say anything?"

Cal hunkered down beside her. "How about cohabit?"

Rachel peered at him from between her fingers. He was grinning, enjoying her embarrassment. She dropped her hands and took a deep breath to re-collect her dignity. "Cohabit. That will do just fine. Thank you."

"You're welcome."

Rachel picked up her cup and tipped it back to finish the rest of the sherry. Good heavens! She was feeling warm all over. She tried to clear her head before she continued. "As I was saying, if we were to cohabit just once . . . well then, perhaps it would be . . . acceptable." She turned her head only to clash unexpectedly with his intense blue gaze. His face was only inches from hers. She squinted at him fuzzily.

"Just . . . once?" he inquired seriously.

Rachel nodded. There. It was out. He seemed to be thinking this over, and she waited.

His gaze dropped briefly to her chest, where the blanket had slipped down below her shoulders, and Rachel was quick to tug it back up to her neck.

"Should we add an addendum?" he asked.

Rachel was confused. "Add a dendum?"

He smiled. "Add an addendum to our agreement."

"Oh! A dendum! I mean, an addendum. Well, I don't think that will be necessary . . . not if we, well, shake hands on it."

He scrutinized her face before offering her his hand. "Shake."

Rachel grasped his hand. It was warm and strong and dry, unlike hers, which was cold and clammy and limp. Even as they shook once, very businesslike, Rachel wondered if she might not have just made a very big mistake.

Cal dropped her hand, then leaned forward to touch his nose to hers. Rachel's eyes crossed as she tried to focus. "Rachel," he said, "you are knee-walking drunk."

She pushed him away, insulted. "I am certainly . . . most certainly not!"

He tumbled back to a sitting position, starting to laugh. "You most certainly are!"

Rachel gaped at him, abashed and indignant. He thought she was drunk, did he? Why, he wasn't even taking her seriously! "Don't laugh at me!"

"Oh, Jesus, princess! You're really pickled! Are you ever going to hate yourself in the morning!"

Rachel glared, simmering to boil. She wanted to bash him over the head with something very hard and very heavy. Forgetting her modesty, she let her blanket drop as she sprang at him, swinging. "Damn you, Cal!"

He was laughing so hard he barely caught her fist before tumbling backward beneath the onslaught of her attack. Rachel tried to twist away from his grip, but he wasn't letting go.

"You weasel!" She swung with her left, but he caught that one too.

He grinned up at her from his supine position. "Honey, you don't know what you're doing!"

She pulled back with all her might, but his grip only

tightened. Rachel now realized she was straddling Cal's hips—a very unladylike, extremely compromising position. It was obvious by the glint in his eye that he was enjoying her predicament, too, and that only made her madder.

She blew a wayward curl out of her face and tossed her head haughtily. "I absolutely positively despise you, Cal Delaney. The thought that I might have let you touch me sickens my stomach."

He lifted a brow. "Are you sure it isn't just all that wine mixing with the sherry?"

"You've ruined my life."

"Have I?"

"Everything used to go so smoothly. I knew what to expect when I woke up in the morning. My days were planned and rational and orderly. My *life* was planned and rational and orderly."

"So stop fighting me every inch of the way."

"Me? It's you! Even now, when I tell you—" she fumbled, embarrassed, "when I tell you . . . well, what I told you, you throw it back in my face. You laugh!"

Cal's smile slowly faded. "I just want to make sure you know your own mind, Rachel."

She stared down at him as her anger slowly seeped away. When she spoke, her voice was tremulous, utterly betraying her. "I haven't known my own mind since the day I walked into the Red Panther Saloon."

Cal's grip on her wrists relaxed, but he didn't release her. "I think that makes two of us."

Rachel's gaze traveled down the length of his torso, then back up again. When their eyes locked, Cal spoke. "You're treading in dangerous territory, Mrs. Delaney."

Rachel felt a tingling sensation in the pit of her

stomach. She licked dry lips and plucked up her nerve. "That's *your* opinion, Mr. Delaney."

Cal didn't answer. He studied her face, then tugged on her wrists, pulling her down to him. Their mouths barely touched at first. Lips whispered over lips, tentative and exploring. Restless for more, Rachel opened to him, inviting him to taste her, slowly, lazily, before their tongues finally mated and mingled.

He dropped her wrists. Rachel felt his palm glide over her breast, and a delicious shiver shot through her. His kiss deepened as he cupped her there, his thumb playing circles over the crest until Rachel thought she couldn't stand it anymore.

She felt him growing hard beneath her, between her legs where they touched through what little remained of their clothing, and she let out a little gasp as he palmed her left hip to better press her body against his. A slight thrust of his hips, and Rachel's belly contracted as a startling rush of heat came from deep inside of her.

She surrendered the last of her inhibitions, placing her palms flat on the floor and pushing up, locking her elbows to take her weight. Feeling drugged, she closed her eyes, and a tiny, involuntary sound escaped her lips. It was something between a sigh and a moan, a sound of sensual pleasure. Although she had no experience, she felt his need with each gentle thrust of his hips and instinctively moved with him.

Never in her wildest dreams had she imagined herself feeling this way, *acting* this way. Then again, never in her wildest dreams had she imagined desire springing to life, coiling tight and sinuous like a waking serpent deep in the pit of her stomach. It made her forget herself. It made her not care.

He groaned and sat up, his voice ragged. "That's it." He slipped the buttons of her chemise. "Honey, I don't care if you shoot me in the morning." Cal hooked his thumbs into the waist of her chemise and started to ease it up.

Rachel lifted her arms as he slid it off in one smooth motion, tossing it over his shoulder into the shadows behind him. He bent his head to touch his mouth to one breast, exquisitely teasing, then suckling. Rachel clenched her teeth and gripped his shoulders as his fingers stroked the bare skin of her back. His touch was so light, so gentle, it was hard to believe these same hands were just as capable of violence.

She struggled to banish this treacherous thought. This was Cal. He was no more a murderer than her own father. Both had killed men—her father during the war, Cal in a line of work that pitted him against ruthless men who killed for greed or bloodlust.

By the time Cal took her by the shoulders and eased her down onto her back, any last minute doubts Rachel might have had about giving herself to her husband were gone. Tugging impatiently at her pantalettes, he pushed them down over her hips, and she quite willingly shed them.

He drank in the sight of her, lush and naked except for the golden locket that gleamed at her delicate throat. Beautiful. She had been created for a man's pleasure. It was almost inconceivable to him that he was to be her first.

Cal quickly divested himself of what remained of his clothing before he moved over her again, bending to claim full, wine-red lips, tasting her eager tongue as his hands roved over the soft satin skin of her belly and the ripe fullness of her breasts, caressing, playing, petting, allowing her awakening arousal to stoke his own. He feasted on the slender column of her throat, her shoulders, her breasts, tasting damp, salty flesh and marveling at the sweet, subtle scent of roses that was Rachel.

He grasped her hips, his mouth playing down, down over the sensitive skin of her navel, down to where he would taste of her most intimately. Hooking one hand beneath her knee, he urged it up and to the side, opening her. She writhed and let out a sharp, startled gasp when his tongue found her essence.

Her thighs clamped together, closing him off, and Cal indulged her modesty, lifting his head. Next time, he thought, moving up over her again to kiss mumbled protests from her lips, for he had already discredited the possibility that this would take place only once between them.

He whispered in her ear. "Relax. Stop thinking so much."

Her eyes were closed, her words breathless. "I can't."

Cal had avoided virgins in the past, but Rachel was different. He had wanted her from the first moment he set eyes on her. And he wanted her to want him.

He whispered again, "Just let yourself go, and trust me a little." And he meant every word as he caressed her thighs, inching his way between them to part her legs and capture her soft heat in his palm. He kissed her neck and her breasts, keenly attuned to her body's responses, as he began to stroke her with practiced fingers.

Very soon, she grasped his shoulders and her hips rose slightly. When she suddenly tensed beneath him, he covered her mouth with his, drinking in and swallowing the tiny cry that came from deep within her throat.

For Rachel, time stopped. She was nothing more substantial than a butterfly's wing. Then, reality began to slowly re-form around her, and she realized she was drenched and trembling.

Her eyes fluttered open. In the ghostly, incandescent light, Cal was positioned above her, spreading her thighs with his knees. He lowered his mouth to hers, then trailed kisses down the length of her jaw to her throat. "Hold on to me, Rachel."

Still in a euphoric haze, she rewound her arms around his neck just before she felt the first painful pressure of him entering her. She tried to wriggle away. "Wait . . . I can't."

But he had her pinned. Escape was out of the question. His breath was ragged, but his voice was steady. "Yes, you can. You were made for me, Rachel."

She closed her eyes and clung to him, wishing fervently that she had never gotten herself into this, wishing . . . This thought barely had time to shoot through her mind. In one bold stroke, he simultaneously tore her and somehow completed her, penetrating, then easing very deep inside of her.

Rachel gulped in a rush of air as he stopped and waited, giving her thrumming heart a chance to slow. She hugged him tight as the pain started to ebb and a blossoming sense of pleasure began to replace it.

He kissed her. "That's the only time I'll ever hurt you."

Then he moved inside of her, thrusting slowly at first. Her pain all but forgotten, Rachel moved with him, falling mindlessly into his quickening rhythm.

Soon, he stopped, tensing as he let out a low groan of release. She trailed her fingers along the length of his sweat-dampened back, feeling a secret thrill that, even in her inexperience, she had somehow managed to satisfy him.

He buried his face in her hair and eased some of his weight down onto her. She accepted him gladly, reveling in his heat from top to toe. After a moment, he lifted his head and gazed down at her in the waning firelight. He wore a small, self-satisfied smile. "Are you still so sure you only want to do this *once*?"

Rachel refused to rise to the bait. She was aglow all over. She couldn't have sparred with him at this moment any more than she could have tossed his six-foot frame across the room. Instead, she accepted the lingering kiss that followed. With regret, she felt him ease out of her.

To compensate, he wrapped his arms around her and rolled onto his back, pulling her with him. They kissed, side by side, their limbs intertwined, for a long time. Finally, Cal sighed, pulling back. "Ah, yes, *that* was worth waiting for."

He sat up and rearranged Rachel's discarded blanket to cover them. When he lay back down again, she rested her head on his shoulder, closing her eyes for the last time. She basked in the halo of the fire, warm and snug as a caterpillar in its winter cocoon. Safe.

She yawned. "Dolores was right."

"Dolores?"

"Mmmmm." Rachel nodded. "It's *not* like what goes on in the corral."

She felt a rumbling vibration in his chest as he laughed out loud. "I hope not."

Rachel smiled. "She told me that if I was lucky, it would last longer."

He kissed the top of her head. "You really have a way of pumping up a man's confidence, Rachel."

She frowned, not sure what he was referring to. "What?"

His fingers were in her hair, stroking absently. It felt rapturous. Rachel wanted to melt into him, fall asleep forever right here in his arms. She barely heard his reply.

"You made me wait too long for you, Rachel. Next time, you'll find out what she was talking about."

Next time. She felt herself dropping off, her thoughts floating free. *"You were made for me, Rachel."* He had said that, hadn't he? In those brief, sweet, fleeting moments just before sinking into a dreamless sleep, Rachel knew that he was right.

Daisy's eyes were closed, but she wasn't sleeping. She was afraid to move lest she rouse Nick, who was finally dozing off by her side.

She opened her eyes to peer at her husband. The light was sparse, only a dusting of moonlight filtering through the window curtains, but she had her night vision by now. His handsome features were relaxed, his breathing shallow and regular. Only a little while yet.

Daisy was getting nervous. Maybe in a little while it would be too late. Maybe waiting even one more minute would make it too late. These thoughts made her stomach twist into new, even tighter knots of worry, and she almost whimpered aloud. Land's sake! It was Tuesday. She hadn't been prepared. What on earth had possessed him to bother with her on a Tuesday?

Daisy closed her eyes again only to be besieged by images of herself waddling down Main Street with a lump the size of a watermelon beneath her skirt. That was horrible enough. She tried not to contemplate the idea of forcing anything that size out between her legs.

Oh, she had heard stories all right. How many times had her mother told her giving birth felt like someone had been ripping her insides out? And Daisy had heard the proof of these words for herself. She had once walked by Lacey Holloway's house on her way home from school only to hear Lacey's mother, who was birthing her eighth or ninth child, wailing and screaming just *exactly* like someone who was having her insides ripped out. Why, some women even died giving birth—died in a pool of blood and agony.

Daisy's eyes popped open again, her heart hammering in her chest. She was perspiring beneath the light cotton material of her nightdress. No, no, no, she wasn't ready yet. She wasn't altogether sure she would ever be ready. But Nick was a man, and he would never understand. Better that he think her barren. Better that he think she wanted children as badly as he. Perhaps someday Daisy would be able to face the idea, but for now she was quite certain she had done the right thing in going to Lacey Holloway for help.

Daisy lay still for another endless minute, listening to her own heart chatter, grinding her teeth and contemplating what it must feel like to bleed to death. Finally, she couldn't stand it any longer. Very slowly, very carefully, she slid out of bed.

She reached for her wrapper and tiptoed across the darkened bedchamber. Her hand was on the door latch when Nick's voice froze the blood in her veins.

"Where are you going at this hour, love?"

Love. He never called her love. Not anymore, anyway. Daisy whirled, clutching the wrapper about her waist in fists. "Why, Nick," she said, swallowing sand, "I thought you were asleep."

"Where are you going?"

One of Daisy's hands fluttered up nervously to pat at loose curls. "I was just going to, uh, freshen up." She was hoping he would take her words to mean she needed to visit the privy and leave it at that.

But Nick sat up in bed. She heard him strike a match, and the room was suddenly flooded in lamp light. "Well, in that case," he began, leaning over to yank open the nightstand drawer, "you'll probably be needing this."

Daisy's mouth fell open in astonishment when she saw what he withdrew. A female syringe! The one and same item she had first purchased from Lacey Holloway almost twelve months before! How had he found out?

"What—what's that?" she asked shakily.

"Are you telling me it's not yours?"

"I—I . . . Where did you find it?"

"I found it in the washroom in the closet tucked beneath your personal towels. Is there something you'd like to tell me?"

"Well, I . . . It's just such a personal item, Nick."

"More personal than what we were just doing?"

"It's just that I—Well, it's a matter of personal cleanliness, not something a woman feels comfortable discussing with a man, not even her husband." Daisy tried to calm her thumping heart. She was well aware the best lies were those that stuck closest to the truth.

"I assume, then, you had no idea that the use of this item goes a long way toward preventing children."

Daisy widened her eyes innocently. "I don't understand what you're saying."

All pretense of equanimity fled as he threw the blanket back and jumped out of bed. "Don't lie to me, Daisy! *No more lies!*"

Daisy took an unconscious step back toward the door. Broad-shouldered and bare-chested, clad in nothing but a pair of drawers, Nick did not, at this moment, appear to be the soft-spoken, civilized man she had married.

She felt tears brimming and was quick to beckon more. "What are you accusing me of?"

In a flash, Nick tossed the syringe on the bed and was across the room. "You know damn well what I'm accusing you of!"

Daisy jumped, frightened by this terrifying, uncharacteristic display of temper from her husband. Before she knew what was happening, he had her by the shoulders. He shook her twice, hard, causing her head to snap back and forth like a rag doll's. "Do you enjoy making a fool out of me? Do you?"

Daisy cowered. "You don't understand!"

"Damn right I don't understand! I don't understand a woman who lies to her husband! I don't understand a grown woman who acts like a vain, spoiled child at every turn!"

Daisy was sobbing for real by now.

"Quit your false tears, Daisy! It's not going to work!"

"I didn't mean to lie to you! I just wanted to wait!"

He let go of her with a shove that sent her reeling back into the door. "I believe you. I believe you didn't mean to lie. You know why, Daisy? You know why?"

She raised a trembling hand to wipe at tears that streamed down her face. "You believe me?"

"That's right. I believe you because lying and deceiving

have become a way of life with you. You don't even know the difference between truth and lies anymore. Rachel was right. I never should have married you."

Daisy felt a sprig of resentment rise in her chest. *Rachel!* He *would* bring up his precious Rachel at a time like this. Perhaps it was Rachel who had betrayed her secret.

Daisy defended herself. "She hates me! She always has! What has she been saying about me?"

Nick shook his head in disgust. "Rachel has nothing to do with this. Don't try to blame your own inadequacies on her."

"My inadequacies?" Her voice quavered in disbelief. "My *inadequacies*?"

Nick turned, crossed the room, and snatched his pillow from the bed. He moved past her, reaching for the door latch.

Panic gripped her heart. "What are you doing?"

Nick's eyes were cold. As they swept over her, Daisy felt as if she had been blasted by a frigid north wind. "You won't have to worry about using that thing anymore, love, because I won't be sleeping anywhere near you."

"What?" Daisy was incredulous. "You're not serious. Nick, please, can't we—"

He shoved her away from the door so he could pull it open, then stopped. He turned, his voice mocking. "You know, on second thought, you might want to hold on to it. Judging by the way I've seen you looking at Cal, I guess you might be needing it."

Daisy was flabbergasted. "How can you say such a thing?"

Nick's eyes flicked over her disdainfully. "Or has he bedded you already, love? Is that the way of it?"

Daisy's head was swimming. Did he really think she had been sleeping with Cal? She covered her face with her hands. "Just get out!"

"Gladly, sweetheart. Gladly. Remember to extend my condolences to your future lovers, will you?"

The door slammed. Daisy swayed on her feet. She wasn't at all sure of what had just happened.

She stumbled across the room and collapsed face-down onto the bed. She cried for a while, then rolled onto her back to sniffle and stare at the ceiling. She had forgotten all about using the syringe to wash away what was left of Nick. Somehow it didn't seem quite so important anymore.

Rachel.

Daisy swallowed hard, almost choking on a lump of seething red anger. *It was Rachel's fault.*

Rachel Girard had been nothing but a source of misery for as long as she could remember. Daisy had always been good in school, but Rachel had been better. If Daisy scored a ninety-eight in spelling, Rachel scored a ninety-nine. Daisy's father, a lumber merchant, had been one of the wealthiest men in town. Rachel's father, of course, had been wealthier.

And then there was Nick. Even as a child, Daisy had adored Nick Girard from afar, frittering away many an hour gazing dreamily at his handsome profile from across Miss Kuppenheimer's classroom. But the only female Nick had had time for in those days was Rachel.

Then, they had all grown up. Daisy had married her childhood love only to find herself doomed to live under the same roof with her childhood enemy. Even so, Daisy had been willing to let bygones be bygones. But not Rachel. Oh, no. She had been poised and ready to pounce from day one.

Daisy was sure it was Rachel's constant badmouthing that had finally turned her husband against her. After all, hadn't Rachel been leading Nick around by the nose ever since they were children? Now, she might have finally succeeded in ruining Daisy's marriage.

Well, this wasn't over yet. Daisy intended to get her husband back, and she would start by unmasking Rachel. She would show Nick just exactly what kind of conniving bitch his cousin really was.

20

The days had passed into weeks, and things were going well. Cal couldn't deny it. The work was good, his relationship with Rachel had smoothed out considerably, and he was feeling better than he had in years.

It was July, late in the afternoon, but the streets were still busy with traffic. Cal didn't even notice the anxious youngster who hovered nearby until he and Paco had loaded the last of the barbed wire fencing into the back of the wagon.

"Mr. Delaney? You Mr. Delaney, sir?"

Cal turned to see a towheaded boy of about eight looking up at him. "That's me."

The boy was dressed in a faded plaid shirt and torn dirty pants. His brown feet were bare. "Mr. McCauley sent me over from the telegraph office, Mr. Delaney."

Cal noticed for the first time that the boy offered a small sheet of paper. Western Union.

Cal took it from the child, then reached into his vest pocket, pulled out a silver coin and tossed it to the diminutive messenger before unfolding the paper to read over the slanted handwriting. Now, who in the world would be sending him a telegram here in Fort Worth?

Cal didn't have to look up to know the boy was delighted with his generous tip. "Yippy-yawhoo! Much obliged!"

Paco chuckled as the child skipped off across the dusty thoroughfare. "If you don't be careful, it'll start getting around you're a soft touch, Cal."

Cal didn't answer. The telegram was from Ezra Evans.

Arrived in Dodge yesterday. All went well. Vern talked to a rider heading your way on the trail a couple weeks back. He gave no name. Big man, black hair. Rides an Appaloosa. Said he was a friend of yours. Give my best to Rachel and Galen. See you in the spring.

Ezra.

Cal frowned. *Except I won't be anywhere near here by next spring, my friend.* He crumpled the strange message in one hand and looked up to survey the sun-drenched street—a street bustling with preoccupied pedestrians and equestrian traffic, everyday people going about their everyday business. Innocent.

A friend? Cal scanned the street again, this time with a more skeptical eye. He was looking for a big man with black hair. There were plenty of those, most of them familiar, local faces. For the first time in a while, Cal felt the loss of his dependable Colts.

Paco piped up from behind. "Trouble?"

Cal shoved the paper into his vest pocket. A friend. Old Tex Granger, maybe? Tex was just about the only old friend Cal could think of who might be riding alone and who also fit Ezra's scanty description. "No trouble," he said to Paco. "Ezra Evans sends his regards."

Paco grunted. "Mighty neighborly of him."

Cal turned and swung up into the driver's seat. "Let's get cracking, Paco, or we're gonna miss supper."

At the Red Panther Saloon, the usual early evening crowd of regulars was in attendance. Lacey noticed the stranger immediately. At this time of year, a new face stuck out like a duck on an empty pond. Still, Lacey suspected she would have noticed him just as soon in a thick crowd as a small one. He was different.

He pushed through the batwing doors, then paused, both hands dropping to rest comfortably on the gun belt that hung low on his hips. Big Bart's fingers fumbled a few notes, then stopped in the middle of "Sweet Betsy from Pike." Silence descended as everyone turned to stare at the newcomer.

With booted feet planted apart, the stranger reached into his vest pocket and pulled out a thick brown cigar. He reached into another pocket, produced a match, and struck it with his thumbnail. The sound of its flare seemed magnified in the quiet saloon.

He shook out the match and pulled the smoking brown cylinder from his mouth. Then he swept the room from east to west with his dark gaze before proceeding to the bar. Dressed all in black with silver spurs jingling at his heels, he didn't seem to notice the apprehensive glances that followed in his wake.

Dolly Jordan emerged from behind a door marked Private next to the backbar in one corner. Quickly, she assessed the situation and gave Big Bart a nod that compelled him to spin back around on his stool and resume the musical entertainment.

Dolly joined Howard behind the bar just as most of the patrons turned back to their own pursuits. The customary background murmur started to pick up once again. Still, the atmosphere, relaxed and carefree only minutes before, had changed. And it stayed changed. A stranger was in their midst.

Unlike the others, Lacey didn't take her eyes off of him right away. She thought he was a striking man. He had the look of a traveler who had just come from the bathhouse freshly groomed and nattily attired. His hair was as black as his clothes, his mustache thick and neatly trimmed, his skin almost the color of rich leather. And he was big. Tall and solid. Lacey thought he must be quite a formidable specimen beneath those new, expensive-looking clothes. She wondered if he was a lawman. If not, she suspected he might be a little dangerous.

"Lacey, honey, wanna get us another round of beers? Hey Lacey! Lacey!"

She felt a tweak on her bottom and she jumped, scowling. Usually she took these routine violations of her person in stride. It was, unfortunately, part of the job, but tonight she was finding it more annoying than usual.

"Hey!" She turned around, glaring at the aging foreman who had addressed her. "Watch your paws, Bernie!"

Bernie lifted thick eyebrows in mock innocence. "Just trying to get your attention, honey bee!"

"Keep your pants on, will you? Can't you see I'm busy?"

Bernie chortled, eliciting similar reactions from the other cowpokes ringing the table. "First time you ever tole me to keep my pants *on*, Lacey!"

Lacey turned away, disgusted. Hell's bells! She couldn't wait to get out of this two-bit town. Dirty, poor-as-church-mice, fumbling cowboys. It seemed like there was no end to them.

She approached the bar and slapped down her drink tray. When Howard looked her way, she raised four fingers, then turned to eye up the stranger who stood near her end of the bar.

Nursing a bourbon and smoking his cigar, he stood aloof from the others, making no effort to be chummy. This brought some disgruntled looks from a few of the patrons whose efforts at chit-chat had already been snubbed. These indignant looks were careful to come from behind the dark man's back, however. The stranger was well-heeled and looked as if he wouldn't hesitate to defend himself if called upon to do so. In fact, he looked like someone who might just shoot a fella stone-cold dead one minute, then turn around to finish off his drink the very next.

Lacey forgot her earlier annoyance. He was definitely different. Not to mention attractive. She wondered where he was from. She wondered even more why he was here. And she wondered still more where he was heading to.

Go on, Lacey. Go on over there and introduce yourself. If you don't, one of the other girls surely will. Lacey glanced over at Maybelle Baxter, who was slinking up against the piano. Maybelle was one of only four other girls working tonight. She was notoriously aggressive, and Lacey saw she was already sizing up this mysterious newcomer.

Plucking up her nerve, Lacey fluffed her hair and sidled over to the stranger. He didn't seem to notice her.

After a moment, she cleared her throat and tilted her head, putting on her best smile. "You from out of town, sugar?"

He still didn't look her way, and for a minute, Lacey got the panicky feeling that he was going to ignore her. After a long moment, though, he finally replied. "Way out of town, missy."

It was an effort to keep her smile from faltering. "Well, uh, my name's Lacey, and if there's anything I can do for you, anything at all, you just let me know."

The man didn't answer. He just kept looking straight ahead, as if counting the liquor bottles stacked in three rows up against the wall behind the bar. It was painfully clear he wasn't interested. Lacey's pride stung, but she told herself not to take it personally. Maybe he didn't like blondes. Maybe he liked redheads or girls with big bosoms or whatever. All men had their little quirks. She knew *that* well enough.

One by one, Howard set four foaming mugs onto Lacey's tray. Disappointed and somehow relieved at the same time, Lacey started to turn away.

"Lacey."

He said it so low and soft that she almost missed it. She stopped in midmotion and wound slowly back around to face him. "Did you say . . . ?"

"You work here year-round?"

Lacey was inexplicably tongue-tied. "Year-round . . . well s-sure I do. Year round, year in, year out."

"You know a fella named Ezra Evans?"

Lacey broke into a smile. This was a friend of Ezra's? She never would have guessed! "Sure I do. He comes down every spring."

"I'm looking for someone."

"Well, you're talking to the right gal, sugar. I know everyone in town."

He turned to look down at her, and Lacey found herself gazing up into eyes so black they seemed, just for a fraction of second, like spiraling, bottomless pits. Then something flashed and registered in those eyes. Interest. He smiled, and she saw that his teeth were white and straight. That smile frightened her—but only a little. And excited her—quite a lot. He was different, all right, about as different as a fella could get.

Lacey rarely found herself attracted to a man. As a matter of fact, until Cal Delaney came along, she thought that part of her had died a frightful death long ago. But now, as she tilted her head to stare deep into the eyes of this stranger, she was caught by an irresistible magnetism. This man had been around. He could take her places. She even knew, with a dreadful kind of certainty, that he could be quite dangerous indeed. And that, oddly enough, was part of the thrill.

"You just might be able to help me, Lacey," he said, raising his glass to finish off his bourbon.

Lacey looked at his hands. They were callused and hard and very, very powerful. Lacey imagined it wouldn't take much for him to snap a girl's neck with those hands.

She raised her gaze again to lock with his. "Anything you want to know, mister. I'm your girl."

21

Rachel studied her reflection in the looking glass, then picked up a silver-backed brush to stroke through tendrils still damp from her bath. The bedroom window was open, but no breezes moved this evening. The late summer air felt as thick and heavy as molasses.

That first night with Cal, the night in the line cabin, seemed like such a very long time ago now. Rachel remembered the morning after. She had awakened with a blinding headache and the half-panicked, half-hopeful idea that what had happened between them had been nothing but an alcohol-induced dream. In the harsh light of day, she was embarrassed to think back upon her own impulsive behavior, but hadn't it been just a little bit wonderful, too? Hadn't some part of her, even then, hoped it wasn't a dream?

From that moment on, things had changed drastically between them. Cal began claiming his husbandly rights with breathtaking frequency, and Rachel, who had been so certain that to succumb just once to temptation would forever free her mind of it, discovered she was more than willing to oblige him.

She liked the way he touched her. She liked the way their bodies seemed to meld together as if they had been created for each other, and she especially liked the curiously secure feeling she got afterward when he wrapped his arms around her and they drifted off to sleep together. There was nothing wrong with that, was there?

Firelights. He had said that to her once. *"Your hair dances with firelights, Rachel."* How peculiar that Cal seemed to find some kind of poetic beauty in the odd color of her hair. Rachel had always wished for beautiful blond hair, for round, blue eyes, and for pale, white skin.

You're behaving like a fool, Rachel Elena. Words mean nothing. He's just passing the time with you.

Suddenly disgusted with herself, she slapped down her hairbrush and rose from the vanity. It might have been Shakespeare who coined a term for her foolish affliction: midsummer madness. Well, summer was at an end, and Cal would be leaving in less than two months' time. Then Rachel would return to her old way of life.

She would forget Cal Delaney. She would forget his face and his eyes, so blue and intense and knowing. She would forget the sound of his voice and that lazy, crooked smile, the smile that could alternately melt her heart or send her into a temperamental fit of anger.

Rachel crossed the room to the window and pushed the curtain aside. From one horizon to the next, the night sky winked with bright stars. The air, perfectly still, smelled of dewy, fresh-cut grass. Summer.

Her glum musings were interrupted when she caught the sound of approaching voices below her window. It was Cal and her father. The essence of cigar smoke rose in the balmy air of the evening, and her father's next words were as clear as if he were standing next to her. "I'm leaving for Corpus Christi tomorrow. I want you to come along."

"Any particular reason?"

"There are some people I want you to meet."

Rachel couldn't help the sudden stab of jealousy that lanced through her heart. Corpus Christi? Her father hadn't so much as mentioned this trip to her. Why should it be so important to Galen that Cal accompany him?

The answer drifted into her mind, smooth and gentle as a passing cloud. *Because maybe he sees Cal as the son he never had.* Rachel frowned. Where had she heard that before?

Galen was still speaking. ". . . the more cattlemen you get to know, the better."

Rachel shook her head as if trying to jostle old memories. The son he never had. It wasn't *where* she had heard it before, it was *when*—many, many years ago.

Rachel thought she must have been about six or seven at the time. She remembered playing in the dirt beneath the parlor window, scattering ant hills with a twig and watching as thousands of the tiny creatures scurried about in a frenzied panic, running into each other, over each other, and around and around in circles.

Her parents were in the parlor arguing. Rachel wasn't particularly disturbed by this. They argued quite often, sometimes so loudly the whole house seemed to vibrate with the sounds of their voices, but they always made up, and after they made up, things were especially nice for a while.

"It's a matter of self-sufficiency, Elena."

Rachel knew it didn't matter if she got dirty. She was wearing a pair of boys' britches, and she was plenty dirty already. Her daddy had taken her out with him to see the men roping and branding new calves. Rachel had been both thrilled and horrified—thrilled that her daddy had thought her "big girl" enough to accompany him and horrified at the brutal treatment of the baby calves. They were children too. Just like Rachel.

She didn't pay attention to her parents' words until she heard her own name, and, even then, she listened with only half an ear. She crept forward and saw that one of the ants had cut a grass blade and was carrying it up the incline toward the side of the house.

". . . the best thing for Rachel. I'm not saying you're wrong, Galen. I'm saying . . ."

Rachel thought that even a grass blade must be quite heavy for a creature the size of an ant.

"You're jumping to conclusions again, Elena."

Rachel decided to name him Hercules. Maybe Dolores would give her a canning jar to keep him in. She could fill the jar with dirt and keep a whole colony of ants.

"Rachel is your daughter, Galen, just a little girl."

Her mother's voice had softened. Maybe that's what made Rachel look up, suddenly attentive. It sounded almost as if she were going to cry.

"Just be sure you're not trying to make her into the son you never had."

Rachel, crouching on all fours beneath the open

window, didn't move as these words settled into her brain.

"I'm sorry, Galen, I just . . . sometimes I wish I could have given you—"

Now her mother *was* starting to cry, and Rachel felt a slash of cold fear. Her daddy was making shushing sounds. *And everything had gotten quiet . . .*

Now, thinking back, Rachel knew what her mother had been trying to say. Rachel knew it in some vague, indefinable way even then. *"I just wish I could have given you a son."*

Cal's voice reached her ears. ". . . and roundup's right around the corner. Are you sure now's a good time?"

Galen sighed. "No time like the present."

"I just meant—"

"I know what you meant, but I still want you along. You should get to know these people. If anything happens to me . . ." There was a pause, then, "You've proven yourself in the last few months. You're smart, you're tough, and I trust the Elena Rose will be in good hands when I'm gone."

"You're talking like you're planning on going somewhere soon, Galen."

Rachel grasped the window sash tightly. Going somewhere. Galen did indeed talk like a man who was planning on going somewhere, didn't he?

She wasn't blind. Over the last month or so, she had noticed the difference in her father. He wasn't looking well, and he wasn't spending near as much time out on the range as he used to. As of late, her robust father looked gaunt and tired. She had mentioned it to him a few days ago, suggesting that he might want to visit Doc Bowers.

He had dismissed this advice by putting on a gruff face and saying, "Who's the child and who's the parent here, Rachel Elena?"

Now, Rachel heard her father laugh, and she was gratified to hear that the sound of it was as strong and healthy, as boisterous and devil-may-care, as it had ever been.

"The only place I plan on going anytime soon is down south, Cal, and I don't mean to the devil's parlor, either! Let's get on inside. I've got a taste for some brandy!"

Their voices faded to a distant murmur. Rachel stood motionless for a long moment, thinking. Where had she gotten the ridiculous idea that he was sick? She closed the window softly and went to bed.

Early the next morning, Cal stuffed a clean shirt into a carpetbag and turned to study Rachel with guarded interest. He had never met a woman who blew hot and cold like this one.

At dinner last night she had been fine. This morning, however, she had arisen to dress in stony silence. She was now seated at her vanity, fooling with her hair and muttering angrily under her breath.

Knowing that he was probably going to regret it, he said, "Are you going to tell me what particular burr has gotten under your saddle this morning, or is it your plan to let me stew for a while?"

At that, she rose to her feet loaded for bear. He could tell by her stance, by the tight line of her mouth, and by the clear flash of challenge in those emerald green eyes when she faced him. Her reply dripped with sarcasm. "How cozy. Just the two of you, off to Corpus Christi."

Cal eyed her cautiously. *Women.* They couldn't just spell it out. "Just exactly what is it you're getting at, Rachel?"

She narrowed her eyes. "Are you looking forward to it?"

"I'm looking forward to maybe learning something. I happen to value your father's experience."

"And he's so eager to impart it to you. Has it ever occurred to you that he might be grooming you to take over the Elena Rose?"

Cal felt his patience slipping. "Well, what's wrong with that? He thinks I'm his son-in-law."

"He thinks you're his son, period."

Ah, so there it was, the burr beneath the saddle, the proverbial bee in her bonnet. Cal threw up both hands, exasperated. "Oh, hell!"

Rachel pounced. "So! You don't deny it!"

"Deny it? Deny *what*?" Cal bellowed back. "That has to be the stupidest thing I've ever heard in my life!"

Rachel's eyes blazed. "Stupid? Are you calling me *stupid*?"

"What the hell do you want me to do about it?" he challenged. "Tell him not to bother because I won't be around in two months?"

"Of course not!"

"Well, then, you'd better get used to it!"

"All I'm saying is that you don't have to lead him on!"

Oh, she was really pushing this nonsense too far. Cal was having a hard time believing what he was hearing, even from Rachel, who somehow managed to be both the most level-headed and most scatterbrained woman he had ever met in his life. "Are you concerned for your father's feelings, Rachel, or just your exclusive place in his will?"

"That's a horrible thing to say!"

"Sometimes the truth is hard to take. I think you're worried about sharing that precious inheritance of yours."

"And wouldn't that be quite a windfall for a penniless cowboy like yourself?" Rachel shot back. "Are you so sure that's not what you've been angling for from the beginning?"

Cal stared at her hard, his annoyance building. "What do you think I am, Rachel? Some kind of fortune hunter? Is that it?"

Rachel balked. "Don't go trying to put words in my mouth."

"Well, here's some stunning news for you, sweetheart. I don't give a damn about the Elena Rose. I don't want any of your money except for what I'm due as stated in that harebrained contract I was fool enough to let you talk me into signing."

"That *I* talked *you* into signing?"

Cal had built up a full head of steam by now. "You're more than welcome to this damn ranch and every damn cow on it as far as I'm concerned! And as for your father, I'm just sorry that he's been saddled with such a spoiled, ungrateful, cold-hearted, greedy, self-centered daughter like yourself!"

"Greedy? Self-centered? Why, you—you—"

Cal snapped the carpetbag shut, snatched it up, and headed for the door.

Rachel gave up trying to find an adjective vile enough to pin on him, and followed at his heels. "Oh, certainly! Throw out a few insults and then leave!"

Cal stopped and swung around to face her. "Your

father is waiting downstairs. After breakfast, we have a train to catch."

"And how do you think that makes me feel?" she demanded.

"Feel?" he asked back. *"Feel?* I think that as long as you know you've got your precious inheritance coming, you're feeling just fine, Rachel."

Their eyes locked for a long, steaming moment. It was only after he turned his back to leave that she lashed out. "An ironic observation considering it comes from a man who probably hasn't felt anything close to a true human emotion in years!"

That stopped Cal cold. His hand was on the knob, his eyes glued to the smooth walnut grain of the door. "I'll be gone most of the week. When I get back, I'll be heading out to roundup. It's probably for the best our contract is soon up after that."

"Well, it certainly can't be too soon for me!"

He yanked the door open, gritting his teeth. "I just hope you enjoy having the bed all to yourself, princess. That's one thing you won't have to share much longer."

Cal slammed the door behind him so hard it rattled the hinges. That effort, however, did little to dissolve his frustration. Cal wasn't at all sure which one of them was the bigger sucker in this sorry scenario laughingly referred to as a marriage—Rachel or himself.

22

The sun had risen. As Rachel rounded the back of the stable, she heard sounds from the bunkhouse, sounds of men stirring awake. Most of them would be heading out today to start the fall roundup.

When Cal arrived home from Corpus Christi late last night, Rachel had pretended to be asleep. She knew he would be heading out again this morning, and if she was lucky, she wouldn't have to face him for a couple of weeks.

This morning, she had arisen before dawn and dressed, casting a wistful glance at Cal's slumbering figure in the bed before slipping out the door. Unfortunately, her morning constitution had done little to clear her head.

Rachel pulled open the stable door and stepped inside. Familiar equestrian aromas greeted her. She listened to the restless snuffling and whickering of horses in their stalls and knew she had come to the right place.

Rachel tilted her head up to survey the empty loft. How many hours had she spent there as a child? A hundred? Five hundred? A thousand? Spurred by a sudden impulse, Rachel crossed the straw-littered earthen floor to the ladder. She lifted her skirt with one hand and grasped the rungs with the other. Carefully, she climbed up to the loft, thinking back to those carefree days when she had scampered up this ladder without giving a thought to the possibility of slipping and falling.

She perched on the ledge, allowing her legs to dangle free. After a minute, she flopped down onto her back and waited for peace to settle over her like a welcome blanket.

It did not.

Her traitorous mind inevitably turned to the argument she had with Cal before he left for Corpus Christi. She had replayed it over and over all week, and with each new rendition, it had only seemed to grow worse.

When, oh, when would she learn to keep her big mouth shut? She had accused him of betraying her, and even as the words tumbled out, it had dawned on her how ludicrous she sounded. The accusation had hung in the air between them for what seemed to Rachel like the longest moment in history. He had regarded her with such utter contempt Rachel felt as if he had poured cold water on her heart. *I'm sorry!* she had wanted to cry out, but that word *sorry* had never come easily for her, and besides, it was already too late.

She was startled to hear the door creak open. *Oh please, not him. Anybody but him.*

"Rachel? Is that you up there?"

Him. Rachel muttered a colorful string of invectives to herself before pushing back up to a sitting position. "How did you know?"

"I'd recognize those ankles anywhere."

She peered down to see that, although currently hatless, he was otherwise dressed for the range—denims, work shirt, leather chaps. He stood, hands on hips, staring up at her in puzzlement. "What are you doing up there?"

"I'm thinking. What does it look like I'm doing? Practicing the waltz?"

"I should think waltzing while lying on your back would take quite a bit of practice, now that you mention it."

"Shouldn't you be going?"

"Actually, yes, I should." He crossed the stable to Friday's stall. Rachel watched as he scratched the stallion behind the ears and mumbled a few words. After a bit, he gathered up his saddle and gear, slung it over one shoulder, and moved for the door.

He stopped and turned around, looking up at her. "Are you planning on staying up there all morning?"

"I haven't decided yet."

She expected him to leave then, to turn right around and disappear through the door, but he didn't. "Do you mind if I join you?"

"Aren't they waiting for you outside?"

Cal glanced at the door, and then, as if making a sudden decision, he dropped his saddle to the floor. "Well, I reckon they can wait a couple of minutes longer."

Rachel felt her stomach clench as he ascended the ladder. What was he doing? He was acting as if nothing were wrong when both of them knew different.

As he settled down beside her, letting his legs dangle next to hers, Rachel looked up to the ceiling to study the spider webs that spanned the rafters. She couldn't bring herself to look at him.

"So," he said finally, "what is it you're thinking so hard about up here?"

"Nothing. I just thought it might help."

"Help what?"

"I thought coming up here might clear my head. I used to come up here a lot when I was little. It seemed to help."

Cal was quiet for a moment. "And is it?"

"Is it what?"

"Helping."

She sighed. "No. Not like it used to. I guess things change when you grow up."

He laughed dryly. "That's where you're wrong. *Things* always stay the same. It's your perspective that changes."

Rachel gave up studying spider webs and dropped her gaze to meet his. She had expected him to be angry with her. Actually, she would have preferred that he be angry with her. Instead, he seemed to be offering up his version of the olive branch, and she wasn't at all sure if she was prepared to take it.

She looked away. "I'm sorry I acted like such a fool. I shouldn't have said half of the things I did."

"Only half?"

She smiled ruefully. "All right. Three quarters."

"Okay. I reckon I said a few things too."

Rachel looked up. "What, like greedy, self-centered—"

"I was a little riled."

"Like you said, the truth is hard to take."

"It wasn't the truth, Rachel. I told you, I was just riled. You have a way of bringing out the worst in me sometimes."

She looked down at her hands. "Oh, it was the truth, all right. And I don't blame you."

"For what?"

"For wanting to hightail it out of here as soon as our contract is up."

"Look, I'm sorry I said you were greedy, self-centered, and spoiled. You're not, not really. I know you a little better than you think, Rachel."

"And so you weren't afraid to speak the truth. I can respect that."

"No. Sometimes I think you act the way you do so that people will be intimidated and back away from you. Maybe we have a little more in common than we thought."

"Then we're two very sorry specimens, Cal Delaney."

"Maybe we are." There was a short pause, then, "As you well know, my dear, I'm heading out today, but rest assured, I'll be back."

She looked up to see that he was smiling. "You don't scare easy, then, is that it?"

He didn't answer as the glint in his eye began to take on a different, very familiar cast. Rachel thought that if she were an innocent pat of butter on a dish, she wouldn't stand a chance under that kind of heat. About two dozen butterflies took flight in her stomach.

With one finger, Cal traced a slow line down along the dip of her neckline. As always, his touch sent a cascade of tiny shivers straight through her body to her pounding heart. "Tell me, princess, were you *really* asleep when I came to bed last night?"

Even though she knew she was only going to get herself into more trouble, Rachel couldn't seem to tear her eyes from his. She wondered what it was she thought she saw there. A reflection of herself? Or just a part of herself she had not known existed until now?

Then, he bent his head to kiss her, and Rachel

closed her eyes to accept him. Soon, he was urging her down onto the floor of the straw-littered loft beneath him, whispering against her lips, "Mmmmm, you know, this may be a good place to philosophize, but there are other things to do up here. Why do you think they call it rolling in the hay?"

Rachel felt his fingers fisting in her hair as he kissed her again. Wrapping her arms around him, she wondered if there were institutions for overly amorous ladies, and if so, did they tie the inmates to their beds at night to keep them from accosting unsuspecting gentlemen in the streets?

Below them, the stable door creaked open, dousing them in a rude splash of early morning light. Paco's deep baritone cut the quiet. "Cal! What did you do, fall asleep in here?"

Rachel stiffened, mortified at being caught in such undignified circumstances.

Cal groaned and lifted his head. "I'll be there in a minute!"

Paco sounded surprised. "What're you doing up there?"

Cal sat up. Rachel covered her face with both hands and prayed Paco wouldn't notice the extra pair of feet peeking out over the edge of the loft.

Cal ran an exasperated hand through his hair. "What the hell, Paco! I'm having a word with my wife if you must know!"

Rachel sat up like a shot and smacked Cal on the arm.

"A word with your—Oh!" Paco apparently experienced an epiphany. "Whoa! I'll be outside!"

The stable door slammed in a hurry.

Cal rubbed his arm and frowned at Rachel. "What'd you hit me for?"

Rachel felt her cheeks flaming with embarrassment.

"'A word with my wife!' I declare to goodness! What's he going to think we were doing up here?"

Cal grabbed Rachel's left wrist and waggled her hand in front of her face. "What are you worried about? Why the hell did I slip that ring on your finger?"

For twenty thousand dollars! Rachel opened her mouth to retaliate, then probably for the first time in her life thought better of it.

The expression on Cal's face was telling. He had been ready for her to snap back. Now, he just smiled wickedly. "If we had a little more time, princess, you can be sure I'd be giving you a proper good-bye."

"By the look in your eye, Cal Delaney, I think you mean an improper good-bye."

"You read that look right."

Rachel's embarrassment began to fade. "I guess I could think of worse things."

"Like getting your fingers smashed in a door?"

Rachel tried hard to suppress a smile. "Yeah, like that."

"Like getting your foot stomped by a twelve-hundred-pound beeve?"

Rachel had to laugh despite herself. "Yeah, like that, too."

"Good." Seemingly satisfied, Cal started back down the ladder. He skipped the last couple of rungs and dropped to the floor. "Take care of Friday for me," he added, bending to retrieve his saddle and gear. "Make sure he doesn't go all soft on me while I'm gone."

"There's nothing worse than a soft stallion."

Cal threw her a lecherous grin before settling his hat on his head and punching the door open. "Why, Rachel, you surprise me. Here I thought you were such a proper young lady."

By the time Rachel could open her mouth to inform

him that she had certainly not intended for her remark to be taken in such a bawdy manner, the door had already smacked closed behind him.

She brushed off her skirt and threaded splayed fingers through loose curls, freeing a few pieces of straw in the process. She must look a wreck. Cal had a way of doing that to her.

She descended the ladder thinking it was probably a very good thing he was going to be gone for a while. She needed the time to get her right-thinking head on her shoulders. And to get used to not having him around. This last thought, uninvited and unwelcome, stopped her cold.

After a bit, she squared her shoulders and crossed the stable to push the door open. Her father stood with Paco by the corral fence as, nearby, Cal bent to secure his saddle to the back of one of the cow ponies.

There was a sudden tightness in her throat. He was going to be gone two weeks. Two weeks had never seemed like such a very long time to her before. Stepping out into the morning light, she called, "Cal!"

He turned around.

Her feet seemed to move of their own volition. Suddenly, she was by his side. Unmindful of the surprised and curious stares they received, she wrapped her arms around Cal's neck and looked up into his questioning blue eyes. "Do a good job out there. I might ride out one of these days to check up on you."

He lowered his voice discreetly. "There are no beds or haylofts out on the range, but there's always the chuck wagon." Then, he wrapped his arms around her, hugged her tight, and kissed her. Rachel drank it in, feeling, at that moment, as if they were the only two people in the world. Too soon, it was over. He looked down into her eyes for a long moment, saying nothing, then he let go of her and turned to mount up.

Rachel stood silent, feeling empty, as he and Paco took their leave. She watched the two departing men on horseback for a long time, having eyes for only one.

Galen strolled up behind her. "Looks like you two settled your differences. That's good. A wise woman once said, Never let your man ride out to roundup angry."

Rachel didn't shift her attention from the figures that retreated into the vast, spreading distance of the Elena Rose. "I think that wise woman might have been Mama."

Galen chuckled. "Come to think of it, you might be right. Now, my motto always was, Never let your woman into the kitchen when she's in a foul mood. That one always served me well."

Rachel's expression turned wistful. Cal was not really her man. Soon, she would be watching him ride away for more than a couple of weeks. Soon, she would be watching him ride away forever.

Something inside of her wrenched, almost taking her breath away, and she was astonished to feel a tear escape the corner of one eye. Hurriedly swiping it away, she turned and headed back to the house.

Eli waited by the rear of the mercantile store, his patience beginning to run low. He pulled a watch from his vest pocket and glanced at its face before replacing it. "You sure she's coming?"

The whore, Lacey, was busy twisting the strings of her reticule into knots. "'Course I'm sure. I know too much for her to go standing me up."

Finding Delaney had been easy—too easy. When Eli set out from Dodge, he had expected to track the ex-bounty hunter for months, but it had turned out that Evans's young cowboy had been right. Delaney had given up his guns and established residence here in Fort Worth. The only thing the cowboy hadn't mentioned was that Delaney had married into one of the wealthiest ranching families in the state, that actually getting to him was going to be about as easy as breaking into an armed fort.

But Eli was nothing if not patient. He had plenty of money, and he could move around without being recognized. The Walsh brothers had never had occasion to wander into this part of the country. Texas was one of the few states in which Eli's face didn't happen to be posted in every sheriff's office.

Still, he was aware of the kind of stir a stranger could cause in a town this size. Word had a way of getting around, and sooner or later Delaney would hear of it. Eli had no desire to touch off his adversary's defensive instincts. Delaney could probably sense a predator coming even in his sleep. The gunslinger might have shed his gun belt, but he was no more likely to lose his finely honed instinct for self-preservation than he was to lose the use of his right arm.

Eli had never met Delaney face-to-face, had never looked him in the eye, but he knew the man as well as he knew himself. They were cut from the same cloth. Delaney might like to believe he was on the side of the holy, but in reality, he was no more than Eli's flip side. Delaney was Eli with a conscience.

Eli was looking forward to meeting his match, but he was committed to lying low until the time was right. He had assumed an alias and taken a room in nearby Dallas. So far, his occasional trips into Fort Worth had been brief, their only purpose to keep tabs on Delaney's movements.

"There she is!"

Lacey pointed to a well-dressed blonde who had just rounded the far side of the building. Daisy Girard did not look pleased to have been summoned to a meeting with the town trollop.

"I declare, Lacey Holloway! What in tarnation is the—" The youthful Mrs. Girard stopped when she caught sight of Eli leaning up against the rear of the mercantile building. He was sizing her up, deciding just exactly who and what she was. His blatant scrutiny brought a pink flush to her face.

He pushed off from the wall and approached her.

Lacey made a hurried introduction. "Daisy, this is Joe Dockett, a deputy marshall from Dallas. He, uh, has some questions."

Daisy Girard looked up at him, blinking rapidly, her pink lips parted slightly. She tried to smile, but there was an inhibiting tightness around her mouth, a trace of apprehension.

Eli wasn't stupid. He was well aware of the effect he had on most people. Even this inconsequential bit of fluff was feeling it—sensing the possibility of danger, much like a rabbit sniffs warily at the night air. But he had long ago learned how to counteract this effect when it suited him. Why, it was as easy as changing one's clothes.

"Mrs. Girard," he said, reaching down to take her small hand in his, "it is indeed a pleasure to meet you. Miss Holloway didn't warn me to expect such an exceptionally attractive lady."

It worked. The trepidation in Daisy Girard's eyes flickered and went out. He had spoken in a language she understood. She now attributed his scrutiny of her figure to nothing more than physical attraction, and that was just fine with Eli.

"Well, I declare!" she gushed, blushing anew as he bent to peck the back of her hand before releasing it.

Eli smiled. "I should let you know right away that I'm not here in an official capacity. It is with a personal matter that I ask your help, my dear lady."

"What is it I can do for you?"

"Miss Holloway has assured me you can be discreet."

Daisy threw a curious glance at Lacey, who was, by now, working out her nervousness by biting one thumbnail down to the quick. Daisy looked back at Eli. "Certainly, Mr. Dockett."

"I understand you're acquainted with a gentleman by the name of Cal Delaney."

"Yes, I am. He's married to my husband's cousin."

"Quite a few years ago, Cal and I worked for the Wells Fargo company in Virginia City. Perhaps he mentioned it to you."

"I heard he worked in some capacity for Wells Fargo, yes."

"I lost track of him after he left their employ, but since coming to Dallas, I've learned he's living here in Fort Worth."

"He lives out at the ranch with Rachel."

"That would be his new wife?"

Daisy nodded, then cocked her head to one side. "I don't quite understand what all of this has to do with me. If you want to speak with Cal, why haven't you contacted him yourself?"

Eli reached into his vest pocket and extracted a cigar. "Do you mind if I smoke, Mrs. Girard?"

"Not at all, Mr. Dockett."

Eli proceeded to light his cigar, ignoring the slight trembling in his right hand. He was aware that the tremor, which had been manifesting itself erratically for the last week or so, was somehow connected to the headaches. There was nothing that he could do about it, and so he ignored it. What he didn't ignore was the nagging sense that it was just one more sign his time was growing short.

Eli shook out the match and continued. "As I was saying, since learning of Cal's whereabouts, I've been reminded of a certain matter left unresolved between us. It's my desire to speak with him alone."

"I don't understand."

"Of course. How could you? I should explain that Cal and I are not the best of friends, Mrs. Girard, and if he were to hear that I'm looking for him . . ."

Daisy pointed a shrewd finger. "I'll just bet he owes you money. Is that what you're trying to tell me, Mr. Dockett?"

Eli chuckled. "Ah! I can see you're not only lovely to look at but very perceptive as well."

Daisy flushed at the compliment. "Well, I'm sorry to tell you that even though Cal married a Girard, he still doesn't have a penny to his name."

"But I'm sure he has access—"

"No more access than I do, Mr. Dockett, and I can assure you, it's limited."

Eli pretended to ponder this before replying. "I'll just have to handle that problem when it arises. First and foremost, Mrs. Girard, I must find the opportunity to discuss the situation with him in private. And that's where you come in."

Daisy frowned. "That won't be easy."

"He mustn't know I'm looking for him, Mrs. Girard."

Daisy glanced again at Lacey, who spoke up now for the first time since she had introduced them. "I told him you would be the best one to know Cal's comings and goings."

Daisy shook her head. "He's out on roundup this week and probably most of next."

Eli interjected. "You'll know when he returns."

"If I decide to help you, Mr. Dockett . . ."

"I will make it worth your while, Mrs. Girard."

Daisy nodded slowly, thinking. Eli waited as she puzzled out the nuances of his proposition. Lacey had assured him that there was no love lost between this woman and Cal Delaney's wife.

Soon, she seemed to arrive at a decision. Squaring her delicate shoulders, she flashed him a dazzling smile. "All right, Mr. Dockett, you tell me exactly what you need me to do."

23

Dolores scrubbed the cast-iron skillet, trying her best to ignore the retching sounds coming from the back porch. This was the third morning in a row that Rachel Elena had lost her breakfast. *Why do I bother cooking?* Dolores thought. She should just throw raw eggs into the bushes and be done with it.

Finally, it grew quiet. The back door hinges groaned as Rachel straggled back into the house. "Feel better?" Dolores asked, turning to eye her skeptically.

Still white-faced and trembling, Rachel nodded. "I don't know what's the matter with me."

Dolores wore a wise look. "When was your last monthly turn, *paloma*?"

Rachel appeared not to have heard her as she sank into a chair at the kitchen table. She raked a hand through thick, auburn tresses and moaned.

Dolores dried her hands on a kitchen towel. "I will find a calendar and we will count the days."

Rachel rested her elbows on the table and buried her face in her hands. "No."

"Rachel Elena."

She lifted her head to look at Dolores crankily. "I don't need to count the days."

"Oh?"

"It was my birthday. The last time was on my birthday."

Dolores wrinkled her brow, calculating silently. "That's almost three—"

"I know, I know."

Now that her suspicions had been confirmed, Dolores couldn't contain her joy. She was surprised to feel tears brimming in her eyes. "This is good news, Rachel Elena! How I wish your mother could be here to see this day! Do you know how happy she would be? Have you told Mr. Cal?"

Rachel glowered. "Of course I haven't told him."

Dolores's smile slowly faded. "What does that mean, 'of course' you have not told him?"

"It means, Dolores, I haven't told him anything, and I'm not sure I'm going to."

Dolores was shocked and more than a little puzzled at Rachel's attitude. She knew as well as anyone that those two had their share of marital spats, but it was also clear to her that they had fallen in love. "How can you say such a thing?" she demanded. "What do you think, in a couple of months he will not notice something is suspicious?"

Rachel snapped. "It won't matter what he thinks in a couple months because he'll be gone by then!"

"Gone? Gone where, *paloma*?"

"Gone to wherever it is his kind gets gone to!"

Dolores pulled out a chair and sat. "Why do you say this? Talk to me, Rachel Elena."

Rachel buried her face in her hands. "He'll be gone because. . . because . . . Oh, damn it!"

"Because?"

Rachel sucked in a tremulous breath. "Because we had an agreement."

"An argument?" Dolores was confused. After all, a day didn't pass that those two didn't manage to have at least one argument.

Rachel looked up, clearly exasperated. "Not an *argument*, an *agreement*! How do you think I got him to marry me, Dolores? I offered to pay him twenty thousand dollars, that's how. After six months, he's free to leave."

Dolores collapsed in her chair, aghast. Never before in her life had she heard of such a thing! Of course, Rachel had told her of Galen Girard's ultimatum, and the timing of Rachel's marriage had been too convenient for Dolores to think Rachel and Cal had truly fallen in love before the wedding, but . . .

It took a full minute for Dolores to find her voice, but when she did, it came back loud and strong. "*¡Válgame Dios!* I don't believe it! I don't believe what I am hearing! My ears are lying! My ears are—"

"Stop it!" Rachel shrieked. "You heard me right!"

Dolores shook a finger in Rachel's face. "*¡Estúpida!*" This is the stupidest stunt you ever pulled, Rachel Elena!"

"I didn't have any choice! Daddy was going to give the Elena Rose to Nick and Daisy!"

"And so you pay a man twenty thousand dollars to marry you and leave in six months? *¡Por Dios!* Only you could think up such a thing!"

Rachel sighed miserably. "It seemed like a good idea at the time."

Dolores rolled her eyes. "Such a smart girl you are! Did you forget how babies are made?"

"Of course not!"

Dolores eyed her doubtfully.

"It wasn't supposed to be like that!"

"Like *what*?"

Quite unexpectedly, Rachel's eyes filled with tears. This was a sight Dolores was not used to dealing with, and her anger wilted. She reached into her skirt pocket and pulled out a handkerchief. "Here, Rachel Elena."

Rachel accepted the handkerchief, snuffling. "The agreement was that there would be no . . . no . . ."

"You plan for everything, then, yes? Except things did not go as planned."

Rachel blew her nose. "Not exactly."

"You must tell him right away, Rachel Elena."

"No. I just can't, Dolores."

"Do you love him?"

Rachel's eyes brimmed full again. A fat tear rolled down her cheek. "I . . . I don't know."

"You must decide what you want."

Rachel twisted the handkerchief. "I don't know what I want."

"Still, you must tell him."

"You don't understand. He doesn't want a wife or a family."

"He told you this?"

"Yes."

Dolores made a clucking sound and shook her head. "I don't think he knows what he wants any better than you do, *paloma*."

Rachel sniffed. "Wise advice."

"*This* is my advice: Tell him, Rachel Elena. For the baby, he will stay."

"But I don't want him to stay for the baby. Don't you understand?"

"Oh yes, I understand well, *paloma*, but he should know the truth. Do *you* understand?"

Rachel swallowed hard and looked at her without saying anything for a long time. Finally, she rose from the table, dabbing at her eyes. "Not a word, Dolores."

The housekeeper pursed her lips and shook her head.

"Not a word," Rachel warned. "I'll handle this my own way."

"You are making a mistake."

Rachel crossed the room to leave. "Well then, you just remember, Dolores, it's my mistake to make."

It was late. The house was dark, all except for that light in the study. Rachel knew it was Nick working late again. It was an occasional practice that had lately grown into a habit. Ever since he and Daisy had had their not-so-private falling out, Nick was now sleeping in one of the spare rooms.

For Rachel, whose own body had lately turned stranger to her, sleepless nights were also becoming a habit. It seemed ironic that all day she struggled against fatigue only to find that when night fell and she finally retired, she couldn't seem to quiet her restless mind.

On her way to the kitchen to make a pot of tea, Rachel almost continued right past the closed study door. That too had become habit—avoiding Nick—and she stopped, wondering how long it had been since she and Nick had talked, really talked, without one of them having some kind of ax to grind in the process. A year maybe. More like two, she thought to herself. Ever since he had started courting Daisy Parker, and Rachel had turned on him like a spoiled child.

She whispered to herself, "Like a spoiled, self-centered, greedy, jealous—" She turned to stare at the closed study door, at the rectangular shaft of yellow light spilling out onto the hallway floor from beneath it.

Retracing her steps, she pushed the door open slowly. Nick was so engrossed in shuffling through a mountain of paper on Galen's desk that he didn't notice Rachel standing in the archway. The collar of his shirt hung open, his dark hair was mussed, and he wore an expression of bedraggled concentration.

"Don't you ever sleep?" Rachel heard her own voice, straining to sound casual and failing miserably.

Nick's head jerked up, surprised. "Rachel." He blinked as if he were seeing a mirage. "What are you doing here?"

The way he said her name, the way he asked that question, as if she were a ghost from the past, made her wince. She forced a smile. "I live here."

He didn't smile back. "I'm trying to get some work done. What time is it?"

Rachel crossed the threshold without an invitation and stood with her hands resting on her hips. "One-thirty."

"Last time I looked, it was eleven."

"Having trouble with something in particular?"

He threw his hands up with a resigned sigh. "Well, I never had your talent for figures, Rachel."

"But you could write poetry."

He eyed her strangely, as if sensing some kind of trap.

Rachel prodded, "Remember?"

Nick held her gaze for a long moment. She noticed the dark circles under his eyes and chastised herself. Why hadn't she seen before now how unhappy he was?

He finally replied. "That questionable talent hasn't proven very useful when it comes to turning a profit."

Rachel settled into a chair facing the desk. "No, that was always my specialty. Maybe that's why we always got on so well together. We made up for each other's weaknesses."

Nick studied his hands bleakly. "Got on. I notice you put it in the past tense. We haven't *got on* so well recently."

"That's probably been mostly my fault."

"Mostly?" Nick looked up, a hint of anger sparking in his eyes.

Rachel recognized the unspoken accusation. She was guilty. When he began courting Daisy, she made no secret of her anger. She let him know how she felt about it right from the start; and it was the beginning of the end for them. Rachel had never really forgiven him—not until now, perhaps—but it was only now, now that she was finally willing to assume responsibility for her own shabby behavior, that a new question formed in her mind, a question that burned so bright and compelling she wasn't sure she could truly make peace unless she knew the answer.

"Why Daisy?"

Nick didn't so much as flinch at the inquiry, and Rachel was a little surprised that he must have been pondering this question in his own mind for quite some time. "Simple. She wasn't you."

Rachel gripped the arms of her chair, her mind numbing over. Had he said . . . ?

Nick shrugged and started shuffling papers. "She

was as 'not you' as a girl could get. I mean, when you think about it, it's fairly obvious, isn't it?"

"There were times when I thought you were doing it just to drive me crazy."

He gave her a self-deprecating smile. "Oh, that was probably part of it, too. If I'd realized what I was doing . . ."

Rachel tried to fight an unbidden grin. "If only I'd kept my big mouth shut."

Nick started to laugh. It was a late-night, too-tired-to-think-straight laugh, but it sounded refreshing all the same. It wasn't long before Rachel joined him.

"All these years," she said when she was finally able to get the words out, "we've been fighting in the schoolyard!"

Nick buried his face in his hands. "It would seem we've worked ourselves into a very fine mess."

After a while, Rachel managed to rein herself in. She felt better, as if she had finally shrugged a burden from her heart. "You know . . . maybe she's not that bad."

Nick stared at Rachel as if she had just announced she was taking a stagecoach to the moon. "My ears must be deceiving me because I thought I just heard you say—"

Rachel raised a hand. "I'm not saying she isn't bad, I'm saying maybe she's not *that* bad. Maybe we've helped create our own monster. I for one haven't been exactly hospitable."

Nick interjected. "Hospitable? I was beginning to think it was just a matter of time until you got around to murdering her in her sleep."

Rachel batted her eyelashes at him sweetly. "It's not like I haven't thought about it, my dear boy."

Nick smiled grudgingly. "I'll give your point some thought."

"Maybe you and she could even begin to mend your differences."

Nick shook his head, sobering abruptly. "Our differences are insurmountable, Rachel."

The finality in Nick's tone made Rachel frown. "You married her, didn't you? For whatever reasons, Nick, you made that final commitment. There had to be something there, whether you like to think so now or not."

Nick picked up a pen and tapped it on the desk thoughtfully. "You might not have made such a bad poet yourself. I never pictured you playing the part of a romantic."

"Well, just keep it under your hat."

Nick eyed her contemplatively. "There's something I think I should show you."

Rachel watched with interest as Nick started shuffling through a mound of papers. He pulled out a folder, then stopped, suddenly indecisive.

"What?" Rachel asked, sitting up. "What is it?"

"You probably won't be happy with me."

"What is it?" Rachel persisted, growing apprehensive.

"It's a report from a detective in Lawrence, Kansas."

Rachel's stomach tightened. It was about Cal. She knew it. Part of her wanted to snatch the folder from Nick's hands and devour it. Another part wanted to flee the room.

"You knew from the beginning I had my suspicions about Cal. I had him checked out. I started in Dodge, of course, since that's where he came from before arriving in Fort Worth. That's where I learned about the boy he gunned down before joining Ezra's outfit. The circumstances surrounding the confrontation were pretty fuzzy depending who told the story. Mostly, though, it looked like Cal was forced to defend himself against a kid too drunk to know what was good for him." Nick hesitated. "Do you want to hear the rest of this?"

Rachel nodded, feeling her throat go dry. "Go on."

"From there, we went back to Virginia City, where he said he worked for Wells Fargo. That part of his story checked out. The man heading up the office now, Jason Farley, had nothing but praise for our man, Cal. Said he was the best damned shot he'd ever worked with in his life."

Nick continued, "When asked about where Cal had come from, Mr. Farley steered us to Wichita, Kansas. The people in Wichita's red light district remembered Cal drifting into their midst as a very young man. They seemed to think he'd come from Abilene."

Rachel broke in. "That's where he said he grew up, in Abilene. I remember him telling me once he lived on a farm."

Nick shook his head. "Not on a farm. At least, not around Abilene, Rachel. He turned up in '67, when the first cattle herds were shipped out. Some of the old-timers remember him pretty well—a kid with a knap-sack, living on the streets until he was able to pick up some odd jobs."

Rachel tried to remember what little Cal had told her of his past. *"It just so happens my first job was sweep-ing up and running errands for a cathouse in Abilene."* But that didn't make sense. That first day, when Rachel had approached him by the corral, he had told her he had lived on a farm, a small farm where they kept a crotchety cow named Daisy. Rachel remembered point-ing this discrepancy out to him later, but she couldn't quite remember what his answer had been.

"So," she said, "he didn't live on a farm around Abilene. He just turned up as a runaway, is that right?"

Nick nodded, his gaze dropping to the file in his hand. "And that's where the trail ended, Rachel. No one knew where he'd come from, not even those people who had counted him as a friend."

"Is there a point to all this?"

Nick looked up again. "It was something Cal said to me later that pointed me in the right direction. He told me to put my feelers out around Lawrence." Nick offered Rachel the folder. "And so I did."

Rachel stared at the folder for a long time before reaching out to accept it. "What's in it, Nick? Do I want to know?"

"Our detective tracked down a man by the name of Jasper MacGregor. He was one of Cal's neighbors. Read it."

Rachel flipped the folder open and forced herself to focus on the handwriting before her. After the first few sentences, she found herself hopelessly drawn in. The detective had written up the report exactly as he had heard it from Jasper MacGregor. Rachel lost herself in the narrative of a Kansas farmer recounting the violent death of a son one hot August night in the year 1866. Rachel read it through in grim silence. When she was finished, she looked up to find Nick watching her.

She offered him the folder. "No wonder Cal has nightmares."

"As you can imagine, I've been feeling a little foolish," Nick said. "It looks like I was wrong about him."

"How so?"

"The man he shot in the back."

Rachel pulled a name from memory. "Leo Walsh?"

"He was one of the suspects in the murder of Cal's family and Jasper MacGregor's son."

Missing pieces fell into place. Cal had told Rachel that his pursuit of Leo Walsh had been personal. But he hadn't told her the rest. *Oh, Cal, you spoke in riddles and half-truths. Why couldn't you tell me the whole story?*

"It explains a lot," Rachel said quietly.

"Yes, it does. And I'm sorry."

"Sorry?"

"Sorry I misjudged him, sorry I tried to stop you from marrying him. Seeing how things have turned out, I was a poor one to be giving you advice on marriage."

Rachel rose from her seat. All at once, she felt quite drained. "It's late. I'm going to bed."

Nick's voice caught her just as she reached the door. "I was wrong, wasn't I?"

Rachel turned back to face him, unsure of his meaning. "About Cal?"

"About you and Cal. You've got yourself a good husband, and the Elena Rose will be yours. Everything's working out as planned, isn't it?"

Rachel hesitated. Working out as planned? She thought about her tidy little marriage contract. The terms of that contract were due to expire in just over a month. She also thought about the child she carried. *That* would come due about five months later. Somewhere, it seemed, she had grossly miscalculated. Rachel felt an urge to blurt out the truth to her cousin.

"Rachel?"

She fought the urge down. "Hmmmm?"

"Is there a problem?"

She shook her head wearily and turned to leave. "No. I'm just tired. Good night, Nick."

24

Feeling guilty for sleeping late, Rachel clutched her wrapper about her nightdress furtively as she walked barefoot across the polished hardwood floor of the dining room. It was already midmorning.

She pushed open the kitchen door and saw Dolores hard at work cutting up vegetables. "I hope you're not expecting breakfast at this hour, Rachel Elena."

Rachel knew that Dolores was still upset with her. She hadn't offered up more than a dozen civil words since Rachel confided in her about the marriage contract.

"Actually," Rachel replied coolly, "I don't think I could stomach breakfast at the moment anyway."

"Coffee?"

Rachel sank into a chair, perched an elbow on the table, and rested her chin in one hand. "Coffee would be good."

Dolores moved to the coffeepot on the stove. "He is back."

Rachel's eyes widened. "What?"

Dolores jerked her head toward the gallery hallway. "He got back early this morning."

"But I wasn't expecting him until—"

Dolores interrupted as she reached for a cup. "He ate enough to fill a horse, took a bottle of your father's bourbon, and went to take a bath."

"What did he say?"

Dolores threw her a pointy look. "He said, 'I'm going to take me one long, wickedly hot bath, Dolores. Don't bother calling me till dinner.'"

"Is that all? Didn't he even ask about me?"

"No."

Rachel pressed her lips together, annoyed with Dolores's prickly attitude as well as the fact that Cal, after almost two weeks away from home, seemed more concerned about filling his stomach and wallowing around in a tubful of soap suds than in asking after his own wife. That self-centered, impregnating weasel.

Rachel narrowed her eyes. "And what did *you* say?"

"I said, 'Fine, Mr. Cal. You take yourself one long, hot bath. I won't call you till dinner.'"

"Then you didn't say anything about . . . ?"

Dolores slammed Rachel's cup down on the kitchen table and parked a hand on one hip. "As you said, it is your mistake to make, Rachel Elena. I don't go sticking my nose where it is not wanted."

Rachel rose to her feet. "Fine."

The housekeeper let out a petulant snort and turned back to her task. Approaching from behind, Rachel reached around to pluck a carrot stick from the ceramic dish by Dolores's right hand. "So, is he still in there?"

"If he's working on that whole bottle, I think he will probably be in there for the rest of the morning."

Rachel nibbled on her carrot, grateful that it was not awakening any queasy sensations in her stomach. *One long, wickedly hot bath, indeed,* she thought, bristling. *Don't bother calling me until dinner, indeed.* Rachel noticed a large pot of water sitting unattended next to the stove. "What's that?"

Dolores looked at Rachel as if she had the brain of a rodent. "It is water to wash vegetables."

Rachel finished off her carrot. "Do you mind if I borrow it?"

"Does that mean you will return it when you are finished?"

Rachel ignored the housekeeper's sarcasm and reached for the pot. "You remember how Mama always said one good turn deserves another?"

"What are you talking about?"

With both hands and a grunt, Rachel hoisted the large pot.

"Well, I think she was right. One good turn *does* deserve another. Keep the coffee warm for me, will you?"

"Rachel Elena!"

Rachel smirked as she marched resolutely down the short hallway. She stopped at the closed door and lifted her knee to push the door latch up. It obliged by clicking open. Slowly, quietly, she nudged the door ajar with her hip.

It was Cal. She would recognize the back of that arrogant blond head anywhere. He appeared to be quite comfortable, settled down as he was in the large porcelain tub, up to his fertile neck in frothy, white bubbles. She noticed the bottle of bourbon—still three quarters full—sitting by the tub and his glass sitting unattended next to it on the floor. A lazy curl of smoke rose from his cigar.

He was leaning back against the curved edge of the tub, about to doze off. So much for the better. She approached from behind, lifted the pot, and upended it over his unsuspecting head.

"*What the—!*" Cal sat up as if he'd been goosed by Mephistopheles himself. Water sloshed out over the sides of the tub in waves. Rachel dropped the pot with a loud *clang!* and jumped back to avoid getting soaked.

Cal twisted around to face her, shaking his head like a dog, blinking water from his eyes. He snatched the soggy cigar from his mouth. "Rachel! What the hell was that for?"

"Just paying you back for last time, Mr. Delaney. How do you like it?"

"How do I *like* it?" He glared at her, dripping. "You think you're pretty smart over there, don't you?"

Rachel folded her arms. "Smart enough."

He flashed her a cold smile. "All right, Mrs. Delaney. I guess this wipes the slate clean."

"For now."

Cal sighed with regret as he eyed his thoroughly doused cigar before tossing it to the floor. "Would you hand me a towel, please?"

Rachel retrieved a towel from the cupboard, moved toward him, then stopped. "Oh, no, I don't think so."

He looked annoyed again. "What?"

"I'm not falling for that."

"Falling for what, for Christ's sake?"

"I hand you the towel and you pull me in, right?"

"Rachel, I think we're both a little old for that kind of thing. Besides, we agreed we're even, right? Just hand me the damn towel."

"Oh, so you're not mad, right? Not mad at all?"

"No, I'm not mad. At least, not yet."

Rachel eyed him cautiously. He didn't look mad. He looked wet. "All right," she said finally, moving toward him with the towel. "We'll just call it . . . *AIEEEEEE!*"

Cal's hand shot out so fast, she didn't have time to react. He grabbed her wrist and yanked hard. Before she knew it, she was pulled into the tub with a rude *splat* and all the grace of a hogtied beeve.

Infuriated, she tried to swat at him, but he must have been expecting as much. He had kept a strong grip on her right wrist and now moved lightning quick to snatch up the left. Water splashed out over the sides of the tub. And he was grinning!

"Cal, you dirty liar! You said—"

"Don't believe everything you hear, princess." Then, he dropped one of her wrists only to wrap a hand around the back of her neck, pulling her to him. His lips came down hard on hers, then his tongue was in her mouth, and he tasted good. Even when she had good reason to be angry with him, she thought she could go on kissing Cal forever. She stopped resisting and clutched at his shoulders, hard and smooth and slippery wet.

He pulled away, tugging on the ribbon at the neckline of her soaked nightdress. "Ooooooh, honey! Whose idea was it to get a big old bathtub with room enough for two?"

"You're bad, Cal Delaney!" Rachel said the words, meaning to mean them, but not quite able to convince even herself.

He spread an open hand over the wet outline of her breast and grinned. "Is this so bad, Rachel? Hmmmm? It feels good to me, real good."

Then, he was kissing her again, and it did feel good.

It felt good to be in Cal's arms again. It was as if he had never left, as if they had never been apart, not even for one single night. He played with her breast, just enough so Rachel moaned helplessly into his mouth, then he slid both hands down along her waist, stopping and pressing, kneading and caressing, along the way. "You, my dear, are in big trouble," he said against her lips, loosening the tie to her wrapper.

Big trouble is right, Rachel thought wryly. She didn't, however, move or even attempt to open her eyes. "Is that so?"

"It is a known fact, Mrs. Delaney, that there are three things a cowboy yearns for after many weeks of deprivation on the range." Cal peeled the soaked outer garment from her shoulders, tugged it off, and tossed it away.

"And those three things are?"

"First, and foremost is a hot bath." Rachel felt him reaching around her legs to nudge the hem of her nightdress up, up . . . up.

"The second, of course, is a good, stiff drink."

Rachel flattened her palms on his chest and rose up onto her knees. "But I bet it's the third thing that gets us in trouble," she said.

"Ah, yes, it's that third thing." He grasped her naked hips, pulling her forward so that she straddled him. The erection he offered her was no insignificant matter. Rachel felt his teeth graze her breast through the thin material still plastered to her skin.

"Oh, Rachel, honey, I missed you," he whispered, one hand dropping to stroke between her thighs.

I missed you too, Rachel thought. More than she had ever imagined.

She sucked in a breath as his fingers slipped inside of her. "Does it . . . does it work in the water?"

"I don't know," he replied. "Fish must do it."

Rachel lowered herself onto him, feeling him slide into her, smooth and deep. "Oh . . . oh, Cal, I think . . ."

"Oh, yes," he said breathlessly, laughing, "I think it works in the water. I think it works just fine."

And it did.

Cal felt like he had contracted a case of leprosy. It wasn't that he minded eating supper alone. He had eaten many solitary meals hunkered over a campfire, and those meals—beef jerky, canned beans, dried fruits, wild rabbit or squirrel cooked unevenly over a fire—hadn't been nearly as tasty as the one he was working on at the moment.

Galen had been the first to excuse himself, mumbling something about wanting to retire early. Nick had followed suit. Daisy had picked at her bird's portion before announcing she had a splitting headache. Soon after, Rachel, who had been looking a little green ever since coming to the table, had suddenly covered her mouth with one hand and dashed from the room.

That had left Cal and Charlotte alone at the huge dining room table. Cal, who had never had much to say to Charlotte in the past, saw no reason to start turning chatty at this late date. He continued with his meal in silence, piling a healthy second portion onto his plate. For a long time there was no sound in the room except for the occasional scraping of utensils.

This was apparently too much for Charlotte, who soon excused herself and left the room looking as if she'd gotten a good whiff of skunk. Cal didn't take offense. Charlotte wore that expression most of the time, anyway.

Dolores burst in from the kitchen, punching the connecting door open with a smack. She swung it closed behind her, equally as noisily. *Everyone's catching it*, Cal thought as he scraped up the last of beef stew from his bowl.

She began gathering up the dishes, her skirt crackling briskly as she moved about the table. She stopped at Rachel's place setting, snatching up a plateful of nearly untouched food. She waggled it at Cal. "She'll have to start eating something soon, or—" She cut off and scowled.

"Or what?" Cal asked.

Dolores gave him a black look. "You done?"

"Yes. It was a delicious dinner, Dolores."

The housekeeper ignored the compliment. "Dessert?"

"Yes, thank you."

Her skirt whish-whooshed as she headed for the kitchen, then, *whump!* as she slammed the door behind her.

Cal wondered what it was he could have done to get Dolores riled. He couldn't think of a thing. Hell, he had only been back since this morning.

Smack! Whump! Whish-whoosh. Dolores appeared by his side and slapped down a plate of apple crisp.

"Looks good," Cal said cautiously.

The housekeeper grumbled as she gathered more dishes, then headed back to the kitchen. *Whish-whoosh. Whump!*

Since coming here, Cal had had his share of troubles with just about everyone in this household, but he had always gotten along with Dolores. Now, he rose from his seat, determined to find out what was bothering her.

When he stepped into the kitchen, Dolores was

busy scraping dishes with a mean-looking butcher knife. She didn't turn around, so Cal cleared his throat and spoke up. "Well?"

"Well what, Mr. Cal?"

"If there's something you'd like to say to me, now's the time. I never took you for one to mince words."

Dolores dropped a plate into soapy dishwater before turning to face him. "I don't know what you are talking about."

"What's the matter with everyone around here?"

"Everyone? Why not start with your wife?"

Cal stared at her. "Is there something wrong with Rachel? She didn't look too good when she left the table, but I just thought—"

"You thought!" Dolores jumped in, brandishing the knife perilously close to Cal's nose. He pulled back an inch just to be on the safe side. "Maybe you should have thought a little bit before now, hmmmmm?"

Cal studied her warily. If he didn't know better, he would suspect Dolores had learned of the marriage contract. "Is something wrong with Rachel?" he asked.

"Nothing that five more months will not cure!"

Nothing that five more months? Cal was accosted by a very old memory, the memory of his mother, pale and sickly, staring down at a bowl of steaming oatmeal. She had bolted from the room, too, but his father had assured Cal and Jessy that she was going to be all right; she was going to be more than all right, because—

Cal swallowed, his throat going dry. "What do you mean?"

Dolores rolled her eyes. "I shouldn't have said anything!" She turned away and snatched up another dirty dish.

"Are you saying that—" Cal stopped, squinting at Dolores's stiff back. "Are you saying Rachel is—" He stopped again, unable to spit out the word. "What exactly are you saying, Dolores?"

"I am not saying anything, Mr. Cal." Dolores turned to face him. "I am forbidden to *say* anything. Do you understand me?"

"No, Dolores, I don't understand." But he thought he did understand. He was starting to understand all too well.

"Ahhh!" She rolled her eyes and returned to her task. "I don't know which of you is more stupid!"

At this particular moment, Cal had to admit he was in no position to argue the point.

Cal stood outside the bedroom door, and, for the first time since his wedding night, debated whether he should knock before entering. He had been walking for hours in the dark, trying to dispel the hazy cloud of confusion that had descended upon him since his conversation with Dolores.

Pregnant.

Well, he had nobody to blame but himself. He hadn't done anything to avoid it, and he had known well enough that Rachel was not the kind of woman who knew how to avoid it on her own, but . . . Well, somehow he had thought it would take longer to actually conceive a child. Or, maybe he had just assumed it wouldn't really happen to them. Or, maybe, as Dolores had intimated, maybe he hadn't done much thinking about it at all. And that didn't make sense for a man who had always been meticulously careful about not leaving any bastard children in his wake, did it?

He was torn by conflicting emotions. There was a part of him that wanted to saddle Friday and head out of here, twenty thousand dollars or no twenty thousand dollars. There was also a part of him—a part he never realized existed—that glowed with a swaggering kind of male pride.

And so, he had walked and smoked and thought and walked some more, and now, as he stood outside the bedroom door, he still didn't feel any more clearminded than he had when Dolores's intimations had first started to sink into his dazed brain.

When he entered the room, he found Rachel tucked into bed, reading a book. She looked up. "Where were you?"

She didn't appear any different, not that he could see from here, anyway. Her hair was loose and wild about her face and shoulders. Her eyes were radiant in the lamplight. Same as always. Beautiful. Although, what had he expected? To stumble upon her knitting a pair of baby booties?

The look on his face must have given him away. Her brows drew together. "What are you staring at, Cal?"

Then he realized that what he was staring at was her stomach. He looked up at her face, feeling foolish. "I was out for a walk."

"Oh." Her puzzled gaze lingered on him for a moment before dropping back down to her book.

He started to get undressed for bed. She had sworn Dolores to secrecy. But why? Because Rachel wanted to tell him herself? Or because she didn't want him to know at all?

Cal climbed into bed beside her and stared at the ceiling. After a bit, Rachel closed her book and extinguished the lamp. It was quiet. Cal closed his eyes.

He could feel a light breeze coming from the open window.

"Cal?"

His eyelids shot open. "What?"

"There's something I should tell you."

His heart skipped a beat. "Yes?"

She paused, and he knew she was gathering her thoughts. Finally, "I had a talk with Nick."

Nick?

She continued, "I had a talk with Nick the other night, and he told me—"

"He told you what?"

"He had you checked out."

Cal fought down a surge of annoyance. "I figured as much."

"He told me about your family. I mean, about how . . . about what happened."

Cal didn't answer.

"I hope you're not angry."

"Why should I be angry?"

He felt her turn toward him, and her hand came to rest on his shoulder. "It was none of his business. Or mine for that matter."

Cal sighed and rolled onto his side to face her in the dark. "It's not a secret."

"I realize you don't like to talk about it."

"Would you?"

"I don't know how I would feel. It must have been horrible for you."

"It was, but it's over. I've finally closed the book on that chapter of my life." He reached out to run an idle hand along the length of her waist.

"Well, he's sorry."

"Sorry?" Cal nudged closer, feeling the urge to

touch a little more of her than just her waistline. Her scent stirred him. He thought that as long as he lived, he would forever associate roses with Rachel.

"Nick," she said sleepily, snuggling closer, accepting his caresses. "He's sorry he misjudged you."

Cal leaned over to touch his lips to hers. He let his hand slide down over her belly, and there it was, the slightest hint of a curve, a soft fullness where there had been none before. If he hadn't already known, he probably wouldn't have noticed it for quite some time yet. An unexpected feeling of elation swelled in his chest, and he couldn't help the grin that spread across his face. It was true. His lovely young wife was knocked higher than a kite!

Unaware of his thoughts, she sighed, draping her arms around his neck. "We already did this once today, remember?"

"That was before," Cal said, nibbling at her neck playfully.

"Before what?"

Before he'd had a little talk with the housekeeper. "Before supper," he replied. And they said no more.

25

Cal stepped up to the bar and slapped down a bill. "Forty rod lightning, Howard, and keep it coming till I hit the floor."

Howard moved to fill Cal's order. He wore a little smile that said he knew men with drinking problems and men with problems to drink. And Cal Delaney was a man hell-bent on soaking himself but good.

It was still early in the evening. Only the double-fisted drinkers were in residence at this hour. Lacey Holloway stood by Big Bart at the piano, throwing furtive glances at Cal. Judging by her manner, she was still licking her wounds from their last encounter. That was fine with Cal. He wasn't looking for a woman. He had enough of that at home.

Howard slapped down a glass and a bottle. "Holler when you're done."

Cal poured out a shot. He was indeed a man with a lot on his mind. Howard couldn't possibly have any

idea how much. And if Cal's problems had even a slim
chance of being erased with liquor, they were surely
going to be erased tonight.

All week, he had given Rachel ample opportunity to
tell him of her condition, but still she had said nothing.
He had watched her each morning as her face paled and
she excused herself from breakfast. He had watched her
as she dressed, struggling valiantly to fasten skirts that
were too tight. How long did she think she could keep
this up? How stupid did she think he was?

His resentment had grown with each day that
passed. He was really beginning to believe she was
waiting for their contract to be up. She was waiting for
him to leave.

Most women would be daunted by the idea of raising
a child alone. Most women needed a man to provide
for them. But Rachel wasn't most women. Rachel had
financial resources of her own, financial resources that
made Cal's ability to earn a living look like a joke. She
had his name, which was all she needed to give legiti-
macy to the child she was carrying.

His proud self urged him to leave. If she didn't want
him or need him, then what was the point of sticking
around?

Cal tossed back the hard-edged liquor in one gulp.
It jolted its way down, leaving a trail of fire in its wake,
but he knew it would take quite a few more of the
same to muffle the confusion in his mind. He poured
another.

The problem was, Cal wasn't sure he could live with
himself if he left. It wouldn't be long before he started
wondering if he had a son or daughter. He would wonder what the child looked like. If it was a son, would
he look like Cal? Would he have inherited the square

jaw Cal had taken from his own father? And what if it was a daughter? Would there be, in the tilt of her mouth or the color of her hair, a passing reminiscence of a girl named Jessica? Would there be a winsome, bright light in the eyes of that child, a light he hadn't seen since a toddler named Rebecca had been laid to rest somewhere far away in Kansas?

Big Bart was pounding the piano keys in a lively tune. Cal couldn't quite place the name of it. He took another shot, like bitter medicine, swallowing it with a gulp and a grimace.

And so, how could he leave? Contract or no contract, he knew he could stay on at the Elena Rose, taking on the permanent role of husband to Rachel and son-in-law to Galen. Cal respected Galen and liked working the Elena Rose. He had even found a stalwart friend in the gentle giant Paco, and Cal knew he had managed to gain the friendship and respect of the other men who worked the ranch as well. It was a good feeling, a hard feeling to leave behind.

"Long time no see, Cal. What've you been up to?"

Cal looked over to see that Sarah Lundquist, one of the working girls, had sidled close. She was a slim brunette, pretty, with a sprinkling of freckles across her nose.

Cal gulped down another shot. This one burned going down, but not quite as much as the two before. He knew he was on his way. "Work mostly," he answered.

"What brings you around tonight?"

Cal looked at Sarah again. She was clean and pretty. That used to be enough for him. Her eyes, of course, were brown, not green. No flecks of amber, no flashes of fire. Her hair was straight and shiny, pulled back into a little twisty-knot with a feather poking out of it.

Cal thought he preferred Rachel's hair, all wild and crazy with firelights and curls, unpredictable, like the woman who owned it.

He looked away, toying with his empty glass. "Just worked myself up a big thirst, Sarah. I reckon I'll get myself good and drunked up and then knock on home."

"Well, it was good seeing you. Come around again soon." And she was gone.

Cal continued drinking in gloomy silence. His job on the Elena Rose was just that, a job. He yearned for something more—a place of his own, a corner of the earth where he could build his own home and work for himself. He was only now beginning to understand what it was that had compelled his father to leave a safe, secure life in Ohio to move to Kansas.

"Woman problems, Cal?"

Cal was chagrined to see that Abner Troublefield leaned on the bar next to him. Abner was a local farmer who often chose to mix here with the cowpunchers; that is, whenever he could manage to sneak out of the house. He had a brood of six whining children and a wife well known to wear the pants in the family. It wasn't any wonder Abner envied the carefree, bachelor life of the average cowboy.

Right now, though, looking into the wounded, grizzled countenance of the man, Cal resented that Abner seemed to be looking at him as if the two of them were a pair of pigs stuck in the same pen. "Woman problems?" Cal snapped. "Hell no! What makes you say that?"

"Ya jest look like a man with woman problems is all."

"Look, Abner, just because you might have woman problems doesn't mean everyone has woman problems."

Abner squinted at him doubtfully. "A mite itchy

there, ain't ya, Cal? I mean, for a man without woman problems."

Cal didn't answer as he poured out another shot.

Abner slurped the last of his beer. "Oh yeah. Uh huh," he continued with a sigh. "The wife done found my last jug of corn likker and chucked it right outen the door of the chicken coop this mornin'. We had a helluva holler over that one."

"The chicken coop?"

"That's where I was keepin' the last of it," Abner answered, staring mournfully into his drained beer mug. "Damn woman sniffed it out somehows. I dunno."

Cal nodded and looked away as the two of them fell into a philosophical silence. He motioned for the bartender's attention. "Howard, pour out another beer for my pal, Abner!"

The sun was dropping into its western pocket. Across the street from the Red Panther Saloon, in front of a livery stable, Eli Walsh pulled a small brown bottle from the pocket of his black duster, uncorked it, and took a swallow. He wasn't concerned that the laudanum would dull his reflexes; he was too keyed up for it to have much of an effect. The waiting was over. The time had come. Soon, he would face his enemy.

Eli was not a religious man by any stretch of the imagination. He was not even inclined to think in the abstract if he could avoid it, but this evening, as he sat waiting for Delaney to emerge from the saloon, he was becoming more and more taken with the idea that fate was at work. Destiny. He had not planned to meet Delaney this night. If Eli had emerged from the livery a moment sooner or a moment later, he would have missed his enemy entering the saloon across the street. As it was, Eli had looked up just in time to catch a glimpse of Delaney pushing through those doors. And he had been alone.

Eli had sauntered across the street only once, just to make sure his enemy hadn't slipped out the back door. He spotted Delaney through a dirt-streaked side window of the saloon and was assured the man wasn't going anywhere soon. Delaney was parked at the bar, his head bent, a half-full bottle of whiskey in front of him. Eli knew then that the man had gotten sloppy. Unarmed and clearly intending to get drunk, Delaney was practically falling into Eli's lap, just begging to be picked off.

As it was, Eli now had plenty of time to wait and think. Maybe he would catch Delaney in an alley like he had Billy Wharton; or, if Delaney left on horseback, Eli would follow him into the night; or, if Delaney decided to buy himself a whore, that would be even better. A man caught with his pants down was hardly in a position to react swiftly. Eli thought he might even kill the girl right in front of him. If Delaney did indeed have a conscience, this would rattle him, sweeten the pie. If not, it would be no big loss. What was most important to Eli was time and privacy. He needed to have a little talk with Delaney, a little talk about Max and Leo. And when the moment finally came that Eli exacted his revenge, he wanted to make sure it was personal, that Cal Delaney knew exactly why he was going to die and by whose hand. Eli wanted to see his face.

Eli lifted his head slowly as he tucked the laudanum back into his coat pocket. He gazed at the false front of the Red Panther Saloon and waited.

*   *   *

Cal stood with his elbow propped on the bar, his chin cupped in one hand. It seemed as if Abner had been droning on for hours, and his head was fuzzing up. He was feeling . . . well, not quite as bad as he did when he walked in the door, and that had been the whole point of coming here. He hoped Friday remembered the way back to the ranch.

Now, Abner finished the last of his third beer at Cal's expense. "Take, take, take! I works my fingers to the bone and the durn woman's never satisfied!"

The crowd had thickened. Big Bart—the best damned *pie-anna* player in Texas, according to Abner—was working up a helluva sweat, and the booze was flowing.

Abner was now dropping valuable pearls of wisdom for free. "Ah yes, once a man gets hisself hitched, the best he can look forward to is gettin' pissin' drunk whenever he can steal hisself the chance!"

Cal tossed off another shot and muttered wearily, "I've gotten better advice from my horse, Abner."

The older man didn't seem to hear. He kept on unabated, knitting his eyebrows fiercely and shaking one skinny fist. "There comes a time when a man's got to ask hisself, is I a man or is I a mouse?"

"A man, cause your wife's afraid of mice," Cal mumbled.

"What you say there, Cal?"

Cal shook his head and straightened abruptly. "I reckon I'm about done, Abner. You want the rest of that?" He pointed to the bottle.

Abner blinked bloodshot eyes, seeming to forget his earlier fervor. "Oh, sure thing! Much obliged,

Cal! Much obliged! Sure ya can't stay for jest one more?"

Cal adjusted his hat, wobbling on his feet only slightly as he did so. "No sir, you just go ahead and . . . go right ahead and finish that sucker off for me, Abner. I can't think of anyone I'd . . . who deserves it more than you."

"You take care of yerself there, Cal Delaney! Don't go lettin' that little woman wear ya down none, no sirree bob!"

Cal turned to leave, imagining with some amusement how Rachel would react to Abner dubbing her Cal's little woman. He pushed through the doors into the cooling temperatures of the evening and stood on the edge of the boardwalk, waiting for his head to clear. The moon had risen. Judging by the position of the stars, he reckoned it was close to nine o'clock.

He had put in a long, hard day. Summer was a thing of the past, but the afternoons were still hot. They had been working on erecting a section of barbed-wire fencing along the southeastern boundary and making good progress.

He had come home tired and not at all in the mood to hear from Charlotte that Rachel had taken off on one of her solitary jaunts. Apparently, this wasn't the first time. Rachel had been known to disappear for days on end when she was in one of these moods. Charlotte had smirkingly passed on Rachel's message that she didn't want to be disturbed.

He knew where she was. She was at the line cabin, the same cabin where they had sought shelter during that thunderstorm, the cabin where they had made love for the first time.

The whole town, all except for the saloons at this end

of the street, looked to be sleeping. Cal suddenly remembered he had left Friday tethered between Fourth and Fifth streets. Searching his vest pocket for a cigar, he started out toward the respectable end of town.

Although annoyed with her, Cal wasn't surprised by Rachel's latest action. She was probably up there moping. Well, he sure as hell wasn't going to go after her. She would have to come back on her own. Maybe by then she would have come to her senses. Maybe she would tell him the truth. After all, the only thing he really needed to hear from her was one sentence: *I want you to stay, Cal.* If not, he would be left to make his decision alone. Go or stay. Turn his back or make a home on the Elena Rose.

The street was empty, eerily silent except for the music issuing from the saloons that were far behind him now. Cal stopped to light his cigar. When he was done, he shook out his match and lifted his head to peer at the sky. Then he heard something.

Eli had removed his spurs and was careful to walk in the street. Even at a distance, he didn't want to take the chance Delaney might pick up the sound of his footsteps on the boardwalk. The streets were deserted, almost too deserted. It was as if God—or Fate—had pushed a people-broom straight down the center of town, clearing out the clutter for the confrontation to come.

Eli's limp was more pronounced than usual, but he was barely aware of it, of the ache in his left leg, the one that usually bothered him only on rainy days. The ache was an old one, years old, and he was used to it. He was also quite positive that the silhouette thirty paces ahead of him on this darkened, deserted street was the man responsible for it.

Eli pulled the laudanum bottle from his coat pocket, uncorked it as he walked, and took a throat-numbing swallow. Then he slipped the bottle back into his pocket and kept moving, limping, quiet as a cat. He was gaining on the figure in front of him, the figure that moved at such a leisurely pace, lost in thoughts of his own . . . begging for it.

Delaney stopped suddenly, and Eli halted not far behind, hardly daring to breathe, ready to duck into the shadows if necessary.

But Delaney was only lighting a cigar. Eli let out his breath and saw in the flare of the match that he stood directly adjacent to a dark, empty alley. Eli knew that particular alley. It was the one between the dress shop and the mercantile. It was where Lacey Holloway had taken him to meet Daisy Girard. Fate.

Eli's fingers flexed and unflexed at his sides as he started to move forward again, slowly, silently. Seconds now. His nerves were buzzing. Blood pounded in his head. Eli twisted his wrist, releasing a tiny metallic spring strapped beneath his shirtsleeve. A silver stiletto slid from its hidden sheath straight into his open right palm.

Something pulled at Cal to turn around. A sound? Later, he wasn't sure if that was exactly what it was or not. And later, he wouldn't give it much more than a passing thought, anyway. It wasn't the sound—if that's what it had been at all—but something that tugged on nerves that had long been dormant.

Like a bolt from hell, those nerves were suddenly screaming, *Behind you!*

"Cal!"

Cal whirled and froze, both hands dropping to clutch at empty air just as he recognized that voice. "Paco!"

A familiar form emerged from the shadows to his right. Cal released a pent-up breath as his friend lumbered forward. "What's the matter, Cal? You look like you seen a ghost!"

Cal swore under his breath and willed himself to relax. "Paco, what are you trying to do? Scare the hell out me?"

Paco approached him and stopped, his thumbs hooked in his suspenders. He chuckled. "I guess I'm lucky you don't wear those guns anymore! I'd be one full-of-holes greaser!"

"Damn straight," Cal muttered, pulling the cigar from his mouth. "And what the hell are you doing here, anyway? You wouldn't happen to be watchdogging for Galen, would you?"

Even in this light, Cal couldn't miss the good-natured twinkle in Paco's eye. "No, sir. Just keeping an eye out for a friend is all. Nothing wrong with that, is there?"

Cal studied Paco's massive form for a long moment before replying. "No, I guess there isn't. You ready to head out?"

Paco laughed and clapped Cal on the back. Cal nearly stumbled and fell flat on his face under the brunt of that friendly swat. As they started to move away, Cal thought Paco could probably wrestle a bull and come out on top of the deal. Not a bad guy to have on your side in a pinch.

"You know, Paco," Cal added as they continued together up the street, "you shouldn't go sneaking up on people like that. Someone's liable to get hurt."

26

Lacey peered into the mirror over the wash-basin in her room and, with trembling fingers, tested the purple welt above her left cheekbone. Her eye was blackening, its lid already half-closed. On her neck were five purpling fingerprints, and a lump the size of a robin's egg had grown on the back of her head. But all of this was the least of her worries. She figured she had gotten off pretty light. Dockett was crazy, and Lacey fully realized that if he hadn't been in such a hurry, he probably would have stayed to finish her off.

As it was, he had only roughed her up and knocked her out. That was early this morning. Now, it was close to ten o'clock. She had been out almost an hour.

Ever since that first night, when Joe had sauntered into the Red Panther, he had started staying with Lacey in her room at Dolly's whenever he was in town. She had known from then on that Joe Dockett was a strange one. Oh, he had paid her well enough, but nothing ever happened. That first night, when she cozied up to him, he had gotten spitting mad, and Lacey had seen for the first time that flash of crazy in his eyes that warned her Joe Dockett was more than just a little bit dangerous.

He had told her he didn't want any part of her, that he was just using her room so he could stay in town without registering at the hotel. He was taking great pains to ensure Cal didn't catch wind of a stranger in town. Lacey should have known then it was more than money Dockett was after. She should have known, but maybe she hadn't wanted to know.

Soon after that, she had taken him to meet Daisy Girard, and, in so doing, had effectively ended her own usefulness. He had stayed over in her room a few times after that, but whenever they were alone, she had gotten the feeling she no longer really existed for him. Whenever she got up the nerve to speak and he looked up, he seemed to stare more through her than at her, and soon Lacey had stopped speaking altogether.

That was, until last night. Something happened last night, and Lacey knew it had to do with Cal, who had stopped in at the Red Panther for the first time in months. Lacey assumed Joe had already left for Dallas by then. And besides, by then, she wasn't so sure she still wanted to let Joe in on Cal's whereabouts anyway. Lacey had reason to want to see Cal put in his place, but that didn't include hurting him, and Lacey was starting to think that was exactly what Joe Dockett had in mind.

Later, Dockett had come to her in a fury, snatching up her water pitcher and hurling it across the room to blow out against the wall in a shower of shattered glass and water. Lacey had stared at the running stains on the wallpaper, her heart pounding in her throat. He had never resorted to violence until then, and in that moment, she knew Dockett was quite capable of murder.

This morning, he had gone one last time to meet Daisy and had returned with a gleam in his eye Lacey hadn't liked at all. She had stood aside while he packed up his saddlebags.

"Going back to Dallas, Joe?" she asked cautiously, hovering by the door, just in case.

He didn't look up. "Not Dallas. No more Dallas, missy. I'm done waiting."

Done waiting? Did that mean he was giving up on Cal or . . . ? She tried to smooth the nervousness in her voice. "You found a way to meet with Cal Delaney?"

"That son of a bitch's luck has just run out."

She hesitated before steeling her nerve. "You're not going to hurt him, are you, Joe? I mean, it *is* just money you're after, right?"

Evidently she had tripped his wire. He raised his head to peer at her, and she could tell he had heard her this time, really *heard* her, the worried tone in her voice. His black eyes narrowed, and when he straightened, leaving his saddlebags open on the bed, his voice froze her blood. "You ain't thinking of turning on me, are you, missy? Because if you're thinking of turning on me . . ."

And before she could move, could even *think* of moving, he had her by the throat, squeezing so hard she thought her neck would break. With one hand, he yanked her forward and then rammed her back into the wall. She saw stars and heard the plaster crumble behind her head, and he was saying something, something awful, she was sure, but she couldn't quite make out the words. All she could think about was the fact that she couldn't breathe. And then he must have used his fist, harder than her father ever had, and, thankfully, she had passed out cold. She truly believed that if she hadn't passed out, he would have killed her.

Now, Lacey stared at the misshapen, stranger's face in her mirror, knowing what she had to do. Cal had to be warned. That was, if it wasn't already too late.

Daisy couldn't believe her eyes. "Oh, no," she breathed, her voice trailing off to a whisper as she stared out the parlor window. A sudden series of hoots and whistles from the ranch hands in the corral had drawn her attention, and now she saw what the ruckus was all about.

"What is it, Daisy?" Charlotte approached from behind and craned her neck to see out the window. Then she gasped, horrified. "God save us! What are *they* doing here?"

Daisy couldn't bring herself to answer. There could be no mistaking the brightly garbed, notorious madam, and now, as they drew nearer to the house, Daisy could see that Lacey was seated next to Dolly Jordan in the buckboard that was now negotiating its way up the dirt drive.

"The nerve! The utter gall!" Charlotte was in a righteous flurry. "Those tawdry women showing up on our doorstep in broad daylight! Oh, just shoot me now! If this gets around town, we'll never be able to live it down! Never!"

Daisy dropped the curtain and pushed past her mother-in-law. She had to find out what was going on. Land's sake! It was Saturday, and Nick was home, working in Galen's study. What if Lacey planned to tell him about their secret meetings? Then another possibility occurred to her, a possibility that caused her heart to pound like a drum. What if Lacey planned on exposing her not only to Nick, but to Galen and Charlotte and to everyone else?

Daisy fairly flew through the parlor doorway and down the hall to the front door. Even so, by the time she reached the corral, both Dolly and Lacey were already climbing down from the buckboard and drawing a crowd of grinning ranch hands. More whistles and raucus calls were coming from the stable.

Daisy lowered her voice. "What are you doing here, you little—" She grabbed Lacey's arm and spun her around. Then her mouth fell open in shock. Lacey wore a floppy sun bonnet to shade her face, but it did little to hide the swelling bruises and angry welts. Daisy dropped Lacey's arm like a glowing coal and raised a hand to her mouth. "Oh, my heavens! What happened to—"

"We need to talk to Cal," Dolly interrupted sternly.

By now, Charlotte was charging up from behind. "See here, Dolly Jordan! You have no business here! You just take that wagon of yours and turn it right back around."

Dolly's dark brown eyes blazed as she straightened her shoulders and pulled herself up to full height. "Charlotte Girard, I am here on important business, and I will thank you to keep your persnickety opinions to yourself. We need to speak to Cal Delaney immediately. It's an emergency."

"I'm here. What do you want?"

All four women turned as Cal approached their corner of the corral, a lariat slung over one shoulder. A few cowhands emerged from the stable behind him to join the small group that had already formed.

Cal's eyes narrowed upon seeing his ex-paramour's bruised face. "What happened, Lacey?"

"He . . . he hit me, Cal. The man who come to town after you."

"What man? Who did this to you?"

"He—he said his name was Dockett. Joe Dockett."

"Dockett?"

Before Lacey could continue, Galen's voice boomed from behind as he approached from the house. "What the devil's going on? Sounds like a blasted barn party out here!"

Daisy turned and saw that Nick was with him.

Galen nodded at Dolly in greeting. "Afternoon, Miss Dolly."

Dolly didn't miss the opportunity to throw Charlotte a triumphant side glance. "Good afternoon, Galen. Nicholas."

"Now, just what is it that brings you and Miss Holloway out to the Elena Rose this afternoon?" Galen inquired.

Dolly inclined her platinum head in Lacey's direction. "We've got trouble, Galen."

The older man's expression clouded upon taking in Lacey's battered face. "Did one of my boys do that to you, young lady? If that's the case—"

"Joe Dockett," Cal cut in, his grim tone causing heads to turn back in his direction. He leveled a hard gaze at Lacey. "What did he want?"

Lacey swallowed, fighting a sudden gush of tears with little success. "He's been in town off and on for about a month now. I—I thought at first he wanted money, you see, and—"

Cal took Lacey by the arm, suddenly urgent. "What did he look like?"

Daisy didn't miss Lacey's instinctive flinch. She was frightened, and Daisy knew very well why. Lacey had been conspiring with Joe Dockett behind Cal's back for the last month. Daisy held her breath, feeling a stab of fear shoot through her belly. Daisy had also been conspiring with Joe Dockett. Just this morning, as a matter of fact. God help her. Was Lacey going to spill the beans?

Lacey sniffled, tears now trickling down her cheeks unchecked. "Well, he's a big fella with black hair and a mustache and . . . very dark eyes, kind of scary eyes."

"Empty eyes," Cal said, his face paling, his voice dropping to a whisper.

The ranch hands had quieted down. There was near silence in the air, all save the whisper of the late afternoon breeze and the ever-present lowing of cows in the holding pens behind the corral.

"I thought he just wanted money, Cal. He told me you owed him money, and so I didn't think there was any harm, you see, and . . ." Lacey started to sob, becoming less and less coherent. "He started acting strange, and I knew something wasn't right, and then, this morning, he said . . . he said . . ."

"What did he say?"

"Oh, Cal, he said that the waiting was over. He left to come after you, and I thought he was going to kill you!"

Nick stepped forward, clearly distressed at Lacey's tears. "Stop crying. Cal's fine. You can see that, can't you?"

Cal was exhibiting less tact in dealing with the weeping girl. He forced her to look at him again. "There's more, isn't there?"

Galen stepped forward, admonishing, "See here, Cal. What's going on? Is this someone you know?"

"Yeah. I know him, all right."

Lacey plunged on. "Joe met with Daisy this morning, and when he came back, he had murder in his eyes, Cal. I don't know what she told him." Lacey's head turned in Daisy's direction.

All heads now turned in Daisy's direction, and she read their faces. Surprise. Curiosity. Accusation. She retreated a step. "What's everybody looking at me for? She's lying. I don't know why, but she's—"

Nick's expression darkened, and he strode forward to snatch Daisy's elbow before she could elude him. "I know you were in town this morning! Did you see this man?"

Daisy's mouth open and closed, but only unintelligible stammers came out. Nick looked angry enough to strike her.

He took her by both shoulders and shook her hard enough to snap her to attention. "Daisy!"

That did it. Words tumbled free. "I don't know how, but he already knew Cal was back from roundup. He wanted to get Cal alone to talk to him about some old debt." Daisy shot Cal a pleading look. "That's what he said. Some old debt that you owed him. I didn't know he was dangerous. I swear, I didn't know he was—"

Nick shook her again. "Stop blathering!"

Daisy looked back up into Nick's furious countenance, cowering. "He wanted to know how he could get Cal alone, and I told him I didn't know. I told him that whenever Cal's working the ranch, he's always with the other hands."

"And that's it?"

Daisy felt everyone staring at her, and grew flustered again. "I—I think so, except . . ."

"Except?"

Daisy tried to think. "Yes, except for the thing about Rachel." She stopped and bit her lip as a very bad, very sick feeling started to creep into her stomach, a feeling even worse than that caused by Nick's molten stare. "I said it was too bad it was Cal who owed him all that money because it's Rachel who's all alone." Her eyes moved fearfully to meet Cal's flat gaze. "Up at the line cabin."

It was September, but Rachel was doing some spring cleaning anyway. If she had been at the ranch house, she probably would have set to work grooming her horses and mucking out stalls. Yesterday, she had spent most of the day riding her best palomino, Misty, who was now tethered in back of the little line cabin, grazing to a fool's content on long grass.

Unlike Misty, however, who was blessedly ignorant of life's vicissitudes, Rachel felt the need to keep herself busy. She had too much on her mind to sit around and read or compose letters or play solitaire. Emptying her mind of worries was not proving so easy this time.

Rachel straightened up slightly, still on her knees. She dropped her scrub brush into the wooden bucket next to her and grimaced as a twinge of pain pinched her lower back. She had been bent over in one position for too long.

Pressing one hand to the ache in her back, the other unconsciously dropped to the softened contours of her burgeoning abdomen. She knew her new plumpness was not noticeable beneath her skirts—not unless one were to look very closely for it—but she could feel the changes in her body most keenly. More and more each day. Today, her belly felt very full and heavy, much like her tender breasts. And she was tired.

She cast a longing eye to the narrow cot in the corner, debating whether to curl up for an afternoon catnap. Just a month ago the thought of sloughing off in the middle of the day would have horrified her. Now, she wondered what other surprises her body had in store for her during the coming months.

After a moment of guilty indecision, she rose to her feet and crossed the room to the cot, lowering herself to a sitting position, then bending to unlace her shoes. She felt the top hook on the waistband of her riding skirt give with a *pop!* and she straightened, her lip curling in disgust. Dolores had let that waistband out just days ago!

"Oh, hell and thunder," she muttered under her breath, reaching back to undo the remaining hooks, then bending again to wrestle her shoes off. "At this rate, I'm going to be big as a barn in a matter of weeks!"

She flopped onto her side, resting her head on the pillow, closing her eyes. *At this rate*, a lecturing voice in her mind added, *Cal's going to be figuring out the truth for himself. And mighty soon, too.*

"Can't hide the truth," Rachel whispered aloud.

The truth. Rachel knew very well what the truth was. The truth was, she had Cal's baby growing inside her, and he had a right to know about it. The truth was, she didn't want a divorce from Cal. Not in a month. Not ever. She wanted him to stay. She wanted him to stay more than anything else in the world— more, even, than she wanted the Elena Rose. But she wanted him to stay because he loved her, not because she happened to be carrying his child.

"He doesn't love you, and he certainly doesn't want a baby," she mumbled, her words starting to slur sleepily. "He said so himself, didn't he? No family . . ."

Rachel opened her eyes, blinking painfully against the sunlight that slanted in the hide-covered window. She must have dozed off. But for how long?

And then she heard it—a horse whickering just outside the window—and she shot up to a sitting position, shaking her head, inadvertently loosening the bun coiled at her neck. That wasn't Misty. Misty was tethered out back, and she was certain the sounds had come from out front. She jumped to her feet, still groggy as she moved for the door.

Then she heard spurs jingling against wooden planks, and her heart swelled. Cal! He had come for her after all. She suddenly wished she hadn't spent most of the morning on her hands and knees, scrubbing that filthy floor. She must look a fright!

She reached for the latch. At that precise moment, she heard a loud clap and felt the door shudder from a jarring impact. It flew back on its hinges so suddenly she was knocked clear off her feet. She landed on her rump, indignant and stunned, but when she opened her mouth to give her inconsiderate husband a piece of her mind, the words died a sudden death in her throat.

The man standing in the doorway was not Cal.

27

The sun was bright. Cool autumn breezes swept across the open range, stirring lush green grasses and pushing lazy white clouds across a dazzling blue sky. It was an ironic backdrop for the small posse's grim mission.

Friday was slick with sweat and blowing out beneath Cal, but the hearty stallion's gallop didn't falter. Squinting against the wind that whipped his face, Cal peered far ahead into the vast distance, scanning the horizon, praying he wouldn't find what he was searching for.

Cal and Nick rode at the head of the group, followed by Galen, his suntanned countenance unusually pale. Paco and ten other ranch hands, all armed with revolvers, shotguns, or Winchesters, brought up the rear. Another ranch hand had been sent into town to notify the marshal, not that it would matter. Cal knew that by the time any official authorities arrived on the scene, it would all be over. One way or another.

The significance of the name Joe Dockett and the horrifying ramifications of Daisy's final words had slammed into him with gut-wrenching force. As Daisy turned to him, her blue eyes wide and fearful, Cal had moved to grasp a corner of the buckboard, a wave of nausea rising up from the pit of his stomach. Joe Dockett. It was an old alias used by the third brother, Eli, the one who was supposed to be somewhere in California. But he wasn't in California. He was in Texas. He was here. And he had Rachel.

For the first time in his life, Cal's hands were unsteady as he buckled on his gun belt and tied down his holsters. Galen had approached him, checking his own rifle loads. "Who is this man? What does he want?"

"Me," Cal had answered flatly, thumbing cartridges into his Cavalry Colt with numb fingers. "He wants me."

"Then maybe he'll let Rachel go."

"No," Cal said, shoving his gun back into its holster.

"But his argument is with you. Rachel doesn't have anything to do with it."

Cal eased the Colt from its holster twice, making sure it didn't hang up, before turning to face his father-in-law. "I have a feeling that's not the way he's going to see it."

"But he doesn't have any reason to hurt Rachel. She's—"

"She's my wife. That's all the reason he needs."

Now, Cal tried to shut out the memory of Galen's stricken expression as Nick leaned forward on his mount, pointing into the spreading distance. Nick raised his voice over thudding hooves and whistling wind. "Another mile or two yet!"

Cal didn't answer. Another mile or two. Would it matter?

He had never met Eli Walsh face-to-face, but he knew the man as well as he knew himself. After all, he had tracked him not only across the miles but across the years. In the long run, Cal had never caught up with that elusive middle brother. Time and fate had intervened. Then Cal made the decision to drop the vendetta that had driven him like a man possessed for years. But now, his own lust for vengeance had risen from the ashes to come about full circle. His vendetta had returned to mock him.

Cal tightened his grip on the reins, trying to put himself into Eli's mind. Why had he taken Rachel? To lure Cal to the line cabin? No. That couldn't be all of it. Eli was murderous, but he wasn't stupid. Surely, he would know that holding a wealthy heiress hostage would practically bring out the cavalry in response. Holding Rachel for the simple purpose of luring Cal to the line cabin was not only foolhardy, it was suicidal. Eli might get one clear shot at Cal, but after that, surely the man knew he would be instantaneously cut down by the others. It didn't make sense, unless . . .

Eli was on some twisted mission of vengeance for the death of his brothers. He would kill Rachel to settle his score with Cal. That was his plan. Eli would be long gone by the time Cal reached the cabin, just like the time Cal had returned too late to save his mother and Jessica. Dear God, it was going to happen all over again.

Cal scanned the horizon, searching for tendrils of black smoke. He kicked Friday into a swifter gallop, shooting ahead of Nick, trying to quell the paralyzing certainty that they were already too late, that all they would find when they reached the line cabin would be smoldering ruins.

Grasping the hot metal coffeepot with a potholder, Rachel crossed to the table where the dark man sat. He was big, big as Cal, with broad, powerful shoulders and thick, muscled arms beneath his black linen shirt. For the past four hours or so, he had mostly ignored her as he paced the small cabin, muttering to himself, then every so often, dropping into a stool by the table to idly spin the chamber of his Colt revolver. He was spinning it now as she poured his coffee.

A thought crossed her mind, a fleeting, impulsive, very dangerous thought—she could fling that pot of hot coffee right into his face and make a break for it, but—

Quick as a striking snake, his hand shot out to grab her wrist. Hot coffee sloshed out over the spout, spreading in a steaming black puddle on the wooden table next to his cup. Her stomach turned over as those black, bloodshot eyes raised to scrutinize her face. "What's on your mind, missy?"

Rachel barely managed to keep her grip on the coffeepot, trying not to show her fear. "Nothing. Nothing's on my mind, Mr. Walsh. If you'll please just let go of my—"

"Not much longer, missy. Not much longer now, eh?"

Rachel knew what he was referring to. "I told you before, Mr. Walsh, there's a good chance he won't come after me at all."

The dark man chuckled. It was not a comforting sound. "An arranged marriage, you said. He doesn't give a damn, right?"

Rachel's gaze dropped to her wrist, where he still held her, squeezing so hard the tips of her fingers were starting to tingle. "That's right. It's my father you're likely to have to deal with, my father and a dozen ranch hands, all of them armed to the teeth, so it would be most wise of you to reconsider your plans and be on your way before they arrive. There's no way you can—"

"I can and I will, missy. That slut in town has probably already warned him. He'll know what this is about, and he'll be here. We have a little score to settle."

"But you'll be killed."

His smile was so cold it froze her heart. "Yes, but I'll be taking a few people along for company."

He let go of her, and Rachel recoiled, dropping the coffeepot with a *clank*. She turned away, afraid the dark man would read the truth on her face. Cal would show up. Part of her wanted him to, needed him to. Another part of her, her rational self, prayed that he would stay away.

Rachel crossed the room to sit on the makeshift cot, not taking her eyes from Eli Walsh as he pulled a brown bottle from the pocket of his vest and poured a dollop of the potent liquid into his coffee. Since he arrived, she had seen him uncork that little brown bottle at least a dozen times to take it straight. At first she had thought it was liquor. Later she realized it was laudanum. By now, the man must have taken enough to knock a horse off its feet, but still, he remained alert and tense.

There was something terribly wrong with him. It wasn't even that warm out, but he was sweating profusely, and occasionally she would see him stop what he was doing to close his eyes and massage his temples. Now his hand trembled as he lifted the coffee cup to his lips. Haunted shadows lurked beneath his eyes. This man was close to the breaking point.

But she had sensed that from the very beginning.

"Don't give me any trouble, missy. I want you alive, but I don't need you alive. You understand me?"

Those had been his first words upon bursting like a phantom from hell into her cabin. He had snatched her by the front of her blouse, dragging her off her bottom and onto her feet in one brutal motion, then swinging her around and slamming her against the wall. From out of nowhere, he produced a sparkling stiletto blade, snipping the buttons from her blouse one by one, then slashing her chemise to prick the delicate skin between her breasts, just enough to draw blood and inject a thread of unbridled terror into Rachel's swirling, confused brain.

Afterward, he had forced her down onto the cot in the corner, and, for one terrifying, repulsive moment, Rachel believed he was going to rape her, but he didn't. In fact, he had shown almost no interest in her at all after that. He had become preoccupied with his own private thoughts as he paced the floor.

Rachel had soon tried talking to him to glean some information about why he was here and what he wanted from her, but his answers were often nonsensical. It took a while before she realized he was using her to lure Cal into some kind of deathtrap, and now she was sick with the knowledge that Cal could not possibly win against him. If Eli Walsh wasn't afraid of dying, he had nothing to lose. How could Cal fight against that? No, her husband was going to die and so, most likely, was Rachel and the unborn child she carried. That was the horrifying crux of Walsh's plan. For the second time in Cal's life, Eli intended to take his family away from him.

This realization in itself was stark and ugly and heartbreaking, but it was the sudden vision of Cal lying motionless with a crimson stain soaking the front of his shirt that finally unleashed Rachel's tears. She bent her head, praying silently that he would not come.

There was a sound, a sound barely discernible, but nevertheless unmistakable. Hoofbeats, lots of them, thudding the soft ground in the distance.

Rachel opened her eyes to see Walsh spring from his seat to the window, his Colt drawn and ready. "Well, missy, it looks like our waiting is over."

Cal had not seen Eli Walsh since the day his mother and sister had been murdered, but the glimpse he'd caught of that face twelve years ago was burned into his memory for all time. Cal recognized Eli even before sliding off his horse to approach the cabin. And Eli recognized Cal too. Those cunning dark eyes immediately picked him out of the advancing pack and focused on him.

"Stop right there! All of you! Or the little lady dies!"

Cal stopped at fifteen yards, his Cavalry Colt cocked and ready to fire. Eli stood in front of the open doorway, his left arm hooked around Rachel from behind, his forearm crossing up between her breasts so that his fingers spanned her throat. She stood stiff and dry eyed, her hair hanging loose.

To Cal, she looked even younger than her twenty-one years, not at all like the haughty, self-assured cattle princess he had first met in the Red Panther Saloon. This was the vulnerable Rachel, the Rachel who cried the night he gave her the heart locket, the Rachel who looked down at him so forlornly the morning he rode off to roundup, the Rachel he made love to that stormy night in this very line cabin. This was the girl he had fallen in love with, despite all his best efforts not to.

Cal's gaze fastened on the front of her blouse, which hung open, to the fringe of her chemise, which was clearly slashed, and he felt an irrepressible rage surge in his chest.

His furious glare clashed with Eli's, and the outlaw smiled, reading his mind. Rachel was his shield. There was no way Cal could get a clear shot, and Eli knew it.

He tapped the barrel of his revolver against Rachel's temple, still grinning. "Hey, Delaney! You got yourself a pretty little woman here, you know that?"

Cal didn't reply to Eli's taunting. He narrowed his eyes, noting that Eli's thumb did not rest ready on the cock. He guessed it was a double-action Colt.

Galen called out from somewhere behind Cal. "You release my daughter, and I'll pay you anything you want! Name your figure, Mr. Walsh!"

Eli's laugh was almost maniacal. "My figure is two dead brothers! You think you can pay me for two dead brothers? One's still rotting somewhere in the Panamint Mountains! The other's planted up on Boot Hill in Dodge City with a bullet in his back! How much you think that's worth, Mr. Girard?"

"The death of your brothers has nothing to do with me or my daughter. You've got no call to involve her in this."

"Well, life just ain't fair, Mr. Girard. It's a sad shame, ain't it?"

"I could make you a rich man, Mr. Walsh. You're a fool to throw it all away."

"Well, what we got here is one of those rare situations that money just can't make right, Mr. Girard. Only Cal Delaney's got the silver to pay me back. You know what I'm talking about, Cal?"

Cal's sights were trained point-center between those glittering black eyes, only inches from the top of Rachel's head, *inches*. "I know what you're talking about, Eli. You said it yourself. This is between you and me. Let her go and we'll settle it."

Eli threw his head back and hooted. "They say you can shoot the eyes out of a rabbit at fifty paces! Is that right, Delaney? How stupid do you think I am? Stupid as Billy Wharton? Stupid as poor Leo?"

Cal struggled to clear his mind of everything but that center point. If it were anyone but Rachel, dear God, anyone but Rachel. He called out, "Stupid was coming out here to take her in the first place, Eli! Now, you're a coward too, hiding behind a woman's skirts!"

Something in those black eyes flickered. Cal noticed for the first time that the barrel of Eli's Colt trembled. Nervous? Cal's eyes shifted back to Eli's cold, glittering gaze. No. Not nervous. Angry, maybe, but not nervous.

"You son of a bitch! All of you! Drop your weapons now or she dies!"

Cal didn't turn to see the others, but he sensed their hesitation.

"Drop them!"

Eli's threat was clear. This was no bluff.

Something thumped to the soft ground behind Cal. Galen's voice rose in command. "Do as he says!"

Cal heard the metallic *scratch-click* of armaments, then more thumps and clicks as firearms hit the ground, one after another after another. Then, everything was quiet. Soft breezes moved across the range around them, ruffling the tall grass.

Galen spoke, his voice tight and low. "Cal, do as he says."

Eli tapped the barrel against Rachel's temple again. "Your turn, Delaney. I'm getting tired of waiting."

"And if I do? Then what? You'll let her go and take me down? Is that the deal?"

Eli smiled. "That's the deal, Delaney. Your life for your wife's."

Nick's voice, a tight whisper from somewhere to his right. "Cal, you're going to get her killed. Give up your gun, and we'll try to get the drop on him before he fires on you. We don't have any choice."

Cal weighed this irrefutable logic. If he could only believe it were that simple—exchanging his own life for Rachel's. That would make it easy. But there was something wrong, something in Eli's eyes.

Cal tried to focus on the line of his sights, knowing that there could be no doubt. He had an innate ability to compensate for the natural trajectory of a bullet at just about any distance. The old gunhand Grady had called it a gift. All Cal knew was he had never had to think about it; not consciously, anyway. But he was thinking about it now.

Make a line, he told himself, *a pure, thin line of concentration.* But, instead, his mind threw up a hopeless jumble of images: Jessica's bent head, wispy tendrils of blond hair hiding her face, the barrel of a rifle trained on his mother's proud figure, hungry flames rising to lick the black night sky.

Eli's voice spiked the air. "You afraid to die for your woman, Delaney?"

Rachel suddenly cried out. "No!"

Cal's heart jumped into his throat, and his tentative aim flinched as Rachel tried to wrench free from Eli's iron hold. "Don't do it, Cal! He's going to shoot—"

Eli's fingers tightened around her throat, choking her off as he jerked her back up against his chest. "Shut up!"

Nick shouted, "Drop it, Cal! For God's sake, drop it!"

Cal ignored Nick's plea and addressed his enemy. "Is killing me going to be enough for you, Eli? After all this trouble you've gone to, is it going to be enough?"

Eli's reply came back, taunting. "What else is there?"

What else was there? Eli was playing a game.

Cal's palms were slick with sweat and his hand was dangerously unsteady.

Eli's finger rested ready on the trigger. The hammer wasn't cocked, but Cal was fairly sure it was a double-action piece. One pull of the trigger cocked the hammer and simultaneously fired the chamber. That's all it would take; one pull of that trigger and Rachel was dead. But they didn't call them thumb busters for nothing. There was a price to be paid for that double action. One split second.

Cal let out a pent-up breath, purposely relaxing his grip on the Colt's trigger and letting the barrel drop a fraction of an inch. "All right, Eli! You win!"

Those hellish black eyes lit up. A triumphant smile began to spread across Eli's face.

No, Cal thought, *you lose*. Then he raised his sights and fired.

28

Fifteen yards away, blood and skull fragments sprayed in all directions. Eli went down. So did Rachel. Cal's vision blurred as he dropped to his knees. *I killed her. I killed my beautiful Rachel.* The Colt slipped from his limp fingers and thumped to the grass. He closed his eyes and bent his head. In his mind's eye, he saw orange flames rising to consume a black night sky.

"Damn! It was a clean shot!"

Cal felt fingers digging into his shoulder. He was vaguely aware that Nick was crying out, exultant, stunned. "She's all right! Cal! Rachel's—"

Cal opened his eyes and raised his head very slowly, straining to focus. Galen and one of the ranch hands were helping Rachel to her feet. Eli Walsh's body lay sprawled on the ground next to her.

He watched as Rachel and Galen embraced. She was all right. He couldn't move, couldn't even acknowledge Paco, who was pulling him to his feet.

Then Rachel was stumbling toward him with tears shining in her eyes. She was suddenly in his arms, her scent, roses, rising to stir his senses, snapping him out of shock long enough to pull her to him in a fierce embrace. He buried his face in a mass of thick, cinnamon-colored hair, thinking that no woman had ever felt as good to him as this one, no woman ever, and he was suddenly overcome with a need to tell her so.

"Rachel, I . . . I . . ."

But the words wouldn't come. She clung to him, whispering in his ear tearfully. "You saved my life, you saved my life. I love you, Cal."

Their ride back to the ranch passed uneventfully. Rachel, who had managed to stay relatively calm throughout the whole horrendous ordeal, had felt herself descending into a state of mild shock. She had wanted so badly to talk to Cal, who rode silent and brooding by her side. She had so much she wanted to tell him, about the baby, about how frightened she had been that she was going to lose him, about . . . well, about everything that was in her aching and confused heart, but with her father and Nick and the ranch hands around, the time wasn't right.

When they arrived back at the house, Cal and Galen and Nick left to pay a visit to the authorities in town. Rachel watched them leave with Eli Walsh's lifeless body slung over the saddle of his Appaloosa.

Dolores soon descended upon her, fluttering and clucking like a mother hen. She poured a hot bath for Rachel, then insisted on serving her dinner in bed. Despite her protests at being coddled, Rachel fell into an exhausted sleep soon after.

When she stirred awake for the first time, it was late. The room was dark except for the light of a half moon filtering in through the sheer summer curtains at her window. The house was night-quiet. Cal climbed into bed, the springs creaking as he slipped wearily between the sheets, then lay very still beside her.

Rachel turned to him in the dark, reaching out for him, needing him to hold her, sensing that perhaps he needed her too. She lifted her head as he wrapped one arm around her shoulders, pulling her up against the solid wall of his chest. She whispered, "Did you just get back?"

"A little while ago."

They lay very quiet for a long time before Cal spoke again. "Rachel, did he hurt you? I mean, did he—?"

"No, he didn't touch me. Not like you mean."

"I don't think I'd ever forgive myself if he—"

"You aren't responsible for anything he did," she said.

"If it weren't for me, he wouldn't have come after you. If it weren't for me . . ."

"I'd be dead," Rachel finished for him. She wished that she could do something to erase the nagging self-doubts that haunted him. "I owe you my life."

"There are some who might say I risked your life to save my own."

Rachel raised a hand to brush fingertips over his chest, wanting to comfort him but not knowing how. He was strong in so many ways, but the hurt he had buried for so many years was deep. "They would be wrong," she said.

Cal reached up to catch her hand in his, stilling it. "Look, I don't care what Nick thinks, or even your father, but I do care what you think. I wouldn't have taken the chance if I thought—"

"I know."

But he continued as if he hadn't heard. "I tracked Eli Walsh for years. After that much time, I got to know how his mind worked. Today, if I had done as he said, I know he would have killed you, Rachel. It would have fit his idea of the ultimate revenge, shooting my wife before my eyes. He wanted to see my face when he did it. He was—"

"A man filled with hate," Rachel finished. "And he wasn't afraid of dying. There was something wrong with him, Cal. He was swigging laudanum like it was water."

Cal paused, massaging her hand idly with long, strong fingers, pressing his thumb into her palm. His voice was soft, contemplative. "You know, I've never been able to forgive myself for leaving them."

The poignancy in his tone nearly broke Rachel's heart. She knew he was no longer speaking of the present. He was remembering his mother and sister. "I wasn't there, Cal, but I don't see that you had any choice."

His fingers stilled on hers. "I could have stayed. I could have tried to protect them. I could have done . . . something."

"You did do something. You did the only thing you could have done. Cal, you had no way of knowing what was going to happen."

"But today I did know what was going to happen."

"Yes."

"You believe me?"

"Yes, I believe you." Rachel tilted her head to look at him, trying in vain to read what was in his eyes. "Don't forget I spent some time getting to know Eli Walsh too. And what's more, I've spent months getting to know *you*, Cal Delaney, even though you've done your best not to let me. I happen to know for a fact you would have given your own life rather than watch anyone else die for you."

Cal kissed the tips of her fingers, meeting her gaze in the dark. Rachel saw the corners of his mouth crook into a wistful smile. "You know that for a fact, do you?"

"Yes, Mr. Delaney. I know that for a fact."

Cal dropped her hand, then moved to encircle her waist with one arm, turning and pulling her full-length up against him. "You sound pretty sure of yourself, Mrs. Delaney."

Rachel heard the change in his tone and felt a familiar tremor of desire course through her. "That's because I *am* pretty sure of myself, Mr. Delaney. Very sure of myself. And very sure of you."

He bent his head, speaking in a whisper against the fluttering pulse point in her throat. "Hmmmm, I'm not sure if I like that, you're being so sure of me. It's . . ."

Rachel let one hand travel down the flat plane of his stomach to find his growing arousal. She shivered when he kissed her neck and whispered, "Mrs. Delaney, you are a shockingly wanton woman."

"Yes, well, as you said once before, that probably has much to do with the company I've been keeping."

His mouth found hers. When he pulled away, he bent his head to bury his face between her breasts, tugging gently at the ribbon-ties of her nightdress with his teeth. He was already pushing the gown up over her thighs to her hips, and Rachel aided him in his quest, moving smoothly to wrap one long leg around his waist.

"Ah, Rachel, Rachel," he breathed warm against her skin, "when will I ever get enough of you?"

She closed her eyes and smiled. "Never, Mr. Delaney. Never."

*   *   *

Rachel opened her eyes to see that the room was no longer completely dark. Just a hint of pale pink predawn light came from the open window. Still groggy with sleep, her mind began to fill with warm, sensual images, images of the previous night. They had made love passionately, as always, their bodies meeting and mating in exquisite harmony. And it had ended as it always did, with Rachel lying nestled in his arms, half-awake, half-asleep, warm and blissful with the knowledge that she had truly been made for him and him alone.

Now, Rachel closed her eyes as a rush of warmth flooded her at the remembrance. Her lips curved into a languid smile as she pulled the sheets up around her naked body. She turned over and reached out to touch . . . nothing.

Her eyes snapped open. Frowning, she ran a palm over the place where Cal had slept. It was cold. Something was wrong.

She rose from the bed and moved to one side of the open window. The sky was still pink and orange in the east, with the sun just rounding over the horizon behind the corral. Rachel crossed her arms over her breasts, shivering as the brisk air chilled her exposed skin. Even the ranch hands weren't out of the bunkhouse yet. Where was Cal?

Then she saw him emerging from the stable, leading Friday by his reins. What was he doing? Where was he going? Something light and barely perceptible fluttered very low in Rachel's belly. Startled, she touched her abdomen. It couldn't be their baby moving. Not yet. Could it?

Rachel watched curiously as Cal knelt down next to Friday, appearing to examine one hoof. Then, her eyes widened as she saw that his saddlebags were thrown over Friday's back. Her heart began to pound.

Rachel turned from the window and rushed over to her armoire, flinging open both doors. Hastily, she pulled out a chemise and pantalettes, then snagged a blouse and skirt.

She dressed hurriedly, frantically, not even bothering to put on stockings before throwing open the bedroom door and flying down the staircase. Her hair was still loose and wild from sleep and lovemaking, but she didn't care. Cal was leaving! Good Lord, he was leaving, and she had a terrible feeling it wasn't just to run some errand in town. Since when did he need fully packed saddlebags to conduct routine ranch business?

Rachel encountered no other waking soul as she ran down the shadowed front hallway to leave the house. Everyone, even Dolores, was still asleep.

"Cal!" Rachel called, skimming across the front yard, a handful of her skirt caught up in one hand. "Cal! Wait!"

By the time she caught up to him, she was gasping for air. "What are you doing? Where are you going?"

He still stood by the empty corral, stroking Friday's neck. "Rachel. What are you doing up so early?" He looked down at her bare feet. "And where are your shoes?"

"Never mind my shoes!" she bellowed, wanting to grab him by the shirt collar and shake him. "You didn't answer my question!"

"Didn't you get my note?"

"What note?"

"On your vanity. I left you a note."

Rachel tried to think. In her hurry, she hadn't even glanced at the vanity. "I didn't see any note. What did it say?"

He sighed, looking pained. "Aw, hell, this is exactly what I wanted to avoid."

"What did it say?" Rachel repeated, trying to keep her voice steady. God help her, she was afraid she already knew what it said.

Cal's gaze fixed on something over her head. She knew he was trying to collect his thoughts. After a moment, he adjusted his hat and looked at her. "I need to go away for a little while. There are some things I have to work out."

Rachel swallowed. "But . . . you don't need to go away to do that. You can take some time off and—"

Cal interrupted, starting to turn away. "I need some time alone."

Rachel could feel him slipping away from her, not just physically, but emotionally as well, and a knot of blind panic formed in her stomach. "But, I don't understand."

He didn't look at her. "I think you do."

"When will you be back?"

"I don't know," he answered, checking Friday's saddle for the last time. Then, he was getting ready to mount, and all that was left of Rachel's tenuous poise fled. She cast about desperately for something to say, *anything* to stop him. "But we have weeks left on our contract! You can't just . . ." Her voice trailed off helplessly, foolishly, as he turned to face her again. She couldn't think of another word to say.

Very slowly, very deliberately, he reached into his vest pocket and pulled out the folded sheet of paper Rachel knew was their marriage contract. She watched, aghast, as Cal proceeded to rip it in half once, twice, three times. He let the pieces scatter in the breeze.

Rachel's eyes raised to meet his flat gaze. She stuttered, "B-but, what . . . ? What are you . . . ?"

"A symbolic gesture," Cal replied sarcastically. "After all, we broke the terms of that contract a long time ago."

"But I don't understand. Don't you want your money?"

His lips curved into a maddening smile, a smile that by now had become deeply ingrained in her heart. "My money?" he repeated. Then, that smile faded and he shook his head. "No, you can keep it." He turned his back and lifted one boot to the stirrup.

"Stay!" Rachel blurted out the word without thinking, then immediately clapped a hand over her mouth, horrified at how desperate she sounded.

But it worked.

He stopped, lowered his foot to the ground and turned to look at her, questioning. "Stay?" he echoed.

"Please stay," she said hoarsely, trying to blink back hot tears.

"Why?"

He was looking at her hard, lending no hint of what he was thinking. Those damned, unfathomable, deep blue eyes. They gave away nothing but at the same time, managed to strip away every layer of skin and bone to bare her very soul.

Rachel brushed at a stray tear before it could run down her cheek. She turned away, feeling humiliated. Oh, she had planned on telling him about her pregnancy, but not like this. Here, *now*, it would come out sounding like she was begging for him to stay. Damn it!

She tried to steel herself. "Because I . . . because of . . ."

"Because of the baby?" he interrupted sharply.

Rachel's mouth dropped open, and she whipped around to face him. "You knew?"

"Come on, Rachel."

"Dolores told you!" she accused.

"It doesn't matter. I would have figured it out on my own."

Rachel's hands balled into fists at her sides. "Why didn't you tell me?"

Cal wasn't sure he could believe his own ears. For Christ's sake, what the hell did she have to be mad about? "Why didn't *I* tell *you*?" he repeated.

Without warning, Rachel sprang forward, raising both fists to pommel his chest. "Damn you, Cal!" she cried, "I've been going through hell and you knew! You knew all along!"

Cal stumbled back a few steps, surprised. Then, all the anger and frustration he had wrestled with these past few weeks suddenly erupted. He snatched up both of her wrists and shouted, "Hold it right there, Rachel!"

Her cheekbones were flushed scarlet. "Let go of me!"

"Why didn't you tell me, Rachel? I'm the father, remember? Didn't you think I had a right to know?"

She stopped struggling as his words apparently sank in. She blinked up at him as if waking from a dream. "W-what?"

With great effort, Cal lowered his voice. "Were you hoping I'd leave none the wiser?"

Rachel shook her head in denial. "What? I . . . no, that's not . . . That wasn't it at all."

"You have my name, that's all you need, isn't it? The child is legitimate. You'll bear no shame for it."

Rachel appeared astonished. "You think all I need from you is your . . . name?"

Cal dropped her wrists, all the fight in him exhausted. "It's true, isn't it?"

Rachel raked unsteady hands through her disheveled tresses and dropped her head, muttering to herself. "I don't believe this."

"What, Rachel? What don't you believe?"

She looked up. "You told me you didn't want a family."

"I told you . . . what?"

She jabbed a finger at his chest, her voice rising indignantly. "You told me you didn't want a family!"

Cal thought for a moment, then realized what she was talking about. Their conversation in the line cabin. Suddenly everything fell into place. He closed his eyes painfully. "My God, you thought I wouldn't want this baby."

"Or a wife," she said.

Cal opened his eyes to look at her. He still thought she was the most beautiful woman he had ever seen in his life. By now, he doubted that fact would ever change. "When I said I didn't want a family, Rachel, I didn't know you were going to go and get knocked up on me."

Rachel raised an admonishing eyebrow. "You make it sound like I somehow managed to do it all by myself."

"Not at all, princess. I was more than happy to do my part."

"It certainly seemed so at the time," she said dryly.

They stood for a long moment, their hurt and anger spent, before Cal finally broke the stalemate. "Will you marry me, Miss Girard?"

Rachel blinked up at him, her eyes seeming to mist over. If he didn't know her better, he would have thought she was getting ready to cry. "I already married you, Mr. Delaney."

"Good point." Cal stroked his chin, pretending to think about this for a moment. "Well then, will you agree *not* to divorce me, Mrs. Delaney?"

Without warning, she was suddenly in his arms, her cheek resting on his chest. "Yes, yes, yes! I would be thrilled and honored not to divorce you, Mr. Delaney." By the tremors in her voice, he knew that he had been wrong before. She *was* starting to cry.

Cal hugged her tight, feeling helpless in the face of all this emotion. This, he knew now, was how she did it to him. Right when he least expected it, she went and turned soft. Fiercely proud and infuriating one moment, tender and vulnerable the next. That was Rachel.

He kissed the top of her head. "What are you crying for?"

"I love you so much. I don't care if I sound like a fool."

"Well, if you're a fool, then I must be too."

"Do you really want this baby, Cal?"

"Of course I want the baby. And I need you too, Rachel. Actually, I've been having a hard time trying to picture a future without you. Somewhere along the way, I guess you grew on me."

Rachel lifted her head to peer up at him dubiously. "Sometimes you say the sweetest things."

Her eyes were wet and puffy and pink. She was a pitiful mess, to be sure, but he wanted to kiss her anyway. "That's because I love you, Rachel."

She stole her arms around his neck and accepted his

lingering kiss. When they parted, he looked down at her. "You think we can learn to work this ranch together without killing each other?"

Rachel smiled and started to answer, but her tart reply never made it past her lips. There was something in his voice. She tried to look more deeply into his eyes, those eyes that rarely betrayed the truth of what went on behind them. But there was truth in them now. Or maybe it was just that she was finally learning to look beyond herself to really know him.

Her smile slowly faded. Why had she never thought of it before? It wasn't the baby Cal didn't want. It wasn't Rachel Cal didn't want. It was . . .

"The Elena Rose," Rachel said in shock, not realizing until the words were out that she had spoken aloud.

"What about the Elena Rose?"

Rachel extricated herself from his embrace as realization hit her full force. "It's the Elena Rose that's the problem, isn't it? You don't want the Elena Rose!"

Cal looked wary, obviously unsure of what she was getting at. "I told you from the beginning I wasn't interested in your ranch or your money, Rachel."

"Oh, yes!" Rachel threw up her arms and started pacing. "You made that very clear from the beginning didn't you? But I wasn't listening. The only reason you married me in the first place was to buy land of your own."

"That's changed," he said, following her erratic movements with his eyes. "I know how you feel about this place. You'd never be happy living anywhere else."

Rachel stopped pacing and turned away, her mind working furiously. Five months ago she might have agreed with him. Five months ago, she had truly believed she could love nothing more than the Elena Rose Ranch. But five months had done much to change her. Cal had changed her. Now, the Elena Rose was just a thing, a possession, a livelihood. It was also her home, true, and it would always hold an important place in her heart, but that was all it was. She had much more to love and live for now. Cal. Their baby. Their life together.

It was then that Rachel was visited with a flash of inspiration. She turned to him, her expression brightening. "We could start our own ranch."

"What did you say?"

Rachel's heart pounded with excitement. "You and me. We could start our own ranch. It'll grow to be even bigger and better than the Elena Rose, and it'll be all our own."

Cal eyed her hesitantly before replying. "Are you sure you know what you're saying?"

"I've never been more sure of anything in my life."

Cal gave her a sly smile, then turned, catching Friday's reins as he swung up into the saddle. He offered her a hand. "Somehow I don't feel the need to be alone anymore."

Rachel insinuated one bare foot in the stirrup and took his hand, allowing him to help her up to settle upon the saddle in front of him. He wrapped his arm around her waist from behind, bracing her against his chest, and Rachel knew with undeniable certainty that she was finally where she belonged.

His voice was warm next to her ear as he gently spurred Friday forward, away from the empty corral and out onto the dirt drive. "Let's go for a ride, princess. We have some very big plans to make."

Epilogue

Doctor Jeremiah Bowers removed the stethoscope from around his neck and shook his head, perplexed. He had traveled out to the Elena Rose to check up on Daisy Girard, who was ready to give birth any day now. He'd known both Daisy and Nick all their lives, so he was glad to see they were getting along much better. Nick was looking forward to the birth of his first child and was noticeably attentive toward his wife. In turn, Daisy had been doing some growing up of her own. These days she seemed less concerned about herself and more concerned about the child she was carrying, Perhaps there was some hope for those two yet.

But it wasn't Nick and Daisy's healing marital relationship that confounded Jeremiah now. It was Galen. While he was here to check on Daisy, he had taken the opportunity to see how his old friend was progressing. What he found positively amazed him.

"I've never seen anything like it before in all my years of practicing medicine."

"Believe it," Galen said with a rakish wink as he finished buttoning his shirt. He moved to settle into the big chair behind his desk.

Jeremiah's brow furrowed. "You say the pain is gone, too?"

"Mostly. It's been getting a little better each day." Galen interlaced his fingers across his middle and leaned back, wearing a big grin. "Hell of a thing, ain't it?"

Jeremiah scratched his bald head and sighed. "I've heard of it happening before, but I've never seen it for myself. Galen, either my diagnosis was way off the mark, or you're experiencing what's known as a temporary remission."

"I don't much care what they call it, Jeremiah. I'm going to take the time I've got left and live life to the fullest, I guarantee you that."

The physician cracked a smile as he replaced his medical instruments in his bag. "You're a tough old dog, Galen."

"Damn right, and this tough old dog is finally going to take some time off."

"Eh? You? I've known you twenty-odd years, Galen, and I've never known you to take a day off yet."

Galen chuckled. "Well, with Paco and that new foreman Nick hired to oversee the ranch, this place practically runs itself now. I'm thinking of taking a trip to Kansas to take a firsthand look at Rachel and Cal's new place. In her last letter, Rachel told me they're raising a couple of Brahman bulls that would put our stock to shame."

Jeremiah nodded as he dropped into the chair facing Galen's desk. "Ah! Now I understand. You also wouldn't mind taking a firsthand look at those new grandchildren of yours either, am I right?"

Galen reached for his cigar box and offered his old friend a stogie. "Twins!" he exclaimed and laughed. "Wouldn't my dear departed brother, George, get a kick out of that? Who would have guessed my Rachel would be raising another set of Girard twins."

"Two girls this time, though, ain't that right?" Jeremiah asked, choosing a thick cigar and caressing it absently with his fingers.

"That's right. Rachel named them after Cal's side of the family, Jessica and Rebecca. I can't wait to see them. If they're anything like their mother, my little girl sure is going to have her plate full."

"I reckon poor Cal is the one with a plateful," Jeremiah countered. "Think about it. Now he's got *three* Girard women to reckon with." Jeremiah sat forward as Galen lit his cigar. He puffed, sputtered, coughed, then plucked the smoking cylinder from his mouth, chasing the smoke away with one hand. "Danged things! Don't know why the hell I even smoke 'em!"

Galen chuckled as he lit his own cigar. When he finished, he rose from his chair and turned to gaze through the polished glass window of his study. From here, he could see most of the working sections of his ranch, the corrals, the stables, and the bunkhouse. Beyond that, nothing but open range. It went on as far as the eye could see. After a long, barren winter, it was once again turning a deep, verdant green. Another spring roundup was right around the corner. This was the Elena Rose, his life's work, his second greatest achievement of all.

His gaze settled on one of the empty corrals, and he

imagined a little girl in copper-colored pigtails and tattered boys' britches precariously straddling that wooden fence, a little girl who had been a sprightly handful since the day she took her first teetering step.

Despite his best efforts to remain stoic, Galen's eyes misted over as that precious picture-memory faded away. That child was gone now, but it was all right. She had grown into a fine young woman with a family of her own and a new life. Rachel had finally found the kind of true and lasting love that Galen and Elena once shared. And that, he knew, was life's greatest achievement of all.

Alone in a Crowd by Georgia Bockoven

After a terrible accident, country music sensation Cole Webster must undergo reconstructive surgery which gives him temporary anonymity. Before he can reveal his true identity, Cole loses his heart to Holly, a beautiful woman who values her privacy above all else. Cole must come to terms with who he is and what he's looking for in life before he can find love and true happiness.

Destiny Awaits by Suzanne Elizabeth

When wealthy and spoiled Tess Harper was transported back in time to Kansas, 1885, it didn't take her long to find trouble. Captivating farmer Joseph Maguire agreed to bail her out on one condition–that she live with him and care for his two orphaned nieces. Despite the hardships of prairie life, Tess soon realized that this love of a lifetime was to be her destiny.

Broken Vows by Donna Grove

To Rachel Girard, nothing was more important than her family's cattle ranch, which would one day be hers. But when her father declared she must take a husband or lose her birthright, Rachel offered footloose bounty hunter Caleb Delaney a fortune if he'd marry her–then leave her! Cal knew he'd be a fool to refuse, but he would soon wonder if a life without Rachel was worth anything at all.

Lady in Blue by Lynn Kerstan

A delightful, sexy romance set in the Regency period. Wealthy and powerful Brynmore Talgarth never wanted a wife, despite pressure to restore the family's reputation by marrying well. But once he met young, destitute, and beautiful Clare Easton, an indecent proposal led the way to a love neither knew could exist.

The Long Road Home by Mary Alice Monroe

Bankrupt and alone after her financier husband dies, Nora MacKenzie's life is shattered. After fleeing to a sheep farm in Vermont, she meets up with the mysterious C. W. Friendship soon blossoms into love, but C. W. is keeping some dangerous secrets that could destroy them both.

Winter Bride by Teresa Southwick

Wyoming rancher Matt Decker needed a wife. His mother sent him Eliza Jones, the young woman who had adored Matt when they were children. Eliza was anxious to start a new life out west, but the last thing Matt wanted was to marry someone to whom he might become emotionally attached.

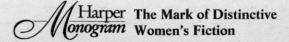